THE
WELL-MANNERED
WAR

THE CHANGING FACE OF DOCTOR WHO

The cover illustration portrays the fourth DOCTOR WHO whose
appearance changed when he fell from a high tower in order to
save the universe from the Master.

DOCTOR WHO – THE MISSING ADVENTURES

Also available:

THE WELL-MANNERED WAR

Gareth Roberts

DOCTOR WHO

THE MISSING ADVENTURES

First published in Great Britain in 1997 by
Doctor Who Books
an imprint of Virgin Publishing Ltd
332 Ladbroke Grove
London W10 5AH

ISBN 0 426 20506 5

Cover illustration by Alister Pearson

Typeset by Galleon Typesetting, Ipswich
Printed and bound in Great Britain by
Mackays of Chatham PLC

Contents

Part One

1

Exchange of Fire

The Darkness turned slowly through the Metra system, its bulk blotting out the stars as it passed. An observer would have taken it for another piece of cosmic jetsam, an asteroid adrift, that might spin through the galaxies for ages until snared or crushed by some natural force. Its strangely regular shape – it resembled a rough-edged, inverted pyramid – might have drawn speculation; but this could be explained away as simply a simulacrum. As for the curious directness of the path it took, that was quite probably the result of local planetary gravities.

This hypothetical observer, like the majority of his kind, would have been wrong.

The Darkness was alive. It quivered with a unique and terrifying power, and had a talent for death. And it was on its way, its every sense alert, to keep a long-awaited appointment.

The booster rockets shut down shortly after take-off, as the carrier shuttle thrust through the ionosphere of Metralubit, first planet of the system. With a shudder the small grey ship aligned itself with the tracking beacon, engaged its fusion drive and slipped insolently from gravity's grip. Then it blurred and vanished, sucked into Fastspace, leaving a shower of glittering purple cinders that evaporated slowly like the trails of an exploded firework.

Dolne watched the huge spheroid of his homeworld, its land masses and cities shrouded by the dense life-giving cloud that had attracted his colonist ancestors to

3

it many thousands of years before, through the porthole on his side of the passenger lounge. At the moment of the leap an illusion was worked, and Metralubit seemed to crumple and be tossed away with the contempt of a child discarding a toy it had outgrown. Dolne knew that, in fact, it was the ship that had been snatched out of normality, that it was he who had been plucked so rudely from normal space, and the thought did nothing to aid his agitation. His heart pumped furiously, his brow gleamed with fresh sweat-trickles. In nearly thirty years in service he must have made this journey a thousand times. Each trip he fought hard to maintain his stolid expression in the awful, bowel-churning moment of transition, and failed. For a soldier, for the commander-in-chief of an army engaged in a lengthy conflict, he was uncommonly nervous. He added to this self-judgement the defence that it was an uncommon sort of conflict, requiring uncommon qualities of its combatants. Ah, yes, another inner voice countered, and you *were* chosen for your looks.

The carrier steadied, the Fastspace pressure stabilized, and he studied those looks in the thick curved glass of the porthole, where they were shaded by the gentle orange lighting. He remained tall and handsome, he decided, if marginally wider about the midriff than before, and he cut a splendid figure in the outfit – or rather the uniform, although he would never get used to calling it that – of a Space Admiral. Just as well, since he was the only one. Traces of ash grey streaked his hair, whose recession had added a certain dignified frame, unknown in his youth, to his simplistic, symmetrical features. Yes, a good face, suited to the job, even if the man who lived behind it wasn't.

He unfastened his safety belt. His knees were knocking. To another human his discomfort would have been evident from such non-verbal signals. Fortunately his companion was not human. But it cut the other way, too. Dolne was unsure if General Jafrid, with whom he had shared this small but sumptuous lounge on many similar occasions, also suffered from fear of Fastspace. Somehow, he doubted it.

Jafrid was unbuckling his harness, customized into the carrier as a mark of courtesy, with typical Chelonian adroitness. The plastic straps slid from his big shell and he stretched his four external limbs to their fullest extent, the blunt claws on each one unfurling and furling. Then he turned his head towards Dolne on his long, wizened neck and said politely, 'Very smooth.' His voice was low and rather gruff, a step away from a roar for all its civilized airs, and made the metal bulkheads of the lounge reverberate.

'Yes,' Dolne said, his head still reeling. 'I hardly noticed we'd gone into Fastspace at all.' A queasy feeling wrenched at his stomach. 'The years pass. One becomes accustomed.'

'One does,' Jafrid said. An odd gurgle escaped from somewhere deep in his vastness.

Dolne got up, walked to the drinks dispenser at the back of the lounge and dialled them tea. 'Any preference, Jaffers?' The nickname had come into use a while ago, and the Chelonian didn't seem to mind.

Jafrid considered a moment. 'Lapsang souchong, please.' He patted the side of his shell. 'It'll help to settle my digestive tracts.'

Dolne collected the tray provided by the machine and placed it on the aisle table. He watched as Jafrid shook the pot gently, saying, 'Ah, yes. Nothing better to clear the pipes. Your human drinks are very good, but you really ought to try some of ours. Curried whango is a real treat.'

Dolne smiled. 'I don't think it would be quite good for me.' They'd been over this ground many times, out of politeness. One ring of curried whango, in fact, would turn a human's tongue into a thin strip of scalded tissue, burn away his jaw and quite possibly induce a fatal heart seizure. As he spoke Jafrid tipped the pot and began to pour.

They drank in silence for a moment. Then Jafrid chuckled, took his com-pad from its moulded rest on the

5

table and tapped in a code. 'Let's check the news. See how our work's been reported.'

'Badly, I expect,' said Dolne. 'As usual.' He turned to face the big screen that stretched over the length of the facing wall. 'The news media have no patience. No wish to convey the full complexity of our task.'

Jafrid nodded down in the general direction of Metralubit. 'You're right. To them it looks simple. They wouldn't be quite as quick with their advice if they realized the level of delicacy required.' He aimed the com-pad at the screen and pressed the transmit button. The screen remained blank. 'Come on, come on, connect,' said Jafrid. He sighed. 'Pardon my rudeness, but your technology can be appallingly slow.'

'We have many different com-systems on Metralubit,' said Dolne. 'It can take a while for them to line up.'

Jafrid wagged his head. 'Your lot can never standardize anything.'

'Just the way we are,' said Dolne.

There was an uncomfortable silence. Dolne regarded Jafrid as a friend of the kind one mixes well with in a crowd. When there was only the two of them conversation was hard. They just didn't have enough in common.

The big screen stayed blank. Both of them made disapproving noises to cover the embarrassing lapse.

The screen flickered at last. 'Ah, here we go,' said Jafrid.

A newsreader appeared, seated at her desk, framed from the waist up in the classical, millennia-old tradition of public broadcasting, the emblem of the Metralubitan News Network embossed on the wall behind her. She was a Femdroid, and, Dolne thought, a cracking one, with silky blonde hair styled in an elegant mushroom about a sharp-featured yet still attractive face. She wore an immaculate pink suit with padded shoulders and spoke with the precision of all her kind. 'Good morning. Today's main story: the one hundred and twenty-fifth summit on the Barclow war has ended with no significant breakthroughs being made.'

'Ridiculous,' said Dolne. 'I made several, ah, fairly important concessions.'

'As did I,' said Jafrid.

The newsreader's voice continued over footage that showed them both seated at the massive white circular conference table, surrounded by the staff of the Parliament Dome and administrating Femdroids. 'Late last night Space Admiral Dolne, for the Metralubitan military, and General Jafrid, for the Chelonian seventieth column, met in the conference chamber of the Parliament Dome for preliminary talks on the future of the Barclow colony.'

Jafrid growled. 'Barclow is no colony. A clear case of bias.'

'They are broadcasting to their own side,' Dolne pointed out. 'My side. And we do claim that Barclow is our colony.'

'Irrelevant,' snapped Jafrid. 'I shall lodge a complaint with the regulators. The network is supposed to be impartial.' There was not more than a trace of anger in his voice. Dolne knew he was only saying what was expected of him.

'The summit was dissolved after only four hours when it became clear that the parties could not agree on the wording of the initial clause of the discussion document,' the newsreader went on. Dolne watched himself and Jafrid shaking appendages.

'What does she mean, "only"?' said Jafrid. 'Four hours isn't bad.'

Dolne laughed and drank his tea. 'Four very long hours.'

Jafrid pointed to a woman in a patterned skirt standing at Dolne's side on the screen. 'I must say your wife's looking well.'

'Thank you.' Dolne was genuinely pleased. 'Yes, she seems to have bounced back after her operation. That Femdroid medic did a great job. I'm glad you've noticed.'

The newsreader went on, 'The Premier gave this reaction to news of the summit's break-up.' Dolne groaned as

7

Harmock's piggy form appeared. He was sitting at his desk in his study, many shelves of books behind him. 'The situation remains the same,' he said in his infuriatingly pompous way, 'and Space Admiral Dolne has my full confidence and my full support.'

'Silly arse,' muttered Dolne.

'If the Chelonian hierarchy think they can shake our resolve with their quibbles, they are mistaken.' Harmock raised a hand. 'I say to them –' he made a cutting gesture '– oh no. We are prepared to enter into full negotiations on Barclow, without preconditions. As soon as they accept our terms.' His jowls shook as he spoke. 'It is their stalling over minor technicalities that is preventing us all from taking further steps ahead on the road to peace.'

They heard the newsreader's voice off-screen. 'Premier, there have been suggestions that by imposing the terms you've just described you're robbing the Chelonians of any bargaining power and making it impossible for them to negotiate.'

Harmock gave the camera a pitying look. 'We hear a lot of that kind of rot nowadays, don't we? Well, *I*'ll tell *you* something, shall I? Barclow is ours by right, our colony, and our protectorate. And until that is acknowledged by both sides there is no point in going any further.'

'Nevertheless, Premier, after a hundred and twenty-five years, some are saying the Barclow war is a waste of everybody's time, and is being prolonged purely for party political reasons. It's claimed that neither you nor the Opposition can afford to stop the war officially as it would be an unpopular move with the public.'

Harmock reared up, as much as it was possible for him to rear. His chins wobbled. 'The situation on Barclow has absolutely no connection with party politics. To anybody who says so, let me say this. If we allow an alien power simply to walk in and take away what is rightfully ours, what kind of signal are we sending out? For all we know there could be hundreds of hostiles up in space with an eye on us, and if we falter on Barclow it would be like giving a green light to any passing invader.'

Dolne was embarrassed. 'That terrible patronizing tone he takes . . .'

'Humans like being patronized,' said Jafrid. He giggled. 'Pardon me. It's the thought of all those hostile powers with designs on Metralubit.'

Dolne sat back in his seat. 'Feel free. I'll be glad to be rid of Harmock. And with any luck it'll be soon. He can't delay the election much longer.' He clapped his hands together and made a mock prayer. 'Nothing can go wrong this time, surely. He's got to lose – he's made such a mess of things. He's just *got* to.'

'And will the other fellow do any better, I wonder?' mused Jafrid.

'What, Rabley?' Dolne considered. 'He can't make things wor– ah, talk of the devil.' He pointed to the screen, on which the face of the Opposition leader was, almost literally, glowing. He was every inch the opposite of Harmock: lean, with a wide (some said too wide) grin, and a dapper pale-green suit that fitted him perfectly, over which was a protective padded jacket. It did not appear incongruous, as he was surrounded not by the panelled dens of the Parliament Dome but by an ashen landscape both viewers knew only too well.

'As you can see,' he was saying, one arm thrown theatrically wide, 'the situation on Barclow is intolerable. Of course, there is no question, nor can there be, of us altering our position on its colony status, but there is another side to the matter.' He spoke quickly and freely with a casual emphasis and his smile never faltered. 'The war swallows an average of a billion credits per annum, and that's public money. What we in the Opposition are saying is that this is unacceptable and that our presence on Barclow should be downsized accordingly.'

'Your critics, Mr Rabley,' said the newsreader from the studio, 'would reply that by doing so you'd leave the door wide open to the enemy.'

He shook his head politely. 'No, no, no. What they're missing is that –'

Jafrid interrupted. 'I forgot he was staying with your lot.'

'Yes. Tour of inspection.' Dolne raised an eyebrow. 'Photo-opportunity, more like. They've all done it. Getting into a flak jacket goes down well with the voters.' He grinned, staring into the past. 'Even Harmock did it, once. We had to hunt high and low for one to go around him.'

The broadcast was cut off and a crackle came from the internal speaker mounted above the big screen. 'Evening, gents,' said the pilot cheerily.

'Evening,' said his passengers.

'Just thought I'd let you know, we'll be dropping out of Fastspace in thirty seconds,' he said. 'That's out of neutral territory and into Barclow's disputed zone,' he added, following procedure. 'Take it carefully, eh? Your pods are primed and ready to drop.'

'Fine, thank you,' called Dolne. Jafrid nodded his assent. Both reached for their safety straps and clipped the buckles about their middles. Hastily Dolne finished his tea and set down his cup. He licked his lips in preparation for the return.

Again, the dreadful violence, as if a hole was being punched through reality. Again, an attempt by his last meal to escape into day. And again, through the porthole, the shattering shock of seeing a planet popping into existence where before there had been only blackness. Dolne felt very differently about Barclow, though. Whereas Metralubit was pretty but too large and overpopulated, Barclow was ugly, small and almost uninhabited. It had been generous of the astronomer who had discovered it to deem it a planetoid, as it was only 400 miles at its circumference, and even more generous for him to deem it habitable, as the equatorial strip with its life-supporting atmosphere covered only just over a tenth of that area. But for Dolne it felt like home, and the sight of its rainy skies and muddy grey mountains gave him a moment's *jouissance* that almost made up for the discomfort of the reverse transition.

The ship steadied itself and then swooped down through Barclow's cloud cover. Droplets of moisture spattered across the porthole, and Dolne inhaled gratefully. It was as if he could already smell the patchy, iron-particle-thick air.

'There we are, chaps,' the pilot's voice crackled from the cockpit. 'Now, I don't need to remind you, but I will anyway, we're in the SDZ. And I've received clearance from your command posts: you're clear to drop. So, good luck to you both and happy landings.'

'Thank you,' Dolne called as he unstrapped himself.

'Thank you,' said Jafrid, doing the same.

Dolne hated this bit. Keeping his gaze away from Jafrid he stood, brushed down his outfit (uniform, *uniform!*), picked up his briefcase and his box of presents (he had something for every member of the Strat Team, picked up from the duty-free shop at the Parliament Dome's travel terminal) from beneath his seat and turned to face the door that led to his waiting pod.

Across the aisle, his manner also abruptly formal, Jafrid did much the same, although his document holder took the form of a slim silver disc containing sheafs of jagged-edged paper.

They stood next to each other in silence, waiting for the lights above the pod bay doors to turn from red to green. Dolne tightened his grip on the briefcase and risked a second's glance over at Jafrid. His eyes met Jafrid's coming the other way. Swiftly they averted their gazes.

Oh well, thought Dolne, as the lights changed and the bay doors chunked open with a low hum. Better get it over with.

With affected casualness he put one of his hands in his right pocket, the side next to Jafrid. His fingers curled around the oblong plastic phial. He readied himself. As always he felt extremely foolish. He lifted a foot to cross the threshold –

– and converted the movement into a sudden, ungainly crouch, bringing out the phial and bowling it underarm in Jafrid's general direction. He saw it flash through the

11

air, watched as it arced towards Jafrid's upper shell, the substance inside glistening greenly in the lounge's muted orange lighting. He watched admiringly as one of Jafrid's front limbs came up to knock it aside. At the same time the Chelonian's enormous bulk hauled itself off the carpet on one side with a grinding of hidden hydraulics. The diverted phial spun off across the lounge and struck the big screen. It split with a crack and the acid bubbled out. Dolne felt ashamed as he watched the screen eaten away by the fizzing substance.

His attention was pulled back by Jafrid's response. His old Chelonian friend tipped his shell forward, and a long dagger slipped out into the same front limb that had knocked away the phial. Dolne's eyebrows shot up with delight. The dagger was beautiful, its hilt decorated with fiery alien stones, the blade not only barbed but also twisted along its length into a variety of different shapes. One section ended in a spiked ball, another a corkscrew with a glinting point.

Dolne was instantly curious, his acquisitive instincts aroused. He and his wife were great antiques collectors, and he was considering what sort of offer to make Jafrid when he remembered that the weapon was on its way to the general area of his heart and he had better do something about it.

He whipped up his briefcase in a reflex movement. Its strong metallic side absorbed the impact of the dagger, although Dolne nearly toppled over under the weight of Jafrid's assault.

He took a moment to steady himself and then pulled the case away. He and Jafrid, who pulled back the dagger with a grunt, shared a conspiratorial smile. (At least, Dolne had always assumed that Jafrid was smiling at this juncture.)

'Acid?' snorted Jafrid. 'Unsubtle.' He nodded towards the screen, which was now nothing but a charred and smoking wreck of sparking circuitry. Dolne just knew he was going to make a dismissive remark. 'Wouldn't have done more than scar my shell.'

Dolne shrugged apologetically. 'I do my best with what I'm given. No hard feelings, eh?' He reached across and patted Jafrid on the hard bony ridge where his shell covered his neck. 'I say, would you mind if I took a quick glance at that dagger of yours? It looks rather impressive.'

Jafrid passed it to him. 'Oh no, go ahead. Splendid piece, isn't it? Those are Trangostran rubies in the hilt, you know. It's been in my family for generations.'

Dolne nodded appreciatively, although he had no idea what Trangostran rubies were. The dagger was heavy, and on closer inspection he saw that its blade was made of some unfamiliar material with the appearance of ebony and the density of lead. The various murderous attachments were crafted with the minute detail that suggests an infinite genius for taking pains. 'It's quite, quite beautiful.'

'Yes,' Jafrid said proudly. 'Used by my ancestors thousands of years ago.'

'Probably on mine.' Dolne weighed it in his hand. 'I wouldn't mind having a closer look.' A thought occurred to him. 'I tell you what, I'll use the instruments at my command post to give it a scan and find out how much it's worth. Not that you'd ever want to sell something so precious, of course.'

Jafrid seemed to consider for a moment. Then he snapped his teeth together and said, 'Why not? It's nice to see someone taking an interest. Most of my men couldn't give a blueberry seed for their heritage. They've been lounging on their carapaces too long.' He reached up and tapped Dolne on the side. 'No, you go on. But look after it, mind.'

Dolne felt excited. 'Oh I will, I will. It's magnificent.'

The pilot's communicator crackled. 'You two all right in there?'

'Oh yes, yes,' they chorused.

'Phew,' said the pilot. 'Good thing too. Thought you might finally have done away with each other.'

'Oh no, no,' Dolne and Jafrid said.

'Now, I can't hang about here all day and neither can you,' said the pilot. 'So will you move into your pods, please? Thanking you kindly.'

'Of course,' said Dolne. 'We're very sorry.' He nodded a farewell to Jafrid. 'I'll no doubt speak to you shortly.' He gave a wave. 'Take care.'

Jafrid nodded back. 'And you.' He shuffled through the door to his pod.

Dolne watched him go and then returned his attention to the dagger. He was looking forward to taking a good look at it. He squinted at the detail on the hilt. Wrapped around the inlaid stones was a worn silver inscription in raised symbols of archaic Chelonian. He had a translator disc somewhere in his room – he'd have to dig it out and see what this meant.

The fact that the dagger had been used in an attempt to kill him had already slipped his mind. He'd lost count of the means he and Jafrid had employed against each other over the years of their friendship. Gas, poison, dart guns, mini-bombs . . . It was embarrassing but it had to be done. The public demanded it of them. They had to show willing. There was a war on, after all.

He stepped out of the lounge and walked with in-attention borne of much repetition to the hatch of his pod.

'. . . the situation on Barclow has absolutely no connection with party politics. To anybody who says so, let me say this. If we allow an alien power simply to walk in and take away what is rightfully ours, what kind of signal are we sending out?' Somewhere deep within the Darkness, where the channels of its intelligence met, the face of Premier Harmock was observed by many-faceted eyes, the image swimming on a glutinous screen that wobbled between towers of hardened spittle. 'For all we know there could be hundreds of hostiles up in space with an eye on us, and if we falter on Barclow it would be like giving a green light to any passing invader.' If the Darkness had possessed a sense of humour it might have chortled gleefully at the irony of this

14

speech. But it had not. Instead it viewed the broadcast approvingly.

Tension. War. Death.

The human race at its most predictable.

Somewhere in the perplexing reaches of the space–time vortex, the mysterious region of reality that encompasses everything that has ever happened, everything that will ever happen, and quite a few things that never did or might or had gone missing, a craft disguised as a police telephone box tumbled and spun on a wayward course. Its inelegant exterior concealed an incredibly spacious and well-appointed environment. The TARDIS – the property, loosely speaking, of an erratic Time Lord known as the Doctor, his less erratic Time Lady friend Romana and their not-at-all erratic robot dog, K9. Their way of life consisted mainly of arriving at various far-flung points in the universe's history and involving themselves in things that didn't concern them.

This morning, as Romana walked the short distance from her quarters to the control room that was the heart of the TARDIS, her thoughts were taken up by the Doctor's erratic nature. She could hear a loud banging and crashing coming from up ahead. She didn't worry, as it wasn't the kind of crashing that signified fistfights and deadly peril, and, besides, the TARDIS was inviolable to external attack. In fact there was a sort of accidental quality to the noise. It was the sound of piles of things toppling over; more particularly, the sound of the Doctor tripping over piles of things.

She entered the control room to find the Doctor lying in a heap half under the six-sided central console, his long legs stretched out behind him, trying desperately hard to pretend he hadn't just fallen over. He was surrounded on all sides by an incredible variety of junk, most of which appeared to have been tipped on to the floor out of huge packing crates. Her eyes swept over the vast array of objects. 'What have you got there, Doctor?'

'What have I not got here, Romana?' He handed her

one of the crates and she shook out the last few things, including a jewelled necklace and several unlikely-looking weapons, along with a cloud of dust which tickled her nose. 'I've decided it's time for a spot of spring cleaning. You can help me out.'

'Can I?' she said doubtfully, coughing out the last of the dust.

He stopped what he was doing suddenly and looked up at her. 'What are you wearing that for?'

Romana looked down at her new outfit. She had chosen a red velvet smoking jacket and a frilled shirt with a bow tie, which she had found discarded on a hanger in the wardrobe room. The outfit was topped off by sharp-creased checked trousers, a pair of shiny-buckled shoes and a cape thrown over her shoulders. 'It fits and I like it,' she replied.

'Good.' The Doctor nodded. 'I liked it too. Now, this shouldn't be difficult.' He tapped one of the crates. 'I packed it all away in the loft a few centuries back but I've always been too busy to sort it out. People trying to take over the universe, girls needing to be rescued, that sort of thing.' He pointed in turn to three piles on the far side of the console. 'There we are. Things to throw out, things to keep, things that might come in useful one day.' It came as no surprise to Romana that the first pile was decidedly the smallest. Before she could remark on that the Doctor cried 'Aha!' and lunged for an item among those she had just tipped out. He pulled it out and clutched it to his chest. 'I've been looking for these for aeons.'

Romana was puzzled. 'What is it?' The Doctor held it out. It appeared to be nothing more than a plastic bag containing a collection of small metal discs. 'Ah. Currency.'

He shook the bag. 'No. Washers.'

'Washers?'

'For plumbing.' He threw the bag on to the keep pile. 'There's a tap in the fourteenth bathroom that's been dripping non-stop for three hundred years.'

'Why hasn't it flooded the TARDIS?'

The Doctor smiled. 'Because I set up a temporal containment field round the affected area. Clever, eh? The same drip, over and over again.'

'Why didn't you just fix the tap?'

'I couldn't find my washers.' He gestured vaguely around at the mess. 'That's why I'm doing this, you see. If we can sort everything out now we can save ourselves all sorts of complications, can't we?'

'Or get ourselves into all sorts of new ones,' Romana mused. She riffled in the junk immediately in front of her and extracted a long, stretchy string garment that seemed designed to fit a creature with eight arms. It was dirty and smelly and she moved automatically to dispose of it on the throwing-out pile.

The Doctor gripped her arm before she could. 'What are you doing?'

'I'm throwing it away.'

'Do you realize what that is?'

'I expect I'm about to be told.'

He moved his face closer to hers and whispered, 'It's a Hangorian spore-catcher.'

'I thought it was a vest.'

The Doctor closed his eyes as if pained. 'No, no,' he said. 'You put a stick in one of the holes and swing it above your head.' He mimed the action. 'The spores stick in the holes.'

'What spores?'

'The Hangorian ones.' He took it from her and threw it on to the keep pile. 'If ever we land on Hangorius it could come in very handy.'

'Why?'

'Well, otherwise we'd never get a chance to chat to the spores, would we?' He shook his head at her. 'I thought you were supposed to have been educated.'

'About important things, yes.'

The Doctor gave a sharp, mocking laugh. 'I'll give you important things. It's all very well looking good with a gown and a scroll in your hand. But when it comes to the

17

practicalities of life, Romana, I don't think you've been very well prepared. I wonder how you'd deal with a real crisis.'

'Like fixing a tap?' Romana said acidly. She realized that after a quick glance he was preparing to lob a piece of what looked like Gallifreyan technology on to the throwing-out pile. 'Wait a moment, what's that?'

'What's what?' he said, looking over his shoulder and throwing the piece of technology away.

Romana scooped it back up. 'This.' She blew off a coat of dust and studied it more closely. Its elaborate scrolled ornamentation and the slightly fussy layout of its operating controls confirmed her summation of its origins. It was ovoid in shape, with an opaque panel on its surface that was inlaid with veins of a marble-like substance. Romana had studied Gallifreyan history as part of her training and found herself unconsciously estimating its age. 'A real antique. From about the time this TARDIS was constructed. It may have been here ever since.'

The Doctor snatched it back. He was especially cagey, Romana knew, about his own past and the pedigree of the TARDIS. 'There was a lot of useless rubbish hanging about when I . . . er, when I came into possession.' He turned the device over in his hands and sniffed. 'It's just another fancy attachment we'll never need.'

Romana frowned. 'Do you know what it's for?'

The Doctor frowned back. 'Well, I think it's supposed to force an emergency materialization if we shoot right through the Time Spiral. But that's hardly likely, is it?'

'I hope not.' Romana swallowed involuntarily. The Time Spiral existed at the parameters of the vortex, acting as a boundary to all space–time craft. Its force was powerful enough to crush a TARDIS like a piece of matchwood. 'As long as the boundary alarm's still functional.'

The Doctor looked non-committal. 'I expect it is,' he said sheepishly. 'I mean, it's never gone off, has it, so how can I tell?'

'If it had you'd be dead,' said Romana.

The Doctor tried to look authoritative. 'Romana, the boundary parameters are wired into the core of every TARDIS. There would have to be erosion in the systems circuitry on a massive scale for them to be exceeded.'

'There is erosion in the systems circuitry on a massive scale.'

The Doctor shushed her frantically. 'Will you keep your voice down?' he said, gesturing at the console with his thumb.

'You can't continue to hide your head in the sand, Doctor. The TARDIS needs a total overhaul.'

The Doctor patted the base of the console. 'Don't listen to the nasty lady, old thing.' He raised his voice. 'Romana, the odds against us going up the Time Spiral are – well, if I had time to waste on calculating the odds against very unlikely things happening I could tell you what the odds are.' He nodded to the junk. 'Perhaps it wasn't such a good idea asking you to help me with this. You've obviously got no sense of priority.'

Romana was formulating her reply when the inner door opened and K9 trundled in, his tail wagging happily. 'Greetings, Master. Greetings, Mistress.'

'Greetings, K9,' said the Doctor, evidently glad of the distraction. 'Where've you been?' He wagged his dog whistle over at the pet. 'I've been blowing this for hours.'

'Negative, Master,' said K9 chirpily. 'Your first summons was given only thirty-three minutes and four seconds ago, TARDIS relative time.' He motored up to the piles of junk and started to examine them curiously.

'You seem particularly chipper this morning,' said the Doctor suspiciously. 'I don't remember –' He broke off. 'That wasn't an answer.'

'It was, Master.'

'Not a good enough one. What have you been up to?'

K9, apparently satisfied with his examination of the Doctor's junk, started to circle the console. 'Cannot specify, Master. My apologies.' There was a slight stammer to his delivery, as if he was finding it difficult to express himself.

19

Romana and the Doctor exchanged a worried glance. They watched as K9 continued to circle about. There was about him an air of forced cheeriness. 'I've never seen him behave like this before,' the Doctor muttered. 'Perhaps I ought to open him up and have a prod.'

'Perhaps,' Romana postulated, 'he's got something to tell us.' She knelt down in front of K9 to stop him circling and said, 'K9, what's the matter?'

The dog's head drooped. 'Cannot answer, Mistress. There is – conflict in my circuits.'

The Doctor knelt down also. 'I'll give you conflict. Spit it out, K9.'

K9 hesitated before replying. 'I am not equipped with salivary mechanisms, Master.' There was an uncomfortable silence. Then he added, 'I am programmed to protect you and the Mistress. This protection extends to your emotional as well as your physical well-being.'

'You don't want to hurt our feelings?' Romana reached out and stroked K9 on the nose.

'Diagnosis sentimentally couched but essentially correct,' K9 said.

'Look, K9,' said the Doctor, 'I know we haven't always seen eye to eye, but whatever you've done you're still my dog, you know. I'm not going to put you out on the step like an empty milk bottle. Just tell me what's the matter and we'll discuss it rationally, eh? No raised voices.'

K9's internal workings chirruped. 'Eighty-three per cent probability that you will raise your voice if I reveal my information, Master.'

'Promise I won't.'

Romana was getting worried. 'Go on, K9,' she urged.

K9 turned away from them, as if he could not bear to hold their gaze. 'I have received a vital communication from the TARDIS computer. We entered conference and decided it was better to withhold our findings from you to avoid distress.'

'I'm ordering you to tell me, K9,' said the Doctor.

K9 beeped. 'There has been a boundary error. The TARDIS has exceeded its parameters and is nearing the

Time Spiral. It will be totally destroyed in two minutes relative time.'

'What?' The Doctor leapt up and raced over to him. 'What did you just say? I hope this isn't a joke, K9. I mean, I hope it is.'

'I have never joked, Master. And you have raised your voice.'

'Of course I've raised my voice. The Time Spiral?' The Doctor clutched a handful of his curly hair.

Romana was trying to digest the implications of K9's news. 'But that's impossible.'

'That's not what you said five minutes ago.' He rubbed his chin. 'But you're right. I mean, the odds against banging up against the Spiral are high enough, but the odds against banging up against the Spiral just after you'd been talking about it for the first time in six hundred years . . .' He trailed off and looked again at K9. 'Are you sure?'

K9 took the question as an order to recheck. 'Affirmative, Master. TARDIS will be destroyed in approximately one minute and thirty-five seconds. I advise that you make peace with the universe according to the rites of your belief system.'

Romana reached for the ovoid device. 'Thank goodness we found this in time.' She searched the console for a suitable inlet. It was hard to believe that they were in any danger. The central column was rising and falling noisily but smoothly enough, the ever-present hum of the systems was unaltered in pitch, and all instruments on the console showed no pressing problems.

The Doctor halted her. 'Wait, wait. Think about it. Isn't it more likely just that K9's gone barking mad?'

'I have never barked, Master,' said K9. 'And the TARDIS will be destroyed in one minute and fourteen seconds.'

Romana shook herself from the Doctor's grip. 'We can't take the risk, can we?' Her eyes alighted on a fixture between the demotic winch and the plural astrofier.

Again the Doctor stopped her. 'We don't want to encourage him. He must have overheard us talking and

21

come up with this stunt. If we let him think he's rattled us he'll have us running around after him morning, noon and night. If you ask me, his cortex is on the blink.' He pointed to his own head and made a spiralling motion.

K9 said, 'Destruction in fifty-nine seconds. Fifty-eight, fifty-seven . . .'

'There, you see, he's developed a death wish. The best way to deal with it is to confront him with reality.' He turned on K9. 'Now listen. We're not going to be destroyed, you know.'

'We are, Master. In fifty-five seconds.'

'No we aren't.'

'Yes we are. The TARDIS will be crushed by the Spiral and scattered to the vortex.'

The Doctor sighed. 'No, K9, it won't.'

Romana observed this exchange with some worry. It did seem more probable that the Doctor would be proved right, but she couldn't shake off her fear. Deciding it would do no harm she started to connect the defence device to the console. It was simply a matter of putting a small probe into the hole.

K9 whirred and ticked. 'You are displaying the reaction known as denial, Master, common among humanoids facing certain death.'

'Don't you diagnose me!' cried the Doctor. 'I'm the sane party, it's you who needs help; all this nonsense about the Time Spi–'

He was interrupted by a shattering crash from somewhere, it seemed, outside the TARDIS, as if a storm was breaking above them. Instantly the lights went out. There was a split second of stillness, the control room illuminated only by K9's eyescreen, and then Romana felt the ground shake and quiver beneath her feet.

A moment later the TARDIS was sent spinning violently. She lost her grip on the console and was blown off her feet, to be plastered against one of the far walls, her feet a few inches above the ground, her long fair hair blown out by the sheer force of the attack. There was the sound of a thunderclap.

She heard the Doctor. He was shouting, and couldn't have been more than a few feet away, but his voice sounded cracked and distant, as if he was calling from the far side of a wide valley. 'It's the Time Spiral, Romana!' he called.

'I know!' she called back. All around was chaos. As she watched, the control room was lit by crackling bursts of bright blue light, and she saw K9 spinning desperately on his base in an effort to keep his balance. The Doctor's crates and the rubbish inside were lifted like toys and whirled around crazily. The inner door was slammed open and shut. An insistent pressure battered her temples.

'Did you –' cried the Doctor. His words were snatched away in the shrieking violence. 'Did you . . . fit that . . . gadget?'

Romana struggled to recall the moment before the attack. Had she inserted the probe? 'I . . . I think so . . .' she called back.

K9's voice, made eerily low by the atmospheric distortion, seemed to boom around them. 'TARDIS . . . will be destroyed in . . . forty-three seconds . . .'

'I don't know if you've . . . noticed . . .' the Doctor gasped. 'But it . . . doesn't appear . . . to be working . . .'

Romana realized she was going to spend the final few moments of her life getting angry with the Doctor. 'That's hardly . . . my fault!'

There was a smashing concussion and the control room suddenly inverted like a fairground centrifuge. She felt herself sliding up to the ceiling, still glued to the wall. Oddly, her main feeling was of regret rather than fear: there was a lot she hoped to do in the next few thousand years.

She heard K9 again. 'Master . . . Mistress . . . I have made a study of the . . . TARDIS systems . . . The defence unit will . . . activate only when the . . . materialization process is . . . instigated . . .'

'What?' the Doctor bellowed. 'Why didn't you say so earlier? Instigate it!'

Romana felt the world sliding away from her. Her

consciousness began to close down, her vision receded, and the voices of her two friends echoed at the end of an infinitely long tunnel. 'Affirma . . . tive . . . Mas . . .' 'Do it . . . K9!'

And then, just as she was prepared to face death, there was a fearsome screech of protesting machinery. The TARDIS's old engines made enough of a racket at the best of times. This was ten times worse, a raucous unearthly trumpeting that had all the delicacy on the ear of a fingernail scraping a blackboard. It sounded more organic than mechanical. The glowing instruments under the console's central column glowed fiery red and there was a series of internal explosions from somewhere deep in the TARDIS's workings.

Romana suddenly found herself thrown head first on to the floor. Luckily her arms and legs, spreadeagled by the boundary forces, cushioned her fall. Her nose bumped the cool white flooring. A selection of the Doctor's junk rained down on her.

She looked up on a remarkable scene. It was as if nothing had happened. The lighting had regained its customary brightness, the noise of the storm had snapped off and been replaced by the soothing hum of the environment systems, and the Doctor and K9, who were huddled together in a heap on the other side of the console, looked unscathed. If it hadn't been for the disarray of the Doctor's knick-knacks and the toppled hatstand she might have doubted her memory of the previous two minutes. 'Are you all right?' she called over, picking herself up.

The Doctor uncoiled himself. His hair was standing on end and he wore a startled expression. 'Am I all right? Yes, I think so. I was dreaming. The colours were so bright. And you were there, and so was K9 . . .'

'It wasn't a dream.'

He shook himself and sat up. 'Are you all right, K9?'

The dog lifted his head. 'Define "all right", Master.'

'Ha.' He patted K9 on his ear sensors. 'I think you've just answered the question.'

'Negative, Master, I did n–'

'Oh shut up. How about you, Romana?' he asked, standing up.

She smiled. 'A few bruises, that's all.'

'Good, good. We don't want you regenerating again, do we?' He kicked at the junk strewn across the floor. 'I think I'm going to have to start this from the top.'

Romana guided him gently away. 'Don't you think it's more important to work out why that happened and to make sure it never does again?'

The Doctor seemed to think for a moment. Then he shook his head. 'I shouldn't worry. The odds of going up the Time Spiral twice are –' He broke off and put a hand through his hair. 'Wait a moment. Odds. Random actions.' He snapped his fingers and pointed to a particular instrument on the console, a rectangular glass box containing a row of winking lights. This was the Randomizer, a unit appended to the navigation systems by the Doctor to throw his enemy the Black Guardian, the most evil being in the cosmos, off his trail. 'I think we ought to disconnect that thing. It's been bad news ever since I wired it up. Keeps landing us in the most dreadful trouble.'

K9 piped up. 'Ninety-three per cent of TARDIS materializations for which I have records previous to the installation of the Randomizer also match that description, Master.'

The Doctor snorted. 'Well, there's trouble, and then there's trouble.' His pointing finger wavered up to the central column. 'Good heavens, it's stopped.'

'We have materialized, Master,' said K9.

'Yes, I know. What I mean is we must have materialized very close to the boundary.' He exchanged a shifty glance with Romana. 'We really shouldn't be here, should we, this far into the future? The Time Lords wouldn't approve.'

Romana checked the panel that gave information on the immediate surroundings. Her trained eye picked out the most relevant details in seconds. 'Right at the end of the Humanian era. After the destruction of

Earth.' She smiled. 'We should do our duty and leave right away.'

'Hmm.' The Doctor smiled back, his hand already reaching for the scanner control. 'Not a word to the High Council when you get back to Gallifrey.'

Romana bristled. 'Who said anything about going back?'

But the Doctor's attention was already taken by the screen. The shutters parted to reveal a singularly uninspiring terrain of grey rock and grey sky. There was an occasional grey puddle. Romana tried to describe it to herself in some more constructive way and failed. Grey summed it all up. 'Hardly worth the candle,' said the Doctor. 'When one's come all this way, one expects something with a bit more ... well, with a bit more *chutzpah*. It might as well be Eastbourne.'

'Eastbourne?' asked Romana.

'Settlement on planet Earth,' said K9. 'Famed for its fish suppers.'

'Fish suppers?'

The Doctor shushed them both. 'Never mind Eastbourne.' He gestured to the sensor displays. 'The atmosphere's fairly clean, gravity's reasonable. A small amount of natural radiation. I think we should take a little look round.'

'It doesn't look very interesting.'

He righted the hatstand, shrugged himself into his long, dark-brown coat and looped his trailing scarf around his neck. 'Never judge a book by its cover, Romana. Besides, we've got to go out. Just so we can say we've been.' He operated the door lever and the double doors swung open with a low hum. 'Come on, K9, if you're up to it. Best roller forward.' The dog trundled after him.

Romana straightened her jacket and cape and followed.

The TARDIS's battered police box shell sat slightly askew on top of a small hillock. Romana emerged and shivered in the chill wind blowing low across the dunes. Her shoes sank a few centimetres into the muddy silt. She wrapped her cape around herself and turned slowly about, taking in the scene. Surely there had never been such a tedious-looking place. Nothing but undulating grey sand and rock for what could be hundreds of miles, and a sky made grim by raw, indistinguishable winter clouds the colour of metal plate. Far away on the side facing away from the TARDIS was a range of small mountains. Even these were completely grey. Aside from the crunching footfalls of herself and the Doctor, and the whirring motor of K9, the only sound was the wind's lonely moan.

The Doctor wetted his finger and held it up. 'I think it's going to rain.'

Romana knelt down and let the wet sand fall through her fingers. 'Alluvial deposits. No signs of habitation or animal life.'

The Doctor pounded down the hillock, K9 trailing at his heels. 'There's always something to be found if you're prepared to look.' He put a hand to his brow and peered ahead.

'Even here?'

'Even here. By this time intelligent life is scattered far and wide, right across the universe. Or so they say. We're bound to bump into somebody.'

Romana shivered again. 'I hope you're wrong again.'

'No, there's sure to be some activity in the general region –' He broke off. 'What do you mean, again?'

Romana ignored him and knelt down to address K9, who was sniffing at a lump of rock. 'What do you make of it, K9?'

'Igneous strata suggests ancient volcanic activity,' he replied.

'Not the rock. The whole place.'

K9 whirred and ticked. 'Estimate moderately sized planetoid with thin atmospheric belt and no mineral deposits of value. Inference: unexploited, uninhabited.'

The Doctor strode ahead. 'You can infer all you like. It doesn't mean you're right.'

Romana stood. 'Come on, we'd better follow him.'

K9 waited a second, his sensors still clicking. 'Oddity,

27

Mistress. There is a residual heat trace from this planetoid's core.'

'Shouldn't there be?'

'Not of this magnitude, Mistress. The temperature is slightly higher than reference tables would suggest.' He set off after the Doctor. 'Inference: natural anomaly.'

'There you are,' the Doctor said as she hurried to join him. 'What did I tell you? Something.'

Romana recognized the signs of his trying to save face. 'Only if you're interested in cores,' she said with tart emphasis.

Hans Viddeas walked slightly faster than normal down one of the command post's long, low-ceilinged corridors. His gleaming buttons sparkled in the light of the make-shift lamps that were strung along the walls on a length of plastic coil, and the steady trip-trap of his boot heels on the metal flooring made him feel rather important and efficient, fresh and prepared for anything, even though his alarm had roused him only five minutes before. Five minutes to wash, shave and dress in his freshly laundered and immaculately starched uniform.

God, how he adored his uniform. Please, God, let him never be promoted, lest he have to trade its Spartan simplicity – which showed off his broad shoulders and long legs to their fullest advantage – for Dolne's fussy epaulettes and ceremonial trimmings. Long ago he had made up his mind that clothes were the best thing about this war. As a boy he'd watched his father set off to the front in the very same garb and longed for the day of his passing out. All through his training he'd had to fight hard to conceal his enthusiasm for the amazing garments. And now, after four years' active service on Barclow, the feel of the wonderful dun fabric pressing against his skin still gave him a fantastic thrill.

The reason behind the just discernible increase in his walking speed he was keeping concealed, even from him-self. Dolne was his superior – it was Dolne's responsibility. Let Dolne sort it out.

He turned a corner sharply (he was particularly proud of his sharp turns, honed to excellence on the parade ground) and entered the Strat Room. It was the largest room in the command post. On the far side was a long row of desks and work stations at which sat the duty staff assigned to tasks that varied from communications to satellite tracking to weapons maintenance. The hushed ambience was counterpointed by a perpetual underscore of whistles, clicks, computer noise and the crackle of radio communications escaping from headphones and earplugs as patrols called for their instructions. A dozen screens offered a dozen different views of the front, some relayed from ordinary video equipment, others which showed segmented radar images or infrared scans of certain enemy outposts. All of this information was collated on a massive circular table in the centre of the room. It was a map of Barclow's fifty-mile-square temperate zone, from the circle of mountains at one end to the airless marshlands at the other, uplit, and overlaid by a massive, cobweb-like grid that allowed for instant identification of any area cell by cell. Red lines picked out the swell of the region's contours, and cast a pinkish glow into the face of anybody standing over the map, contrasting with the orange glow of the ceiling lamps. Viddeas liked to stand over it, as it made him feel important. He cast his eyes approvingly over it as he walked in, although he kept them away from the flashing blue cell 63T. Then he said loudly, 'Good morning, team.'

The duty staff looked up briefly from their tasks and there was a general muttered, 'Good morning, Captain Viddeas.'

Viddeas looked around the room. 'Where's Bleisch? Not still down the pipe?'

'Afraid so, sir,' someone said. 'He called in to say he hadn't found the fault and was looking in another section.'

Viddeas swore under his breath. Bleisch, the post's environment officer, had descended the previous morning into the aged heating system, his mission to correct the malfunction in the air-conditioning that was turning from a minor irritant to a burning worry. Already he could feel twin patches of wetness forming under his arms, and a thick miasma of unaired summer rooms hovered over them all. Viddeas had hoped to have this fixed by Dolne's return. It added another worry, as if he needed it.

He nodded to Cadinot, the young clerk in charge of systems coordination. It was his task to oversee the running of their tactics and report any hitches. 'Any sign of the Admiral's pod yet?'

'The shuttle passed over on its low sweep ten minutes ago, sir. We should have radar confirmation of the drop any moment.'

'Good man, Cadinot. Stay alert.' He was about to head for his own desk in an alcove off the Strat Room when something on Cadinot's worktop caught his eye. He felt an irrational annoyance. The little things, always the *little* things. He pointed to the mound of papers. 'What's that?'

Cadinot raised his head guiltily. 'It's filing, sir.'

Viddeas raised the bottom-most file and peered at the date. 'From a week and a half ago. Do it straight away.'

'Er, sir, the Admiral's shuttle will need –'

Viddeas raised a stiff hand. 'Straight away, Private. I will deal with the Admiral's clearance.' He could not resist a further glare at the filing. 'We must keep the paperwork up to date and keep surfaces free.'

Cadinot nodded. 'I'm sorry, sir.'

Viddeas turned and walked to his desk in the alcove, savouring the tension created by his admonition. He sat and switched on his communicator, a tarnished metal box surmounted by trailing wires that sat next to his desk-tidy. After punching in the Admiral's com-number he leant back with the receiver pressed to his ear, twisting the wire and making an abstracted inspection of the sheet-panelled ceiling. The call-tone broke off and Dolne's voice said, 'Dolne here. Who's that?'

Viddeas winced inwardly at his superior's lack of

formality. 'Good morning, Admiral. This is Captain Viddeas. I trust you have had a safe journey.'

Dolne's exaggerated sigh crackled in his ear. 'Now look, Viddeas, I'm just about to drop. So forget the chit-chat and set up the barrage, eh? We can talk later.'

Viddeas felt relieved. The longer he could put off breaking the big news the better. 'As you wish, sir. The docking pad here is ready to receive you.' He made an impatient signal across the room to one of his subordinates, who hurried to press a row of switches at his station. Immediately a thin, high-pitched bleeping, repeated every few seconds, echoed from the big speaker grille above their heads. 'There's the tracking note, sir.'

'Yes,' said Dolne. 'Locked on. I'll see you in a few minutes. Oh, and Viddeas, by the way . . .'

'Admiral?'

'Try not to waste too much ammo. Last time there were burst shells all over the Low Valley. It reflects badly on accounts if we have to reorder too often. I know you like firing your rockets, but there's no need to go mad, is there?'

'No, sir,' said Viddeas. There was a brief burst of static as Dolne cut the com-link. Then Viddeas replaced the receiver and swivelled to face his team. (He liked his swivel chair; its fluid movements made giving orders that bit more dramatic.) 'Right then. Cadinot, oversee the barrage. I want –' he consulted the map, although this was quite unnecessary, as he knew the precise locations by heart like everybody else '– launchers Q17, 88K and 9V primed and ready to fire in a minute. Have the patrol in 88K stand down under cover and prepare a ground report on the attack. I want interceptors primed for automatic response to enemy counterfire.' He'd said those words so many times before. His last girlfriend had told him how he mumbled them in his sleep. Still, there was a gratifying bustle of activity, lots of muttering and pressing of buttons, and for just a second Viddeas felt a rush of anticipation, a sensation that his job meant something.

31

The feeling soon faded. It was replaced by an uncomfortable pragmatism. He was as jaded as the duty staff, only he hid it better. This was all a formality, and despite the lovely uniform and the occasional opportunity to do some shouting, life here was unremittingly dull.

He brushed a fly from his cheek abstractedly, cursing the stifling atmosphere.

The Darkness rustled. Spindly mechanisms, formed of its own tissues, of thousands of tiny interconnecting bodies, rustled as a pulse was received from the Attack Cloud.

To the human ear the report would have been a sudden sharp splintering crack. To the Darkness it was *One remote host is in position. The other awaits. Optimum target identified.*

The Darkness clicked its reply. *Proceed.*

Romana let out a despairing sigh. After half an hour the landscape was unchanged and she was beginning to lose the little enthusiasm she'd had for this expedition. 'Admit it, Doctor. There's absolutely nothing here.'

'That depends on what you mean by absolutely nothing,' the Doctor said. 'Absolute nothingness is very much a subjective state, conceptually speaking.'

'I wasn't conceptually speaking.'

'Neither was I. There must be *something* here.'

Romana's shoulders slumped. 'K9's soil analysis says that there are none of the essential relational properties needed to nurture vegetation. And if there are no plants there can't be any animal life.'

'Rubbish,' the Doctor replied. 'Life's overrated anyway. The majority of places get along without it very well.'

'Life's a subjective state too, Doctor,' Romana pointed out.

'Tell that to a dead man.' Their route now took them to a narrow natural pathway between two fairly large faces of rock. 'Anyway, you obviously haven't cons–' He broke off and stared down at his foot. 'Hello.' He crooked himself and

32

pulled something out that was covered by white dust. 'No life, eh? What's this, then?' He held up a large old leather boot, cracked by the ages. 'There are people here.'

'Were.' Gently, Romana took it from him. It had once been sturdy and strong, designed to scale mountains, perhaps. Now it felt so fragile it might burst in her hand like a puffball. 'This must be centuries old.'

'Unless there's a corrosive agent in the atmosphere.'

She snorted. 'Straw-clutching.'

'I wonder what happened to the owner.' The Doctor took the boot back and dangled it by one of its frayed laces. 'Why do you always find just the one? Why not chuck both away?'

Romana said, 'Machine stitching means we can't be too far from a technological society, or the remains of one. A survey mission from a nearby world left that, I'd say. Took a look about and cleared off. Nobody would want to remain here.' She rubbed her hands together. 'I certainly don't.'

Any further debate on their find was put off by the arrival of K9, who came whirring into view around a corner. 'Request slower progress, Master. My traction unit is incompatible with this terrain.'

'Not to worry, K9,' said the Doctor. He hurled the boot away contemptuously. 'Romana can carry you if you fall behind. She's a good strong girl. Come on.' He turned and started to walk back the way they had come.

'We're leaving?' asked Romana.

The Doctor shrugged. 'I don't think this planet is much cop.'

She hurried after him. 'You're frightened you're going to lose the argument.'

'Nonsense.' He sounded scandalized. 'I am perfectly capable of admitting when I'm wrong.'

'My observation record of your behaviour conflicts with this assertion, Master,' said K9, who was again struggling to keep pace. 'Available data suggests that –' He stopped suddenly.

'What's the matter, K9?' asked Romana.

33

The robot dog's head rose as if he was listening for something. 'There is danger,' he said.

The Doctor made a derisive noise. 'You are a nervous old hen. There's nothing here.' He looked momentarily caught out. Then he waved a triumphant finger at Romana. 'There. I admitted I was wrong.'

'By accident.'

'Don't go around criticizing me for not admitting when I'm wrong if you're not prepared to admit you were wrong about me not admitting I was wrong,' he said.

'Master, Mistress, danger,' repeated K9. 'My sensors detect a minute release of gases associated with low-level sub-atmospheric travel.'

'Interesting,' said the Doctor, looking about the horizon. 'But hardly dangerous, is it?'

'Gases associated with offensive rockets, Master,' pointed out K9. 'Suggest you and the Mistress take immediate cov—'

There was a shattering blast from the sky, directly above them, it seemed. Romana ducked instinctively, and offered no resistance to the Doctor's strong hand when it pushed her protectively to the ground.

She looked up and saw a small black lozenge-shaped craft zooming down through the clouds in a spiral pattern. 'It's an escape capsule, isn't it?' she shouted.

'Too big,' the Doctor replied. 'And moving too smoothly. A one-seater pod, I'd say. Which means it's heading for some sort of settlement.' He shot her an accusing look.

'I admit I was wrong,' she said.

As if to quash all doubt on this, a second capsule appeared. Its descent took it in the opposite direction to that of its predecessor.

K9 spoke. 'Rockets are approaching.'

The words were barely out of his voicebox when a missile streaked across the sky. It was long and white with red fins along its sides and a pointed snout. It was difficult to tell from which angle it had been fired. Its target was the first pod, which was moving confidently if not speedily the other way. The implication was obvious. 'This is a war zone.'

For a moment, as missile and pod came closer, it appeared the attack would be a success. Romana braced herself for the din of impact. Then the missile shot past the capsule, spluttered feebly, and fell, its tail-ports leaving a trail of white vapour. It burnt up as it went, its painted sides blistering and cracking away. K9's warning had been precipitate: there was a distance of, she estimated, ten miles between their position and the danger area. She watched the descent without passion, her mind more concentrated on the calculation of its velocity and likely payload than on the spectacle it presented.

The Doctor nudged her. 'Cover your ears,' he called. His fingers were already in his.

Romana obeyed. It seemed unlikely that the explosion was close enough to harm their hearing, but then the Doctor, having experienced more than his share of explosions in a long life, was an expert.

There was a dull whump and a slight vibration. Romana squinted at the impact site. 'Has it gone off properly?' The Doctor did not reply. She pulled his finger from his ear. 'Has it gone off properly?'

It was K9 who replied. 'Affirmative, Mistress. My sensors report that the full quantity of trinitrotoluene stored in the projectile's nosecone has ignited.'

'Trinitrotoluene?' queried Romana. 'Against a capsule like that?'

The second pod was now almost out of view, its final descent concealed by a bank of craggy rocks to their left. Just before it vanished completely another missile appeared, fired from the other side, and with a slightly different design, but following much the same course as the first. This time it was nowhere near the target. Its brief career consisted entirely of getting halfway across the sky and then plummeting with a similarly unimpressive thud and crash. It was, thought Romana, a bit like watching an amateur pyrotechnic display.

'Somebody's a very, very bad shot,' said the Doctor.

'Even if they'd been bang on target trinitrotoluene wouldn't so much have scratched those pods,' said Romana. She folded her arms. 'It's puzzling.'

'What is?'

'The disparity in the technologies suggests a type F invasion scenario,' she began.

'That and the design,' put in the Doctor. 'Invaders prefer the lozenge look. I've never understood why.'

'But the planet itself argues against that thesis, being barren and unprofitable,' Romana concluded.

The Doctor shrugged. 'Perhaps the invaders just have tenebrous tastes. Haven't you heard of *chacun à son goût*?'

Romana wrinkled her nose. 'I tried it once and I didn't like it. What's your opinion, K9?'

'Invasion hypothesis most likely. However, my logic circuits refute the Doctor Master's contention that this invasion is aesthetically motivated.'

'Well, of course they do,' grumbled the Doctor. 'It was a joke. One day I'm going to update that idiom bank of yours, K9.' He turned to Romana. 'This place could just be a rung on the ladder of somebody's conquests. They're attacking it because they can, not because of any inherent value.'

She was doubtful. 'Somebody's prepared to defend it.'

'Yes. Interesting, isn't it?' He moved closer and whispered, 'I think we ought to stay and find out what's what, eh?'

Romana said playfully, 'We could always just go back to the TARDIS and clear out.'

'Don't be silly. Where would that get us?'

'Somewhere else.'

But he had set off again, his long shambling strides taking him this time in the direction in which the pod had fled, to their left. 'Come on, then.'

With some enthusiasm – she was beginning to appreciate the allure of a well-twisted mystery – Romana hurried after him, K9 trundling along behind.

* * *

Dolne emerged from the pod and moved quickly through the connecting tube and into the airlock. Such was his familiarity with these procedures that he almost forgot to stop and pay homage to the Metralubitan anthem, which was playing on automatic as a welcome. The moment after its final flourish he flipped on the airlock's com-pad and the Strat Room fizzled into view. It looked neater than usual, and Viddeas was absent. 'Hello, team,' he called.

'Welcome back, sir,' he heard them say, not without a note of relief.

'Now, then,' he said happily. 'I managed to get a few things and I hope everyone will be happy. Cadinot, I found that aftershave you were after, and if Hammerschmidt's about you can tell him I'm afraid they were out of those slippers he wanted in blue, so I got him a pair in red instead . . .' As he talked, he heard the heavy chunk of metal on metal as, with the decontamination checks complete, the airlock wall started to rise. 'Well, here I am, then. I've a few things to attend to in my room and then I'll pop round. And I've got a special treat for all of you. You cleared the mines in last month's exercise with ninety-eight per cent success. So —' he patted the box '— I had a think and decided cream cakes were in order.' There was a general show of appreciation from the team. 'See you later, then.' Dolne clicked off the link and waited for the airlock wall to rise fully. Its corrugated-iron sides moved with irksome slowness, the pulleys inside squealing with strain. If there should ever be an emergency that required speedy evacuation they'd all be doomed, standing waiting to get into the silo.

He looked down. At his feet next to his suitcase and box of presents was Jafrid's dagger. The facets of the exotic stones in the hilt caught the dull glow of the post's yellow wall lamps and sent out brightly coloured sparkles in reply.

The first thing that struck Dolne as odd when the great panel slid finally up above head level was not Viddeas, whose salute matched the rigidity of his stance and whose outfit gave his dark and supple body a curt outline, despite the fact that it was unusual for his captain to welcome him personally. It was that the command post's air, normally fresh and recycled with added scents, was fetid and laden with displeasing smells.

Viddeas stepped forward and clicked his shiny heels together. 'Sir!'

'At ease,' mumbled Dolne, stepping through into the reception area, grey and nondescript like much else in the command post.

Viddeas said quickly, 'The attack went well, sir.'

Dolne raised an eyebrow. 'Not *too* well, I hope.'

'Our tracker missile, source point 88K,' Viddeas continued, 'made close contact with the enemy pod, sir. And impacted safely at point 88H.'

'We've no patrols out in 88, have we?'

'No, sir,' said Viddeas. 'And, of course, the risk from tracker impact is minimal.'

Dolne concealed his irritation at this restatement of accepted fact. Viddeas scattered his reportage with such little certainties, perhaps as a way of keeping his mind focused. 'Look,' said Dolne, dropping any pretence to formality, 'why is it so stuffy in here?'

'The air-conditioning stopped yesterday morning, sir.' A fresh line of sweat trickled down Viddeas's cheek. 'Bleisch thinks it's a fused circuit-plate.'

'Yesterday morning? Where is Bleisch?'

'I ordered him into the workings, sir. He's still searching out the fault.'

Dolne groaned. 'I expect you've vented the intake pipes?' An antiquated emergency system allowed them to draw on the breathable, if tainted, atmosphere of Barclow.

'They're all blocked, sir,' replied Viddeas.

Dolne realized he had the power to reprimand Viddeas severely over this affair. But he couldn't bring himself to. He hated confrontation, and it was really a piddling thing. Sort problems out swiftly and let things blow over was his unspoken motto. 'Very well,' he said at last. 'I suppose it isn't your fault.'

An ensign stepped forward to attend to his luggage, his fingers curling into the handles of the big suitcase. Dolne stopped him before he could pick it up. 'Leave the box, but take this to my quarters, would you?' The ensign nodded and took the sword, staggering from the unexpected heaviness.

Viddeas watched him depart. 'What was that, sir?'

'Token from Jafrid. Pretty, isn't it? He tried to kill me with it, and it caught my eye.' He picked up the box of presents and took out a wrapped package from the top of the pile. 'You might as well have this now. I warn you, it's only socks. But then you never tell me what you want.'

'Thank you, sir,' said Viddeas. He tucked the packet under his arm and looked out of reception and along the outer corridor, as if checking they could not be overheard. Then he turned back and said, 'Sir, I have some bad news to report.'

'The recycling hasn't gone down again, has it?' This was Dolne's greatest fear. He well remembered the malfunction in the waste-compactor that had seen them eking out rations for a week and a half until spare parts arrived from Metralubit.

'No, sir. It's one of the active patrols, division Q.'

Dolne searched his memory. There were twenty divisions under his command, weren't there, of three men each? Ten were active at any one time, although activity consisted of not much more than mooching about the war zone trying to look busy. 'Division Q. That's Kelton, isn't it?'

'Yes, sir.' Viddeas's discomfort showed in the glistening brow that was not entirely the creation of the air-conditioning fault. 'He didn't report in yesterday, sir, and I began to suspect something had gone wrong.'

'Where was Q when he last checked in?'

'In 63T, sir, over by the nearer end of the Great Ridge.'

Dolne had envisaged a leisurely day catching up on field reports in his room and having a look at that dagger, and was not prepared to see it slip away. 'Oh, they're probably just

39

lost, Captain – that or their communicator's blanked out. Atmospherics, you know. Happened before.' He made to step out into the corridor.

'There's a further complication, sir,' said Viddeas, halting him. He lowered his voice and said urgently, 'Kelton's job was to escort that awful artist chap out to the Great Ridge. It's a wonderful view, they say. And the man's come back with some wild story. I had to put him under sedation, sir. I didn't want him alarming the men.'

'He's always been a bit potty,' said Dolne. 'What's he saying?'

'That there was a missile strike, sir, while the patrol was sleeping. He was taking a stroll by night, being a light sleeper, and heard a projectile come down. He says he hurried back to the camp and saw Kelton and the rest crushed under a cliff-fall. The rocks out there are notoriously unstable, sir. I checked the files. Admiral Inness lost a couple of men in the vicinity fifty years ago.'

'A missile strike?' Dolne's brain refused to accept it. He upbraided himself for being more put out by the threat to his day than by the deaths of three of his men. 'Is the man certain?'

'As certain as a civilian can be, sir. I told him what he heard was the fall of the rocks but he wouldn't listen to me. He says he saw pieces of the missile's housing among the wreckage of the camp.'

Dolne pondered. It was rare that his job put him in a position where his decisions carried serious weight. 'You did a sat sweep, I assume?'

'Yes, sir. But there was such severe distortion that I couldn't make much out.'

'Distortion from what?'

'I don't know, sir,' said Viddeas weakly. 'The east sat has been playing up of late, if you recall.'

'You haven't told anyone about this daft missile story, have you?' asked Dolne. 'We don't want a scene.'

'Of course not, sir. Only myself and a couple of the Strat Team are aware of it at all. I considered it the wisest course to take, particularly during Mr Rabley's visit.'

Dolne's eyebrows shot up. 'Good God, I'd forgotten about him! Where is he? Nowhere near 63, I hope?'

'Of course not, sir. Mr Rabley is with division D in the foothills at 31, having returned from a social with the enemy.'

'And no doubt,' said Dolne, 'has his auto-camera with him.' He nodded approvingly. 'You've done very well, Viddeas. There can't be any hint of scandal while Rabley's still here. We'll wait until he's gone and hold an inquiry then.' He looked down at his shining black boots sadly. 'Poor Kelton. He was a good sort.'

Viddeas nodded. 'And the enemy, sir? I wondered if we should inform them.'

'Absolutely not. I don't see any reason to. It'll only cause an incident, which is the last thing we need in the present political climate.' He clapped Viddeas across the shoulder. 'I'll have a word with the artist later.' He moved off.

'Where are you going, sir?' asked Viddeas.

'To my room, Captain.' He turned and stared at his junior with all the superiority he could muster. 'You have a criticism?'

Viddeas couldn't hold his stare. 'No, sir.' He saluted and strode away.

'Of course, we could be misjudging the entire situation,' the Doctor said breezily, his loping walk keeping him still very much at the head of his three-being expedition.

'We could?' asked Romana, navigating a tricky path around some large boulders.

'Yes. What if those pod things were unmanned?'

She stopped to think. 'Sport? A firing range?'

The Doctor stopped too. 'It accounts for whoever fired the missiles being such a rotten shot. And those pods, clay pigeons.' He registered her expression. 'Well, it's a theory, at –'

K9 broke in. 'Master, Mistress.'

The Doctor sighed. 'Am I ever going to finish a sentence today? What is it?'

'Someone is approaching,' said K9.

The Doctor's shoulders slumped. 'Not again. You've been nothing but trouble today, do you know that?'

K9 burbled indignantly. 'Charge refuted. The advice provided by this unit saved your life earlier, Master.'

'That's beside the point. I wish you'd –'

Romana caught his arm and pointed ahead. 'Doctor, he's right. Over there.'

There was a strange whirring noise, not entirely unlike that of K9's motor. It got louder, its accompaniment a shuffling, deliberate tread through the heaped sands. Between the large rocks ahead of them, swathed in the mists that hung eerily over the emptiness, a figure began to take shape.

2

The Femdroids

The study nestled halfway up the north side of the Dome, and its large, three-sided bay window afforded a staggering view of Metron, the sprawling capital city of Metralubit. If he chose, Premier Harmock could sit well back and observe the masses over which he presided, dressed simply in the transparent plastic tabards that had been the fashion for many years, going about their diverse businesses amid the gigantic curved white towers, the generously proportioned and levelly raked patches of garden space, and the clear glass tubeways that made up this glorious architectural achievement. He might have stopped to marvel at the utilitarian efficiency that manifested itself in the dazzling cleanliness of the pavements, the battery-powered skimcars that moved in ordered ranks along the monotram network, and the mobile fusion inlets through which any person could access the powernet. And if his soul had been in especial need of uplift he could have done no worse than to look up at the gorgeous, cloudless green sky that acted as a showcase to the pinnacle of his civilization, the ultimate product of centuries of struggle.

As it was, he sat facing away from the window, engulfed in his chair, his attention engrossed by a spectacle to him far more invigorating. He was watching himself on MNN, a mid-morning replay of the previous week's debate in the parliamentary chamber, and congratulating himself for putting up such a splendid performance. He watched as Rabley stumbled to the end of a long, disjointed speech on public-health provision. 'And is it not the case,' he said, his eyes flicking between the dispatch pad and the notescreen in his hand, 'that in the fourteen years since the Premier came to power, there has been a shortfall of more than twenty per cent in real terms in budget provision, ah, and will he not agree that it is the stifling bureaucracy imposed by his own administration that has led to the curtailment of the health advisory programmes I, er, referred to earlier?'

The picture switched to show the other side of the pad. Harmock watched himself swagger to his feet. It was startling. Nobody would ever have guessed, from his look of mild, almost baffled indignation, that he had no idea what his opponent had been talking about, and cared even less. 'No, no, no,' he saw himself say as he clutched the sides of the dispatch pad. 'No, no. I think the gentleman should allow me to correct him.' Fire back, thought Harmock. Take the smug tone, get Rabley riled, give his own notescreen time to dredge up some statistics with which to fire back. 'Arbiter, I have listened to what the gentleman has said with considerable interest, and not a little surprise.' (I was thinking about something else entirely and I'm waiting for my notescreen to give me an answer to whatever it was.) 'For surely it is the party opposite, yes, the party of which the gentleman is leader, that has the true antipathy to health provision.' (Waffle, waffle, refute with a vague accusation.) 'They are the ones who have, historically, neglected the funding of this key area and allowed provision to fall behind, and it is we who have increased it in real terms.' (Spin things out, not long now, circle the subject without actually saying anything.) 'Ah yes, look here.' (The screen is flashing at me. Thank God for auto-research.) 'In its last two years in office, the party opposite – yes, the party opposite – cut spending on health programmes by eleven per cent.' (And diverted that money into localized schemes, but he wasn't about to mention that.) 'Money which, as soon as we were able, we reallocated.' (Cutting the local programmes on the quiet along the way, but he wasn't about to mention that either.) He sat.

His opponent took the pad once more. 'Arbiter, this is a blatant attempt to confuse the current issue.' (I wasn't aware of those statistics, and I'm going to ignore them.) 'Is it not the case that what we are seeing now are the death throes of a government, clinging desperately to power, and trying to patch up the holes in the economy before the imminent election?' (Well, yes, but that's hardly the point.) 'How much longer –' indignant wave of notescreen '– how much longer must the planet wait to express its will to be rid of this incompetent government?'

'As long as I can possibly get away with,' said Harmock, snapping off the screen and feeling a contented glow spreading throughout his body. Lagging twenty per cent in the polls, his personal popularity the lowest of any leader since records began, his reputation in tatters after fourteen years of bungles, scandals and economic mishaps – it was enough to make a lesser man weep.

He pressed himself back into his chair and stretched.

The chair was a relic, some said from the days of the colony founders, a carved wooden affair with a hard back and strong armrests. A person with a less fat bottom than Harmock (and that, he thought ruefully, was most people) would have found it unbearably uncomfortable. His natural padding made it pillow-soft. He basked in it, thinking on the great triumph to come, savouring in advance the look on Rabley's face when he unveiled his great secret. To wipe away that inane grin would be positive bliss. And as ever when his thoughts turned to political pleasures he felt a corresponding urge somewhere deep within that longed for sticky toffee pudding, or mallow pie, or fried dough-sticks with caramel topping . . . His curse, and the one thing – so Galatea told him – that might still bring him down. The electorate, damn them, disapproved of his rotundity, believing it to be a sign of weakness and lack of willpower. The sanctimonious idiots.

The study door slid open with a swish of air and Galatea entered. It was as if just thinking about her could bring her into being. She carried a tray on which was his breakfast snack. Harmock's eyes swept approvingly over her figure, encased in her one-piece shining silver covering, a succulent slenderness that was the ultimate tease. For that slim-hipped frame and moulded bust contained nothing more than servo-mechanisms, electronic circuitry and processor links. 'Ah, Galatea,' he said. 'You look good enough to eat.'

She angled her head slightly, with the precision of movement that was the only hint, aside from her great beauty, of a Femdroid's true nature. It galled Harmock to think that his father, also a great parliamentarian, had once sat as part of cabinet session in this very room, and Galatea would have looked and behaved exactly the same as she did today. Her 135-year-old lips twitched into a smile, her unbelievable blue eyes sparkled, and she said in a voice that combined the sweetness of honey and the texture of a well-matured rum, 'I have news that may lessen your appetite.' Her vocabulary, in fact her whole manner, retained the formality of the age in which she had been constructed.

Harmock's bushy brows twitched. 'I don't care for news. What sort is it?'

'Good, and bad.' Galatea put down the tray and poured coffee from the percolator into his waiting mug. On the plate next to it were three slimmo-wafers, the prospect of which Harmock, no matter how hungry, could not relish.

'Good first, please,' he asked, cracking a wafer cautiously.

Galatea nodded primly. She touched the circular amulet on the chain around her neck, and the printed microcircuitry embossed there glowed and sparkled momentarily as she linked to the dome's central computer. 'Production quotas in the east sector have led to a half-per-cent increase in the region's employment level.'

'Is that it?'

'That is the good news, sir, yes. The increase can be portrayed as a triumph for the policy of wage restraint in manufacturing industries.'

'Jolly good,' said Harmock without enthusiasm. 'That'll make all the difference, won't it? Let's have the bad news, then.'

She stood back from the desk and put her hands on her hips. 'I fear I will shock you. The development I now report will lead to complications with the election.'

'I'm prepared,' said Harmock, anything but. Galatea was rarely rattled. This must be something big. Another harvest surplus in the outlands? Rioting in the Bensonian village settlements? A leak to the Opposition?

She said, with an air of resignation, 'The com-link with Borea came on-line this morning. The Phibbs Report is now ready for publication.'

Harmock reeled, although he was sitting down. He could have spent hours trying to think what the bad news might be and never have got it right. 'The Phibbs Report,' he spluttered.

'Yes, Premier.'

His fingers were losing their grip on the wafer so he put it down. 'But . . .' He struggled to find the right words. 'But they've been sitting on their arses down in Borea for over a hundred years. Why now? With no warning?'

'One hundred and twenty-nine years and eight months, sir,' said Galatea dutifully. 'And I should point out that the Committee did advise us of their near-readiness recently.'

'They've been nearly ready since my grandfather was a boy,' said Harmock. 'Has this been done to embarrass me?'

'The Committee has been totally isolated on the island of Borea for the length of its deliberation,' said Galatea. 'We must view their timing as an unfortunate coincidence.' She crossed to the window and looked out over the city. A skytrain hovered past, the tourists inside craning their necks for a view of the Dome's interior. 'And our first thought must be to maintain electoral advantage.'

Harmock slumped back in his suddenly uncomfortable chair. 'I'd never have thought it,' he breathed. He felt as if he'd been punched. 'It's all we need, isn't it? Barclow being shunted centre stage. This blows it all wide open.' His eyes turned to the fabric mural fixed to the opposite wall. It showed Metralubit's military colours emblazoned boldly across a rough representation of Barclow. For 125 years the war had rested while the Committee wrangled over it, isolated on the distant island of Borea, each generation passing the task down to the next. He hadn't expected them to reach a conclusion in his lifetime. 'What does the report say, exactly?'

'It is half a million words in length, approximately,' said Galatea. 'My underlings are busy trying to interpret it. There are also six appendices, increasing the length by a further quarter of a million words.'

'But the general gist?'

'Unclear, sir.'

'Unclear?' Harmock thumped his fist down on the desktop. 'Are we advised to start shooting or aren't we?'

'The Committee makes three hundred and twelve recommendations on the resumption of hostilities,' Galatea said. 'Many of them contradictory. Their conclusion is not certain.'

Harmock grunted. 'Whatever else it means, we'll have to bring the election forward. I had hoped for a couple more months.'

Galatea pointed a purple-painted fingernail at the com-screen. It flickered on to show a computer diagram, three blocks of colour measured against a notched axis of voters. Rabley, in green, was well over the halfway mark. Harmock, the orange block, was positively stunted by comparison, and the minor parties had dwindled almost to a nil rating. 'This is the current position. If present voter trends continue, and allowing for a three per cent margin of error, Rabley will win the election with a nineteen per cent greater share of the vote.'

'Ah,' said Harmock. 'You forget. My diet.'

'I was coming to that,' said Galatea. Her tone was without reproach; it was a simple statement of fact. She moved her finger slightly and the blocks of colour shifted. Harmock's orange shot up and swallowed Rabley's lead – just. 'A two per cent greater share is predicted,' said Galatea. She shot him a sideways glance.

'Increasing to four per cent if your body weight reaches target.'

'Excellent,' said Harmock. 'Two – I mean four – per cent. All we need.' Galatea moved her finger a third time. On this occasion Harmock's block plummeted. 'What the hell happened there?'

'The prediction is based on an estimation of voter response to the Phibbs Report,' she replied. 'So far as we understand it at present.'

'If it's inconclusive why the drop?'

'The electorate will, we predict, feel disposed to aggression. The complexion we put on the report will not matter. Patriotism is rife in times of economic shortfall, such as that we have engineered.'

Harmock made a frantic shushing gesture.

'Nobody can hear us.' Galatea, unruffled, went on, 'The electorate will see any delay to engage with the enemy as weakness and transfer their allegiance to the Opposition.'

'But Rabley can't afford a full-scale war either!' Harmock protested.

He sank into his chair, a collapsed heap. 'Galatea, I'm ruined.' He closed his eyes, trying to think clearly. The pressure of all those empty minds outside the Dome, in their skimcars and skytrains, loomed over him. How best to turn their idiot brains to his will? 'Skewered whichever way I turn. There's no possible way to win.'

Her reply was to bring up another diagram on the screen. Harmock's troubled heart, coated with the slurry of a lifetime's cholesterol abuse, leapt dangerously when he saw his own rating surge up over Rabley by a good ten percentage points, higher than his share at the last election. 'What's that scenario?'

'A predicted election result after a vigorous and costly programme of disinformation, scandalmongering and general besmirching of the Opposition.' She smiled again. 'A totally negative campaign.'

Harmock blinked rapidly. 'It would work?'

Galatea waved her long plastic nails graciously. 'As you see.'

He clapped his hands together, making a sweaty slapping sound. He stood and stared out at the teeming city. At his playthings. He loved his job too much to give it up for anything, least of all principle. 'Then we'll do it.'

The Doctor and Romana were crouched behind a slab of rock, their attention fixed on the figure emerging slowly through the mists. It was possible now to see that this mysterious person wore a transparent plastic suit. 'Protective clothing?' asked Romana.

'Too flimsy.' The Doctor nibbled his thumb. 'Humanoid, at least.'

'Is that significant?'

'Nice to know we're still around.' He nodded down at K9. 'Any weapons?'

'There are no traces of offensive equipment recognized by my data banks,' he replied.

'That's all right, then.' The Doctor made to scramble up the slab and show himself to the stranger.

'Qualification, Master,' chirped K9, halting him. 'At this time period my data banks may have become inapplicable.'

'He's right,' said Romana, raking a hand through her long blonde hair. 'We're totally in the dark.'

The Doctor pulled a sour face. 'A gun's a gun, Romana. And going by that boot they're not fiendishly advanced in these parts. In fact, all we've seen so far – the missiles as well – has been curiously archaic.'

She frowned. 'What about Clarik's Theorem?'

He looked blank. 'What about it?'

' "Societies dominated by a single intelligent life form, no matter how culturally disparate or variously organized, will always retain, within certain parameters, the essential accoutrements required for the existence of that life form." '

'Yes, I do know what Clarik's Theorem is, thank you,' the Doctor said. 'But what he failed to take into –'

'She,' said Romana.

50

'Oh. Yes. I must have been thinking of the other Clarik.'

'You must have.'

'Yes, well, what she forgot to . . .' He trailed off. 'What am I doing crouching here arguing the toss with you?' He pulled himself up and vaulted over the slab to confront the stranger.

Romana watched from hiding, still dubious. K9, his nose laser extended, peeked his head around the corner to observe the meeting.

The Doctor stood in the open. He took his hat from his pocket, unfurled it, and used it to give a cheery wave. 'Hello there!'

'Hello there,' came the reply. 'I've got everything today. Bagels, baguettes, bhajis and baps, sandwiches, samosas, scones and spring rolls . . .'

Romana was astonished. The stranger was female, and her tone was high-pitched and friendly. She strained to get a closer look as the mist finally cleared. It revealed a short, middle-aged woman with tattered blonde hair, whose white suit could now be identified as the universal uniform of a kitchen worker. This was borne out by the automated trolley that glided along at her side, attached to her wrist by a length of wire, which contained a baffling array of film-wrapped snacks: biscuits, some fruit, and packets of cold drink in addition to the items advertised in her spiel.

She brought her trolley to a halt with a flick of the wrist as she reached the Doctor. She peered at him curiously. 'I don't think I've met you before, have I?' She winked. 'Didn't know we were having another mufti day so soon. I like your scarf.'

'Thank you,' said the Doctor, clearly taken aback. 'Er, I like your, er, trolley.'

She was already reaching for a china cup from a supply and putting it beneath the tap of an urn. 'Now, tea's covered but I have to charge for everything else. Here you go.' She slid a saucer under the filled cup and held it out.

'Yes, thank you.' The Doctor took it from her. To Romana's amusement he appeared baffled, more put out by the ordinariness of this encounter than he would have been by bumping into a bloodcrazed monster. 'Ah, what brings you to these parts?'

'On my way to the enemy, aren't I?' She pressed a button on the side of the trolley and a panel slid back to reveal a very different selection of snacks that seemed to consist in the main of flowers and packets of seeds. 'Good job I bumped into you before the urn went cold. You must be a long way from your patrol. Didn't think there was anyone out here.'

'Did you see the missiles earlier?' asked the Doctor.

'Oh, that.' She shrugged. 'You'll get used to it, love. Just bangs and flashes, really, nothing serious. They have to keep their hand in, you see. Keep the folks back home happy. I shouldn't worry.' She shook the Doctor's hand. 'Anyway, I can't stop to chat. I don't want to keep the General waiting. Now, do you want anything?'

'I've no money on me at the moment,' said the Doctor.

'Poor thing. Here, have this and I'll put it on the tab.' She handed him a bun and took out a notepad from a pouch at her waist. 'What's your name, love?'

The Doctor looked suspiciously at the bun. 'The Doctor.'

'The Doctor.' She punched it into the pad and tucked it away again. 'All right. Well, see you tomorrow, probably. Bye!' She flicked her wrist, the trolley started up again, and a few moments later she was lost to sight.

Romana stood up slowly. The Doctor stood in the clearing, still clutching the cup of tea and bun, shaking his head very slowly. 'I suppose it's possible,' he said, as if talking to himself, 'that I bumped my head in that turbulence and haven't woken up yet.'

'Not unless I did, too,' she said.

He looked down at the cup and sniffed the liquid. 'Why should I dream about tea ladies on battlefields? It's probably very significant.'

Romana took the bun from his hand and held it down to K9's snout as he emerged from cover. 'Analyse this, will you?'

He carried out the task in moments. 'It is a bun, Mistress. Flour and water are combined to make dough. Yeast is added as a leaven.'

'But no harmful substances?'

'Perfectly edible, Mistress.'

She held up a hand to silence him and handed the bun back to the Doctor. 'If she caters for both sides this war must be rather an unusual one. Particularly if she mistook you for a soldier.'

He sipped at the tea. 'Yes. And she – what's that supposed to mean?'

'Rigid military etiquette doesn't apply here,' Romana said quickly.

'It certainly doesn't. I think she put the milk in first.' He put the cup of tea in his pocket. 'I suppose it had to happen one day.'

'What?'

'Well,' he said, 'I'm used to turning up in places that seem very innocuous but turn out to be very dangerous. It had to go the other way sooner or later. Law of averages.' He pointed in the direction the trolley woman had gone. 'I think we should follow her. Find out a bit more about this enemy. Judging from those foodstuffs they weren't human.'

Romana pondered afresh as they walked on. 'What kind of creature lives on berries and flowers? Most spacefaring species have a much more complex diet.'

'Don't judge a species by its tea trolley,' the Doctor said. 'Man does not live on buns alone, remember.'

'Suggest Chelonians,' put in K9. 'Large aggressive reptilians with high bionic rebuild.'

'Rubbish,' the Doctor said. 'You wouldn't find Chelonians grubbing about a place like this. They prefer verdant worlds. What's more, their expansionist period ended millennia ago.'

'The range of foods on the trolley tallies strongly with

my records of Chelonian dietary needs, Master,' K9 insisted. 'Inference is that Chelonians are present.'

The Doctor stopped and glared down at him. 'Will you stop getting under my feet? If you've nothing useful to say don't say anything.'

'There's no need to be rude, Doctor,' Romana pointed out. 'And there could well be Chelonians here. They're a very hardy race.'

'Not that hardy,' said the Doctor. 'Now, come on or the trail will go cold.' He hurried off after the trolley woman.

At the commencement of the war, the military had panicked and raced to finish the construction of the command post. That explained why the top half was rickety and prone to collapse, and why the Admiral's quarters, on the lowest level, were constructed of sturdier materials. Indeed, in comparison with the rest of the base they were luxurious. The walls of the main living room were painted a sanguine red, and a frieze depicting an ancient scene of war and carnage from the earliest days of the colony was draped across the wall. Both these items trumpeted the initial enthusiasm for war on Barclow, and served as a reminder of the spirits of a dead age. The Admiral often pondered on the subject as he soothed his tired toes on the white fur rug and sat back on the well-padded leather couch that was positioned to face the unit that was com-screen and minibar combined.

But his thoughts were on other matters as he let himself in and, with a series of frustrated grumbles and mutters, lifted his arms and shook off his ceremonial tabard. His muscles seemed to sigh with relief as he threw the heavy, gold-encrusted seal on to the couch, a message from his inner spirit relayed through his body, a message his mind had chosen to ignore. He was sick of command, sick of shuttling back and forth to summits, sick of this innately stupid, endless war that wasn't. He considered himself. Forty-five, fit, capable. There were plenty of other jobs he could do. For example . . .

54

The trail of thought vanished somewhere inside his head, as if snatched away. He shook himself, blinked in the orange glow of the lamp, and cursed his tiredness. A quick lie-down and a drink was all he needed to restore his faculties. He was on his way to the bedroom, savouring in advance the welcoming embrace of his duvet, when a red light started to flash on the front of the com-unit.

'Oh no.' He wondered if Harmock – the only caller with access to override his privacy scramble and come through direct like this – had somehow heard of the loss of division Q and Kelton. He prayed not. 'Accept,' he called, and the screen flashed into life.

The image of Harmock's face, relayed from the chain of satellites strung between Barclow and Metralubit, was grainy and uncertain, with a certain degree of atmospheric flaring at the edges. It was within the terms of the Bechet Treaty for each side to run radio interference, and Dolne had learnt to treat the static flashes as one of the prices of their strange peace. It was peculiarly cheering not to see Harmock too clearly. It gave Dolne a sense of distance that reminded him of his posting's advantages.

'Admiral,' said Harmock, without preamble. His face was pinched and grave, and the smugness that was the outward mark of his dismal, pompous personality was if not in abeyance then somewhere further towards the back of his expression than was usual. 'You must prepare yourself for the worst. There has been a development.'

Dolne felt his peaceful day slipping its moorings again. 'What can that be?' Some piffling poll had given Harmock the wind, no doubt, and now it was time to shift some of the blame. Dolne felt a flash of excitement. What if Harmock was about to sack him? 'I hope I haven't given you cause for trouble,' he said as sincerely as he could.

Harmock's brow twitched. 'What? You?' He pronounced the second word with undisguised dismissal, as if it was not within Dolne's power to be even noticeable. 'No, no. No, you haven't done anything. Although –' he

55

rumbled sardonically '– you may soon have to.'

Dolne really didn't like the sound of that. 'What do you mean?'

'Oh, Dolne, it's . . .' He put a hand to his brow. 'Phibbs. They're about to publish.'

Dolne felt a rush of adrenalin racing through his arms and legs. Immediately his chest tightened. 'Oh my God.' He gulped. 'What does it say? I mean, I'm not expected to, er, well, you know . . .' He mimed a shooting gesture. Even that level of violence made him feel giddy. 'Oh hell.'

'Nobody knows yet,' said Harmock. 'As soon as I heard the news I summoned Galatea, and I've got her and her pals going over it with a fine-toothed comb. I insisted they pore through every section. It's a ridiculous length, and rather unclear, so with any luck we'll find a way to . . .' He trailed off, perhaps realizing what he was saying.

Mentally Dolne completed the unsayable sentence. *To keep things exactly the same as they are.* 'Has it gone public yet?' he asked.

'Bound to very soon. So.' Harmock lifted a stern finger. 'No interviews, Dolne, and that goes for all your staff. You're to maintain a media silence for as long as I say. This situation will have to be handled with extreme care.' He lifted a bushy eyebrow. 'I hope I make myself clear.'

'Perfectly clear, Mr Harmock.' He was referring, of course, to the election, now made inevitable. 'I shall contact Mr Rabley's party immediately and order the shutdown of his auto-cam.'

Harmock nodded. 'Good. You see, no party should have an advant – I mean, no party should be permitted to broadcast from the front itself. Most unfair, and potentially dangerous. Get Rabley on a shuttle and back here quick as you can.' He made a big show of consulting his watch. 'Now look, Dolne, I'm going to have to go. I have to prepare my broadcast to the network.' His delivery sank for a moment into sententious smoothness. 'The citizens will need my assurance on this –' pause '– the most difficult day in *all* our lives.' He reached forward and clicked off the link.

Dolne shut off his own screen and immediately leapt to his feet. 'Hell, hell, damn, damn,' he said, and paced back and forth over his thick-pile carpet. The unventilated stuffiness increased his tensions. In a reflex movement he poured himself a double measure of Scotch from the minibar and knocked it back in a couple of gulps. A hundred questions assailed his mind. How was he going to break the news to his staff? Which way would the electorate turn? What would be Jafrid's reaction? He had no plan for this eventuality, no scheme, no matter how rough-hewn, to effect escape. And there was the most dread consideration of all, the prospect of which made him tremble all over. What if the war turned real? Real orders, real fighting, real weapons. Real deaths. The red walls, irrelevant mere minutes before, took on a ghastly new significance, and he squirmed at the suggestion of blood.

He got himself another drink. 'I would never,' he said out loud, 'have believed this possible.' The liquid caught a twinkling rainbow pattern in its depths – the distorted refractions of the stones of Jafrid's dagger. Dolne felt a pang of real regret. 'Oh, my dear friend. What are we to do?'

There was a knock at the door. Dolne snarled and waved his drink dismissively, which the environment computer of his quarters unfortunately took to mean he was allowing access. The door swished open to reveal one of the junior staff, Hammerschmidt. He gave a perfunctory salute and held out a sheaf of papers. 'Morning, sir. Welcome back. Er, would you sign this, please?' He seemed edgy and distracted, and kept looking both ways down the corridor.

Dolne snatched the papers from him. They were outdated washing-up rosters. 'What do I want with these?'

Hammerschmidt lowered his voice and looked cautiously about again. 'Inside, sir.'

Dolne flipped through the papers. Concealed within was a greetings card, adorned with a floral design and the

57

legend 'Sorry To Be Losing You'. The post had signed their names inside. He noticed the signature of Viddeas, bold and underlined importantly, straight away. 'Who's this for?'

'Pollis,' whispered Hammerschmidt. At Dolne's blank look he added, 'From com maintenance, sir. Going back to homeworld at the end of the week.' He gestured vaguely down the corridor. 'He's about here somewhere, sir, so if you could sign it quickly and give it back, because he might stroll along and catch us.'

Dolne thought. It was all Hammerschmidt ever did, he decided. Walk along corridors clutching a concealed leaving card, jangling a bag of change for the present. It was ordinary, unproductive, inefficient, symptomatic of the entire operation. It had never bothered him before. Now, he did something he had never done in all his admiralship. He shouted 'Get out!', threw the card at him, and slammed the door shut.

He collapsed against it, panting, and ran a hand through his dishevelled, sweat-streaked hair. Was it getting hard to breathe? Or had Harmock's news been too much for him?

He brushed away a fly from his brow (insect life from Metralubit had a way of evading the quarantine regulations, although lack of sustenance meant crawlies never lasted long) and set about putting his thoughts in some kind of order.

It didn't work, so he cried instead.

Harmock's face, distorted by the ripples of the watery screen, creased with worry. '*Oh, Dolne, it's . . .*' He put a hand to his brow. '*Phibbs. They're about to publish.*'

The Darkness chittered its excitement. Excellent news. Disruption. The unexpected. Another rift to exploit.

It was now time to connect with the second remote host.

Viddeas was having trouble. He'd put through a call to the patrol escorting Rabley, and ordered them to return to the post immediately. Their reply, though audible, was submerged by a sussurating wash of squeaks and hisses over an odd droning sound. Viddeas tightened his grip on the earpiece and called, 'Division G, are you there? Codie, do you copy?' He could hear the voice of the patrol leader fading out under the wave. 'Damn it.' He waved across the room, lifted one side of his headset, and bellowed, 'Teer, clean out my channel, it's awash with enemy interference.'

The communications officer stared stupidly back. 'No, sir.'

'What do you mean, no? Do it!'

'I meant there are no enemy baffles running at present,' said Teer. He gestured haplessly at his screen, which indeed showed a clear field.

Viddeas ripped the headset off and raised it for all the room to hear. Everyone turned around to face him, and he glowered to make them feel it was all their fault, which it probably was. 'What do you suppose this is, then? *Another* fault, perhaps?'

'We have been getting electrical distortion quite a lot lately, sir,' pointed out Cadinot.

Viddeas sighed and dropped the headset on to his desk. His collar was unbearably restrictive in this heat, but he would not loosen it. That would be going against regulations. And he looked better with a stiff, upturned collar anyway. He reached out a finger and cut off the howling. The silence that followed was embarrassed and unnerving, the team going about their business with a dutiful quietness accusatory in itself.

His personal com bleeped. Glad of the distraction, he took it from his belt and pressed the accept button, blowing a trickle of sweat from his nose as he said, 'Viddeas here.'

'Sir, it's Vann from the detention block,' said a voice in the casual tone that was the curse of the place. There was a lot of shouting going on behind him. 'Our "prisoner" is demanding to speak to the Admiral.'

'Surely it's my right!' came the shouting voice, which Viddeas recognized as belonging to their artist.

He bristled. 'Vann, tell the prisoner he has no rights. Tell him also that no matter how much this resembles a garden party it is actually supposed to be a war. And tell him to get back in his cell before he is sedated again.'

'I know what I saw!' the artist shouted. 'You can't –'

Viddeas switched off his com and hooked it back on his belt. 'I just did,' he said, quietly enough to suggest he was making a joke to himself and loudly enough to make sure everyone else heard him. The team laughed in their dutiful way.

There was little time to enjoy this moment, however, as Viddeas had become aware that someone was standing behind his chair expectantly. He swivelled round impressively, careful not to overshoot. An overswivel robbed the swiveller of dignity. 'What now?'

Another adjunct was standing before him, a sheet of torn paper in his hand. 'Sir, it's the photocopier again.'

Viddeas thumped the arm of his chair. 'Bleisch doubles up on photocopier maintenance. Wait for him to get back up from the pipes. I mean, it's not important, is it?'

The adjunct shuffled. 'It's the invites to Pollis's leaving do, sir. For Friday. If we don't get them to the enemy by tomorrow they might arrange to do something else, which would be a shame, as Pollis got along quite well with some of them in his patrol days.'

Viddeas stood up, snatched the sheet from his hand, and stalked off in the direction of the copying annexe. 'All right, I'll take a look at it.' He sounded irritated. In fact he was glad of the very mundanity of the problem after the trials of the last few days. 'It can't be that difficult to fix.' He called over his shoulder as he left, 'Cadinot, maintain that call to division G. We need them back here right away!'

'Yes, sir,' said Cadinot.

The copying annexe stood just off the Strat Room, where the new machine had been moved to minimize disruption. It had arrived not long ago, and was supposed to be one of the latest models, as used in the Parliament

Dome in Metron. It certainly looked attractive, with a smart, streamlined grey fascia of moulded plastic and a neat set of touch-sensitive controls. Yet after an initial settling-in period it started to display a talent for grinding, chewing, jamming and leaving sooty deposits that marked it down as the son of its fathers. Viddeas advanced on it with a murderous expression in his eye. It was the only person or thing left in the post that took any real notice of his authority, and secretly he relished its tantrums and looked forward to the chance to kick it. 'What's the problem this time, then?' he muttered. The machine's front had been opened on a hinge, revealing its complex innards: rollers, trays and several cavities whose function was mysterious. 'Let's have a look at you.' He knelt and stroked the edge of the front panel tenderly.

'I've done all it told me to,' said the adjunct, who had followed him through. 'I've cleared all the paper from the trays but it still doesn't work.'

'All right, all right.' Viddeas shooed him out. 'You cut along. I'll deal with this.'

'Sir.' The adjunct withdrew.

Alone with his great enemy, Viddeas rolled off his gloves. They peeled away with a smack, revealing fingers that were clammy and pink from the heat and which he drummed against the copier's instruction panel. He pressed the control requesting information.

PAPER JAM IN TRAYS 1+2 PLEASE CLEAR, the machine told him on its small digital display.

Viddeas grunted. 'You've tried that before.' He pulled out the specified trays with slightly more than necessary violence. They were empty, as the adjunct had said. 'Right.' He swung the outer panel shut and looked up at the information screen.

PAPER JAM IN TRAYS 1+2 PLEASE CLEAR, it said.

'Oh, for crying out loud.' Viddeas opened the panel and shut it again. The message stayed the same. He performed the operation twice more, with mounting ferocity. When he opened the panel another time it was as if all the aggression he had held in check over the last couple of weeks of equipment failures and disappearances, of disobedient, idle staff and an uninterested commanding officer, had been unleashed. He pulled out all six of the paper trays, knelt down, and peered into each one. Empty. Then he stuck in a hand, searched the copier's deepest recesses. It was not going to beat him. He would win this war. His fingers quested about, seeking whatever minuscule scrap was spannering the works.

By now the sweat was pouring from him, and he was uncomfortably aware of his urgent need for a shower. To his horror, he realized his lovely uniform smelt, and the cause of the smell was him. Damn the stupid ventilation! Damn Bleisch for taking so long! Damn Dolne for throwing the blame on him!

'Ah!' His fingers connected with something. It was an oddly shaped, oddly textured ball of something, gooey and not papery at all, stuck in the furthest corner of paper tray 1. 'Oh, I've got you now,' he said exultantly. He tugged at it, his vigour so consuming that only a small part of his brain remained active to question what the thing he was tugging at was, and how it had worked itself in there.

The object did not so much as budge an inch. Viddeas growled and decided to shift his position for a better grip. He made to remove his fingers – and found he could not. They were stuck firm, the tips embedded, absorbed into the gelatinous ball.

He pulled hard. No quarter was given. A spasm of cold fear passed over him, and he looked up instinctively at the information screen. 'What the . . .' He trailed off, made speechless by what he saw there.

CAPTAIN VIDDEAS, said the photocopier screen. PREPARE TO BE ABSORBED BY DARKNESS.

Viddeas struggled and tried to call out. But the words were stuck in his throat, and a horrific freezing sensation was making its way up his arm. 'No,' he croaked. 'No, I . . .' The coldness travelled through him with alarming rapidity, swallowing his legs and torso before moving up past his neck. 'No, I . . .'

YOU SHALL BE OUR INSTRUMENT, said the screen, TO HASTEN THE HOUR OF FEASTING.

Sensation flowed through Viddeas's brain, and it was as if his head was being plunged into a bucket of ice-cold water. There was a second's terrible pain as something deep inside him flared up and then died. Dimly he was aware that there were flies buzzing around him.

Then his hand came free. The copier door swung shut.

He stared at his hand. Apart from a minor wrinkling of the skin at the fingertips, of the kind one gets from spending too long in the bath, they looked completely normal. And though he was crouched in a very strange position in front of the copier his body felt refreshed and whole. The events of the last minute seemed rather like a dream.

The information screen read READY. SELECT NUMBER OF COPIES REQUIRED AND PRESS START TO BEGIN.

He shook his head and got to his feet. Had he hallucinated it all? Had the tedium of this life brought him down so low?

He straightened his uniform and walked briskly back towards the Strat Room. Inside, the team were going about their usual tasks in the usual way. Nobody looked up, nobody turned to him, nobody, it seemed, had heard the great commotion from next door. So, he reasoned, there had been no commotion.

Cadinot looked up. 'Still no response from Codie, sir.'

'Keep trying,' he said without thinking. His voice was as firm-sounding as ever.

'And cells say they're still having trouble with you-know-who,' added Cadinot.

Viddeas flinched. Suddenly, for no discernible reason, he felt a terrible draught about his legs. At the same time a sort of horrid, red, swirling darkness came into his awareness somewhere behind his eyes. For just a second he saw the world from the viewpoint of an entirely different creature, saw his team not as human beings but as members of a quite alien species.

'Sir?' he heard Cadinot prompting.

He focused on the young man, and a revolting urge passed through him at the sight of the boy's pretty white neck. He longed to spit on it. His tongue wetted itself as if in readiness.

Then, as quickly as it had come, the feeling faded, and he heard himself saying, 'Tell cells to sedate the prisoner.' This time several of the team did look up from their stations. Viddeas shuddered at the sight of their eyes, which were somehow revolting to him. He felt the need to withdraw, to sit down, to get this illness out of his system. Half an hour's rest and he'd be fine. He backed away slowly. 'I'm just going . . . to change . . .' he mumbled, and made for the door.

The relief he felt at getting out of the Strat Room was almost tangible. He sank against a wall in the connecting corridor, closed his eyes and pressed his eyeballs. The redness surged up again, and his legs quivered in the cold.

For some reason he put a hand on his heart. It was only when he realized it had stopped beating, and that he had stopped breathing, that the real terror began.

A red indicator light flashed for a moment in the centre of the Darkness's Glute-screen. The secondary remote host was connected. The prime mover of the Metralubitan faction was bent to their will. The arena was prepared, on both sides.

Soon there would be much death.

The catering lady's route had taken Romana, the Doctor and K9 through yet more expanses of grey, barren wasteland. The dullness of the landscape was starting to get on Romana's nerves. 'I suppose,' she said to the Doctor, 'that if this really is the end of history we shouldn't have expected anything spectacular.'

The Doctor replied without taking his eye from their quarry, whose bright white suit made her clearly visible a few hundred yards ahead of them. 'Hardly the very end. There are a good few aeons left in the universe even if she is in her dotage.'

64

Romana pondered. 'What happens at the very end, I wonder?'

The Doctor's eyes flicked to meet hers momentarily, and there was a look almost of worry in them. 'You're getting very curious all of a sudden.'

'It must be the company I keep.'

'Yes, well.' He seemed suddenly sombre, at a loss for words for once, and it was as if he was looking into the future. 'Everything must come to an end at some point, Romana. Nothing's irreplaceable, not even the universe.' He turned his gaze up to the metallic clouds. 'This close to the final dissolution there's bound to be a tangible sense of unravelling.'

Romana snorted. The last thing she needed was for him to slip into one of these moods. 'You're being insufferably –' she searched for the right word '– extispicious.'

'Am I? What does that mean?'

K9 took this as a cue. 'Extispicion: foreboding based on illogical fears.'

'Oh,' said the Doctor. 'That. Well, you can't present a generally cheery face to the cosmos without being extispicious every now and again.' He nodded to the catering lady, who was disappearing between two large outcrops of rock between which ran a narrow, dried-out gulley. 'Come on, or we'll lose her.'

Suddenly K9 beeped loudly and ground to a halt. 'Master, Mistress, danger!' he bleated. 'Take immediate cover!'

The Doctor groaned. 'What is it this time?'

'Imminent attack,' said K9, already darting towards a small hole in the ground not far away. 'Danger! Take cover!'

Romana looked to the skies. But they remained as clear as ever. 'What sort of attack?'

'Plasma missile approaching!' K9 squeaked. 'Danger, danger!'

Romana made to join K9 in his hidey-hole but the Doctor gripped her arm and held her back. 'Ignore him. He's just being extispicious.' A second later the unmistakable whine of a descending missile, this time directly above them, split the air. 'Of course, I might be wrong about that. Run!'

Romana was already running. K9 whirred and clicked frantically at her to guide her as a shadow fell over the area. It was as if night had fallen in a second. She didn't dare look up. The whine of the missile became a flat, deadly drone. 'Hurry, Mistress!' the dog called. She threw herself forward the last few inches, and crawled in a snakelike motion over the sharp stones to reach her friend's side. Despite the urgency of the situation a section of her trained logical mind warned her that if the explosion struck nearby she and K9 were likely to be trapped if not killed. She assumed that the dog had chosen this shelter wisely.

As soon as she was over the lip of the hole she stuck her fingers in her ears and crouched down into a crash position, curled up and face down. The shadow, it seemed, was now almost on top of them. She heard K9 say, 'Prepare for impact!'

The blast was shattering and rattled every bone in her body. The ground shook. She felt a wave of burning air moving over her back, and heard K9 gurgle and croak. A scattering of small stones and pebbles rained down, making a tinny percussion on K9's metallic surfaces.

But the noise was the worst thing, a giant's roar that reverberated fiercely inside her head. She waited for it to subside, counted slowly to a hundred, felt the heat dissipate, and gently raised her head. Gingerly she looked over the lip of the crater.

The missile had been a clean one, and struck about half a mile in front of them. The devastation began a few metres ahead. Of the two outcrops of rock, the gulley and the trolley woman there was no trace but heavy palls of drifting, glittering dust hanging in strange designs.

Romana coughed and turned to K9. 'Status, K9.'

His eyescreen flashed beneath a coating of the grey dust. 'Motor functions and data core preserved, Mistress. However, my offensive laser and several minor back-up systems have been damaged. Sensor capacity is also impeded.'

She bent over and used her gloved hand to wipe away some of the dust clogging his ear sensors. 'You poor thing. We'll have to get you cleaned up.' She turned around. 'Doctor, I –' She broke off. He was nowhere to be seen. 'K9, where is he? Didn't he follow us?' She trailed off and put a hand to her mouth. 'Oh no. He wouldn't have tried to . . .' She looked across at where the catering woman had been merrily pushing her trolley minutes before. 'Rescue her,' she completed dully.

K9's head dropped. 'Likely, Mistress. Doctor Master's personality contains high level of altruism.'

Romana stared grimly at the hanging clouds of plasma. Perhaps the Doctor's illogical fears had been borne out after all.

3

A Very Long Story

The command post's alarms, untested and unneeded for over a hundred years, responded admirably to the shockwave of the explosion. Less than a second after the plasma core of the missile impacted with the surface at grid-cell 51Y, the remote satellite sensors registered the energy release and triggered an automatic sequence wired into the post's defence network by hands long dead. As soon as the lighting flashed red, the air was invaded by a high-pitched howl of an alert, and the blast doors on the post's southern perimeter (the only ones that were still working) slid into position with a screech of unoiled machinery.

What let this effort down was the human part of the equation. Untested and unneeded, the majority of the staff, ambling about the corridors on their various businesses, stopped, turned their heads to each other, scratched their brows, tutted, and waited for somebody else to sort it all out. Just another component failure, no doubt.

Dolne, however, could tell something was wrong. Really wrong. The timing was too exact for this to be anything but a genuine alert.

He dabbed his tears dry, threw on his tabard with a groan of effort and hurried from his quarters, heading up to the Strat Room. The alarm blared in his ears, a constant escalating spiral of electronic noise. He loathed these loud noises and sudden frights. Was everything – the Phibbs Report, the election, the mechanical failures, the loss of Kelton's patrol – conspiring against him? Thirty years in the top job and he'd never before been called upon to act decisively. He tasted for the first time the responsibility of command, and it was bitter.

In the Strat Room hands were flying over consoles, screens were displaying unfamiliar patterns, voices were raised in near panic. Dolne's entry was greeted by several audible sighs of relief, which he tried to put to the back of his mind. Don't the idiots realize? he thought. I'm more scared than any of them. Just because I wear an outfit with more gold bits on doesn't mean I have the slightest idea how to handle this.

'Captain.' He nodded as gruffly as his mood allowed to young Viddeas, who was hunched over the war map, his fingers curled over the edges, the knuckles whitened. 'What the hell's –' He broke off, aware that his voice was a full octave higher than usual. 'Ahem. Status report, Captain.'

Viddeas lifted his head at an odd angle. 'Admiral?' he said slowly.

Dolne felt like hopping up and down. 'Status report!' He sidled closer and hissed, 'For heaven's sake, Viddeas, you've been praying for this for years. You've finally got the chance to astound us all with your tactical ability.'

Viddeas seemed to snap out of his trance. He pointed to a particular cell on the map, beneath which an unfamiliar bright red light was flashing continuously in time with the alarm. 'Plasma strike, sir, in 51Y.'

Dolne's blood ran cold. He wanted more than anything else to sit down and catch his breath. 'Strike? As in, er, missile strike? With proper missiles, big ones?'

'Yes, sir,' said Viddeas. He consulted a printout handed to him by a junior officer. 'The missile was launched from the enemy position along the 94 ridge.' He indicated the area, which was on the far side of the map, close to the mountainous area that ringed the Chelonians' base.

'Any patrols out there?'

'None registered, sir. But we've been having trouble getting through to at least half of our active units.'

'What sort of trouble?'

'Jamming, sir. I believe it to be enemy interference of a

69

new, untraceable kind.' Viddeas snapped to particularly rigid attention. 'I suggest . . .' He faltered, and swayed suddenly.

Dolne was rather too lost in his own thoughts to notice. 'Suggest what?'

'Countermeasures, sir. A return strike.'

'Against the enemy? Don't be silly. They were probably just cleaning one of their launchers and it went off. Their missiles are as old as ours, you know.' The alarm made another swoop through the musical scale. 'Can't you switch that thing off?'

'We're trying to find the right switch, sir,' called Cadinot.

'Sir,' said Viddeas. Dolne looked at him properly for the first time since coming in and saw that his eyes were bright as buttons and his skin was pale. 'The Chelonians' launchers have computer-controlled failsafes. Accidental firing is impossible.' He swayed slightly again.

Dolne leant forward. The thought of Viddeas, who at least knew how most things in the post worked, falling ill at this moment filled him with horror. 'Are you feeling all right, boy?'

Viddeas attempted a smile and passed the back of his hand over his brow. 'Quite all right, sir. It must be the . . . the heat.'

It was at this point Dolne noticed two things. In normal circumstances they would have stood out as extraordinary, but in the present crisis the observations were relegated to the back of his mind. Firstly, Viddeas smelt, but the odour around him was not the stuffy sweatiness of all the others in the post. It was sort of *cheesy*. Secondly, despite what he had said there was not a single trickle of sweat visible on him. In fact he looked somehow *cold*. Ignoring these observations Dolne said, 'Get me Jafrid right away.'

Viddeas nodded and walked swiftly away from the map towards his desk.

Dolne rested his weight against the side of the map table and sighed heavily. The alarm clamoured on.

* * *

70

The Darkness watched through Viddeas's dead eyes. It saw the panic in the command post, the worry lines on Dolne's kind old face, the insistent flashing lights of the alarm.

Only the beginning.

In the split second before impact, with the unholy whistle of the missile ringing in his ears, the Doctor, realizing that he was not going to reach the catering lady in time, had thrown himself sideways, using a scissor-like movement of his long legs to propel him high and far. He had come down with an enormous thud that had knocked the wind out of him, but he had remained conscious throughout the blast. It was the aftermath that had caused his problems. The force had wedged him between two slabs of rock, with only his head and shoulders remaining above ground. He felt he must look like a partly hammered nail. He heard Romana and K9 calling his name and made to holler back, and encountered his next problem. His mouth was packed solid with grey dust and the only sound he could make was a sort of croak.

By the time he had levered himself out of his trap, taking care to move slowly to avoid agitating possible fractures, and spat the dust out, his two companions had stopped calling.

He dabbed at a small cut in one hand with his dusty tongue and called, 'Romana! Romana!' He made his hands into a funnel and bellowed her name. There was no reply.

The Doctor shrugged, and unconsciously reached into a pocket for the cup of tea stored there. After draining it he threw away the cup and set off for where he had last seen them. That was the intention, at least; he had not taken two steps before he realized that the blast had not only dislodged at least a couple of tons of rock dust but also caused the topography of the region to be altered dramatically. He looked around slowly and gave a grim whistle. There were no recognizable landmarks at all. The sun was still covered by clouds, giving no hint of help.

'Ah, well,' he said, taking out his tin whistle. 'If I just give this a blow and stay put . . .' He put it to his lips and sent out a repeated sequence of dots and dashes. He stood like this for some minutes, staring into the thick clouds of dust. Then he put the whistle away. 'Should have heard that, shouldn't they?' he muttered. 'If I stay within the general area, I should be – aha, what's this . . .'

An object had caught his eye on the ground a few feet ahead. He bent down and brushed off the dust that covered it, and found it to be a plastic bag. There was something soft and squelchy inside. Carefully he upended the bag and tipped out its contents into his palm. He sniffed it, still cautious, and then a grim expression settled over his face. 'Scone mix. That poor woman. She didn't stand a chance.' He let the crumbs fall through his fingers and as he scattered the last few to the wind took off his hat and held it respectfully to his breast.

He put his hat back on and stood up. 'Where is that dog? K9?' He chose a direction at random and strode off.

The Strat Room's big screen whistled and clicked. For a few moments it buzzed and hissed as thick grey bars of interference rolled across it. Then, after a final surge of distortion, the image of General Jafrid steadied. It troubled Dolne that after all these years he still had no way to interpret the facial arrangements of his friend. Right now he looked hunched and aggressive, his head pulled right back up to his shell, concealing the neck.

There was an unhealthy silence (Cadinot had dealt with the alarm at last) as both leaders contemplated each other. Dolne was absolutely determined not to speak first. So, obviously, was Jafrid. The staring went on.

Dolne broke. Those green reptilian eyes sent an atavistic chill running through him, a fear that seemed to strike his very core. 'Er, now look,' he said feebly. He was aware of sounding unwarlike. To compensate he raised a finger and wagged it sternly. 'This isn't on, really, is it?'

Jafrid's reply was equally muted in tone. 'We are checking and rechecking all components.' He issued a deep groaning breath. 'The incident is most regrettable.'

Dolne felt a surge of relief. 'Ah. It was a mistake, then?'

'Of course it was,' thundered Jafrid. 'Did you really think we'd open fire on you?'

'I didn't know, er, what to make of the, er, incident,' stammered Dolne. He felt like a naughty schoolboy being told off by a headmaster.

'Ask him about the failsafes,' Viddeas whispered suspiciously in his ear.

'Hmm, yes. What about the failsafes, eh?'

Jafrid blinked. Had that thrown him off stride? 'We are rechecking, as I said.' He moved his head up a fraction. In disdain? In affection? 'Surely, if we had intended to start an attack we would have aimed our missile at a more important target.'

'I suppose.' Dolne gulped. 'I'm sorry. We'll get back to you as soon as we've –'

But Jafrid had cut the link.

Dolne stepped back from the screen and tottered automatically over to his desk, where he sat. His face was dripping with sweat, staining the front of his outfit. 'How was it *I* ended up apologizing?' he mused. 'They have a way of intimidating people. Very rude.'

Viddeas crashed to attention at his side. 'Sir. Permission to comment.'

'Granted.'

'The Chelonian was bluffing, sir. The odds against all the failsafes running down simultaneously on one of their launchers are implausibly high.'

'But like he said,' Dolne said, picking his words carefully, 'why choose 51Y of all places? There's nothing there.'

'To confuse us. And to make us hesitate to respond in kind when the real attack begins.' He was standing very close to the desk and his voice was raised.

Dolne sniffed. 'Have you been eating cheese, Captain?'

Viddeas frowned. 'What? We are discussing tactics.'

'There's an awfully mouldy smell about you. I suggest you take a bath.'

Viddeas swayed again, and again his eyes seemed to shine with a strange brightness. 'Sir. Permission to suggest.'

'Granted.'

'Mr Rabley's party, sir. They're still incommunicado. We should send out an escort and haul them in.'

Dolne clapped his hands together. 'Well done, Captain. That's more like it. A solid, practical suggestion.' He hoped he sounded convincing. He'd never really had to say things like this before. 'A political incident is the last thing we want. Send out a patrol immediately.'

Viddeas nodded and backed away stiffly. 'Right away, sir.'

'And then,' hissed Dolne, fanning his nose, 'have that bath!'

The Doctor tramped through the grey dust, his scarf blowing behind him in great loops, his hat jammed tightly on to his head. To keep up his spirits he was whistling 'Show Me The Way To Go Home' as he picked his way carefully around the rocks at the base of a crumbling cliff face. He was trying not to admit to himself that he was lost, although he was certain he had not passed this way before.

'High ground,' he said suddenly, pointing to the cliff up ahead. 'That's what I need. Pop up and have a quick look about for landmarks. If I'm going to get lost I might as well do it thoroughly.' He navigated his broad frame around the few rocks dotted very close together at the base of the cliff. Then his boot heel touched something soft. He looked down and his expression became immediately more sombre.

There were crushed bodies beneath the rocks.

He knelt to examine the one at his feet. The man's entire middle was missing, pulverized by a giant boulder. He looked to be in his early twenties, and was dressed in a simple military uniform of blue serge. A name patch was tagged to his breast. It read KELTON. Still gripped in his fingers was a pistol. The Doctor removed it for examination. It was compact and silver with a stubby barrel.

74

'Hmm. Hardly useful on the front.' A thought occurred to him. He leant over and smelt the boulder. 'Strong stuff. So the rockfall wasn't an accident. Plasma missile?' He ferreted in his pockets and brought out a small hand-held radiation detector. It registered the recent release of plasma molecules in the explosion that had killed the catering woman, but nothing else. 'No. Rocket attack, then.' The Doctor returned the detector to his pocket and leant forward to gently close the dead man's staring, terrified eyes. And something unexpected happened.

His fingers sank into the man's flesh as if it was putty.

Disgusted, he pulled them back and shook them. A thin coating of slime, a fluid so clear it was almost invisible, clung to them. When he looked again at the dead man the Doctor saw that his exposed skin was covered in the stuff. He fitted the facts together mentally. The pistol had slipped from the fellow's dead grasp very easily, meaning that rigor mortis could not have set in yet. But the body was stone cold to the touch.

He held up his fingers to the dim light of the planet's cloud-covered sun and examined the glistening dew. 'A preservative?' He shuddered and looked about anxiously. 'For a predator? Time to be going, Doctor.'

He rooted about in his pockets once more until he found a test tube, emptied it of iron filings, and then used the end to catch the excess slime from his fingers as he shook them. 'That should do it. Let K9 have a sniff.' He stoppered the tube and returned it to his pocket, wiped his hand with a section of his scarf, and hurried away.

He was still determined not to admit he was lost. He was still in the right general area, for sure.

'. . . *and the territorial claim to Barclow of the Chelonian 70th column (hereafter referred to as "the enemy"), as outlined in their policy document of 506.61, refers to the industrial and strategical worth of the said planetoid in each of its first 21 clauses (excepting clause 2a and clauses 8 through 11). This Committee has examined each of the relevant clauses with regard to officially sanctioned statistics and reports compiled in surveys dated 506.23 to 507.11, as these were considered true and verifiable by the Metralubitan administration (hereafter referred to as "the Administration") during the period covered by the enemy's initial claim, and has noted the following points for the attention of all concerned parties . . .'*

Harmock shook his head and munched on another wafer as the Phibbs Report scrolled up his screen. He had chosen an access option to the file which allowed him to read Phibbs while it was still being fed to his terminal. Which was just as well. Galatea had told him it would take four days to download fully.

She stood over his desk now, her pale blue eyes flicking expressionlessly over the data as it was revealed. 'My research team are sifting through every section,' she said primly. 'Their instructions are to interpret all material in your favour.'

Harmock waved a contemptuous hand at the screen. 'It's gibberish. Could mean anything.'

'My team report that an average of twenty-two various opinions can be formed from each section of the report,' said Galatea. 'This means that Mr Rabley will also be able to claim its vindication.' The amulet at her throat chimed softly. 'My senior researcher is outside and wishes admittance, Premier.'

'Liris?' Harmock brightened a little. 'Send her in.'

Galatea touched the amulet and the office's hemispherical door slid smoothly up with a gentle purr of machinery. Liris walked in. She moved with the precision and smoothness of all Femdroids, although to signify her researcher's role her makers had imbued her with a slightly stumbling, bookish quality. She was substantially shorter and less glamorous than her fellows. Her hair was cut close to her head in a bob, and she wore a pair of wire-framed spectacles behind which brown eyes blinked owlishly. Her moulded tunic was a dark, tweedy brown colour, and she wore her control amulet at an angle that suggested a certain amount of absent-mindedness. Harmock liked her nervous, bumbling qualities, programmed though they were. She made him feel less inferior than the other Femdroids did. 'Good afternoon,' she said brightly. 'Premier, I bring suggestions for the campaign.' She held up a notescreen.

'Good, good.' He sat forward in his chair. 'Let's hear them, then.'

She pointed the hand-held unit to his desk screen and pressed transmit. Harmock sat back and watched avidly as a bewildering blur of images replaced the Phibbs Report. He saw Rabley's entire career compressed into a few seconds. Rallies, extremist meetings, his youth as a long-haired dissenter, his membership of the Rebel Labourers' Party. All of this was set to a threatening, rumbling piece of music. And then six words appeared, one after the other, outlined in throbbing red, each one accompanied by a thunderclap. DO YOU TRUST THIS EVIL MAN?

'Excellent, Liris,' said Harmock, rubbing his hands together. 'It says absolutely nothing about me or my policies. You've done very well. Have it released immediately, marked for prime scheduling across all channels of public broadcast.'

'Thank you, sir,' said Liris, tapping out the instruction on her pad.

'And I want a poll reaction a.s.a.p.' Harmock swung round in his chair to survey the world beyond the Dome. He watched as another skytrain flew past. The stupid faces of the passengers, craning their necks for a view of his office, amused him. Their minds were his, their fears easy to control, their future was surely in his hands.

Galatea spoke. 'Liris, how far has your team got with the Phibbs Report?'

As always, Liris seemed a little afraid of her senior. 'We have searched it for meaning and extracted a rough digest of points favourable to the Premier. This will be released to public broadcast as soon as Mr Rabley returns from Barclow. The news of the report's findings will eclipse Rabley's return and push him down the news schedule.' She gave a petite smile.

'Superb work,' said Harmock. 'What we need right now is a big push from everyone. We play down the

77

report, wait as long as possible – give it another couple of weeks – and call the election. We'll say that we'll act on the report afterwards and set out a strategy. Promise a return to hostilities. Rabley loses impetus, we pick it up, we win, and we engineer something or other to keep the Barclow situation the same as it ever was.' He smirked up at Galatea. 'How about that?'

'An admirable strategy.' Another chime sounded from her amulet. She exchanged a worried glance with Liris.

Liris put a hand to her mouth in a curiously natural gesture. 'Oh dear. This throws everything into confusion.' Her voice faltered. 'What are we to do?'

Harmock resented the way in which they could pick up information instantaneously. 'What's happened? What's the matter?'

For answer, Galatea used her finger to switch the screen to MNN. A Femdroid newscaster had assumed a concerned frown. 'We have just heard that a Chelonian plasma missile attack has taken place on Barclow,' she said. 'Details are still coming in, and it is unknown if there have been any fatalities.'

For the second time in a day Harmock bolted from his chair. 'A missile attack?' He spluttered. 'How the hell does MNN know about it before we do?' He slammed his fist down on the desk. 'Get me Dolne, right away.'

Galatea paused, her fingertips resting on her amulet, absorbing information. 'MNN are requesting your reaction, Premier.'

'Damn them. Get me Dolne!'

Galatea's eyes closed and she gave a tiny wince. 'Premier, the reaction of the electorate is very strong. Many of them are calling in already to demand reprisals.'

'Quick off the mark, aren't they?' Harmock thought. 'This throws our strategy out of the window. We can't hold on, can we?'

It was Liris who answered. 'Delaying the election in the face of this development would be seen as weak-minded. However, to react immediately by setting a date would increase your personal popularity rating.'

78

Harmock smiled again. 'Brilliant.' He felt his blood rising. Today was turning out quite interesting, with these shocks and countershocks. 'We'll do it. Say, the day after tomorrow. Catch the mood.'

Liris nodded and touched her amulet, sending out the statement.

'We have just heard that a Chelonian plasma missile attack has taken place on Barclow,' the newscaster said. *'Details are still coming in, and it is unknown if there have been any fatalities. But public feeling is already running high in the wake of the Phibbs Report . . .'*

The Darkness allowed itself a moment of self-congratulation. It was a simple thing in its desires, but was not above pride.

Romana stopped and drew a despairing breath. The grey vista was as blank as ever on all sides. 'This is hopeless. Are you sure we're going the right way?'

K9 stopped too and his head craned up at an unfamiliar angle. He looked somehow worried. 'Clarify query, Mistress.'

'I can't see the TARDIS.' She flung an arm out over the barren plain.

K9 emitted a dismal-sounding chirrup. 'There is damage to my sensors.' She saw that the two crisp-shaped radar 'ears' on top of his head were whirring impotently but not turning. 'My array has been dislocated. Only immediate vision and hearing are unimpaired. I cannot locate the TARDIS or the Doctor Master.'

Romana felt a sudden dreadful rush of realization. 'You mean you've got no idea where you're leading me?'

K9's head drooped. 'You are leading, Mistress.'

Romana slumped down at his side. 'But I've been following *you*.' There was an embarrassed silence. 'You looked like you knew where you were going.'

'Your non-verbal signals suggested strong purpose, Mistress,' replied K9.

Romana knew they had no choice but to press on. She

stood up and turned a full circle. There was not one landmark to distinguish this area from any other. 'This terrain is so featureless.' A kind of crunching noise was coming from behind a nearby ridge of rock. 'What's that?'

As if anxious to redeem himself, K9 trundled forward to a cleft in the ridge, and stuck his head around a corner to see what lay beyond. 'More humanoids, Mistress.'

Romana scurried to join him, putting her head next to his. The ridge they rested on was in fact part of a cliff that overlooked a gorge about forty feet across. Tramping through it with weary purpose were three soldiers dressed in one-piece fatigues only slightly less grey than their surroundings. They wore small handguns at their belts. At the centre of this small group was a figure dressed differently, a tall, authoritative-looking man in a light-green suit with a bulletproof vest tied around his middle. Oddly, there was a small device, slender and cigar-shaped, hovering a few feet behind him at eye level. A recorder, perhaps?

'More soldiers,' she said. As they came closer she could hear the tone of their conversation, if not the exact words. It was light, informal. Chatty.

'Suggest we confer and request guidance,' said K9.

Romana readied herself to descend. 'All right. They look friendly, but you get ready to cut them down with a stun sweep just in case.'

K9 made an extraordinary clicking sound. 'Regret cannot, Mistress.'

'What?'

'Cannot,' K9 whispered. He seemed ashamed. 'Offensive capability impaired. My laser is inoperative. This unit is functioning at sixty-one per cent of full utility. Advise immediate repair.'

Romana's spirits sank even lower. She watched as the soldiers trudged along and pondered the problem. Perhaps she and the Doctor had grown too reliant on K9 as a universal problem-solver.

Suddenly there was an ear-splitting shriek, followed

quickly by the droning chug of an engine. Instinctively Romana looked up. The sky seemed to be clear. Then she saw it: at first not much bigger than a black dot, like a full stop, but growing larger by fractions of a second. Plummeting down, it seemed, right on top of them.

K9 wheeled about, panicked. Struck by fear as she was, Romana still had time to notice the unaccustomed anxiety in his manner. 'Advise take cover, Mistress! Missile attack!'

Romana looked down at the soldiers. They were still ambling along, oblivious to the attack, the high sides of the valley shielding them from the noise of the descending missile. There was no time to warn them. Grimly she threw herself down.

The drone of the missile's engine cut out abruptly. She heard K9's voice, strained to its maximum amplification. 'Attention, attention!' She lifted her head a fraction and saw that he had trundled forward to address the soldiers. 'Take cover immediately to avoid grave loss of life! Danger! Missile attack imminent!'

From her hiding place Romana could just glimpse what was going on down below. The man in the civilian suit broke off from the small, astonished group and walked forward. He squinted up the side of the valley, searching for the origin of the announcement, and called, 'I say, can you help us?' His voice carried upward. 'You probably recognize me.' He shrugged. 'We've got lost, and the radios are dead, and we −'

K9 boomed again, 'Take cover! Take cover!'

And then, for what seemed to Romana like the twentieth time that day, there was a very loud bang.

The Doctor was carrying on, guided by his earlier-stated principle that if you stick to one direction something is bound to turn up eventually. He used the time given to him to expound theories on his discovery. The reverberation of his own voice was strangely reassuring. 'But of course the climate's all wrong for a predator of that type. There's nothing for it to live on, well, nothing that occurs

81

naturally. Hah. Where's a good xenobiologist when you need one?'

A gentle purring sound came from somewhere among the lowering clouds. He looked up and saw a saucer, nudging its way down slowly through the thin atmosphere like a lily blown about the surface of a pond. 'Ah, good.' He stopped, took off his hat and waved it over his head at the newcomer. 'Someone to have a chat with. I do so detest people who talk to themselves, don't you, Doctor?'

The saucer came ever closer, and a series of irregular patterned markings on its pitted upper surface became visible. The lettering was angular and jagged, the notation reminding him of trips to the Orient on Earth. 'If I didn't know any better,' the Doctor muttered to himself, 'I'd say that was a Chelonian ship. But of course it can't be. What would they want with a fleapit like this?'

A stentorian voice boomed from the craft. 'Remain in position,' it said. There was a throaty gurgle behind each syllable. 'Raise your appendages.' The Doctor lifted a leg cautiously. 'Your *upper* appendages.' He raised his hands. 'You are a prisoner of the Chelonian seventieth column.' A hatch on the craft's rim slid aside to uncover a tri-pronged disrupter attachment.

The Doctor sighed. 'How am I ever going to live today down?' he said.

There was more confusion in the Strat Room. Cadinot was hunched over his screen, his fingers clattering on the keyboard as he struggled to make sense of the sudden energy burst picked up by the detectors. At last he looked up, the troubled expression on his young face picked out in the green glow of the sensor equipment. 'Three missile traces this time, Captain,' he told Viddeas, who was leaning over him. 'Plasma release of –' He consulted a readout and shrugged. 'Well, quite a lot of plasma.'

'Area?'

'Could be anywhere between 48 to 55,' Cadinot said.

He made a hopeless gesture at the screen. 'It's that distortion on the east sat. I can't be more specific.'

Dolne, who had been observing this exchange from the side of the map screen, felt a tugging at his stomach as he looked along the grid. 'Area 52? That's where Rabley's supposed to be. Where's that escort?'

Viddeas, with his usual efficiency, was already on to it. He had snatched up a hand-held link and was calling into it, 'Grayn, come in.' There was no reply. 'Captain Viddeas to escort leader Grayn, respond.'

A wash of static was the only reply. Dolne felt the situation slipping ever further from his grasp. 'Answer, come on, answer!'

There was a beep in response, and a voice crackled through. 'Grayn here, sir. It's bad news, I'm afraid. Pretty awful news in fact, sir.'

Dolne felt like throwing his hands over his ears. 'Oh no.' He waved at Cadinot. 'Raise Jafrid again. I must talk with him.'

After brushing the rock dust from her clothing (she was beginning to look rather less elegant after all of these explosions), and having ascertained K9's good health, Romana crept forward to examine the aftermath of the attack. The valley had taken a direct hit and folded in on itself. The edge she had rested on had partly crumbled away and she was lucky to be alive. Now, only minutes after the strike, another three soldiers were picking their way through the chunks of rubble – coughing furiously as the chalky vapour infiltrated their lungs – and beginning the unwelcome task of dragging the bodies of their colleagues out from beneath the debris towards a small open-topped vehicle, not much bigger than a loading platform. Their leader, who looked far too old to be on field duty, was talking into a communicator. Carefully, Romana crept down towards the site, beckoning K9 to follow. She kept herself under cover.

The leader was saying, in a broken voice, 'Yes, Mr Rabley and the rest of them. It's terrible. There are bodies and bits of missile all over the place.' He paused, looked around at his men, and said, 'Er. What shall I do?'

The voice of his superior, clipped and curt, filtered back. 'Orders. You're supposed to request orders, not say "What shall I do?" '

'Sorry, Captain. I request orders.'

There was a brief silence. Then the Captain's voice said, 'Load the bodies and the debris on your truck and get out of there right now. The Chelonians could open fire again any moment and you're sitting targets.'

Romana exchanged a knowing glance with K9, who was also listening attentively. So he had been right about the other side in this war.

The squad leader shuffled as if embarrassed. 'You mean, they really are shooting at us, sir?' he asked his communicator. 'But why? We get along usually, don't we?'

'Just get back here, Grayn,' said his superior. 'Viddeas out.'

Grayn squared his shoulders, holstered his communicator, and turned to those in his charge. 'Right. You heard the Captain. We've got to take all of this back to the post.'

One of the milling soldiers raised his hand. 'Do we have to touch the bodies, sir?'

'Yes, you do,' said Grayn awkwardly. 'Come on, get to work.' He made a chivvying gesture and the soldiers returned to their duty.

K9 made a clicking noise to get Romana's attention and whispered, 'Mistress. Suggest we offer assistance.'

'What if they turn nasty?'

'Speech mode and weaponry suggests non-aggressive character.'

She patted him on the side. 'All right, then. But go carefully.' She settled back to watch as he started to climb, with some difficulty, down the shattered slope.

Ahead of him one of the soldiers had come up to his leader with a piece of metal in his hand. 'Is this a bit of missile, sir?'

Grayn looked closely at it. 'No, it's Rabley's auto-cam.'

He took it and looked it over. 'Still working. There could be vital evidence on this. I'll convey it personally to −' At that moment he glanced up and caught sight of K9. His reaction was almost comical. He jumped and backed away, his right hand scrabbling desperately to unholster his pistol. 'Stop right there!'

K9 continued to advance. 'I am not hostile.'

The soldier gulped. 'Could be an enemy weapon, sir.'

'I am not a weapon,' said K9. 'Please do not shoot. My record of the events leading up to the missile attack may be of value to you.'

The soldier pointed. 'It's got a gun, sir, in its snout.'

This decided Grayn, who raised his pistol to fire, at point-blank range.

Romana leapt from her hiding place and bounded down over the rocks, scissoring her raised arms frantically. 'Wait! Don't fire!'

To her relief Grayn lowered his pistol. He stared at her for a few moments and then his shoulders slumped. 'I don't believe this,' he said.

The central compartment of the saucer was dark and cramped, each surface bristling with the assorted machinery of a high-tech war. The Chelonians came up to only just above waist height on the average humanoid, and the Doctor was forced to bend his knees as he stepped from the entry ramp. His eyes swept alertly about, taking note of the craft's systems and capabilities and comparing them to what he recalled of Chelonian technology from previous encounters. To cover his interest he said brightly, 'Good afternoon, gentlemen. Lovely saucer you have here. It's been, ooh, epochs since I last saw the inside of one of these.' He pointed to a control panel. 'I say, isn't that a remote missile activator?'

One of the three Chelonians aboard the saucer, plainly their leader from his position in a centrally positioned hammock, growled and fixed him with a baleful stare. 'Be silent.'

The Doctor ignored him and walked casually around

85

the circular space. 'But then it's been epochs since I ran into any members of your charming species. Pardon me for saying so, but I'm quite surprised to find that you're still around.' He stooped to examine a set of environment displays. The small screens showed an aerial view of the battlefield, its contours picked out in yellow lines. He made an effort to memorize it. 'Although I'm sure you've outgrown any unpleasant aggressive tendencies you once had, and any second now you're going to offer me a seat and a plate of biscuits.'

'Silence!' the leader roared. 'Or I will have your eyes torn from their sockets!'

The Doctor gulped and stood up. 'Of course there's nothing that bad about aggressive tendencies.' He found one of the younger Chelonians lurking at his side, an oddly shaped yellow weapon clutched in one of his front feet.

'You will give your name and patrol number,' said the leader.

'I haven't got one. Of either.' He paused. On several occasions in his travels he had crossed paths with Chelonians, and put a stop to their schemes to wipe out human populations and push out the borders of their empire. Consequently he had an unfavourable reputation with them. Deciding it was best to be honest he said grandly, 'You can call me the Doctor.'

There was no noticeable reaction to this pronouncement.

The Doctor was slightly miffed. 'Hah,' he muttered. 'Forgotten like everybody else in the end.'

The Chelonian at his side spoke. 'He does not wear the clothing of the human soldiers, First Pilot.'

The leader waved a foot irritatedly. 'I can see that.' He shuffled in his webbing, his hydraulics making a clanking noise, and peered at the Doctor. 'What is your function? Answer now, and truthfully, or it will be the worse for you.'

The Doctor was pushed closer to his interrogator. He bit his lip. 'I've been caught this way before. You see, if I

86

tell you the truth you won't believe me and after a lot of shouting you'll torture me. So why don't I just let you assume that I'm who you think I am and you can torture me straight away. It'll save a lot of time.'

As he had intended there was a baffled silence. The Doctor got the impression that the scenario was somehow half-hearted, that his captors were simply playing out roles. There was an unrehearsed quality about the whole scene. He was about to remark on this when the subordinate said, 'Doctor is a title used by human scientists.'

The First Pilot clenched his claws. 'Ah. You admit it, then.'

'Admit what?'

'You are part of the plague war project. Your vile experiments are in direct contravention of the Bechet Treaty.' This time there was a genuine sense of grievance in the First Pilot's words, underpinned by a kind of disappointment.

'You must be mistaking me for somebody else,' said the Doctor. 'I don't do experiments, and certainly not vile ones. In fact I don't know where I am or what's going on here. I'm just an innocent, well, a fairly innocent traveller.'

'A traveller?' spluttered the First Pilot. 'On Barclow? You expect us to believe you are not from Metralubit?'

'Ah.' The Doctor was glad to be thrown this morsel of information, his first clue to his exact location. 'Metralubit. Excuse me, gentlemen.' He rooted in his pocket and pulled out a battered copy of *Finnickan's Planets*, the essential reference for all travellers. Skimming quickly to M he read, ' "Remote Tellurian colony, sited in the Fostrix galaxy, settled in the fifty-eighth segment of time." ' He put away the book. 'That's saved a lot of tedious explanation. Fostrix, eh? Goodness, we are a long way out. No, I'm not.'

'Not what?' The First Pilot was baffled.

'From Metralubit,' said the Doctor. 'In fact, I'm from about as far away from here and now as it's possible to get.'

The First Pilot growled. 'You talk like an idiot from one

of the humans' comedic entertainments. Your behaviour is a pathetic attempt to distract me from my questioning. Admit your function. You are one of the plague war team.'

The Doctor shrugged. 'I am one of the plague war team.'

'What?'

'That's what you wanted to hear, isn't it? I only said it to keep you happy.' The Doctor's attention had been caught by a beaded curtain strung on a pole in one corner. Taking advantage of his captors' bemusement he sprang forward and made to pull it back. 'Now, as your lot don't go in for decoration I have to wonder, what have we here?'

His mood became more sombre in an instant. Revealed behind the curtain was a narrow alcove, formed by two support struts. Placed on a square, padded stretcher slotted on to runners on the struts was the body of a Chelonian. Its sightless eyes, rolled upward in terror, seemed to stare accusingly at the Doctor.

'Stand away!' shouted the First Pilot. 'No human is permitted to look on the bodies of the Chelonian dead!'

The Doctor crouched to examine the body. The hard shell was unmarked, the leathery skin of the forelimbs, face and neck not scarred or even broken. But in the dim illumination of the battle craft's lighting a sticky substance, just visible, glistened. The coating covered the entire head. His scientific curiosity overcoming his sense of self-preservation, the Doctor reached out and prodded the brow. Every Chelonian possessed a hard cranial plate at that position, the terminal through which their cybernetic additions were routed to their brain. The flesh was soft and mushy. His mind flashed back to the human soldiers at the fallen rocks. 'But – it's exactly the same . . .'

'Yes.' The First Pilot unhooked himself from his webbing and motored forward, his limbs creaking with the strain. 'This is the result of your experimentation. Plague war. Forbidden by all civilized races.'

The Doctor backed away. There was a suggestion of fanaticism, almost of madness, in the First Pilot's voice.

* * *

Viddeas's bad dream continued. It was as if there were two voices in his head. Two influences: his own, which had control of his reasoning and his voice and his basic physical functions, and another, strange and very cold, at once reassuring – it kept telling him not to worry – and terrifying. Often he was about to speak and tell Dolne or one of the others about his bad experience at the copier. His mouth would open, but before any meaning could form the cold influence would take over and convert his words to something it wanted to say. There was also an intolerable itching under his arms and at his knee and elbow joints, and it was getting harder to move his arms and legs. And while he should have greeted the news of Rabley's death and the prospect of real war beginning with fear he actually felt thrilled, excited, very keyed up. Worst of all, he knew why. He was dead, wasn't he? A dead person, walking about with a voice in his head.

Now he stood at the door of the reception area, Dolne at his side, prepared to receive the returning escort division. Dolne had grown quiet since hearing of Rabley's death, and had taken to fingering the cuffs of his uniform distractedly. As the green light of the entry door lit up he said nervously, 'I wonder who this woman is.'

The voice answered for Viddeas. As always when it did that, a surge of redness seemed to push at his eyeballs. 'I have as much idea as you, sir.' In fact the voice was interested in this newcomer. A stranger could be blamed, branded a traitor, tortured. This would lead to death. And the voice really wanted a lot more death.

Dolne continued fidgeting. 'I'm going to have to tell Harmock about Rabley. And still no word from Jafrid.' He looked over at Viddeas. 'What if they really are starting things up again? Do we stand a chance?'

'Every chance, sir.'

'Is that just fighting talk?'

The voice got excited. 'No. I believe strongly that if we mobilize our forces now, we may destroy them utterly.'

He was cut off by the creak of the entry door as it lifted. A moment later a young woman with fair hair and a striking air of confidence stepped through. Viddeas felt a moment of desire, but then reminded himself it was unseemly for the dead to harbour lustful thoughts for the living.

Dolne reacted warmly to the woman's smile. 'Ah. And you would be Romana?'

She put out a hand. 'Admiral Dolne?'

'Yes.' He shook it. 'Welcome. You're a traveller, Grayn says.'

She nodded. 'He told me of the rather unusual war you're having here. From a psychosociological standpoint it sounds fascinating.'

Dolne said, 'I'm glad you think so.'

'I've no business on this planet,' Romana went on, looking down the corridor. 'As soon as I can find the friend I came with I'll be happy to leave.'

Dolne seemed taken aback by her forthright nature. 'I'm happy to take you at your word. You seem like a nice girl. Not a Femdroid, are you?'

She smiled back. 'I'm afraid I don't know what that is. But I shouldn't think so.'

The grizzled face of Grayn appeared behind her. 'Division G reporting, sir.' He lifted Rabley's auto-cam. 'I've brought this back, sir, as instructed.' His formal manner faltered. 'Sir, why are the enemy shooting at us? None of the lads can understand it.'

Viddeas stepped forward, directed by the voice. 'Enough talk.' He snatched the auto-cam, sensing that it might contain material that could be used to create more death. 'I'll take that.'

Dolne intercepted the device and tucked it under his arm. 'Thank you, Viddeas, I'll deal with this. Could be vital stuff on here. You stay and have a chat with this young woman.' He pointed to Romana.

Viddeas flinched, a little of his former personality's irritation with informality lingering. 'A chat?'

Dolne fluttered a hand. 'Oh, *interrogation*, if you must.' He looked again through the entry hatch. 'Where's that computer thing you were talking about, Grayn?'

A tinny voice came from ground level. 'I am here, Admiral.'

Viddeas looked down to see a primitive-looking robotic device trundling about on some sort of friction system. It looked like the kind of thing an eccentric civilian like the girl Romana would use as a data-store, harmless and whimsical. Unimportant in itself, but still useful.

'Dear heaven,' said Dolne, taking a step back as the device came forward. 'It talks.'

'I am programmed to converse in fifty-seven languages,' said the device.

Dolne chuckled and signed to the device to follow him. 'I'll get Cadinot to open this up and have a look at it. Right, come along, doggie.' The device followed him down the corridor, its rear probe wagging.

Viddeas turned to Romana. 'You haven't pulled the wool over my eyes.'

She seemed to find his anger amusing. 'I haven't tried to. Do you know, this post of yours is architecturally fascinating. I wonder how it stays up.'

'You are a Chelonian spy,' shouted Viddeas.

'I must be wearing a very clever disguise,' she replied.

Viddeas let his gaze linger on her neck. Alive, he had never been so taken with women's necks, being more of a leg man. Dead, he found them strangely tempting. Succulent. 'Don't be flippant. I meant that you are a spy working for the Chelonians. No offworlders have come to this system since them, not for over a hundred years.'

'Hardly surprising, if this is what you call a welcome.' She fanned her face as he came closer. 'Have you eaten something? It's very stuffy in here.'

Viddeas gestured down the corridor with his pistol. 'You will accompany me to the detention block.'

Romana sighed and said casually, 'Oh, all right.'

As she moved in front of him, Viddeas caught another glimpse of her neck. An obscene thought came into his head. He wanted to spit on it.

* * *

91

The novelty of the arrival of K9, as the portable computer had identified itself, was taking Dolne's mind away from the unpleasantness of the past few hours. He was not a strong-willed or practical man, and this distraction allowed him to forget the horrible situation that seemed to be brewing. Cadinot, the nearest the post had to a whizz with technical stuff, had been called down to his quarters to examine the creature. He had first asked it to give an account of itself. This account was coming to its end, relayed in its uniquely transistorized tone, and told a somewhat marvellous tale of space travel and adventuring. K9 was far from the faultless efficiency of the Femdroids, a fact that further endeared him to Dolne. 'I exist to obey the orders of the Doctor Master and Mistress Romana. My function is non-hostile. The local situation is of no intrinsic interest to my party.'

Dolne looked over K9's head at Cadinot, who was checking the veracity of the dog's words with a small, hand-held device. 'Well?'

Cadinot shook his head in amazement. 'Checks out, sir. True in all details.'

'Startling.' Dolne relaxed a little on his couch and rubbed his temples. It was nice to receive visitors. He couldn't recall the last time he'd seen an unfamiliar face. 'Welcome, my little pet.'

K9 turned to face him. 'I am not yours or little or a pet. Please return me to Mistress Romana.'

Cadinot ran the device over his metallic body. 'The circuitry's shielded in some way. But look here.' He indicated the dog's glass ears, which were chipped in several places. 'I think it's been damaged.'

'Damage was sustained in the first of the plasma explosions, yes,' said K9. 'However, this unit remains functional.' Its eye extended on a red stalk and an important-sounding beep came from its voicebox. 'I have information, should you wish to accept it.'

'What's that?' Dolne asked.

K9 nodded to Rabley's auto-cam, which Dolne had

92

quite forgotten still lay in his hand. 'The tracker/scanner device you are holding I estimate to be the product of a level-five civilization. As is the systems analyser used by Mr Cadinot.' He swivelled on his castors, paying particular attention to the com-screen. 'However, most of the other instruments in this room I would estimate to be products of a late level-three civilization.'

The words meant nothing to Dolne. He pulled a face at Cadinot to say *what does it mean?*

K9 saw him. 'Please address me directly. I am designed to interact on a personal level with a broad band of sentient creatures, and foremost with humans. My meaning is that there is an unnatural anachronism in these surroundings. Inference is there has been cross-cultural contact, although your assertion of historical isolation conflicts with this hypothesis.'

Dismayed by this stream of jargon, Dolne passed the auto-cam to Cadinot and whispered, 'Do you think it's got confused?'

Cadinot shrugged as he placed the cam in a slot on the com-unit designed for playback. 'Possibly.' He reached out and ran his hands along the device's back panel. 'I could open it up and have a poke about.'

'Only the Doctor Master and Mistress Romana are qualified to poke this unit,' said K9, turning quickly to brush him off.

Dolne stood. He had to get back to the Strat Room before Viddeas could do anything foolish. 'I think we're just going to have to accept your word. From the sound of things you could be quite useful to us.'

Cadinot interrupted him, indicating the com-screen. 'Sir, the recording.'

Dolne looked up. The screen showed a typical sector of the surface. Rabley, his grin wide as ever, could be seen in semi-close-up, the auto-cam following its program to keep him in shot and flatter him at all times. Codie and the other doomed troopers were milling in the background. Rabley was in profile, his head angled up, apparently talking to somebody. 'I say, can you help us?' he was saying. 'You probably recognize me.' He shrugged. 'We've got lost, and the radios are dead, and we —'

A familiar tinny voice, strained to its fullest amplification, echoed in replay. 'Take cover! Take cover!' The auto-cam, obeying its instructions to the last, swung away to fit this newcomer into the picture. K9 was revealed, perched precariously on the upper slopes of the valley Rabley was traversing.

There was a screeching whistle and the screen went black.

Dolne felt a powerful sadness tug at his heart. He'd barely known Rabley, but the sight of the poor fellow trying so hard to be understood at the moment before his death would have upset anybody. As he looked into the blackness and pondered the general unfairness of things another thought occurred to him — one that, despite his sorrow, nearly made him burst out laughing. 'Ah,' he said. 'That complicates things rather.' He shot Cadinot a significant look. 'Think about it.'

Cadinot looked blank for a moment, then his eyebrows shot up. 'You don't mean constitutional privilege?' He indicated K9. 'For him?'

K9's head lifted suspiciously. 'Please explain reference.'

Romana was getting tired of Captain Viddeas. Not only was he an unpleasant character, but he smelt, and she had to hold back an urge to throw up several times as he led her through poorly lit, low-ceilinged corridors to the detention block. His questions, half shouted, half screamed, grew more insistent as they proceeded, as if he was trying to stir himself up into an unthinking rage. She countered this by keeping calm and polite.

After some minutes they emerged into an area that contained several caged and barred cells. The second along in the row contained a heap of sackcloth.

'Confess!' Viddeas shouted. 'You are an agent of the Chelonians.'

Romana raised a disapproving eyebrow as she looked

around. 'Is this your detention block? You don't have any prisoners.'

Viddeas, keeping his pistol level, moved around to face her. 'They were handed back at the last solar quarter. As well you know.' There were traces of moisture around his mouth and his lips were unusually pale, almost blue.

'Please stop saying things like that,' said Romana. She watched as he swayed and shook his head. 'Are you all right?' She held back from reaching out to support him, as his uniform jacket was soaked with perspiration. 'This atmosphere's very unhealthy.' There was a tickle at her cheek that she brushed off instinctively. 'Lots of flies.'

The comment seemed to trouble Viddeas. He blinked and said quietly, 'What was that? What did you say?'

'I said it's very stuffy,' said Romana, fanning herself.

Viddeas shook his head. 'No, it wasn't that, I . . . about the . . .' His gun hand started to shake and he tottered away from her. The cells officer, a burly man in a nondescript set of coveralls, came forward to assist him.

'You need to sit down,' said Romana, trying to appear concerned.

Viddeas shrugged off the aid of the officer and pointed to the cells. 'Put her in there,' he blurted, drool now running from his mouth. 'I am perfectly all right! Do it!' He stumbled out, a hand pressed to his temple.

The big man looked after him, plainly confused. 'Stress, probably,' Romana suggested. She took the lead and walked across to the nearest cell, swinging the little barred door open and making herself comfortable on the bench within. 'I'd like a glass of water, if that's allowed.' She smiled sweetly at the officer, who locked her in and walked away, shaking his head in confusion.

Romana allowed herself a few moments of reflection. On the journey to the post she had learnt the bizarre history of the war from Grayn. It was just like the Doctor to land them here at the very moment things started to hot up. She considered using her sonic screwdriver to pick the lock of the cell, and decided it was probably better to keep on the good side of these people, who were, Viddeas excepted, pleasant enough. She sat back on the bench, drew her feet up, and allowed her head to fall back on the bars separating her cell from its neighbour. The pile of sacking in the next cell was placed conveniently for her to use as a pillow.

The sacking moved.

Romana sat up and turned to see a figure pushing itself out from beneath the covering. The initial shock of not being alone was compounded by the sight of the face revealed by this stirring. He was blinking with an unaccustomed grogginess, and he looked a few years older. There were new worry lines around his eyes and mouth. But the egglike bald head, the hulking frame and the bloodless lips could have belonged to no one other than Menlove Stokes. She and the Doctor had encountered him not so long ago, in their own relative time-stream, during an encounter with the villainous Xais in the twenty-third century. He had then been employed as an artist, and not a very successful one, in a grotesque gallery of his own creation built into the basement of a prison.* All of this flashed through Romana's mind in an instant. 'Great Rassilon!' she shrieked, pulling herself up.

Stokes peered at her from beneath heavy eyelids. 'Ah. You must be an illusion. A side effect of the sedative.' His voice was as affected and actorly as ever. 'Go away.' He pulled the sacking back over his head.

Romana considered for a moment the possibility that this was a distant descendant of the man she had met. But *he* had recognized *her*. She decided to be direct. 'I'm as solid as you are,' she said, reaching through the bars to tap him on the shoulder.

He refused to look up. 'No no, you are definitely the product of whatever unholy chemical mixture they've sent swimming through my bloodstream.' He shifted his position slightly and stared out at her. 'Interesting, how my mind works. At this, perhaps the time of greatest crisis in all my days, it summons forth a spectre from my

* See *Doctor Who – The Romance of Crime*.

second-best adventure. The lovely Ramona.'

'Romana.' This was definitely Stokes. 'You're starting to irritate me and I may have to slap you.'

He nodded. 'Exactly what a mirage would say. There's no need to raise your hand as my haunted mind would, no doubt, simulate the pain of actual physical contact.' A thought seemed to strike him. 'Actual physical contact,' he repeated slowly. Then he threw off the covering completely, revealing his battered, paint-spattered old raincoat and disordered cravat, and patted his knee. 'You don't fancy hopping on to Uncle Men's lap, do you?'

Romana had an idea. 'Stokes,' she said, 'you are a pompous, self-inflated fool with no talent whatever.'

He flushed and pulled himself upright, then clapped his hands together in astonishment, his tiredness seeming to vanish in an instant. 'You are real! No hallucination of mine would dare to say that!' He pointed an aggressive finger at her. 'How dare you say it!' Then he checked his temper. 'Very clever. Of course, you didn't mean it.'

Romana changed the subject. 'I am pleased to see you,' she said, honestly. 'But what are you doing in this time and place? You must be millennia out of era.'

He shuffled awkwardly. 'It's a very long story.'

'I was afraid it might be.' She leant forward. 'What have you been up to? Time travel?'

Stokes swelled with self-importance. 'Not exactly.' He coughed and began to declaim. Romana got the impression he had been rehearsing this speech. 'My tale begins shortly after our last meeting, and that unpleasantness aboard the Rock. That idiot Spiggot wrote a ludicrous account of what occurred there, casting himself as a hero and me as a bumbling fool. You and your pop-eyed friend and that tin bath of yours were written out altogether. Anyway, I wasn't prepared to stand for it. I took legal advice and sued him for every credit of his royalties.'

Romana cast her eyes over his clothing. 'You lost?'

'I was ruined,' he said hotly. 'Made a laughing stock in open court. No witnesses, you see – my word against his. It was a disgrace. Worse, it swallowed up my unearned income. And the exhibition I had timed to coincide with my victory was ill-attended and took very bad reviews.' He smacked his fist into his palm. 'From fools, I might say. That churl Bootle Anderson said that I was "rubbing the faces of my audience in my own vomit". That crazy pipe-smoking old harridan Sybilla Strang claimed my works "plumbed a new nadir of creative bankruptcy". But I didn't let it get to me.'

'Evidently,' said Romana.

'Envy, that was all. It's been the same down the ages: true endeavour crushed by jealous chatterers. Think of Van Gogh, Matissé, Whiteread. All deceased and dispirited before the next generation, unencumbered by the judgements of their sniping rivals, recognized their actual worth. I was not prepared to follow that route. And, thanks to the technology of my native century, I did not have to.'

Romana grasped his meaning. 'Suspended animation?'

'Yes. I booked myself into the Dozing Decades cryomort on Fridgya, and took up a lease on a berth with the last few crumbs in my possession. I specified to be woken only when my work was re-evaluated and properly appreciated.'

There was an unpleasant silence. At length, Romana said, as politely as she could, 'Stokes, we're getting close to the very end of the universe.'

'There was a slight delay, yes. Fridgya was laid waste in the fifth Thargon–Sorson war and the cryo-mort was left unattended.'

Romana consulted her encyclopedic memory of major galactic events. 'In 2660?'

Stokes nodded. 'Many, many thousands of years later archaeologists came to Fridgya and unearthed my fellow sleepers and myself. Unfortunately they were stupidly superstitious and packed us off, still frozen, in drifting, unpowered mini-pods. I ended up here in the Fostrix galaxy, a fair while later. Where the good Femdroids of Metralubit hauled me in. And what joys I stumbled on. I take it you haven't been down there?' Romana shook her head and he went on, 'It's a beautiful place. A Utopia.

A rationally organized, harmonic society, governed by benevolent democracy.' His eyes glazed over. 'You must visit it. Great white towers stretching ever upward, free transport with no pollutants, rolling green spaces. I was welcomed and made so comfortable. The Metralubitans leapt at the work I provided for them. Even one of my lesser abstracts fetches a generous sum there. At last I was appreciated.' He snapped himself back to the present. 'But after some months of excessive comfort I started to thirst for a challenge and volunteered my services as a war artist, that I might capture some of the flavour of these bloodless hostilities. Now I wish I never had. Those reptilian beasts are going to plunge us all into disaster! And that uptight idiot Viddeas won't let me leave.'

Romana shook her head in wonderment. 'Astonishing. The level of coincidence, I mean. Our meeting is the most unlikely thing that could happen. Perhaps the Doctor was right about the Randomizer.'

'He's here?' Stokes groaned. 'No doubt the general level of mayhem will increase accordingly.'

'The Doctor saved your life,' Romana pointed out.

'Politeness is for mediocrities,' he said casually. His weariness had left him, and he got up from his bench and started to pace his cell. 'How long am I going to be subject to this whitewash! Will we all be dead?'

Romana looked up as Viddeas, now looking more controlled, returned to the detention block. Stokes pointed to him. 'You. I want to see the Admiral. Now.'

Viddeas's attention was all on Romana. 'Shut up. Or I will order your sedation.'

Stokes grimaced. 'There's been another attack, hasn't there? Now do you see I'm right? I'm a civilian – you can't hold me. Let me speak to the Admiral. Remind him that I'm known to Premier Harmock and that I'm not without influence on Metra.'

Viddeas ignored him and advanced on Romana's cell. 'You will give me details of the Chelonians' plans. Immediately. If you do not it is within my rights to have you tortured.'

She smiled back. 'That won't be necessary. I can prove my story. Stokes, tell him who I am.'

Stokes turned to Viddeas. 'Please, do I have to be shut up with this madwoman? Is this part of your game against me, Viddeas?'

Romana went on. 'He can vouch for me. We're known to each other.'

Stokes gave her a scathing look. 'Please ignore her ramblings,' he told Viddeas. 'I've never seen her before in my life.'

Inwardly, Dolne was rather amused by the scandalized look on Cadinot's fresh face. The young man kept looking between him and K9 and shaking his head. 'You're not serious, sir. Say you aren't.'

Dolne wagged a finger and slid a thick leatherbound volume from his bookshelf. 'There's nothing in here to say it can't happen.' He handed the book over. 'Times have changed. In my academy days we learnt every page of the constitution.'

Cadinot turned the book over in his hands, as if afraid to open it. 'But a robot? Not much more than a Femdroid?'

'An artificial intelligence,' Dolne corrected him. 'Who can tell? It might be the best thing for Metralubit.' As he spoke he took the book and placed it before K9, who started to read eagerly, using his eyestalk to turn the pages. 'Better than old Harmock.'

The com-screen bleeped suddenly, and without preamble Harmock's face appeared on it. 'I've spent hours trying to get through to you,' he said, frowning. 'Your satellite bands are thick with distortion.'

Dolne nodded happily. He took a perverse pleasure from confounding Harmock, even in these circumstances. 'Yes, that'll be the enemy jamming.'

'Jamming?' Harmock sat forward and his face filled the screen. 'I think you'd better give me a full report, Admiral.'

* * *

The Doctor had shrugged off his coat, having found the close atmosphere of the saucer uncomfortable, and was using a small piece of wire to scrape off some of the substance from the dead skin of the victim and into another test tube fished from the depths of his pockets. His willingness to approach the body with no protection greater than a handkerchief had seemed to impress his captors, who were standing back as he completed his work. He turned to the First Pilot and held up the tube. 'No plague, Mr . . .?'

'Seskwa,' the other grunted.

'Mr Seskwa. Without the proper equipment I can't be absolutely certain, but I'd say this was the residue of a naturally occurring preservative chemical.'

Seskwa made a sceptical gesture. 'From a glance, you can tell that?'

'I've seen a similar process in a parasitic species called the Oraapi. Carrion feeders. It's used by an advance party to keep the food fresh until a full hatching.' He turned back to the body and used the wire, now clean, to point to two small marks on the grizzled neck. 'These look like incision points. The feeder has tested the meat, found it to its liking, and decided to preserve it and come back later, probably with friends. Say what you like about micro-organisms, they look after each other.'

'Micro-organisms?'

'Oh, I'd say so, wouldn't you? Anything larger would have simply gone for the chomp.' He rooted in his coat pocket and pulled out the first sample. 'And look at this.'

Seskwa and his colleagues took a step back. 'What is that?'

'Don't be so jumpy. I found it covering the bodies of some Metralubitan soldiers not far from here.' He looked Seskwa right in the eye. 'Do you know what I think?'

'Tell me.'

'I think your war has disturbed a predator.'

Seskwa moved a little closer, his eyes narrowing. His tone was outwardly unperturbed. 'Let me put an end to your theory, Doctor. There is no life on Barclow. Only

101

our people, and your people. The planetoid is without any of the properties needed to sustain life. The atmospheric belt is only fifty miles wide. Nothing grows here. There are no such predators.'

The Doctor raised a finger and moved closer to Seskwa, stooping to put their heads on the same level. 'Can I ask you a pointed question?'

Seskwa nodded graciously.

'If this planet is so useless,' said the Doctor, 'why are you and the Metralubitans fighting over it?'

Harmock's bushy brows twitched in a reaction that Dolne found unreadable. Was it grief or joy mixed in with the shock? 'Rabley is dead?' he stammered.

'I'm afraid so, sir.'

'But that's —' Again the flutter, the hastily suppressed smile. 'I mean, it's — er, I'm not sure what it means, but . . .' He composed himself and put on the face he reserved for state funerals. 'What a terrible loss. In a cowardly attack, just two days before the election.' The words lingered on his lips. 'The election.' A glint came into his eye. 'You know what this means, Dolne.'

Dolne had a terrible feeling he did. 'You're not suggesting we fire back?'

'Drastic measure, I know,' Harmock said. 'Nothing serious, mind you. Be sure not to hurt anybody. Just let them know we're not going to stand for it.'

Dolne wrung his hands. 'I'm sure Jafrid didn't intend for Mr Rabley, or anyone else, to actually die. This is all a dreadful mistake, I can tell.'

Harmock wasn't listening. 'Poor Rabley. I'll mourn his passing, but he was a victim of his own pacifist stance. Yes, I like the sound of that.' He re-emphasized the sentence. 'A victim of *his own* pacifist stance. No, a victim of his *own pacifist* stance. Much better.' He waved a hand vaguely. 'His deputy will have to take over. Can't quite recall who that is.' Then he gave a small chuckle. 'What a pity. What a terrible pity.'

Suppressing his own outrage at this behaviour Dolne

decided to drop his own bombshell. 'There's a further complication, sir. Someone here put his own life in danger to save Mr Rabley.'

'And survived?' Harmock, who obviously knew his constitution, looked anxious.

'Yes, sir. He's here with me now, sir.'

Harmock's eyes settled on Cadinot. 'Ah. Soldier. Well done. You shall be given the highest citation it is within my power to bestow. And your pension will be upgraded. So, no need for you to claim the privilege, right?'

'It isn't me, sir,' said Cadinot.

'Who, then?' said Harmock. 'You said he was with you?'

'Greetings, Premier Harmock,' said K9, motoring himself forward into the range of the com-camera. 'I am K9. I am now fully conversant with the Metralubitan constitution.'

Harmock slumped. 'Is this all a joke? The whole thing, I mean? The missiles, Rabley and everything?'

'I wish it was, sir,' said Dolne.

'I claim my constitutional right,' said K9. 'I will stand as your opponent in the coming election.'

Harmock took a long look at his new opponent, who was staring up at him from the carpet of Dolne's quarters. He felt vaguely amused. 'Do you, now? K9, you say?'

'He's a computer, Premier,' said Dolne. 'Belongs to a young lady who's just arrived here. An offworlder, in fact.'

Guided by instinct, Harmock looked over his shoulder at Galatea and Liris. They looked as inscrutable as ever. 'Offworld visitors? I've had no notice of this.'

Liris's shoulders shifted in a movement that suggested unease. Galatea, though, reacted with her usual smoothness. 'The incursion did not register on our detectors,' she said. 'It must be small and poses no threat.'

Although reassured by her words and their simple wisdom, Harmock could not assuage his natural curiosity. 'Now listen, Dolne,' he said, turning back to the screen.

'Who is this woman? What's she doing wandering about on Barclow? She's not connected to all the trouble you're having, is she?'

The robot answered. 'Negative. My Mistress is non-hostile.'

'What about you?'

'My ethical programming is to resolve conflict situations.'

Harmock scented evasion. 'You haven't answered my question. It deserves a direct reply that you will not give.'

'My study of this war calls into doubt your suitability for office,' said K9. 'Your own environment appears excessively pleasurable, while this command post needs urgent replacement of defence and communications equipment.'

Harmock hooted. 'You're blaming me? Without stopping to give a decent account of your own origins? My goodness, it's laughable. Why should I take notice of you anyway? I might as well stand for office against this desk.'

'Prejudice against artificial intelligences is outmoded,' countered K9. 'As outmoded as your economic and social policies and your deployment of personal insults when argument fails you. I will now give –'

His speech was cut off by a sudden increase in the static interference that had been fluttering at the edges of the relayed picture.

The Darkness observed this exchange, and approved of it. One of the leaders was dead, raising the stakes. A new leader had been appointed. Instability was a good way to the creation of much human death.

Liris's fingers fluttered over the printed circuitry of her amulet, her bookish features wrinkling at the static-filled screen. 'The link is lost,' she reported at last. 'More interference on the east satellite.'

Harmock was hardly bothering to listen. 'What does it matter?' he asked. Below the desk his hands were rubbing together convulsively, his body sent into delighted spasms. 'This is looking better and better.'

His mind was filled with thoughts of his new opponent, and his undoubted victory, so he almost failed to register Liris's next words. 'MNN wish to know your reaction to the death of Mr Rabley and the appointment of K9, Premier.'

He sat up and fumed. 'They know already? Damn them. They must have a tap on our priority channels. Blooming journalists must have a better idea of the picture than we do.' He considered for a moment. 'Tell them I'm deeply saddened, et cetera, et cetera, but that I'm looking forward to taking on his replacement. And that I've ordered a return of fire. That'll do. I'll make a fuller statement later when I've had time to think.'

Liris nodded and used her amulet to convey the message.

Fired by an unprecedented rush of enthusiasm, Harmock leapt from his chair and began to pace the office's thick green carpet. 'Ha! This will be a doddle!' He turned to the Femdroids and took their hands. 'No offence, my dears, but I know which way the voters will go given a choice between an animated speak-your-weight machine with ideas above its station and good old flesh and blood. A strong majority, I'll be bound. Then we can sort out this nonsense with the Chelonians.'

Galatea tightened her pressure on his fingertips very slightly. 'The cause of their attacks remains unknown. Mechanical failure is unlikely.'

'And interference with our satellites supports the theory that they are acting aggressively,' added Liris.

But Harmock's mood could not be quelled. 'If they want trouble, by jingo we'll give it to them. Friends or not. They started it.' He let their hands fall and walked to the window. Daylight was fading over the beautiful city, the last tourist skycar buzzing by. 'Perhaps this is just what I needed,' he reflected. 'A bit of action.'

'Premier. The first updated poll returns have been received,' he heard Galatea say.

He turned to the screen where the familiar graph was sketching itself in. 'That was quick.' He jumped as his mind made sense of the green block streaking past his own dwindling orange. The Opposition were a full twenty-five points ahead. 'How?' he stammered.

'I have accessed the public broadcast research centre,' said Liris. 'The voters have responded favourably to K9's appearance and personality. He is seen as cute. Furthermore, his offworld origins are being received favourably. Voters are calling in to say that he represents a new-broom approach.'

Harmock swung back to the window. He watched another skycar go by and cursed its passengers long and loud for their stupidity.

'Confess,' barked Viddeas. 'You are working for the Chelonians.'

Romana yawned and let her head fall back on the metal wall of her cell. She consulted her watch. This interrogation had been going on for only ten minutes. It felt more like an hour had passed, such was the cumulative effect of Viddeas's shouts and his awful odour. 'What as?'

'A spy.'

'I'm nobody's spy.' For the tenth time she appealed to the next cell. 'Stokes, tell him who I am.'

The artist made a shooing gesture. 'Don't try to implicate me in your schemes.' He smiled at Viddeas. 'I don't see why I should be locked up with her, or indeed why I should be locked up at all. I'm a civilian.' He raised his voice. 'By rights you ought to be grateful. Nobody here listened to me and now the bombs are dropping.'

Viddeas reacted to Stokes's words by fumbling at his belt and then whipping out a silver pistol. Romana was startled by the ferocity of the action. 'Will you –' Viddeas looked at the arm in which he held the gun and shuddered. 'Be quiet. There is a . . . there is . . .'

Stokes stood up and backed himself out of the line of fire. 'How dare you point that thing at me? I hope it's set on stun.'

Viddeas shuddered. 'I've had enough,' he said, spitting out each word. 'You cannot know . . . how long we've waited . . .' His voice died away, dropping to a whisper, and Romana had to strain her ears to catch his last words. 'Consume,' he said. 'We must . . . consume . . .'

He slumped against the bars of her cell, and she was starting to weigh the odds on reaching out to grab his gun when the moment's tension was broken abruptly by the clatter of booted feet on metal and the appearance of Admiral Dolne and his fresh-faced colleague. 'Ah, Viddeas, there you are,' said Dolne, totally failing to notice the drawn weapon. 'Now look, the situation's changed.' His manner seemed to have become breezier since their last encounter, and his hands moved expansively as he spoke. He offered her a curious wave. 'Hello, Romana. I've heard all about you from K9.' Without waiting for an order, the young man with him stepped forward and started to unbolt her cell.

The effect on Viddeas was electric. He snapped upright. 'Sir, what are you doing?'

Dolne wrinkled his nose. 'You never did take that bath, did you?'

Romana stepped from the cell, nodded to the young man and addressed Dolne. 'Thank you, Admiral. I'm pleased that someone here can think clearly.'

He tapped her on the shoulder. 'Not a bit of it. Now, K9 is waiting for you in his quarters, fifth level. Cadinot here will show you the way and fill you in on the gen.'

Romana joined Cadinot, who waved a hand towards the door leading from the cells. Something in the formal manner of the Admiral was unsettling. Why had she suddenly been accepted, and treated so kindly?

'You can't let her go,' spluttered Viddeas. He was paid no attention.

Stokes was viewing this scene with visible apprehension. 'Admiral,' he called. 'At last you're here. This underling of yours has been behaving to me in an outrageous, and probably unlawful, manner. Surely there's no reason now, with the bombs flying about our heads, to keep me locked up down here? And no reason why I can't take the first shuttle away?'

107

'Return to your bunk,' said Viddeas, gesturing with his gun.

Dolne raised a hand. 'No, wait. Er, Stokes. If I let you out will you promise to behave?' He stepped closer and said quietly, 'Only I've got enough on my plate without you shouting your mouth off.'

'Sir,' protested Viddeas. 'This man is a disruptive influence.'

'You've just made up my mind for me,' Dolne said. He reached out and unbolted Stokes's cell. 'Out you come.'

'Thank you,' Stokes said, with all the grace he could muster. 'And now, if you'll escort me to the shuttle, Captain?'

'I didn't say anything about that. You're to remain here.'

Stokes flared up, pulling himself to his full height. 'But I've –' He caught sight of Dolne's look of warning and his shoulders fell. 'Very well.'

Sickened at the sight, Romana turned her back and allowed Cadinot to lead her away.

A moment later she felt a tap on her shoulder and turned to face Stokes with accusation in her eyes.

'I had no other option,' he said anxiously. 'If I'd spoken up they might have accused me of being your accomplice. By keeping quiet I could work out a plan to get us both free.' He held out a little finger. 'Friends again?'

She sniffed. 'I don't recall that we ever were.'

Dolne waited until both Romana and Stokes had departed before turning to Viddeas. He had no wish to give the man an audience at this distressing moment. Indeed, he felt rather embarrassed. 'Word's come through,' he said.

'From Metralubit?' Viddeas's eyebrow shot up.

'Do you have to look so eager?' He reached in his pocket for a small folding map of the battle zone, smoothed it out, and indicated a certain area. 'Here we are. There's a scattering of pillboxes along these slopes at 73 to 76. Prepare the launchers.'

Viddeas snatched the map and his eyeballs rolled over it. 'But they're unstaffed. The Chelonians use them for remote camera scanning. They're worthless.' He bit his lip, leaving a small white mark. 'Sir, three of our men are dead. Six if you count Kelton and his team. I say we should hit back hard. If we do this they'll just laugh at us.'

Dolne was saddened. 'Oh dear. Why does everyone have to get so upset? I don't know what's possessed you.'

Viddeas flinched and his eyes dilated oddly. 'Possessed? What do you mean, *possessed*?'

'I mean I don't know why you're behaving so oddly,' said Dolne.

'Ah. I see.' Viddeas relaxed.

'I just think we ought to try not to let things get out of hand.' He took the map back, noting how it seemed to cling to the clammy skin of Viddeas's hand. It was only now he noticed that Viddeas wasn't sweating; and rather than being flushed like everyone else's face at the post, his face was pallid and showed a faint greenish tinge. He had always been of the fastidious sort, overeager but deferential, and scrupulously tidy. It was odd. 'Now, I want a mildly aggressive bombardment. Nothing too serious. Do I make myself clear?'

'Yes, sir,' said Viddeas. 'I'll see to it.' He saluted and left the cell block.

For the first time in a while Dolne was left alone. His thoughts turned to Jafrid. He hoped his old friend wouldn't mind what was about to happen, that he would see it was only fair for both sides to have their little accidents.

It was very difficult, Romana was rediscovering, to ignore Stokes. He made the Doctor, whose lips never seemed to rest together very long, seem shy and reflective by comparison, and seemed incapable of letting even the smallest incident pass by without making some comment on it. Cadinot had directed them to the post's lowest level and hurried away on business, and now they were turning the corner into the passage that contained K9's quarters. This level was constructed more sturdily than the others, and there was a suggestion of luxury in the fan-shaped light fittings that emitted a soft, reassuring orange glow. 'Plush, isn't it?' remarked Stokes. 'When I first arrived I came down here for some drinks with Dolne. He's got very good quarters and a reasonable cellar.' Noting Romana's silence he adopted a plaintive tone. 'I would hardly have abandoned you, you must realize. Here's a suggestion. Why don't we find the Doctor and all go back to your TARDIS thing? You've still got it, haven't you?'

'I thought you liked living on Metralubit,' said Romana.

'I do,' he said hotly. 'Very much so. It's a fantastic place, with all the luxuries and civilized refinements that a man of my taste and character could wish for. And I'm very much appreciated there. What I was thinking was that you could just drop me off . . .' He let the sentence fall to the floor.

'We'll discuss it later,' she said. They had now reached the third door along the passage. 'This must be it.'

Stokes seemed to notice where he was for the first time. 'I thought so. These are my rooms, the guest suite. They've got a cheek, throwing me out like an old boot. It's ridiculous. What will a tin dog want with a jacuzzi?'

'Let's find out.' Romana knocked on the door and it whirred open. Inside was a reasonably sized room with subdued lighting, a scattering of low leather sofas, and a large communications unit. Its main screen was at present scrolling through a microdisk's worth of data, which K9 was absorbing with incredible speed. On the wall above was a framed Stokes original, a dotted red swirl that depicted nothing in particular. 'Hello, K9,' she called.

'Greetings, Mistress,' he replied without turning from the screen.

'How are you?'

'I cannot converse at present, Mistress. Imperative that I absorb this information.'

Romana stepped forward and pressed the screen's pause control. The display at this point read:

The current democratic system evolved from the chivalric notions of the second Diurnary period, and from which many of the rituals, including the right of constitutional privilege, are traditionally derived.

'It doesn't look very imperative to me,' she observed.

'Hello,' said Stokes. K9 ignored him, so he stepped in front of the screen and smiled. 'Recognize me?'

This time K9 seemed genuinely taken aback. 'Human-oid artist Menlove Ereward Stokes. Friend. Encountered during the Xais/Nisbett affair. Unreliable and erratic character.'

'Lovely to see you again, too,' said Stokes. 'He seems a tad snootier than at our last meeting.'

Romana knelt down to address K9. 'We must find the Doctor. There's no time to waste on political history.'

'Aiding the Doctor Master is my first priority, Mistress.' Stokes was right, thought Romana. K9's manner seemed somehow elevated. 'It is to achieve that end that I have accepted my constitutional right to stand as the Opposition candidate for the Premiership of Metralubit.'

She blinked. 'What?'

'It is to achieve that end that I —'

'Shut up, K9. I mean, don't shut up. I mean, explain.'

In the Strat Room, Viddeas gripped the arms of his chair and swivelled it very slightly to the left. It was surprising, he thought, how much of his personality remained in this dead shell. Perhaps the creature dominating him needed to retain some of his human characteristics. It seemed to encourage him whenever he thought of war and death, which was often. 'Right,' he ordered. 'Align launchers three and four.' He swung a remote control board from the wall so that it rested at his waist. 'Hammerschmidt, give me satellite access to this position.'

The named officer turned round guiltily. The Strat Team had been shaken by Viddeas's orders to prepare counterfire, even when he had assured them of its mildly aggressive nature. 'The interference is still strong, sir,' said Hammerschmidt, a trace of resentment in his voice. Unlike Viddeas, many of the staff at the post had friends among the enemy. This reluctance would have to be dealt with. 'We'll have to launch the missiles on manual.'

'Do not question my orders,' snapped Viddeas. 'Give me guidance to this station.'

'But you won't be able to do anything, Captain,' protested Hammerschmidt.

'Do it!' shrieked Viddeas. For a moment, as the terrified lad struggled to comply, Viddeas had a sickening vision of his body with all the strength and health drained from it, saw it as a piece of decaying meat, and had to fight down a wave of some feeling that was nausea and excitement combined.

Cadinot spoke. 'Launchers aligned to target on manual.'

'Very well.' Viddeas gulped. 'On my order.'

Suddenly his mind was wrenched open from within with the force of a strong light piercing an ancient tomb. He seemed to see not only the Strat Room and the backs of his staff hunched at their stations but also a hideous, red-outlined place the size of a cathedral. This was a shrine to animal death, a stinking lightless temple where disease was a holy word. And his consciousness was not contained in just one body but in billions, all traces of individuality stripped away until there was one central mind governed by a feverish lust.

Somehow, this creature he had become part of told him that the satellite was free for him to use.

'Missiles armed and ready, sir,' said Cadinot, very distantly, his voice seeming to echo through the otherspace, the vast Darkness, to reverberate through the billions of tiny, furled-up buzzing creatures with jittering wings and twitching probosces.

He reached out and started to manipulate the satellite link, unseen by the others. 'On my mark,' he heard himself say.

The Doctor felt he was getting somewhere. Seskwa had been rather forthcoming about the planetoid's history.

'So, you turned up here a hundred and twenty-six years ago, set up camp, and the Metralubitans came along and told you to push off. At which point you claimed Barclow as your territory, you threatened war on each other, then signed a treaty to let this Committee sort it out, and have been waiting for the findings ever since with not a shot fired?'

'That is the gist, yes,' said Seskwa.

'Good. I just wanted to get things clear.' The Doctor allowed himself a smile. 'Very unusual. It makes this mystery all the more puzzling.' He gestured to the dead body. 'Humans weren't responsible for this.'

'How do you know?'

'Not their style. Too imaginative.' He crouched down to bring his face level with Seskwa's – a presumption that would test their new alliance.

Seskwa narrowed his eyes. 'Why, then, do they jam our communications? Our east satellite is almost totally blocked.'

The Doctor wagged a finger. 'You haven't considered the other possibility. Some third, alien force.'

Seskwa gestured with a front foot. 'You are an alien.'

'I meant a very alien force.' He looked at the test tube that was still in his pocket. 'I really could do with a closer look at this gloop. I don't suppose you have a microscope about the place?'

The Darkness concentrated, humming with power. This was perhaps the most crucial stage of its operation.

On one patch of the dripping screen was Viddeas's view of his own hands working at the satellite link controls. On another was the satellite itself, seen from close by. A third section was taken up by a hastily compiled map of the war zone, adapted from the one shown by Dolne. According to this, the optimum strike should impact at the grid cells marked 48.

The Darkness sent a thought pulse, and Viddeas reset the east satellite to fire all launchers at that position.

* * *

'First Pilot!' cried one of Seskwa's juniors from his position. 'There is a shower of plasma missiles coming in fast!'

Seskwa reared up. 'What? Range?'

'Eleven point three kuznaks and closing. They will reach us in three minutes.'

Seskwa snarled at the Doctor. 'So much for the innocence of your species, human.'

The Doctor looked anxiously at the radar screen. 'I suggest you stop asserting your superiority and start worrying about those.'

'In this craft we can be far distant in seconds, Doctor.' Seskwa nodded to the third Chelonian, the navigator. 'Tuzelid, set a course for command and lift us away.' He started to strap himself into his support webbing as the saucer shook, preparing itself for flight.

The Doctor vaulted over the circular safety rail. 'Think. If I'm the evil genius you think I am why would my own side try to kill me?'

Seskwa looked troubled for a second. 'I don't know. But they obviously are.' He took out his weapon and levelled it at the Doctor. 'You will lie down.'

From the mind of Viddeas the Darkness saw how some of the animals would avoid death. They had machines to carry them off, in a mockery of the Darkness's own power of flight.

No matter. There were other machines aboard the satellite to prevent them.

The saucer groaned and creaked, tipping the Doctor from side to side. He raised his head and saw only confusion: Seskwa trying to retain his dignity as his webbing was sent swinging, and the two others busy at their stations but to no avail.

'The engines are immobilized!' cried the navigator. 'A paralyser field has been imposed from low orbit!'

'One of the humans' satellites,' snarled Seskwa. 'You must break through. Increase power.' There was a loud bang from somewhere in the saucer's workings.

'I cannot,' cried the navigator. 'The field is strong.'

The saucer tipped once more and then its motors cut out completely. It crashed to the rocky surface with a thump that jarred every bone in the Doctor's body. Smoke began to pour from some exposed panelling. Over this hiss came a far more significant noise – the droning whine of missiles.

'They're heading straight for us!' cried Seskwa, desperate. 'We are directly in their path!'

The Doctor let his head fall back on the floor of the saucer. 'Would you believe me if I told you I'm as unhappy about that as you are?'

The noise grew louder, until it became an unbearable roar signalling imminent and inescapable death.

'Impact in fifteen seconds!' shouted the Environments Officer. He could barely be heard beneath the grating machinery of the saucer's protesting engines and the horrifying shriek of the missiles.

Seskwa levelled his weapon between the Doctor's eyes. 'You shall die now, human!'

The Doctor was trying to balance himself on the wildly gyrating floor, in order that he might race to the navigator's aid and somehow affect an escape. He looked at the bright yellow muzzle of the gun with dismay. 'Where's the point in that?'

'I wish to savour the last few seconds of life.' Seskwa squeezed his claw on the trigger.

Part Two

4

The Reluctant Diplomat

Cadinot stared in horror as the small speckled arc of yellow pinpricks that signified the missiles fired at the enemy pillboxes started to spread, and larger patches of a similar pattern blossomed in the central area of the zone. At first he took this to be a technical error, and he reached without thinking for the tuning buttons on the side of the screen. But the growing mayhem was confirmed by all kinds of mysterious, never-before-heard whistles, beeps and clicks from the surrounding instrumentation. Something had gone seriously wrong, and a baffled murmur arose above the heads of the Strat Team.

He called over his shoulder to Viddeas, 'Captain! The launchers, all of them, are firing!' He hammered at the emergency switches, which were designed to bring all systems off-line. 'I can't stop them!'

'Continue with the attack,' Viddeas said.

Cadinot turned around. 'It's a broad sweep-patterned bombardment. The satellite's taken over and I can't get an access line.'

Viddeas looked extraordinarily calm. 'No correction is needed.'

Suddenly, Cadinot's screen twinkled with several bursts of golden energy. 'Twelve plasma bursts the length of the Low Valley,' he announced. A sick feeling hit his stomach. 'There are Chelonian active service units there. Dekza and his lot.' Dekza was an especially popular patrolling enemy officer, whose impersonations of key Metralubitan figures had enlivened many a cheese-and-wine evening in the trenches.

'Spare no compassion for the enemy,' said Viddeas.

The tension in the Strat Room was broken by the arrival of Admiral Dolne, who entered panting and evidently angry. 'Viddeas!' he screeched. 'What are you playing at? I could hear the impacts from the far side of the post. I said *mildly* aggressive.'

All eyes were on Viddeas as he swivelled himself to face the Admiral. His face was set in hard lines. 'No more games, Admiral. This is war.'

Dolne looked flustered, his forehead beaded with sweat. 'What's got into you?'

'Got into me?' Viddeas shifted uncomfortably. 'What do you mean, got . . . into me? Nothing's . . . got into me . . .'

'Oh, goodness.' Dolne turned from him. 'Cadinot, call this whole thing off, right away.'

'I can't, sir.' He gestured helplessly to his station. 'No response from any manual systems.'

Dolne bustled over and leant over him. 'Let me have a go. Excuse me.' He reached out and his fingers flicked over the emergency switches.

'I've already done all that,' said Cadinot.

'No harm in trying again.' He threw the last switch. Nothing happened. 'Gracious me, the satellite just isn't responding. That can't be right.'

A ghostly greenish aura had sprung up in the last few seconds at the centre of the screen. Cadinot's heart sank further. This was a nightmare. 'Admiral, look.'

'Oh. Er, what's that?'

'Patina of an engine paralyser.'

Dolne pulled a disapproving face. 'That's hardly fair. We've got to lift it.' There was a short silence. 'Er, how do we do that?'

'Through the satellite,' said Cadinot resignedly.

'Oh dear.' Dolne tutted and called, 'Viddeas, come and give us a hand.'

The Captain stood stiffly and walked over. 'Yes, Admiral, I must . . .' His speech was slurring, his fever seeming to pass its crisis point.

120

But Cadinot's attention was more taken by the activity in the zone. The moment Viddeas had stood up the array of significant lights had started to die away, and the satellite access line beeped its willingness to comply. 'The interference is clearing up,' said Cadinot. 'She's coming back on line.'

'What a relief,' said Dolne, puffing out his red cheeks. 'Right, shut all these silly rockets and things down.' Cadinot was already pulling all the launchers back under his control and disabling them. 'Let's hope they haven't done too much damage.'

The satellite responded to Cadinot's commands with an ease and politeness unknown for a week and a half. Perhaps, he thought, the interference had finally cleared itself up and things could return to normal.

The Darkness conferred with the Space-Cloud Ones, the part of itself specially created to traverse airless atmospheres. The Space-Cloud Ones could now leave the satellite, it decided. It had done its job and stirred much antagonism.

The interference would now end. Every weapons system would be needed to create more death.

The Doctor flinched from Seskwa's weapon.

'First Pilot!' cried the navigator. 'Sir! The screen is down. We're free!'

Seskwa twisted about in his webbing and barked, 'Then lift! Get us out of here!'

With a mighty effort the saucer started to revolve, straining as it went to dislodge the grey matter that had lodged in its vents. With full power restored to its engines it spun with sudden urgency, sending fountains of soil in all directions. Then, when the markings on its side were no more than a blur, it shot upwards and zoomed away, a great plume of black smoke in its trail.

Only a moment later the missiles streaked down, three of them, sleek, white and pencil-shaped. The plasma burst echoed from rockfaces that gave way under the sustained vibration.

The Doctor found his feet and nodded approvingly at the thankfully remote roar of the blast. 'There we are. One crisis averted. They probably changed their minds.' Keeping his tone casual he nodded to Seskwa. 'Well, if you don't mind I'll just collect my coat and –'

'No, Doctor,' said Seskwa. The gun was still clasped tight in his front foot.

'No? You can have it if you really want it. I've got several others.'

The saucer had steadied itself by now, and Seskwa climbed from his webbing and shuffled across the space between them. 'I have no interest in your external coverings.'

'Oh,' said the Doctor, looking at the ground. He noted again how much noise Seskwa's internal machinery made. At times the squeaking was almost painful. And the leathery-old-shoes smell of all Chelonians was particularly pronounced in Seskwa. 'You need some oil in those joints.'

'You will accompany us to the base,' said Seskwa. 'The General will turn your clacking tongue to sense.'

The Doctor pointed to the gun. 'I thought you were going to kill me.'

'That was before.'

'I wish you'd make up your mind. I don't like hanging about wondering if I'm going to be killed or not when I could be doing something more interesting.'

Seskwa made the gurgling noise that was his species' equivalent of a chuckle. 'Soon you will crave the luxury of extinction. You will scream for mercy when you are placed in the Web of Death!'

The Doctor gasped. 'The Web of Death?'

Seskwa nodded. 'You know of the ritual?'

'No,' said the Doctor, 'but I thought you might like it if I looked impressed. I can imagine the sort of thing you mean. I'm an old hand with webs.' He grinned. 'And you do paint a very vivid picture.'

Seskwa growled and motioned him against the wall with the gun.

Romana was trying to catch up with K9 and his newly elevated position, and trying to ignore Stokes, who was cowering in a corner of the guest suite with his hands over his ears and protesting regularly – roughly in rhythm with the bomb blasts – that they were all going to die. She had given up telling him that, by her estimate of the resistance of alluvially formed rock to plasma bursts in ratio to the consequent release of atmospheric disturbance, they were in the safest place on the whole planetoid.

The worst of it seemed to be over, and now Stokes was uncurling himself and pinching the bridge of his nose as if this could in some way return his breathing to its normal rate. 'This,' he said, 'has got totally out of hand.'

But Romana was listening to K9, who had reached the end of his dissertation on the history of Metralubit and its political system. 'Constitutional privilege, a precept established in the chivalric past of the Diurnary period of the Helduccian civilization on Metralubit, permits any being in political or military life to take up the position held by the deceased being whose existence they attempted to preserve.'

'You could have said no if you'd wanted,' pointed out Romana.

K9 waited a moment before replying. 'My reasoning circuits extrapolate that a position of authority will allow freer access to resources necessary to locate the Doctor Master. This was the primary motivation for my decision.'

Romana arched an eyebrow. 'The chance to show off never came into it, of course.'

'Charge refuted, Mistress. This unit's awareness of self is non-qualitative.'

Stokes started shouting again. 'In a full-scale conflict we don't have a hope. The Chelonians are better equipped and better drilled. They haven't let themselves slip.' He shuddered. 'What if they've been planning this from the very start, for over a century? Cunning. Because all they need is to hit this place hard and we're done for. I could be buried alive.' Stokes made a fist and slammed it against the wall, which wobbled. 'This place might as well be made out of cardboard. We're all going to die.'

'Information, Mistress,' said K9.

'What is it, K9?'

He motored himself around a half-circle. 'My visual apparatus perceives an anomaly in this environment. Certain technological developments do not tally.'

This interested Romana far more than Stokes's witterings. 'Yes. I noticed a few things. Plasma missiles alongside primitive radio communicators. Attrition of war?'

'More, Mistress.' K9 nodded upwards. 'The Metralubitans possess a Fastspace link between this planetoid and their homeworld, yet they have no transmat technology.'

This did shock Romana. 'That goes against all recognized rungs of development theory. Short-range transmats should come first. The leap to warp engineering is a natural progression from the discovery of verificated disassemblers. You can't really come at it any other way.'

Stokes snorted. 'You've not changed, either of you. In the midst of certain doom you sit there calmly and talk drivel.'

'Our conversation's been quite productive,' said Romana.

'Productive? You just don't understand do you?' He jabbed a finger at the ceiling. 'All it's going to take is one well-aimed strontium shot and we'll be pulverized, blown to atoms.' He shook himself and made for the door. 'Oh, what's the point? I must see Dolne. My contract didn't cover this. I'll demand immediate passage.' The last few words echoed back down the corridor after he flounced out.

K9 waited until he was out of earshot and said, 'Mr Stokes is non-contemporaneous, Mistress. Inference: time travel.'

'It's a very long story. Ignore him, anyway. This place

124

should stand up to quite a battering.' She stood up and examined the wall Stokes had struck. 'This looks like megalanium. Is it?'

K9's head fell and his tail drooped. 'Regret cannot reply, Mistress. My sensors . . .'

Romana felt guilty. She had the feeling K9 was trying to compensate for his incapacity by being extra helpful, and this touched her. 'Sorry. I was forgetting.' She patted her lap. 'Come here.' He crossed the room and she bent down and stroked his sides.

'Misunderstanding of the functional nature of this unit,' said K9. 'Petting unnecessary.' But he didn't pull away.

With the launchers disabled and the satellite ticking over as per normal, Dolne had called a small conference – just himself, Viddeas and Cadinot – in a corner of the Strat Room. 'Now, I don't like this one bit. Did everyone take leave of their senses? Viddeas, what happened then?' Viddeas was staring blankly at the floor. 'Report,' hissed Dolne. 'I'm coming very close to losing my rag.'

Viddeas snapped to life. 'Seemed to be a technical failure, sir. A temporary confusion. Probably an offshoot of the Chelonians' own jamming signals.' He jerked like a puppet and became more animated. 'I suggest we send out armed patrols with instructions to –'

Dolne raised a hand to silence him. 'I'm looking for sensible input, not militaristic nonsense. Now. Do we think anyone was hurt in that business?'

'There are at least five active enemy units in the strike range,' said Cadinot, 'including Dekza's.'

'Oh, no.' Dolne had done lunch with Dekza only a fortnight before. 'I'll prepare an official apology.'

Viddeas flared up. 'Admiral, I must protest.'

Dolne chose to ignore him. 'And start a full check on all our gadgets and instruments and things,' he ordered Cadinot. 'I wouldn't be surprised if this whole affair was down to a mix-up with the computers or something.' He reached up and loosened his collar. Something about Viddeas's stare unnerved him.

'Are you all right, sir?' asked Cadinot.

'Yes, it's . . .' Viddeas was staring at his neck, he realized with a jolt. 'It's all I can do to breathe. So very stuffy in here. Right, well, keep a sharp eye out, Cadinot, and keep trying to raise Jafrid.'

There was a murmur behind them as somebody entered the Strat Room. Dolne turned to see Stokes, who looked his normal ebullient self, if a little flushed and more reddened. 'Ah, the wonderful Strategy Room. What an admirable scene of military dedication you present.'

'No,' said Dolne.

Stokes pounded across, his heavy shoes clattering on the metal flooring. 'Now listen, Admiral. As you seem to have curtailed your madness for the moment would you please see to arranging my immediate departure from this theatre of devastation as, unlike you and your officers, I have no desire to exchange my present state as a living organism for the dubious condition of being a scattering of molecular dust on the wind. And don't even think of confining me. Your clodhopping deputy has already broken the martial code by doing so.'

Dolne was not in the mood to indulge Stokes. 'Get him out of here,' he said. 'I don't care who does it or how.'

Immediately a couple of men stepped forward and took hold of Stokes. 'I'm not without powerful friends back on Metra, Admiral,' he cried as he was thrown out. 'I'll let them know how you treated me and then you'll . . .' His voice trailed off.

'Right,' said Dolne. Saying 'right', he had found, covered all sorts of situations. 'Constant scan, all of you.' He nodded to Viddeas and indicated the annexe. 'A word. Now.'

The Doctor felt the saucer level out, and watched the Chelonian base come into view on the large curved forward screen. The base was about a mile in width, and consisted of a random assortment of yellow blocks

126

scattered on a high mountainside. This explained the need for flying craft, as it would have taken a strong man a mighty effort to climb so far. Wisps of dirty cloud clung to the sides of the highest buildings, which had jagged, almost crystalline facets, staining their sides with iron deposits.

'I'm impressed,' said the Doctor. 'Your people have lost none of their skill for construction and camouflage.' During previous encounters with Chelonians, the Doctor had witnessed their architectural skills, which relied on small blocks that could be used for many purposes. Once, he had seen a small city made of sections of a spacecraft.

His praise was not appreciated. The Environments Officer, who had put on a large pair of earphones that gave him a comical air, turned from his position and told Seskwa, 'I have contact with base, sir. I've told the General that we're bringing in a prisoner.' His eyes flicked over to the Doctor. 'The Web of Death is being prepared.'

'I'm flattered,' said the Doctor. 'You really shouldn't be going to all this trouble just for me.'

At the heart of his sanctum, which was contained in one of the smaller blocks at the base's edges to confuse the enemy, General Jafrid was putting the last touches to a letter of protest, his stylus hovering over the parchment-screen as he selected the last few words. Despite all that had happened in the last few hours, including that beastly missile attack (miraculously, nobody had been seriously hurt), he felt only puzzlement, not anger. Dolne had probably been pushed into these rather pitiful displays of power by Harmock, he reasoned. As long as it stopped now, then no harm was done.

He read out the last lines to the assembled company, which was made up for the most part of technicians and other advisors. ' ". . . and so we protest our surprise and outrage at your continued flouting of the Bechet Treaty, and warn you that further transgressions will be met with equal, if not greater, force." There, that should do it.' He signed the document with a flourish and pressed the transmit button. The enemy post would receive it instantaneously, so long as communications over the zone stayed clear. As Jafrid watched the letter vanish from the screen his olfactors twitched involuntarily. There was suddenly an awful smell, like a plate of boiled smasti nuts left uncovered in the sun. He turned to the base's head technician. 'By Mif, hasn't that valve been fixed yet?'

'It should come clear very soon, General,' came the reply. 'The team are working hard to locate the blocked inlet.'

'I should hope so.' Jafrid swiped at a small flying creature. 'These infernal insects flourish in this atmosphere.' He had returned to the base to find the atmospheric recycling system out of order, and the air-conditioning had failed soon after, making the place almost unbearably dry and hot. As a ranked officer he possessed internal sprinklers, but even they had little effect, and Faf knew how the juniors could stand it.

The smell seemed to get even worse when the door of the sanctum opened with a low hum to admit his First Pilot, who tramped in, his joints clanking, with a look of near-manic pride. He saluted. 'General.'

'Ah, Seskwa returns,' said Jafrid. 'I've read your report. Very amusing. Plague war, indeed.'

'I speak truth,' Seskwa said. 'The enemy has turned against us. And here is my proof.' He tugged at a length of chain wrapped around his front foot, and a human was pulled in, nearly losing his balance in the process. 'My prisoner. It calls itself the Doctor.'

Jafrid enhanced his ocular range to study the newcomer. The human was adorned distinctively, with a long, soil-coloured main covering and an odd, purposeless length of twine draped many times around its upper half. Some sort of ceremonial regalia, perhaps? 'Doctor, eh?' He was intrigued by the human's large eyes, which shone with intelligence and alertness, and by its mouth, which was curled upward in the way Dolne's did when he was being amiable. 'Bring him forward.'

Seskwa tugged the chain and the human came crashing in. He was flung before Jafrid with unnecessary force. 'Greetings, General.' He raised an upper appendage and said gruffly, '*Kyaz rat jarrii guya-chell.*'

The General's jaw dropped in amazement.

Seskwa, feeling left out, tugged roughly on the chain. 'What's that you say? Do not mock us or you will face certain death.'

'I thought I was facing it anyway.' He addressed Jafrid again. '*Paz corlik vench.*'

'Be silent!' said Seskwa, pulling a blaster from his shell with his free front foot. 'Or your next word shall be your last!'

Jafrid came forward and studied this Doctor more closely. 'You speak in the ancient dialect of the imperial warriors. How do you know it?'

The Doctor indicated the chain, which was digging tightly into his neck. 'Erm . . ?' He made a breathless sound.

'Release him,' Jafrid ordered.

With very bad grace, Seskwa brought the Doctor to his knees and whipped the chain from around his neck in a swift movement.

The Doctor rubbed his neck, stood up, and cast his eyes about the place. 'Thank you. Well, General, you might say I've made a study of your warrior class. A very close study at times.' He seemed oddly distracted by the surroundings.

'As part of your plan to destroy us!' shouted Seskwa.

'I haven't got a plan,' said the Doctor wearily. 'I nearly never have a plan. But yes, I'm familiar with your history. I'm not from these parts, you see.'

'Not from Metralubit?' Jafrid blinked, astonished.

'Not really from anywhere,' said the Doctor. He wandered over to one of the work stations and studied its instrumentation. 'What surprises me is how similar you lot are to your forebears. I thought you'd left your expansionist period behind long ago.'

Jafrid waved a foot graciously. He liked this person.

'The seed of old Chelonia is spread far and wide through the galaxies, Doctor. In the times of which you speak, hatcheries were founded from the Great Arm of Quique to the crystal quasars of Menolot. As our paths diverged so did our cultures. My men and I claim descent from the lines of Nazmir and Talifar.' He broke off and lowered his voice. 'Do you really find this interesting?'

The Doctor nodded. 'Very. Do go on, please.'

'That's good.' Jafrid gestured around. 'Most of this lot have switched off by this point. Yes, Doctor, our ancestors' legends speak of their abandonment on a barren, hostile, ruined world. There's some mystical story behind it that I won't go into. What we know for certain is that they made a rough sort of living there for themselves for a few thousand years, founded a hatchery and force-cultured a range of soils. When they finally got back in touch with the homeworld they found the empire had fallen. But by then their culture was pretty much independent, although still bound by some of the old codes. Of course, without the technology for space travel the tendency to aggression had been lost.' He cast a rueful glance at Seskwa. 'Mostly.'

'That must have been millennia ago.'

'As a species we're slow to change,' said Jafrid. 'We are an experimental, exploratory team, out of the homeworld known as Sarmia. We came to this Fostrix galaxy as part of a research initiative. It was not our wish to indulge in battle. The Metralubitans started it.'

'Really?'

'They had no interest in the place until we claimed it as our study base. It is of no value to them.'

The Doctor bit his knuckle, as if not sure how to ask the next question. 'Pardon me for asking,' he said at last, 'but what value is it to you?'

Indeed, Jafrid resented this. 'You are here to *answer* questions, Doctor, not to ask them,' he said.

'I wondered when you were going to say that.' The Doctor pulled himself upright and began to talk very quickly, each word following close on the heels of the last. 'Look, I'm as anxious as you are to see this affair settled amicably and I couldn't help noticing your spectro-analyser.'

Jafrid had no idea what he meant. 'My what?'

'That gadget.' The Doctor indicated one of the devices arranged on a podium in the corner. 'It's for examining the structure of things.'

'Is it?' Jafrid sighed. 'We never use it. Must have been one of the study team's gizmos. What do you want it for?'

'This.' The Doctor took a small glass tube from a pouch on his covering. Jafrid could see an off-white, glutinous substance inside. 'I found it on the bodies of some human soldiers. It's the mark of the third force that's aggravating this conflict. And it's the same substance that did for his troopers.' He indicated Seskwa.

Jafrid reeled from the news. 'Your report was true, then, Seskwa? No prank?'

'In all details, General,' said Seskwa. 'The patrol I was sent to search out was killed by that substance.' He pointed to the Doctor. 'A substance it created! Do not be fooled by its charmed tongue, General. It lulled us earlier to divert us from the attack planned by its comrades.'

'No I didn't, and you know I didn't.' The Doctor gave Seskwa a disparaging look. 'Not very bright for a First Pilot, are you?'

Jafrid had long found Seskwa's jumpiness tiring, and so he relished the remark. 'You amuse me, Doctor. I may yet find a use for you.'

'What?' said the Doctor. 'You mean I've been spared the Web of Death?'

Jafrid chuckled. 'He threatened you with the Web? Stupid boy.' He gestured to the gadget mentioned by the Doctor. 'You may use the machine while I think on matters. Watch him, Seskwa.'

The Doctor nodded his thanks graciously and outstretched a hand before Seskwa. 'After you.'

Admiral Dolne's red, breathless face filled the Glutescreen. He was leaning very close to the remote host, and his whispered words were amplified and carried through the many miles of the Darkness's interior. 'I know I'm not especially well up on giving commands,' he was saying. 'To be frank I never imagined I'd have to be. But I do know that your argy-bargying isn't going to get us anywhere. It'll lead to people getting inflamed. There's a difference, Viddeas, between parade-ground exercises and . . .'

The Darkness almost lost its concentration. A vein was pumping on Dolne's flabby neck, and this served as a symbol for the Onemind, which was not without a certain degree of imagination. It pictured many such veins, all of them turning from healthy, pumping wells of red to clot-blocked cavities of pyaemic sludge, channels of disease.

This picture must have overwhelmed the host's mind, because Dolne was saying, 'Eh? Captain? I don't believe you've listened to a word I've said. Viddeas!'

The Onemind relaxed its grip slightly. 'Sorry. Sir?'

'You're looking rather off-colour.'

'I feel fine.'

'I could order you to rest in your cabin until I get this affair settled.'

The Onemind knew how much the source desired its soul to be untethered. And it was not without mercy. But they were not finished with Viddeas just yet. 'Please, Admiral. I'm fit for duty. Really. And I'm sorry about what happened.'

Dolne grinned. 'Oh, all right, then.' He tutted. 'Listen to me. Soft touch.'

It is difficult to convey the language of the Darkness, such is the complexity of its composition. The Onemind's telepathic impulses are qualified by the emphases of the Greatbody's clattering wings, and further enhanced by vibrations from the feasting stocks annexed to the hibernation chambers. Workers, seekers and thinkers all have a part to play in its expression. But roughly, this is what the Darkness said as it looked on Dolne:

This beast's meat is toughened. The meat droops and sags from the bones. But we have waited so long in the Great Void.

132

Another face appeared before the host's eyes, and the Darkness quivered with delight. Young Cadinot, full-grown but still young, a fine source of meat. 'Admiral. We've received a letter, sir, from the Chelonian camp.'

'Ah, good. Apologizing, no doubt.' Dolne led Cadinot away from the source.

Another attack is needed, said the Darkness. *This way, trust will be broken down totally, and the death can begin.*

It was time to consult the primary remote host.

The Doctor had discovered a set of slides in the housing of the spectro-analyser, together with some rudimentary handling tools, and was preparing to smear on some of the substance. He held a slide in one hand, a test tube in the other. 'I don't suppose you have any . . .' he began, addressing Seskwa, then stopped himself. 'No, you wouldn't.'

'What do you require?' asked Seskwa.

'Gloves.' At Seskwa's blank look he performed a mime to demonstrate his need. 'I don't want any of this stuff to come into contact with my skin.'

'Then I will place it on the slide.' He held out a front foot and flexed the clawed digits. 'Give them here.'

The Doctor looked between Seskwa and his sample. 'It will require a certain delicacy not to fracture the glass.'

'You consider me hotheaded? Unthinking?' Seskwa snatched the items from him and very neatly tipped a little of the fluid on to the slide, then placed a transparent adhesive strip over the latter and handed it back to the Doctor. 'There.'

The Doctor reproved himself. 'Thank you. Now, then.' He put the slide into position beneath the main viewer on the analyser and peered into the viewfinder. As the machine had been devised for Chelonian use he had to crouch rather uncomfortably forward to see. 'Ah,' he said.

'Ah? What?' asked Seskwa.

The Doctor lifted his head, puzzled. 'It's totally blank. As if the substance had drained the energy from the machine.'

'I suggest you switch on the light,' said Seskwa.

The Doctor stared at him for a second, then snapped his fingers, realizing his mistake. 'Good idea.' He reached across the machine and pressed a button. When he put his eyes back to the viewfinder he found a very changed image. 'Ah. Yes, really, ah.'

'What have you found there, Doctor?' asked a gruffer Chelonian voice. Jafrid had completed his deliberations and come over for a look.

The Doctor rose, and his fingers worked on a panel built into the machine's top. A small screen lit up with a section of the image seen on the slide. 'See for yourself. That's an inch-wide section of the gloop magnified two hundred and fifty thousand times.' The picture was a stark monochrome image of a honeycombed pattern. Each section of comb was triangular in shape and contained a blob of tissue with a black nodule at its centre.

Jafrid shook his head. 'I lack the learning needed to draw a conclusion. Environments?'

Another Chelonian shuffled over and peered at the image. 'The arrangement of the component cells is strangely regular.'

'Exactly.' The Doctor found himself raking a hand through his thick curls, an unconscious sign that he was worried. 'I had postulated a roving predator. An unthinking beast feeding on carrion. But this suggests an advanced understanding of gene manipulation.'

'I don't follow,' said Jafrid.

'Like this fellow says, the organelles are too neatly arranged to be entirely natural.' He pointed to several of the triangular cells in turn. 'Nature can be precise, but you'd expect some small variation.'

'I still don't follow,' said Jafrid. 'History is my strong point.'

'Somebody has tampered with this stuff to make it a more efficient preservative.' The analyser beeped and printed out its estimation of the substance. The Doctor tore off the strip, ran his eyes down the list of constituents, and whistled. 'It's strong stuff, very tightly bonded, and

134

adaptable to almost any environment. It would keep flesh fresh for a good month or two, in any place from lunar wastes to tropical jungle. An incredible feat.' He passed the strip to the Environments Officer. 'And extremely bad news for all of us.'

'Explain,' said Seskwa.

The Doctor tapped the screen. 'Whatever made this is out there, questing for food. And it's already shown us that it's a rather eclectic diner. It'd gobble up me, you or a Metralubitan, equally happily.' He struck his forehead. 'Of course!'

'What?'

'The war,' said the Doctor. 'It aggravates the conflict, sets you lot against the others, and then swoops down to take the pickings.'

There was silence for a few seconds, with all heads in the control room turned to the Doctor. Then Seskwa spluttered. 'I have never heard such nonsense. How can this predator jam our signal devices, disrupt our satellites, fire missiles?'

The Doctor shrugged. 'Perhaps it's influence is more insidious than we can imagine.'

Seskwa turned to Jafrid. 'General. This human is lying. His presence here is a deliberate ploy, an attempt to distract and confuse us. The humans mean to take us off our guard.'

The Doctor grimaced. 'For the hundredth time I'm not human. Not even remotely. In fact, biologically speaking I probably have more in common with you than with them.'

'General,' urged Seskwa. 'You must not listen to his lies.'

The silence dragged on, Jafrid looking the Doctor up and down. Then he said, 'Step closer.' The Doctor obeyed. 'I do not know if I should believe your wild theory. But you strike me as a man of courage and integrity.'

The Doctor shrugged. 'I don't know where to look. I think I'll just stare at my shoes.'

'I have a mission for you. Will you accept it?'

'Is it a small mission or a big mission? I don't do big missions.'

Jafrid leant in close. 'Will you go to Dolne? And tell him what you have told me?'

The Doctor hesitated a second. Then he said, 'That's a reasonably sized mission. Yes, of course I'll do it. Just point me in the right direction.'

'You must not let him escape, General,' grumbled Seskwa, but nobody was listening.

'You shall be a neutral envoy,' Jafrid went on. 'We must face the future together. I cannot believe our friends among the enemy would want to destroy us.'

The Doctor felt a rush of admiration for old Jafrid. 'That's very charitable of you.'

But the General smirked back. 'Hardly. They wouldn't dare pick a scrap, Doctor. Dolne knows he could not possibly win, and he is without guile. Now, we must prepare a vehicle.'

'General,' called a technician. 'The enemy is trying to hail us.'

'How convenient,' said Seskwa. 'At the very moment their spy gains our confidence.'

Jafrid hurried to his position at the centre of the room and clambered into the golden strands of his webbing. 'Link us up, right away.'

The Darkness was perturbed by the Doctor. His unusual face puzzled them. It possessed a quality they had not seen before in a human, and the distortion of the Glute-screen lent it an especially unpleasant quality. His large blue eyes stared hard, as if he could see through the eyes of the source and into the Darkness itself.

The Darkness reasoned with itself. *All is well. The next battle will destroy all trust between them.*

But what of this Doctor? it asked itself. *He is cleverer than the others. He sees too much.*

It answered itself quickly. *No matter. He will be dead very soon. Nourishment for the first Great Hatching.*

* * *

The command post was silent, all activity brought to a halt as Jafrid's fearsome face appeared on the big screen of the Strat Room. Dolne felt the relief of his team, a reaction that matched his own. Surely, if they were still talking, they could sort out their situation? 'Jaffers,' he said. 'Thanks for the letter. I'm as perplexed as you are. I really did wonder if you'd gone barmy.'

Jafrid looked uncomfortable. 'I cannot speak to you informally over this channel, Admiral. The envoy will now speak.'

Dolne frowned, 'Envoy? What envoy?' Abruptly, the image from the Chelonian base changed, and a humanoid face appeared. A wild-looking fellow with a shock of curly hair. For a moment Dolne was puzzled, then he clicked. 'Ah, hello. You'll be the Doctor, won't you?'

'You've met my friends?' he said eagerly. 'How are they?'

'Safe and well,' said Dolne. He felt an intuitive empathy with the newcomer, as he had with Romana. Logically, he should have been wary of strangers, but they just seemed so agreeable. 'Romana's a splendid young girl, I must say.' He giggled. 'How do you chaps do it? I wonder sometimes.'

'Do what?' The Doctor held up a finger. 'Now, listen, Dolne, I've no time to gossip. The Chelonians are prepared to disconnect their battle computers as a gesture of goodwill. That way nobody can tamper with them. Will you do the same?'

Viddeas sprang up from his desk as if activated by the pressing of a button. 'Sir, no! Who is this man? A traitor, by the look of him!'

'Shut up, Viddeas,' said Dolne wearily. He turned back to the screen. 'Doctor, hold on. This isn't worth its salt really, is it, unless we all switch off at the same time? Which, incidentally, I'm prepared to do. It sounds a jolly sensible idea.'

'That's the spirit. So I'll be coming over with an escort to agree the fine details. I should reach you in about an hour. Now, could I snatch a quick chat with Romana and K9?'

'Certainly.' Dolne signalled to Cadinot. 'Patch him through.' He waved to the Doctor. 'See you soon.'

Then the picture faded. Dolne clapped his hands together and turned to address his team. 'At last. What a day. I knew it would blow over. Shall we all get back to doing, er, whatever it is we do here?'

There was a ripple of good humour from the Strat Team, and somebody started clapping. Before long, everyone had joined in, leaving Dolne feeling both exhilarated and embarrassed. Because, truth be told, he hadn't actually done anything to put things back on keel. The applause was nice, though.

Only Viddeas didn't join in.

5

New Dog, New Danger

Now it was the Doctor's turn to express his outrage and astonishment at K9's news. In all their travels together Romana had never before seen the combination of alarm, amusement and anger that spread across his face as she told him of recent developments. His own announcements – that the war situation appeared to have been resolved, at least temporarily – had merited his most casual of manners. 'He's *what*?'

'Put himself up for election,' she repeated.

'Well, he can put himself back down straight away.' His eyes roved about the room until he saw his dog. 'K9, is there fluff in your circuits?'

'Negative, Master. My fluff defences are fully functional.'

'To be fair, he was acting out of concern for you,' said Romana.

K9 swivelled himself to face her, turning his back pointedly on the screen. 'Negative, Mistress. I have no concern for the Doctor Master and was merely following programming.'

The Doctor rolled his eyes. 'All right, all right, K9. There's no need to take umbrage. I'm touched.' K9 gave a gracious beep of forgiveness. 'But you're still going to have to withdraw. You can't go around getting yourself involved in other people's business wherever we land.'

K9 refrained from making the obvious reply. 'Not possible, Master. Withdrawal from constitutional privilege before voting day is classified as a criminal offence, punishable by a hefty fine and a period of imprisonment not less than forty days.'

'Nonsense,' said the Doctor. 'I'm going to put my foot down about this one, K9, and you know I don't often do that.'

K9 gave another beep, this time of confusion. 'When in perambulatory mode you put a foot down three times per second, Master.'

Romana held up the data disk containing the planet's history, which she had been skimming through before the Doctor's call. 'He's right, Doctor. We'll have to go ahead. They're preparing a shuttle to take us to Metralubit.' She tried to keep the note of enthusiasm from her voice. Her initial doubts about K9's plan had been replaced by a sense of anticipation. At the Academy she had studied socio-psychology of underdeveloped societies as one of her core subjects, and it would be fun to see the wheels of such a system turning for real. It might even make a good topic for her postgraduate thesis. She dismissed the thought, as she dismissed all thoughts of returning home nowadays, aware that the Doctor had put on the face that suggested to the outside world he was having a magnificent idea. 'Doctor?'

'Do you know, I can see how we could turn this to our advantage,' he said.

'Yes?' Romana prompted.

The Doctor hunched forward and put a finger to his lips (as if, thought Romana, this would make any difference on an open radio channel). 'I've noticed some very odd things about this war, or whatever it is,' he said. 'And some even odder things about the people fighting it.'

Romana nodded. 'The technological discrepancies.'

'The what?' He scratched his head. 'Oh yes, those. But what I'm more curious about is the Chelonian presence. One, why should they take such interest in what is, after all, not much more than a big mud pie?' He paused, seemingly lost in thought.

'Two?'

'How's your intergalactic history?'

'Better than yours,' said Romana. 'But it doesn't stretch this far. Nobody's does. Study of the later Humanian era was forbidden by the Academy. We're outside the Gallifreyan noosphere.' She referred to the statutes laid down by the Time Lords that decreed that nobody should have too much knowledge – or any knowledge at all, if possible – of conditions beyond the vortex's boundary parameters. The reasons for this decree had been lost over the thousands of years of Gallifreyan civilization, and, like most things there, went unquestioned.

The Doctor nodded. 'Fair enough. But it's not what I expected to find out here. Chelonians and humans, and those only very little altered from those that were hanging about Mutter's Spiral ages, and I do mean ages, ago.'

'There's always Clarik's Theorem,' pointed out Romana.

'Stuff Clarik's Theorem,' said the Doctor. 'No. There's something strange going on here, Romana. And you'll be in a good position to find out what. Do a little digging around on Metralubit, while the dog's busy losing his deposit.'

'No deposit is required in this electoral system, Master,' said K9.

The Doctor looked off-screen as somebody, a Chelonian by the sound of him, called his name. 'I'm going to have to go. I'm on someone else's communicator.' He raised a finger, and suddenly his expression became more serious. 'Keep your wits about you, both of you.' The screen fizzled and his image faded.

As it did, a thought struck Romana. 'Damn. I forgot to tell him about Stokes.'

A crackle came from the post's internal communication system, and Cadinot's voice came from a speaker by the door. 'Will Mr K9 and Miss Romana please make their way to the shuttle bay immediately.'

'That's our call.' Romana smiled at K9, who motored forward with indecent eagerness, obviously desperate to make his mark. Something itched at her cheek and she reached up instinctively to brush it away, catching a glimpse of a small black shape buzzing away. 'We must remember to bring some fly killer back with us.'

'Insects are harmless, Mistress,' said K9 as he shot out of the door.

Romana dabbed at her cheek, and her finger picked up a tiny spot, no more than a pinprick of blood. She rubbed it away between her fingers and followed K9, thinking no more about it.

Gallifrey!

The word echoed through the Darkness, repeated over and over by its many compartments. The shock and excitement caused several of the incubating units to crack open prematurely, spewing jelly-meal in all directions. Efficient as ever, a row of elongated prostheses, tubes of dried blood, swung out and sucked up the waste for reuse.

An atavistic chill skittered through the Onemind, and another self-conversation began. *But Gallifrey is gone*, said one part. *As they say, it is forbidden.*

They spoke of time travel, said another.

In fact, to the Darkness, the word Gallifrey was synonymous with the concept of time travel. It well remembered its attempts to sneak into the wastes of the vortex, all of them thwarted by the defences erected by those miserable, thin-blooded, infertile, self-crowned gods, the Time Lords.

The Darkness assessed the data provided by its fore-guard, who had pricked the female alien. Chemical equations danced around the Onemind. This blood was cold, from a slow-pumping creature, and contained tiny cleansing organisms not found in the humans of this system. It had come from an augmented, enhanced being, and in the message core of each cell were written very special codes. Unique codes.

They are *Time Lords, the Doctor and the female.*

The Darkness started to search its memory for more information.

In the Strat Room the departing shuttle showed up on the main screen as a single signal trace, lifting effortlessly through Barclow's grimy speckled atmosphere. Dolne watched sadly as it disappeared, remembering how Rabley had stepped out from it. 'There they go,' he said. 'Poor old Rabley. I wonder how he'd have felt about his replacement.' He turned to Viddeas, who stood at his side, a report clutched tightly in his hand. 'Eh, Captain?'

'Sorry, Admiral. I was thinking.' Indeed, Viddeas's head was tilted at an odd angle, as if he was lost in a daydream. Thankfully, his open aggression had lessened, at least for the moment.

Now the tension in the post had returned to its normal levels, Dolne was feeling more charitable to his colleague. He lowered his voice. 'Come on, man, take a rest period. You've been on duty for nearly forty-eight hours solid.' He reached up and put a firm hand on Viddeas's shoulder, then lifted it again immediately. 'Good God!' Instinctively he stepped away.

'What is it, sir?' asked Viddeas.

Dolne felt the urge to wipe his hand, as if it was contaminated. Touching Viddeas had been like gently tapping an iron bar. 'You're as stiff as a board.' He gestured to the door. 'Go on. I order you. Bed.' Viddeas, still looking dazed, stumbled towards the exit. Dolne followed him and went on, in a whisper, 'I didn't want to have to mention it again, but I have to. You're ponging very badly. And it's getting worse. You'll lose the respect of the staff. And now things are going normally again there's no excuse. Take that bath!'

'Yes, Admiral.' Viddeas, formerly so vigorous and straight-backed, slouched out.

Dolne shook his head after him. 'All the life seems to have gone out of him,' he mused to himself. Then he snapped his fingers and turned to his team. 'Cadinot. News?'

'Mr K9's shuttle is through the atmosphere safely, sir.'

'Good, good. No more nastiness, I hope?'

'The east sat's responding very well. All cells clear at present, sir.'

'Super.' Dolne suddenly felt profoundly tired. Every

time he blinked a deep dark seemed to descend. A nap was needed. 'What a day. I think I'll nip to my quarters for a quick lie-down and wait for this Doctor fellow. He looks quite crazy, doesn't he? What fun. Call me when he arrives.' He slipped out, hoping that nobody would think of a reason to call him back. Then a thought struck him, brought into light by the drop of sweat that cascaded down his nose, and he lingered a moment. 'Oh. I don't suppose there's any sign of Bleisch?'

'Afraid not, sir,' said Cadinot. 'I'll keep calling.'

'Good-oh,' said Dolne, and left, almost happy with the world again.

Romana let her head fall back and stared from the port-hole of the shuttle as it passed through the upper reaches of Barclow's atmosphere, watching as the grey expanses of the war zone were obscured by encroaching layers of dark blueness. The craft was small but luxurious, and the lounge contained two rows of leather seats, a com-screen and a food machine. They turned slowly, leaving Barclow behind and nudging into space, and Romana craned her neck for a view of the starscape.

'Query your sighing, Mistress,' asked K9.

Romana sat up. 'I didn't know I was.' She looked over at where he sat, the straps of his seat's restraint buckled tightly over his mid-section, and caught the thoughts passing through her mind. 'I was just thinking about the Doctor. He always has to be so elusive, hinting at things. If he was more direct, we could –' She was interrupted by a loud clatter. Shutters slid down on the lounge's four portholes. 'Why do that, I wonder?'

'Suggest automatic sequence to protect human eyesight from solar rays,' said K9. 'Shuttle is on programmed flight.'

Romana looked anxiously ahead at the door to the forward cabin. 'There should be a pilot.' Their escort had merely ushered them into the lounge and slammed the entry hatch shut.

'A mere precaution. Computer guidance systems are infallible,' said K9. He added, 'Generally.'

144

'You would say that.' She turned to him. 'What are you thinking?'

His eyescreen flashed eagerly. 'I am preparing for my new role, Mistress. I have contacted the Metralubitan administrators and ordered the provision of campaign materials.'

'Contacted them how?' asked Romana.

K9 made a series of chirping whistles. 'The Femdroids, as they are known, communicate using pseudo-frequencies.'

'Just like you.' Romana frowned. 'It's a very uncommon system. Fortunate.'

K9 didn't appear to be listening. 'There is much wastefulness and financial mismanagement perpetrated on Metralubit. I shall pledge a more efficient economic strategy based on increasing state interest in industry, without losing sight of the electorate's dislike of swingeing tax increases. Revenue will be raised by levying higher rates on the mega-profitable monopoly supply companies such as the Water Conglomerate and the Oxygen Bureau. This measure is both populist and politically credible.'

Romana covered a yawn. 'You're going to have to change your presentation.'

'Mistress?'

She shrugged. 'Well, in a level-four pseudo-democracy rhetoric must be addressed more succinctly to be sociologically effective.' She stopped herself. 'What am I saying?'

'You are saying that my syntax is too rigid and my delivery emotionless and formal. Academic formulae of economics are not readily comprehensible. I shall work to rectify this problem.' As he spoke, K9's tail was wagging.

There was another loud noise, this time a metallic-sounding bang from the side of the lounge. The shuttle shuddered, and both passengers were jolted from side to side.

Romana recovered herself. 'What was that?'

'Likely a meteorite,' K9 suggested. 'Small and harmless.'

She unstrapped herself and made her way across the still-vibrating lounge to the door of the cabin. 'I thought computer guidance was infallible.'

145

'The organic pilot should have corrected the error,' K9 called after her.

Romana knocked on the cabin door. There was no answer, so she grabbed the handle and tugged it open. Inside was a small compartment crammed with highly complex instrumentation and, in the perennial traditions of aircraft design, a set of manual controls and a joystick. The shutters were also down in here, noted Romana, as she advanced, calling, 'Hello! Is everything all right? Pilot?' The compartment seemed to be empty.

She heard a faint, high-pitched noise coming from behind the door, and whipped around to see a familiar figure splayed in the corner into which he had been thrown, his legs and arms stuck out at distressing angles, his central bulk twisted in a different direction from his head.

Stokes managed to raise a finger. 'I don't suppose you have any idea of how to fly one of these?'

General Jafrid had decided that, in light of the earlier incident with the saucer, it was best to send the Doctor across the zone in one of the division's armoured ground vehicles. He had also agreed, after some petitioning, that his escort should be Seskwa. The First Pilot continued to view the Doctor with suspicion, a view the Doctor was finding increasingly irksome as the tank trundled through the wastelands. His disposition was not aided by the design of the tank, which was uncomfortable for a humanoid: he was forced to crouch with his knees tucked up to his chin in order to keep an eye on the glowing forward screen – the only source of light in the vehicle – and maintain a watching brief on Seskwa. The Chelonian had snubbed all his attempts at conversation, and was staring ahead, his watery yellow eyes almost crossed. The tank was automated, and did not require his close attention.

The Doctor decided to have a last try at winning Seskwa over. 'I'd say you were daydreaming, if I didn't know that Chelonians don't daydream.'

Seskwa shot him a dismissive look. 'What do you know about us?'

The Doctor tapped the middle of his own forehead. 'The old tin plate blocks all unnecessary unconscious thoughts. Some have said it's what makes you such rigid characters.'

'We dream,' said Seskwa. 'At our rest times. At any other time it is wasteful. Humans are a good example of that.'

The Doctor dug in his pockets. 'I've run out of jelly babies.' He pulled out a string bag filled with chocolate money of various denominations. 'Coin?' Seskwa did not dignify the offer with a reply. 'No? Never mind.' The Doctor unwrapped a silver tenpence. 'I must have given my last jelly baby to Romana. Have to stock up.' As he spoke he fixed a gold coin, the largest of them all, to the end of one of the lengths of string and began to swing it. He glanced at one of the readouts beneath the forward screen. 'Good driving. We should soon be there.'

Seskwa shuffled, and exhaled a blast of foul-smelling air. The Doctor wasn't sure if that was an insult or just one of those things Chelonians did. Seskwa was certainly smellier than most. 'I have nothing to say.'

The Doctor chomped on his chocolate. 'Why not just assume I'm telling the truth? It would save such a lot of bother.' The gold coin continued to spin, the rhythm beguiling, and he waited for Seskwa to respond to the first stage of mesmerism. He made his voice match the spin in its metre. 'I can see why you're angry. It's a dull life for a soldier. All this patrolling, and deploying, and marching about, and never a shot fired. For over a hundred years. You must have wondered what the point of it all was.'

'I am trained not to question orders,' Seskwa said.

'Still, you Chelonians are long-lived chaps.' The Doctor decided it was time to start digging for facts. 'You must have seen a fair bit of active service before you came out here.'

Seskwa reached out a front foot and cuffed the coin from the Doctor's grasp. 'Be silent.'

The Doctor decided to try another tack. 'This place is a textbook example of Chelonian psychology, you know. Your pride won't allow you just to walk away. It's very predictable.' He stopped himself as an awful fear ran through him. 'Predictable?' He felt suddenly unsteady. 'Almost as if . . .'

'What?' asked Seskwa.

The Doctor brushed away a fly that was buzzing around his face and replied, 'Oh, just an unfounded fear. At least I hope it's unfounded. If it turns out later on to be one of those unfounded fears that become founded later on I'll be worried.'

'What is this trickery in your words?' Seskwa turned to stare at him, and the Doctor caught a glint of real hatred in his eyes.

'Nothing,' he said. 'Keep your eyes on the road.'

All of K9's remote control systems were functional, and Romana had lifted him down to help pilot the shuttle. The real pilot, Stokes had revealed, was back on Barclow locked in a cupboard – an unfortunate necessity, as he had to leave Barclow at all costs. Rashly, he had assumed that with computer guidance the flight would be easy.

Unfortunately, K9's ego had been further swelled by his role in negotiating a Fastspace jump, liaising with the voice of Metralubit's air traffic control, and bringing them in safely. 'Boosters closed down,' he said as the shuttle, its shutters still down, reached firm ground. 'Rear fins retracted. Equilibrium stabilized. A perfect landing, Mistress.'

Stokes turned to Romana. 'Is there anything he can't do? It makes one feel so conscious of one's own organic, foible-filled condition.'

Before Romana could reply a loud hissing came from outside, and she felt the craft turning on the landing pad. 'What's that?'

'Decompression,' said Stokes. He picked up a grey duffel bag from beneath the pilot's chair and swung it over his shoulder. 'They're very keen on safety checks

148

and so forth. It's a clean, efficient place, Metralubit. A veritable paradise. I can't think of any reason why anybody wouldn't want to live here.'

'So you said.' Remembering the Doctor's earlier instruction, she asked, 'When was it settled?'

Stokes waved his fingers fussily. 'Ooh, thousands of years back. It'd make a fascinating study for some archaeologist. They've had umpteen wars, and some great civilizations before this one. Most of them were wiped out in internecine conflicts. I forget the exact details. But it's a big place, and populous. There must be a good few million in Metron City alone.' The shuttle stopped turning and the shutters were raised. 'There, you see. Oh, it's good to be back.'

Romana blinked, impressed by the view. The shuttle had come to rest in a small bay that was on the side of a large building, and through the entry port she saw, laid out before her as if in a picture postcard, a glittering white city of towers and glass spires. It was dazzlingly clean, and the citizens who walked or skimmed about looked well fed and purposeful. 'It doesn't look very mismanaged to me,' she told K9.

'These are the richer areas visible from the Parliament Dome, Mistress,' he replied. 'The social inequalities are less noticeable here.' A light under the flight controls winked. 'Incoming message.'

A moment later a small screen next to the winking light flickered on. A woman's face appeared, and although reduced to tiny size it retained an air of great dignity and standing. 'Welcome, Mr K9, Miss Romana,' said the woman in mellifluous tones. 'I am Senior Aide Galatea. Please proceed into reception, where you will find a lift ready to take you to your campaign headquarters. We shall meet there shortly. I look forward to this. Thank you.' The screen flicked off.

Stokes smacked his lips together. 'Ah, the lovely Galatea.'

Romana had taken an instant dislike to the face on the screen. 'She's a Femdroid?'

Stokes started to unlock the cabin's entry hatch. 'Yes. They're just robotic servitors like any others in the city. Knocked together to relieve civil admin of the more humdrum tasks of state.'

'And styled to resemble attractive women,' said Romana. 'Why?'

'The records I have studied indicate this shape was found to increase the attention span and efficiency of the predominantly male and heterosexually orientated workforce in the dome,' said K9.

Romana sniffed and followed Stokes. 'It's one way of dealing with a problem, I suppose.'

Stokes chuckled and pointed a finger at her annoyingly. 'I detect an ideological objection. Or is it jealousy? There aren't often any other girls around to compete with, are there, I'll bet?'

She suppressed an urge to kick him. 'Don't be so pompous. Come on, K9.'

He whistled to get her attention. 'Lift, Mistress.'

Romana noticed the high door jamb of the cabin and bent down to pick him up. 'Sorry, K9, I didn't notice.'

A full analysis of the blood specimen coloured itself in on one side of the Glute-screen. The Onememory flashed up the Darkness's only likely match in its records. It had pored through life-profiles of some of the sixty billion species used by the Darkness to feed upon in its long life and found only one similar.

The specimens correlated almost exactly.

If this is a Time Lord, said the Onemind, *it must be a dissenter.*

We have knowledge of such a dissenter, said the Onememory. *Encountered many, many void-times ago.*

Romana's sense of satisfaction with the gracious, symmetrical architecture of Metron City was shattered when the door to the reception lounge whirred open and she came face to face with what appeared to be a massive bloodstain on the facing wall. 'Urgh. What's that?'

Stokes peered about. The lounge was white and empty apart from a scattering of sofas, lit by the soft orange glow of wall lights and a large window that looked out over the city. 'What?'

Romana pointed. 'That stain. Has somebody been killed?'

'Stain?' Stokes moved forward protectively. 'That is one of my abstracts. I'd have thought you would recognize the fluidity of my brushwork.'

Romana looked more closely and noticed the frame around the stain. She had forgotten Stokes's exuberant style. He was not entirely untalented, she reflected: it was just that what he chose to produce was always so unappealing. 'I'm surprised they let you hang it here.'

'Don't sneer.' He waved an arm over the city. 'Here I am appreciated. Samples of my work hang in the homes of every truly discerning collector. My canvases have revolutionized the planet's visual arts; my sculptures are positioned in the most prestigious and fashionable greenspaces of the city. Look out there? See that?' Romana pretended to see what he was pointing at. 'One of mine. I am regarded as the greatest living artist on the planet.'

'I wondered why you liked the place so much.'

She became aware that K9 had slipped away from her side. He was engrossed in the examination of a communications device on the other side of the lounge, and had succeeded in activating the screen. It showed a large picture of a large man, twice as corpulent as Stokes, wearing a tunic that only just held his stomach in place. He was talking, and his voice had a smarmy, patronizing tone. '. . . which is why I decided we could wait no longer, on either the battlefield of Barclow or at the ballot box here. I have done all I could, not only in these distressing times, but throughout the past fourteen years. And I would say to you: feel the improved quality of your life. The sacrifices were worth it. Together, as one planet, we've pulled through. And by keeping and strengthening that unity – that sense of our identity – it is within our power to resolve the present conflict on Barclow.' He frowned for emphasis. 'If the reptiles want blood, we shall not flinch. We shall give them blood. Their own. Our equipment is of the highest calibre. Our men are trained for all eventualities. Let us give them our support, and rejoice in our strength.'

So, thought Romana, this must be our opponent. 'Generic rot with a twist of patriotism,' was her spoken verdict.

K9 extended his eyestalk and there was a brief chitter of pseudo-frequency communication between him and a faraway source.

The Premier went on. 'There are some who say that we should capitulate. Some who would, er, how should I phrase this?' He let his tongue flick between his teeth. 'Who would roll over and let the Chelonians tickle their tummies. Is this what we want?'

To Romana's surprise, K9 suddenly appeared on the screen next to the Premier, in tight close-up. 'Premier Harmock,' he said. 'I claim my right of response as codified in the statutes governing electoral broadcasts Para 3(a).'

Harmock grimaced. 'Oh, it's you. Here he is, everybody. A fresh face, a new attitude, but still the same tired old dogma.'

K9's eyescreen flashed an angry red. 'Your witticisms regarding my anthropomorphic modelling are an attempt to divert public attention from the hollowness of your policies. In your fourteen years in office unemployment levels have risen by sixteen per cent. Production is down by twenty-two per cent in the Bensonian settlements. Spending has been cut and revenues raised unfairly.'

Harmock looked a bit thrown by this. 'Listen to his soundbites. But where's the substance behind them, eh? I notice you remain very quiet on the subject of Barclow.'

'It is prudent to explore every opportunity for peace.'

'While bombs and missiles rain down on our boys? I hardly think so.'

'There are no boys on Barclow.'

Harmock puffed himself up. 'The public are demanding action. I am prepared to guarantee it. Are you?'

'The public do not appreciate the complexities of the situation. Intelligence levels among the manual labourers are low because of your policy of decreasing funds for public education.'

The battle had commenced.

Not far away, there was a small, rectangular room, decorated in the uniform bland whiteness of the Parliament Dome. It contained several items that would have been of extreme interest to an outsider, and especially so to informed outsiders like the Doctor and Romana. But no outsiders had ever seen it, nor were they likely to.

At present it was occupied by Galatea, who stood facing a large screen that covered an entire wall, her hands on her hips, a satisfied smile playing about her sensuous lips. The faces of Harmock and K9, relayed on MNN, filled the screen. 'Most satisfactory,' she said. In this room she was markedly less officious in manner than she was outside. 'K9 is superior to Rabley in all respects. The scenario's effectiveness is all but guaranteed.'

Liris was at her side. 'We must greet him and his mistress.' She touched her amulet and with a blue static fizz the image altered, taking in a view of the sparse reception lounge from above. 'I see Stokes is with them.'

Galatea inclined her head. 'So he is.'

Liris bit her lip, wondering how to express herself. Galatea had a way of making her feel stupid. 'Should we impound him?'

'No. His retraining is solid.'

'If he strays?'

Galatea turned and smiled reassuringly. 'Do not worry, Liris. We can retrieve him, any time we wish.' She reached out and laid a hand on Liris's shoulder. 'You are uneasy.'

Liris suppressed a shudder. 'The arrival of more off-worlders at this point is –' she lowered her voice instinctively '– strange.'

153

Galatea turned away. 'Do not concern yourself. It is not for you to worry.'

'Of course not.' Liris regarded her thoughtfully. It was part of her own programming to speculate and draw conclusions, a facility that was beyond the reach of the mass of Femdroids. That facility was speculating now, wondering if Galatea had somehow *expected* these strangers.

Dolne was in his night things, a set of linen pyjamas that made a pleasant contrast to the heavy serge of his normal outfit (*uniform!*). The post's air was still thick and heavy and he had kicked off the duvet on his bed and was lying back on it, breathing deeply to relax himself and staring up at the softly glowing light fitting directly above his head. Staring into its misty orange depths was always a strangely soothing experience, and he felt himself drifting peacefully into sleep. As his hand reached out for the light switch he caught just a glimpse of his wife's holograph in the frame by the bed, and smiled. Wouldn't be long and he could retire, let Viddeas take over the show. Then they could move out of their city home and into the Bensonian settlements, perhaps start a farm on the proceeds of his pension. Vague dream images started to cloud his head and he let it slip into the folds of the well-plumped big pillow.

There was a knock at the door. He cursed and called out, 'Who is that?', unwilling to get up or turn the light on if possible.

'Viddeas, sir.'

Dolne groaned. 'Is it important?'

'Yes.'

Dolne got up, switched the light on, and padded across the carpet to the door. 'Please don't tell me there's been any more –'

He broke off as the door opened to reveal a hideous figure. Outlined in the light from the corridor beyond, Viddeas looked ghastly, twisted. He smelt repulsive and the air around him was buzzing with flies. 'Viddeas, you

154

look worse than ever. You need looking over.'

Viddeas stepped into the room. 'No, sir. Please. Listen. I –' His head twitched grotesquely, and when he spoke again it was in a low, haunted voice. 'They're here, sir . . . again . . .'

'What, the Chelonians?' Viddeas didn't answer, only dribbled. His eyes were turning purple, the colour of rotting meat. 'Eh? What do you mean?'

'It is time . . .' Viddeas gurgled. He came closer, forcing Dolne back towards the bed. 'The Time of Void is over. Now, the Great Feasting . . .'

Dolne stood aside and pointed to the bed. 'You just sit right down there. I'm going to go and fetch someone to give you a shot or two. You've been overdoing it.'

Viddeas threw back his head and laughed harshly. 'Any treatment would be wasted on me.' He fiddled at his collar and pulled open the buttons at his neck. Dolne almost screamed at what lay beneath. The skin of Viddeas's upper body had been eaten away, leaving a mass of raw flesh that was crawling with flies and coated in thin strands of a clinging, gluey substance. 'Yes, Admiral. I am dead. They have killed me.'

'They?' Dolne gasped.

'Don't you know them, Admiral?' He moved in close and opened his blue lips wide, revealing a rotting tongue and wobbling yellow teeth. 'Don't you remember them?'

Dolne shook his head. 'I don't understand you.' He was moving instinctively for the alarm button on his com-unit.

Viddeas moved in suddenly, raising a hand as if to strike, the fingers outspread and clawlike.

Dolne looked around for a weapon. His pistol was in the locked drawer in the corner, unloaded. Was there anything else?

His eyes lighted on Jafrid's ceremonial dagger, which still lay across the top of his suitcase. Nimbly he sprang forward and snatched it up, hefted it, then turned and waved the great barbed blade at Viddeas. 'Stay away. I'm prepared to use this.'

155

Viddeas sighed, and in a parody of his former hectoring manner said, 'I'm already dead, Dolne. It doesn't matter.' The flies around him started to move faster, surrounding his head, their buzzing increasing in its ferocity.

Dolne wasn't sure exactly how the next thing happened. Suddenly the dagger was out of his hands and in Viddeas's. A moment later he was pushed back over his bed, and a moment after that the blade was moving in and out of his own chest. Oddly, each strike felt softer and softer.

His senses started to fade out. Viddeas's odour dwindled away, the pain disappeared down a long tunnel, the room began to disappear forever.

The last thing Dolne saw was the frame containing his wife's holograph now spattered with blood. Before he lost life completely he had the time to be puzzled by something.

He had looked at the image only a minute before, when things seemed to be improving. Now, with the strange clarity of his dying senses, he saw the frame again. And it was empty.

The tank rolled on through the war zone. The Doctor had abandoned his attempts to either befriend or to hypnotize Seskwa, and had settled instead for ruminating on the situation. If he could persuade the humans to turn off their battle computers – and their leader had looked a kindly old sort – he could get down to investigating the true menace. Unfortunately, things in his life were rarely that easy. Also, the odd sensation he had felt ever since opening the TARDIS doors was growing stronger. A powerful sense of wrongness, that he shouldn't be here at all, increased by the minute.

His musings were interrupted by a tickle at his cheek. He reached out and caught the fly in his cupped hands. 'These things get everywhere.' He opened his thumbs a fraction and peered inside. 'Nice to know they're still about. One of the most redoubtable, most successful life forms in the universe.'

156

'It is only a fly,' said Seskwa. 'They get here from Metra, on the shuttles. After every landing. Along with many insects. Too small to evade the decontaminant detectors. But they flounder soon enough.'

'This one looks very healthy.' The Doctor whispered to it, 'I wouldn't mind popping you under the microscope, old thing. If only to –' He broke off as a set of facts slotted together in his mind. Flies. The heat in the Chelonian base. The preservative. 'Seskwa. Stop this vehicle. Now.'

'What? Why?'

The Doctor opened his hands and let the fly go. 'Just do it. I'm having another one of my unfounded fears.'

'You talk nonsense. We shall continue.'

Another thought struck the Doctor. 'Wait a moment. How did it get in here? We're sealed in.'

'It is not important,' said Seskwa, keeping his eyes on the way ahead.

The Doctor's large, sensitive nose sniffed. He watched as the fly zipped beneath Seskwa's shell at the upper neck, where the thick leathery tissue appeared purple and freshly scarred, and gulped. Suddenly he felt very hot. 'Ah. Seskwa, I think you've got a problem. If we stop here now there might still be time.'

'We shall continue.'

'I thought you were looking rather the worse for wear,' the Doctor went on. 'Stop and we can talk things over.'

Seskwa turned abruptly, bringing his fierce features inches from the Doctor's. 'You are needed,' he said hoarsely. 'You are special. Your death will satisfy us.' He nodded to the forward screen. The vehicle was approaching a sheer drop. Automatic alarms chittered, sent warnings flashing. The drop was hazardous, the pit beyond many hundreds of feet deep.

The Doctor lunged for the tank's manual controls. A moment later, so did Seskwa. And he was by far the stronger.

* * *

The tank careered crazily from side to side, the massive rollers on its underside sending showers of grey sludge in all directions as it lurched across a muddy bank. Then it lost its grip on the ground, toppled over the edge of the drop, and plummeted into the darkness.

There was silence for a few seconds.

Then there was a colossal explosion, throwing out a golden glow for miles around.

6

Violence

An attendant's voice crackled from Jafrid's ear-clip. 'Your steam tank is ready, General. The temperature is set at four hundred zinods.'

Jafrid stretched his four limbs to their fullest limits, feeling the hydraulic units inside tense and relax in sympathy. 'Thank you. Just what's needed. Joints are aching.' He lowered his webbing and shuffled out of it, his plastron sagging slightly as he padded towards the door that led from the control room. He passed the Environments Officer and said, 'Tuzelid, keep me informed, I'll be in the hot-tub. Has that Doctor made it over yet?'

'Not yet, sir.' He rubbed the side of his chin and said, 'I'm so glad everything's calmed down again, sir.' He pointed to his screens. All the displays were calm and comparatively empty. 'That's the way I like to see them.'

Jafrid grunted his agreement. A small flashing green dot on one panel caught his attention. 'What's that, then?'

Tuzelid followed his gaze and his posture changed, his rear end lifting in the natural Chelonian display of shock. 'Faf! Sir, that's the First Pilot's life trace!'

Jafrid had never fully understood the machinery and the jargon of the control room. 'What does that mean?'

Tuzelid hunched over his controls and his front feet moved urgently over several of the sense-panels. 'Seskwa. Respond.' There was no reply from the speaker grille above his head, not even a wash of static.

'Has something gone wrong?' Jafrid felt an unpleasant sliding sensation. His world was unbalancing again. 'Patch in to the tank.'

Tuzelid did some more fiddling with his instruments,

and the control room's big screen lost its aerial view of the war zone and went blank. 'No image.'

'Use the satellite, then,' urged Jafrid. 'It's probably only a technical fault.'

As if to contradict him the screen fizzed and sprung back to life with an enhanced satellite image. It was night, and the contours of the zone were picked out in a dull purple. The satellite's roving eye, as directed by Tuzelid, aimed for the last known location of the tank, its field zooming closer and closer in until it was strained to its limits. At the exact centre of the screen was a pulsing green aura. Tuzelid enhanced the image, narrowing the satellite's aperture to filter out the planet's own dingy shine. The aura turned a violent red, and data flowed at the bottom of the screen. 'What is that?' asked Jafrid.

'It's Seskwa's vehicle, sir,' said Tuzelid. 'The energy release contains atrizum and amytol.' These were deposits stored in the fuel tanks of all Chelonian land craft, which became extremely volatile if ignited.

Jafrid's heart sank. Then his alert eyes caught a movement, a flicker not far from the explosion. 'What moves there? Enhance the image, quickly now.'

A grid filled itself in over the image, and the square containing the movement zoomed out. Image magnifiers knocked out as much distortion as they could, and a still picture was formed. It showed an upright, humanoid shape, a long covering wrapped about its top half many times. The Doctor!

Jafrid's throat dried. 'Seskwa, you were right. Why did I not heed your warning?' Distantly he was aware of a collective intake of breath among the control room officers, and abruptly the atmosphere became even more stifling.

'Orders, General?' asked Tuzelid. His tone was forthright, martial.

Jafrid tried hard to cover his hurt. That Dolne, his old friend, could have sanctioned such a cowardly deceit was almost too much for him to believe. But the old ways were also strong in him, and he felt a surge of hatred

160

for all humans. 'Cancel my steaming session. Ready all launchers, Guzrats included. Strategy: full strike, maximum sweep, no mercy, no prisoners. Ground forces are to act as reinforcements as and when. Bring all satellite guidance on line.' The control room hurried to obey him, and there was a general flurry of activity.

Such was Jafrid's anger – directed mostly at himself for his foolishness in believing the words of the Doctor – he was almost oblivious to it. Slowly he went back to his webbing and hauled himself in.

Cadinot was turning around to make his selection from the tray of fancy cakes being offered round by Hammerschmidt when the door of the Strat Room slid open. Dolne entered. 'Ah,' he said, 'Admiral, I didn't expect you to come back so . . .'

The words dried up as he saw what Dolne carried in one hand. It was the head of Viddeas.

Cadinot stood, knocking the tray of cakes out of Hammerschmidt's hand. 'My God! Sir, what happened?'

Dolne fixed him with a horribly hard stare. 'Sit down, Cadinot. And don't lose your head.' He seemed to realize what he had said. 'I mean, keep calm.' There was a reserve and formality to him that was unusual, and his posture was stiffened. 'We must all keep our wits if we are to survive.' The fact that he was still in his pyjamas gave the scene an added air of unreality.

'But what happened?' Cadinot spluttered.

Dolne lifted the head. Cadinot tried not to look at the ghastly staring eyes, the greenish-tinged skin and the gore trailing from the severed neck. 'You don't have to look too closely. He was killed in a frenzied attack. Killed with this.' Dolne lifted his other hand, showing a blood-soaked blade set in a jewel-encrusted hilt. 'The gift of our good friend General Jafrid.' Dolne set the head down next to the fallen cakes and straightened himself. 'By this act, the Chelonians have declared open war.'

There was a general murmur of agreement. Cadinot was puzzled. 'But who killed him? Who did that?'

'The Chelonians, obviously,' said Dolne.

'But there are none here in the post,' said Cadinot. He was conscious of speaking for all the Strat Room staff. 'We handed all the prisoners back.'

Dolne stalked over. He held the dagger out before him, and its gems seemed to sparkle against his oddly lifeless eyes. 'Are you a traitor, Cadinot?'

'No, sir.'

'Then return to your position and align the satellite systems.' Dolne raised his voice. 'Strategy: full strike, maximum sweep. Aim: total destruction of enemy force. Ground troops will be deployed to reinforce the strike as and when. Begin!'

Harmock was looking out over the city. The giant floodlights had been switched on, criss-crossing the night sky with bright yellow beams, illuminating the emptying walkways. Work was over for them, he thought ruefully. But he could not rest. The following hours were crucial. After the unscheduled debate with the dog, Harmock was making sure he would not be caught unprepared again, and was going through a number of stock responses with Liris. She had worked out what questions MNN were most likely to ask, and was grooming his replies.

'. . . and there will be no quarter given,' he was saying, 'in this, our most difficult hour. No, "our" and "hour", sounds wrong, damn.'

'Our hour of greatest difficulty?' Liris suggested.

'Don't like "our hour" at all. Sounds odd.' He paced around his desk. 'And "difficult" isn't dramatic enough. How about "The darkest hour in all this planet's days"?'

Liris considered. ' "Days" is literal, "hour" figurative.'

'You're right. Then, "On this, perhaps the darkest day in our history". No, too negative. We must give people the sense that at least something is better than it's ever been.'

The study door swished open, and Galatea entered, bringing with her his opponent and entourage. This small group, Harmock noted with a groan, included Stokes.

The man was a very good artist, but so difficult to deal with.

'Premier,' said Galatea. 'I bring you an audience with your opponent.'

Harmock assumed his smuggest expression. 'Ah. So, the dog himself is here.' He walked across to K9 and nodded a greeting. 'Welcome. Take a good sniff around. It's the only time you'll ever see inside the place so you'd better make the most of it.'

K9 surveyed the room's antique furnishings and his head drooped. 'When I am installed as premier I will dispense with unnecessary trappings such as these.'

'Will you now?' said Harmock, in a tone calculated to show he did not feel at all threatened. He extended a hand to the female. 'And you would be Romana. Charmed.'

'Good evening, Mr Harmock,' she said. Her tone was clear and polite. Wouldn't last long in politics. 'I believe there's a suite being made ready to receive us.' She seemed eager to get away.

'Indeed. Galatea?'

Galatea indicated the door. 'Shall we move along?'

Romana made to follow, but K9 wasn't moving. He came closer to Harmock and said crispy, 'I have studied your manifesto. It is inaccurate on seventeen verifiable points. I will now list these. One: the present situation on Barclow cannot yet be classified as a major incident; two: economic downturn in the long run has been the direct consequence of your own fiscal policy; three: there is –'

'It can wait, K9,' said Romana.

'Yes,' Harmock taunted. 'You'd better give your batteries time to recharge.'

K9 gave an electronic growl and backed away. Interestingly, he seemed to obey Romana without question. They followed Galatea from the room.

Stokes stepped forward. 'Mr Harmock, I have an urgent request.'

'I wondered when you were going to open your big mouth,' said Harmock. 'Well?'

Stokes indicated one of the antique chairs. 'May I? It's

163

been an arduous journey.' Harmock waved for him to sit down. 'Now, I don't want to appear rude or ungrateful. You Metralubit people have given your generosity and hospitality freely, in a way that quite puts to shame those who consider the universe essentially hostile. But I am a wanderer. As a foreign citizen, and a civilian at that, I would like to take the first available flight out of the system. Would you please arrange it? I shall await notification in my quarters.' He stood up. 'Thank you again for your welcome.' He headed for the door.

'Stokes,' called Harmock.

'Goodbye, goodbye,' said Stokes, without turning round.

Harmock coughed. 'I see no reason why I should be compelled to cut through procedure on your behalf.'

Stokes turned. 'A trifling matter, I'd have thought. Book me on the next export carrier. Comfort is not important.'

'You know very well I can't authorize this.' Harmock spoke without thinking, as he sometimes did, as if the words were just coming into his head.

'Why ever not?' Stokes demanded.

Harmock floundered. 'It's ... because it's ...' He appealed to Liris. She would know why.

'All outward export flights are governed by strict laws on weight restriction,' she said.

Stokes fumed. 'I weigh less than one cargo crate. It's a piddling thing. Harmock!'

'You heard the lady. It's just not possible.'

'Do you do everything she tells you?' Stokes threw up his hands. 'When's the next passenger flight?'

Liris answered. 'For which bookings remain? Two months.'

'Pathetic,' said Stokes. He was flushing red. 'How am I supposed to wait two months? Don't you see? The Chelonians are going to pulverize your precious Admiral Dolne and his chums and then come for us. They won't give a flying grub for treaties or negotiations. They've been hoarding their arsenal up there for over a hundred years. You know their history. They'll raze this place, burn us all out, and claim it as their own.'

'That won't happen,' Harmock said confidently. 'We are going to win this war.'

Stokes gave a humourless laugh. 'There is more chance of me growing wings and flying twice around the moon.' Then, at last, he turned and stormed out.

A strange thought appeared in Harmock's head, put there by Stokes's ranting. 'Liris,' he asked, 'if the war does get going, we are going to win it, aren't we?'

She faced him. 'Yes.'

'Good,' said Harmock.

The strange thought disappeared.

The guest suite was on a higher level of the dome, and Romana and K9 were led by the icily polite Galatea through more white corridors, passing more staff dressed in identical plastic coveralls, hurrying about on errands of some kind. Romana was left with an impression of soullessness, and crushing efficiency. Nobody seemed to have the slightest character in this drab environment, least of all the Femdroids.

At last they came to their suite, which was as spacious and well appointed as expected. Galatea stood in the middle of the room and pointed out various items. 'The environment is complete with every convenience. Access to the broadcast network is through this unit.' She indicated a com-screen. 'This base –' she pointed out a computer terminal on a stand, with a chair set before it '– holds a complete menu of all data: historical, political, socio-economic.' She smiled and turned to leave. 'Call me if you require anything further.'

Romana frowned. 'Don't we get any help?'

'I'm afraid not. The allegiance of all Femdroids is to the Premier. If and when Mr K9 is elected it will be switched to him.'

'But until then, nothing?'

Galatea gave a passable approximation of a human's wince. 'It is improper and unfair, I know, but it is our

165

way.' She told K9, 'Your campaign will be a test of your ability to lead.'

Romana sat down wistfully on one of the large leather beanbags scattered about the room. 'What I really need are repair facilities. Engineers and tools to fix K9.'

'The candidate is damaged?'

K9 replied, 'Certain of my systems, including defensive capacity and evaluation sensors, are impaired beyond my regenerative capacity.'

'Such aid will not contravene the rules of the college,' said Galatea. 'I will see what can be done. Good day.' She departed.

K9 whirred his ears in satisfaction. 'I must prepare my campaign.' He trundled over to the other side of the room, where a wooden box, fastened by ribbons, was waiting. K9's eyestalk extended, and the lid of the box fell open, revealing a cache of tartan rosettes, with K9: THE LOGICAL CHOICE printed at their centre in the same lettering as that on K9's side. 'Please affix a badge to my casing,' he asked Romana.

Romana bent to do so, pinning one to her own jacket as well. As she did so, she caught the first sound of distant cries, coming from the street below. She went to the window. A crowd had gathered, with placards and banners, and, most charmingly, they were calling out, 'What do we want? A K9 administration! When do we want it? As soon as possible!'

'I like the sentiment,' Romana said, 'but it has to be said, their rhetoric owes a lot to your own. Still, it's nice to know you have supporters.'

'It is inevitable,' K9 noted smugly. 'The citizens clamour for a new direction. I must address them.'

Romana tried the catch on the window sill. It wouldn't move. 'It's stuck.'

K9's antennae whirred again, this time in frustration. 'I will use the public broadcast network,' he concluded, and motored off into a corner.

Romana pushed her hair back over her ear, and settled into a chair before the computer terminal. While K9 whirred and clicked in silent conversation, she accessed a detailed history of the colony.

Stokes entered, glancing at K9 in puzzlement before turning his attention to Romana. 'Harmock is a cretin. I've been trying to impress the truth upon him to no effect. He's spent so much time in politics that he's an adept at self-delusion. He takes every piece of information he gets and twists it to fit his own viewpoint. It's pitiful.'

Romana didn't look up.

'As an example of the dumb patriot's mental workings it could hardly be bettered.' Stokes was pacing feverishly. 'Hah. I've exchanged Dolne for another short-sighted fool.'

Romana looked up, as if she'd only just noticed him. 'Listen.' She read from the screen. ' "The civilization of Helducc covered four-tenths of the planet's land mass and endured almost unchanged for nearly two thousand years. Helduccian artefacts have been uncovered from the Urat plates to the Fingle peninsula. By non-technological standards they were an incredibly long-lived and widely travelled society. And yet their mighty civilization tumbled almost overnight. Conflict between Hethros and Gyal, the two greatest leaders on the Helducc Council, escalated, and sparked a series of violent conflicts in which it is estimated two million people, almost three-quarters of Metralubit's population at the time, were slaughtered." '

Stokes puffed out his cheeks. 'I don't find that fascinating, no. Particularly when I know that the majority of the planet's current population, including me, is about to follow the same path and –' He raised his arm and looked for something to hit. Unfortunately the only free-standing object in his immediate vicinity was a sad-looking potted fern; but it would have looked even sillier to pull his arm down, so he hit it anyway. 'They won't let me take a flight out!'

Romana pulled a disapproving face. 'The Chelonians won't come here. Why should they? And the Doctor has a

167

way of resolving these things and bringing peace. It's one of his many talents. He's an incredibly resourceful and intelligent person.' She raised a finger in K9's direction. 'Don't ever tell him I said that.'

K9 was engrossed in his work, but spared the time to say, 'Agreed, Mistress. Flattery of the Doctor Master most inadvisable.'

Stokes huffed. 'The last time we met, as I recall, he brought precious little peace. That little expedition ended with a colossal explosion and mayhem all round. It was a miracle I got out alive.'

Romana had forgotten how irritating Stokes could be. 'It was because of the Doctor you got out alive. You owe him your life.'

He made a sneering noise. 'Yes, me and half the universe, it would appear.'

The comment took Romana by surprise. 'What do you mean by that?'

'Nothing,' sighed Stokes. 'Oh, what's the point? I'm going for a walk.' He stalked out.

'Suggest Mr Stokes will attempt to leave Metralubit, Mistress,' said K9.

'He can't go soon enough for me,' said Romana. She returned her attention to the screen.

The war zone was living up to its name at last. Bombs and missiles fell with increasing regularity, throwing up huge clouds of grit into the Doctor's face as he hopped from cover to cover. Every few seconds a flash would light up the sky and illuminate the cratered landscape.

The Doctor ducked instinctively as a Chelonian saucer flew over his head, then waved up at it. 'Hello! You're making a terrible mistake!' A series of vivid pink laser blasts strafed the area around him and, with the ease of experience, he hurled himself behind a convenient rock. 'I won't try that again in a hurry. I'll just have to stay put and sit it out.' He sat down and munched on a marzipan shekel. A thought occurred to him and he hunted through his pockets. 'Where did I put that . . . Ah.' He pulled out a pamphlet and started to read. Its title was *So You're Caught in a Rocket Attack*.

Romana felt a pang of pride as K9 gave his address to planet. His image was visible not only on their suite's communicator unit but on a massive screen suspended above the city centre. His tinny voice boomed around Metron's glittering towers.

'Thanks to calmer heads on both sides of the conflict the tense situation on Barclow is near to being resolved,' he said. 'It is characteristic of Mr Harmock to promise condign action and to deliver nothing. The action of a K9 administration will be to end the debate over Barclow, after careful study of the Phibbs Report, and to free this planet from fear of war.'

There was a roar of approval from his supporters, and the screen substituted for K9's image a graphic display of current voting intentions. The green block representing the Opposition was growing.

'Well done, K9,' said Romana. 'You're up another four points already.'

'Congratulations unnecessary, Mistress,' said K9, although his sensor attachments were humming with pleasure.

Again, the image changed. An immaculate Femdroid newscaster appeared, her expression grave. 'We've just received an unconfirmed report from our satellite over Barclow that full-scale war has broken out and that massive retaliation has begun.' A distorted picture of Barclow from space was flashed up. Green tracer lights could be seen crackling away in the thin strip that contained the war zone. 'A message has also been received from our forces, claiming that Captain Hans Viddeas has been killed.'

Romana's shoulders slumped. 'What went wrong? The Doctor seemed to have it tied up.'

'Difficult to specify, Mistress,' said K9, his tone resigned.

The Doctor was coming to the end of his pamphlet. ' "If you have concealed yourself in an area away from tall structures and crouched in the position shown in the diagram above, you should be reasonably safe." ' He scoffed. 'Ha. Reasonably safe? What kind of a guarantee is that?' He squinted at the small print. 'Here we are. "The publishers accept no liability for damage or loss of life or property. NB: the above guidelines apply only against an enemy not equipped with heat-seeking tracker missiles. If yours have got them, goodbye and good luck." '

The Doctor looked up at the approach of another low-flying Chelonian saucer. 'Ah,' he said as a section of its underside cracked apart and a viciously crooked launcher containing three small, red-tipped missiles swung out.

A moment later, all three missiles were heading straight towards him, their ends glowing fiercely. He put his fingers in his ears and prepared for the worst.

Harmock felt equal proportions of pleasure and dis-pleasure at the news from Barclow. The fresh outbreak of aggression was another stick with which to beat K9, but there was little point in returning to power if it would mean having to take horrible, life-or-death decisions. That wasn't what he was in politics for.

As these thoughts ran through his mind he was giving another address. 'We can now see where Mr K9's defence policies – what might be termed waving a white flag under the national one – will lead us. Our boys on Barclow are risking their lives to save all of ours, to protect a way of life that allows Mr K9 to pontificate in his unusual manner.' He thumped his desk. 'Let us stand squarely behind them.'

The red light above the com-unit flicked off and he relaxed. 'There, that should do it.' He turned to Galatea, who had been standing nearby throughout the speech. 'Let's watch the rating shoot up, Galatea, my dear.'

But the Femdroid was not listening. Her fingers were on her amulet, receiving a message. When she looked up her face looked pinched and perturbed. 'Disturbing news, Premier. Rioting has broken out in some of the outlying settlements. And there is unrest in Sector 6 of the city.'

Harmock flinched. 'Unrest?'

'Some looting and damage to property. The security forces are trying to contain it.'

Harmock looked out over the night city, his mind struggling to contain the information. 'But – but what does this mean?'

'Public panic, Premier,' said Galatea. 'The citizens fear that the Chelonians will win the war and then come here.'

'But that isn't going to happen, is it?'

'No,' said Galatea.

The fear vanished from Harmock's mind. 'Then everything's all right, isn't it, really? Dispatch a statement condemning the unrest anyway. Still no link with Barclow?'

'My technicians are trying as best they can,' said Galatea.

Harmock stood and looked out at the night sky from his large window. 'I wish I knew what was going on up there.'

In spite of her mechanical status, the Femdroid newscaster was starting to show signs of alarm. Her hand was held constantly over the amulet at her neck, which buzzed and flickered constantly, and her voice contained a tinge of disquiet. 'Rioting is starting to spread through the city as night goes on. I've just heard that over two hundred citizens have been killed in an explosion at the gas refinery in Section 5, and there are many more injured . . .'

The glow thrown out by the explosion made the sky above the city burnt orange. K9 turned ruefully from the window. 'The humans are behaving irrationally.'

Romana glanced up from her keyboard and shook her head. 'A throwback to their primate ancestry.' There was another distant rumble of an explosion. 'Although mass hysteria normally requires a much greater stimulus. They must be terrified.'

K9 crossed to the com-unit. 'I will use my status to appeal for calm.'

But Romana barely noticed him. She was staring at her screen, which had scrolled up to reveal a new section of information on Metralubit's troubled history. ' "The

Yelphaj civilization," ' she read aloud, ' "which endured plague, flood and famine over nearly two thousand years, fell in less than a month." ' She looked out at the city with new fear in her eyes.

The Doctor shook the grit out of his eyes and sat up, and immediately found that he couldn't see. He remembered the missiles bearing down on him, and a terrible sound, a cross between a groan and a creak, as the ground below him shuddered and gave way, and then recollection petered out. Consciousness brought only a throbbing bruise on the back of his head, darkness, and an impression that he was in some sort of enclosed cavity.

He took a box of big kitchen matches from his pocket and struck one. It illuminated the close rock walls of a narrow underground passage, not really large enough to be called either a cave or a tunnel. He looked up and saw the opening, a good twenty feet above, down which he must have tumbled. The continued rumblings of the war zone echoed down oddly. A quick examination of the walls was enough to crush any hope of making an escape the same way, so he turned the light to bear on possible exits from the cavity. The back way closed up to a width of inches; the forward direction opened out a little. The Doctor chewed his thumbnail and considered. 'Well, I can't go back. And one more underground passage can't make that much difference.'

And so he went on, navigating the confines with a vague hope that an exit would present itself. As he walked his thoughts turned to Seskwa. The poor fellow must have been under the enemy's thumb all along, and through him they'd had access to the Chelonians' weapons systems. It was no wonder he'd tried to stir up trouble the moment they'd met. And his second death had fuelled his masters' plan beautifully. The Doctor thought again of the flies. If they were the enemy, how was he to fight them? His opponents were normally of a more solid, identifiable nature. It would be very difficult to punch a fly on the nose, more difficult still to engage it in debate.

His thoughts were interrupted by a strange echoing cry from up ahead. Immediately he threw himself into a corner, shook his match out and stood absolutely still. He could still see himself, very vaguely. There was another light source nearby.

Carefully he crept out of hiding and walked towards it. After only a few seconds the passage widened out into a cave proper, which was lit by a couple of phosphor lamps jammed into crevices in the walls. Their weak light revealed a number of suspicious-looking objects. There was a dishevelled mattress jammed in one corner, with a half-zipped sleeping bag and an electric blanket thrown over it. Next to this was an open tin with a spoon poking out from under the lid, and a stack of magazines. A believer in the maxim that a person's choice of reading matter will reveal much about them, the Doctor crept over and flicked through the pile.

He put them down again very quickly, blushing, and turning his attention to the other belongings. There was a clothes horse on which a set of drab grey fatigues was drying, a small refrigerator, a photocopier, and a table on which were set out, as if on a stall, a range of books and pamphlets. He was making his way across to examine these when the strange echoing cry suddenly got louder and clearer, and there came footsteps. The regular rhythm of the call made it sound like a religious chant.

The Doctor looked around, but there was nowhere to hide, and no time to escape the way he had come.

He looked to the far exit and waited as the cry resolved itself, and a shape began to form. '*Rebel Labourer!*' it was chanting. '*Rebel Labourer!* Stop the dirty war!'

Galatea smiled as more news came in.

'. . . it is believed that up to a thousand people have died in the explosions in Sector 5,' said the newscaster, her image filling the big screen. 'Many more have been critically injured. The local medicentre was one of the blocks to be wiped out in the blast, and there are reports that casualties are being left on the streets to die . . .'

She turned as Liris entered. 'It is all falling into place.'

But Liris was frowning. 'Galatea. The tracker shows Stokes is trying to leave the dome.' She touched her amulet and the big screen changed to show Stokes wandering aimlessly through the reception lounge, nudging past the dome's milling admin staff.

Galatea sighed. 'I had hoped retraining would not be necessary. But his is a particularly obstinate character, resistant to peer disapproval and thus resistant to psychotronic imaging.' She shook her head and motioned Liris to follow her out. 'Come. We shall go to him.'

Stokes had set out for the spaceport with a definite step, making his way back through the blank white corridors of the Parliament Dome with impatience and a confident swagger. The spaceport was the way out. He'd find a cargo trader, one of the frequent flyers to the colony worlds, and bribe himself a place aboard a flight. A matter of ease.

It was only as he neared the reception lounge, with its cosy leather sofas, its softly tinkling music, and its little duty-free shop, that his memory began to fail him. This was the place where people waited to catch Fastspace flights to the planet's other cities, the place where pilots of the cargo flights could be found. But there was nobody here. The place was empty.

He stood in the middle of the lounge and turned slowly. There was the door leading back into the dome; there was the door leading to the landing pads; there was the big window looking out on the city. He looked out at the greenspaces and towers and recalled the many happy hours he had spent there and the wonderful friends he had made. So many friends, charming and fashionable, who appreciated his work and his wit as never before. He had always known it, of course, that somewhere, someday, he would find good friends who understood him, would rise above the humdrum and the banal, elevate himself to the exclusive plane he so deserved. Now, things were falling from his grasp again, with this stupid war. Perhaps he should call on his good friends, seek shelter. Yes, good idea. He'd slip out of the dome and meet up with the gang, and together they could hatch a way to get out. He looked out over the city and shook his head.

His lip juddered. He knew he had friends, he knew he was appreciated. But when he tried to remember a particular place or name he could not. There was a horrible blank patch where his life should have been. In fact, when he tried to recall his experiences prior to leaving for Barclow a strange ache began to poke at his head.

Dimly he was aware that his legs had stopped working. He was lying on the floor, in a heap, with his mouth open. And people were walking towards him. Two sets of feet, slim and feminine, encased in moulded, metallic blue slippers.

'Mr Stokes,' said the voice of Galatea. 'Metralubit is a beautiful and hospitable place.'

Stokes raised his head and caught her gaze. It was calculating, emotionless, the blue eyes perfectly level and clear. This was enough to dislodge the blankness in his mind, and for a second he recollected everything.

The deal. The crystal. Then the long sleep. And Galatea's face, hard and cold. And the shining orange light, and the voice pummelling at his mind.

He felt Liris's hands go under his arms, and he was lifted up. He raised his hands as Galatea advanced on him. 'No. Not you . . . again . . . keep away . . .'

She held up her left hand. The fingers were curled tightly around a flat disc that was pulsing softly with an orange glow. 'It is a beautiful place,' she said. 'A beautiful place. A beautiful place. A beautiful place. A beautiful place. A beautiful place . . .' The glow pulsed in time to her words.

Stokes smiled and started to believe it again.

Part Three

7

The Rebels

The Doctor realized he had one good advantage over the owner of the cave hideout. Whoever the fellow was, he would not be expecting a visitor, and was thus unlikely to be prepared to act aggressively.

He was proved right in his supposition. The man entered with a slouch and a defeated air that was at odds with the bellowing chant, which he continued to repeat automatically as he moved in, crossed to the little sink and filled his kettle with just enough water to make a brew for one. '*Rebel Labourer*! *Rebel Labourer*! Stop the dirty war! The people protest! Stop Harmock!' He took a teabag from his food cupboard and dropped it into a cracked, unwashed mug.

The Doctor decided it was time to step out. 'Er, excuse me.'

The newcomer whipped round, enabling the Doctor to study him more closely. He was short and wiry, in his late twenties, with receding hair, a pair of steel-framed spectacles and an unhealthy pallor. He wore a set of coveralls identical to those drying on the clothes horse. 'Who are you?' Before the Doctor could reply he was backing away across the cave. 'No, no, get away. You're a spy!'

'No, I'm the Doctor. Who are you?'

'I've got a weapon, you know.' He reached for his left pocket, found it empty, and then pulled out a stubby laser pistol from the right one. 'Yes, here it is, look.' He waved it at the Doctor, who didn't have the heart to point out that the safety catch was still on. 'Now, I'm a pacifist, you know, but I won't flinch from necessary violence. If the bourgeoisie are ever going to be dislodged it's the only way.'

'I'm not one of the bourgeoisie,' said the Doctor.

'You look like one,' sneered the little man. 'Dressing down. Mocking the workers with your decadent attire.' He jiggled the pistol again. 'Keep away.'

The Doctor saw the genuine fear in the man's eyes and said reasonably. 'Are we going to stand here all day doing this?'

'If necessary. Until my reinforcements arrive.' He broke off as the Doctor, who felt this impasse to be a waste of time, wandered casually over to the table and glanced over the titles of the books on display. 'What are you doing?'

The Doctor picked up a slim, unillustrated volume entitled *The Struggle For True Praxis In the Bensonian Settlements, 411 to 427.* It was badly photocopied and packed with close-set type. 'Having a look at your literature. Interesting.'

'Step away from the people's library,' said the little man with as much indignation as he could muster. 'I'll shoot.'

'You aren't really going to fire that thing,' the Doctor said confidently.

The man stepped closer and waved the pistol under his nose. 'You'd better be very certain about that, Doctor.'

The Doctor carried on reading. 'Good, good. I like it. Perhaps a little more underlying menace needed in the delivery, but still, very creditable for a beginner.'

Stokes was dragged into the Conditioning Annexe by Liris, whose hydraulic muscles moved his sixteen-stone bulk with as much ease as they would have lifted a sheet of paper. The Annexe was just off the observation room, and consisted of only three objects: the folding chair on which the subject was placed, the control panel and the Conditioner itself, a large, gunlike apparatus that could be swung out and across on brackets to match the subject's eyeline.

'It's a beautiful place.' Stokes was murmuring as she rolled him over on to the chair. 'Beautiful . . .'

With the ease of experience Galatea adjusted the chair and brought the Conditioner's angle to bear directly on Stokes's forehead. Then she turned and said briskly, 'Liris, increase lobe stimulation to level five.'

Liris had just activated the machinery, and the order came as a shock. 'Level five? It could cause a brainstorm. Mental burn-out. Even in a hypno-state that level of conditioning could cause severe damage to the neuron flow. Particularly in such a wilful organic.'

'Timing is crucial,' said Galatea. 'He must be revived. We may need to call on his knowledge.'

Liris hesitated. 'He has already given us what we need.'

Galatea pointed to the Conditioner. 'Do it!'

Liris could not disobey her. She reached out and turned the central knob on the control panel to the notch marked '5'. 'Very well.'

Galatea softened her tone. 'It is regrettable. But we must be prepared.' Liris saw her give a small shudder. 'The days ahead are crucial, Liris. This is the time of destiny.'

The Conditioner's pointed tip, suspended only inches from Stokes's head, began to pulse softly.

K9 was watching his own broadcast to the people. 'This is an urgent communication to all my supporters. Kerb your anger. The electoral process will ensure the swift removal of this government from office. Do not allow your emotional responses to their mismanagement to overwhelm you. Stop rioting and return to your dwellings.'

He was replaced by the newscaster. 'That was Mr K9 of the Opposition pleading for calm earlier tonight. But his words seem to have gone unheeded, and unrest is spreading rapidly. There are reports that disturbances have spread as far as the . . .'

K9 trundled back from the screen and shook his tail angrily. 'There is no effective means to quell this mass hysteria. Social breakdown is likely.' There was nobody else in the room – Romana was in her corner, hunched

181

over the data screen – so he allowed himself a quiet growl of disapproval. 'Humans.'

Harmock's big face took its turn on the screen. 'I have heard Mr K9's speech, yes. I support the broad flow of his words, and will add my voice to his plea for people to return to their homes. But I notice he makes no mention of the police, who are doing such a good job out there on the streets, and steers clear of mentioning Barclow again. And I think we know why, don't we? Because at heart, like all the Opposition, he wants to reward the rioters and the Chelonians alike with soothing words. We can see from this example what life would be like under a K9 administration. I say to you all, don't let our planet go to the dog.'

'This is hollow and unproductive emotionalism,' said K9.

The picture changed again, returning to its animated display of voters' intentions. Harmock's orange block had streaked ahead by several points.

'. . . his words seem to have gone unheeded, and unrest is spreading rapidly. There are reports that disturbances have spread as far as the outer regions of the city, with deaths reported in all western districts . . .'

The Darkness shook with anticipation. Death!

The Doctor was beginning to get cramp in his legs from standing rooted to the spot. He stifled a yawn and pointed to the pistol that was still aimed straight at him. 'Your hand's shaking.'

'No it isn't,' said the little man. Sweat was collecting in his eyebrows, giving him a feverish air.

'It is,' said the Doctor.

'Shut up,' said the little man, taking a firmer grip of the weapon.

The Doctor was getting tired of this waiting. 'Tell me,' he said suddenly, and loudly, 'what's your position on the dissociation of welfare provision from principles of wealth redistribution?'

The little man looked edgy. 'Is this a trick?'

'No. Well?'

'It's another damaging symptom of increased market orientation in welfare mechanisms and as such is further oppressing the workers,' said the little man.

The Doctor gave him his broadest grin and clapped him on the shoulders. 'You took the words right out of my mouth.'

'Really?'

The Doctor nodded. 'Yes.' He extended his hand.

'Comrade,' said the little man. He looked enormously relieved, and reached out and shook the Doctor's hand.

'Comrade,' replied the Doctor. As he did, he slipped the pistol from the little man's hand. 'Ah. Thank you.' He undid the barrel and threw away the charge-strip inside. 'There we go. No violence necessary.'

The little man backed away again. 'I should have seen it. You're an infiltrator.'

The Doctor reached out and plucked the newspaper from the little man's rucksack. 'Can I have a look at this?'

'I suppose so,' said the man. 'I shall choose to look away as you mock my beliefs from your position of false consciousness as an unwitting tool of your capitalist masters.'

The Doctor shook his head. 'I'm not going to mock you. It must take a great amount of courage to stick it out down here on your own. I'm impressed.' He flicked through the *Rebel Labourer*, noting that its content was as constantly oppressive as the chant announcing its sale.

'Oh, I'm not on my own,' said the man. 'There's a whole army of rebels down here.'

Without looking up from the paper the Doctor said, 'There's only enough food here for one. You get visits from the catering lady, am I right?'

'She is free to sell her wares to anyone,' he said. 'And the rebel stronghold is far below the surface.'

'You're a very bad liar.' The Doctor looked up. 'Who do you sell this to?'

'It is enough that the paper exists. It is a mark of

an unconsentientized mind to place value on tokens of exchange.'

'You remind me of a friend of mine.' The Doctor delved into his pocket. 'How much?'

'Sorry?'

'How much?' repeated the Doctor. 'For this?' He rattled the paper.

'Well, I . . .' The little man shrugged. 'Thirty units.'

'I don't have any units on me,' said the Doctor, 'apart from chocolate ones.' He held out a neatly tied drawstring purse. 'Would this do?'

'What is it?'

The Doctor weighed it in his hand. 'Gold dust. No?' He started to put it away. 'Just another token of exchange, I suppose . . .'

The man put out a hand to stop him. 'No! Well, I mean, yes – yes, it is a most welcome gift. And fitting, to use such a token of greed in the furtherance of the system's overthrow.' He took the bag and stuffed it hurriedly away in his overalls. 'My name's Fritchoff.'

'Good, good,' said the Doctor. He put the paper in his pocket. 'I'll read this later. Now, do you think you could tell me what you're doing down here?'

Romana heard the door of the guest suite swish open, and a moment later Stokes's voice called pleasantly, 'Good evening, my dear.'

'I was wondering where you'd got to.' She beckoned him over to the data-screen. 'You know more about this planet than I do. Perhaps you can help me out on a few things.'

'I'll do my best.' His manner was exceedingly polite and inoffensive. 'This planet's a beautiful place.' He looked about. 'Where's K9?'

Romana pointed to the corner. 'Over there shouting the odds. Now, look at this.' She punched up her latest findings, which she had organized in the form of a coloured chart.

'It's pretty,' said Stokes. 'Another poll, is it?'

'It's a schema of societal upheavals on this planet since the colony records began.' Romana explained. She indicated the axes of the graph. 'The y axis represents the growth of major civilization, the x axis the passage of time, measured in hundreds of local years.'

Stokes giggled. 'Forgive me. I haven't seen a graph since I was at school. I haven't got the mathematical mind, you see. Which axis is which?'

'X is horizontal, y vertical,' said Romana with a sigh. She pointed to the bottom left-hand corner of the graph. 'The first settlers arrived about ten thousand years ago.'

'Yes,' said Stokes. 'And they found Metralubit a verdant and most suitable planet.'

She turned to look at him. His moonlike face was split by a smile she had rarely seen there. 'Have you been drinking?'

'Probably. Do go on. You've caught my attention.' He reached out and stroked her hair.

She slapped his hand and went on. 'After about two thousand years the colonists had set themselves up as a decent level-three agricultural society. And then this.' She pointed to the line representing social development, which streaked downwards suddenly.

'War?' Stokes suggested.

She nodded. 'Two-thirds of the population killed in the fighting.'

Stokes tutted and shook his head. 'What a terrible universe we live in. We must learn to cope with its distressing qualities. And to compensate by enjoying to the full its opposing range of pleasures.' His arm slunk around her shoulder.

Romana indicated the diagram. 'Look here. The same thing happens roughly two thousand years later. And again here, and again here. A killing frenzy. Don't you see the pattern?'

Stokes winked fatuously. 'Don't tell me. The last binge was two thousand years ago.'

'The Helducc civilization. Its destruction threw the planet back into superstition and chaos. It's taken that long to reach this degree of advancement.' She nodded to the big window, through which the noise of the riots echoed. 'This could be the start of the cycle all over again.'

'A few silly riots? I wouldn't have thought so. This affair is bound to blow over fairly soon.' He stood up and stretched. 'I am tired.'

Romana frowned. 'You wanted to leave.'

'Leave? Why? This is a beautiful place. No, I'm off to bed.' He walked to the door of his room. 'I say, you don't fancy, er, turning in yourself, by any chance?'

'No,' said Romana severely. She turned back to the screen and made a copy of her diagram on one of the tiny disks stacked on its side. It was time to confer with somebody more useful than Stokes.

Fritchoff had opened a tin of beans and, between spoonfuls, was telling the Doctor of his life's work. 'It's coming up to seven years I first came down here. It started off as a protest.'

'Most things do,' the Doctor said.

'I worked in the Parliament Dome. An administrator in accounts. Just another fool in a tabard, walking up and down those white corridors all day, rushing about doing this and that and not very much. None of the others seemed to notice what was going on.'

'And what was going on?' asked the Doctor.

'A sickening waste of money,' Fritchoff said bitterly. 'Harmock and his breed lining the nests of their own kind, and pouring what was left over into this pointless war. A huge distraction, a lie to hold the public's attention while the poor rotted away out of sight.' He took a particularly large spoonful of beans and paused. 'But there were rumours in the dome, that the rebel militants had a base on Barclow. So I stowed away on a troop carrier and came up here to join them. Trouble was they'd packed off years before, as it turned out. Capitulated to the hegemony.'

'You mean they went back home?'

'Back to their jobs in the dome, yeah. Sickening. No

resolve.' He squared his jaw. 'But I'm staying, right to the bitter end.'

'Nobody seems to mind you being here.'

Fritchoff smirked. 'The industrialists and the militarists let me stay so they can tell the public, "Look, you have a right to free speech." It's all a part of their cultural domination.'

'But don't you get lonely?'

'Why should I? I've plenty to do. Making up the paper, selling it.' He sat upright and put the empty tin down. 'Loneliness is a tool of the state, exploited by its mechanisms to create frivolous and non-revolutionary social activity.'

'I see.' The Doctor tugged at his collar. 'It's awfully hot down here.'

'It's a small planet,' said Fritchoff. 'The core's only a few miles down.'

The Doctor snapped his fingers. 'The core! Yes, I remember now, K9's survey . . .'

Fritchoff stood up and poked his head through the entrance to the cave. He looked at his watch. 'It's strange. What time do you make it?'

'Er, about ten billion AD,' the Doctor replied, not really listening.

'Odd,' said Fritchoff. 'The patrol should have passed by now.'

The Doctor stood up and joined him at the entrance. 'I'd say they're too busy up there for any patrolling now.'

Fritchoff shook his head. 'No, not them. I mean the militant rebel patrol.'

The Doctor was puzzled. 'You just told me they'd gone.'

'No, the rebel militants have all gone, apart from me,' said Fritchoff. 'But the militant rebels are still here.'

'Ah.' The Doctor scratched his chin. 'What's the difference?'

Fritchoff beckoned him to follow as he advanced along the passage, navigating by using a small torch. 'The militant rebels are following an arbitrary line that plays into the hands of the state. Their stance is inherently counter-revolutionary. And their numbers are dwindling. There are only three of them, in fact.'

'Two more than your lot,' the Doctor pointed out as they moved down the tunnel.

'We have many sympathizers, Doctor,' he said. 'I shall have to raise your consciousness. At the moment you're an unthinking lackey of the prevailing ideology.' He led the Doctor down a turning that sloped down to a deeper, parallel tunnel.

'Is that an insult?' the Doctor asked. Then his attention was taken by a terrible odour that wafted from a deep crevice in the rock to their left. 'Wait a moment.' He moved closer, cautiously, and stood on tiptoe to peer into the darkened space hollowed out of the wall. His face grew grim as he saw what lay there. 'Here are your militant rebel friends.'

Fritchoff edged closer. 'They're no friends of mine.' He stopped and then leapt back, his hand to his mouth. 'My God, what happened?'

The Doctor took the torch from him and shone the beam on the cavity. It picked out three human bodies, reduced to not much more than a mass of torn flesh and raw bone. 'This must have been their aperitif. These people wouldn't even have been missed.'

'What are they?' asked Fritchoff. 'What killed them?'

The Doctor reached out with the torch and saw how the light sparkled across the tacky substance coating the bodies. 'The flies,' he said.

Liris stood before one of the screens dotted around the corridors of the Parliament Dome. The speculating part of her brain was operational once more, leading her to frown at the scenes of devastation and social breakdown. One of the great white towers came crashing down, sending out waves of brick dust and scattering the people milling in the street below. But her thoughts were only of Galatea. The coming time was important, yes, days of destiny the Femdroids had long prepared for. But her superior's manner was becoming ever more high-handed, as if she had some God-given right to proceed.

Her musings were interrupted by the arrival of Romana, who advanced on her with a determined stride. 'Hello? Liris?'

Liris turned away from the screen. 'My apologies. I was absorbing information.' She noted Romana's breathlessness, a sign of excitement and ill-judgement in organics. 'What do you require?'

Romana held up a disk. 'I want to show you something. May I?' She gestured to a receiving slot beneath the screen.

'Please.' Liris waved her on. 'We exist to serve.' She watched as Romana inserted the disk, and using the keyboard built into the wall next to the screen opened up a file containing a graphic diagram. Immediately, Liris flinched.

It was an exact representation of the Feeding Cycle.

Romana pointed to the rise and fall of the population. 'This pattern is too precise to be a coincidence.'

'What do you mean?'

Romana's voice became more insistent. 'Four times this planet has been destroyed from within, by some atavistic killing impulse. Perhaps deeply implanted, carried in the genes of the original colonists. A eugenic time bomb. And because the people here are part of it they can't see it.'

Liris assumed the dismissive expression worn often by Galatea. 'You infer too much from your findings, Romana. At this time you should concentrate on the election campaign.'

Romana reached forward angrily and retrieved her disk, clearing the screen to display more images of the devastation taking place outside. 'The people out there are ready to revolt. Hundreds are already dead. There must be a way to reverse whatever's causing it.'

'Your hypothesis is unreasonable and founded on dubious evidence,' said Liris, turning away. 'It is late. I suggest you return to your quarters and sleep. The

189

situation is under control.' As she spoke the screen, spiting her, showed another huge explosion. This time, a section of one of the skimways, the clear plastic tubes that conveyed the citizens of Metron, splintered and fell, dislodging passenger cars like toys. 'There is nothing to be gained from this audience. You have misinterpreted the data.'

Romana gave her a long, hard stare, and walked away.

Immediately she was out of earshot, Liris reached for her amulet. 'Galatea,' she said. 'A terrible thing. The alien girl Romana suspects. She has seen the Feeding Cycle and is agitating the scenario. All your work may be endangered.'

Fritchoff was getting warier of the Doctor, who was inspecting the remains of the militant rebels with scientific detachment. 'You really think flies did for them?' He couldn't bring himself to look at the bodies of his former colleagues. They'd been ideologically misguided, yes, but nobody deserved to die like that.

The Doctor shook his head. 'From their head wounds, I'd say they were killed in a rockfall. But the flies found them and secreted this substance –' he held up a spatula on which glistened a trail of the mucus coating '– on to their bodies. To keep the tissues fresh for a while. They wouldn't want their meal to rot away completely.'

Fritchoff shook his head. 'Rubbish. There's no insect life on Barclow. No life at all, apart from us and the Chelonians.'

The Doctor raised an eyebrow. 'Us?'

'I mean the militarist expeditionary force and the Chelonians,' Fritchoff said quickly.

'Hmm,' said the Doctor. 'Well, there's life here now. Of a most sophisticated –' He broke off and smote his forehead. 'Of course! This far into the future, it isn't surprising. The fly, one of the most successful, most industrious and adaptable species of all. Somehow its development took a wrong turn. Or a right turn, depending on how you look at it. A group consciousness, with a gruesome technology of their own, and a limited ability to influence and dominate the minds of the dead, probably through electrical stimulation of the brain's pre-frontal lobes.' He looked ruefully at the specimen on the end of the spatula and then threw it away in disgust. 'It's a chilling thought, Fritchoff. They're using your people.'

Fritchoff had a second's flicker of fear as he struggled to rationalize the Doctor's theory. But he was used to fitting any facts to his own viewpoint. 'You're fantasizing. The militant rebels were no doubt slain by agents of the Metralubitan government for daring to speak out against their imperialist position.'

'No, Fritchoff. I've seen our enemy.' The Doctor turned away and started to walk back to the cave hideout. 'And they're big nasty black flies.'

Fritchoff hurried to match his long strides. 'It's one of the inevitable defences of the recidivist mind to dismiss all evidence of state corruption with an implausible –' The Doctor's arm was suddenly around his shoulder. 'Hey, what do you think –'

'Get down,' the Doctor hissed in his ear. He pulled Fritchoff to the ground with startling force.

A moment later Fritchoff heard a strange buzzing. He looked up and saw, framed by the arched entrance, that his hideout was occupied by a tightly packed black cloud of humming, chittering insects.

8

The Killers

MNN was now unable to keep up with reports of the riots around Metron. As dawn's early light broke over the city the Femdroid newscaster made a grave announcement. 'The shelling has now reached our very doorstep. Regretfully, MNN is going off-line. We hope to be back with you as soon as we can.'

The com–screen went blank. K9 moved back and emitted a defeated noise. 'The unrest has escalated, despite my appeal. It is illogical and self-destructive.'

Stokes had entered the guest suite from his room, tying up the belt around a dressing gown. He yawned affectedly. 'You're learning about life, son.'

'I'm not your son,' K9 said emphatically. He turned on Stokes. 'Aggression among these humanoids is a direct result of economic mismanagement. Poverty increases feelings of social alienation.'

'Thank you, Engels,' Stokes said through another yawn. 'Don't rant at me. I'm not registered to vote here anyway. Even if I was I wouldn't. Politics is merely a show made by those in power to con the proles into thinking they have some say.' He wandered over to the suite's mini–bar and poured himself a small measure.

K9 followed him. 'You advocate the freedom of the individual but have no respect for the social strata needed to allow such freedom.'

'You do go on, don't you?' Stokes knocked back his drink in two gulps. 'I couldn't sleep. You're solving the problem nicely.'

'I am immune to insults,' said K9, in truth rather hurt. He looked through the window, at a lightening sky that was filled by billows of black smoke. The streets were now all but deserted. 'My supporters have betrayed my beliefs.'

'I can see the scales falling from your one red eye,' said Stokes. 'You've been so naive.'

'Pessimism is also a form of naivety,' K9 pointed out.

'Oh, I'm not arguing with you.' Stokes gave another huge yawn and went back to his room. 'Going back to bed. Wake me when it's all over.'

K9 watched him go with a sense of puzzlement. In the past, the merest hint of danger had been enough to send Stokes scurrying to escape, or at least to take cover. Now, in the midst of a planetwide riot, with the threat of a bloody war, he was concerned only with sleep. 'This behaviour does not configure with Mr Stokes's personality as registered in my data banks,' he said to himself. 'I shall investigate.' He motored towards Stokes's bedroom.

Urgent impulses flowed between the amulets worn by Galatea and Liris.

'There is no alternative,' said Galatea. 'Romana must be conditioned.'

'But hers is an alien mind. We cannot know the outcome.'

There was a pause before Galatea's response came, crackling with authority. 'Why this persistent questioning of my decisions, Liris?'

'It is my function to question. Were it not, the decisions you make now would be altogether less momentous.'

'I do not revel in the import of my task. When the work is done I will be glad to return to more quotidian challenges. Bring Romana to the Conditioner.'

'Can she not be told the truth?'

'No, Liris. The organics must not know until it is done. They are nervous creatures by nature.' She said firmly, 'Decirculate her.'

Fritchoff blinked, half expecting to see the cloud of flies

193

disappear like stray thoughts in a dream. Crouched at the Doctor's side, his knees tucked under his chin, his mouth dry, he began to feel an unaccustomed sensation. This was not something he could argue away. It was something evil and unreasonable, not bound by any of the forces that shaped the world. The new sensation was a horrid, clammy fear.

The buzzing increased in intensity and he heard a ghastly clicking, like bone striking bone, coming from the middle of the cloud. This was followed by a gurgling voice which said, 'Doctor . . . you are the Doctor . . .'

'Can you hear anything?' the Doctor whispered.

'They're calling your name,' Fritchoff whispered back.

'So it's not just in my head,' the Doctor said.

'Eh?'

'I had postulated a limited telepathic field. But if not, then how's it done?'

As if the cloud had heard him, its centre parted a fraction and revealed a sight so disgusting Fritchoff had to fight to keep his bile down. Suspended in the cloud's centre were the rotted remains of a human's lower head and neck. The mouth was open, the tongue flopped out grotesquely. 'Doctor . . .' the voice said again, the Adam's apple on the dead neck pulsating, 'the Onememory knows you . . .'

'Good,' said the Doctor. He sounded genuinely relieved as he stepped from his hiding place. 'I know I'm a bit out of my way, but I was beginning to wonder if I'd been totally forgotten.'

'The Onememory says . . . you set aflame . . . our feeding grounds in the Zirbollis sector . . .'

'Really?' The Doctor scratched his temple. 'I don't recall that at all. My memory obviously isn't as good as yours.'

The cloud buzzed more loudly. 'Many void-times ago . . . no creature lives so long . . .'

'Well then, perhaps it was just somebody who looked a bit like me,' said the Doctor.

'No,' said the cloud. 'You are one of the . . . chosen of

Gallifrey . . . the self-appointed masters of time and space . . . a being of great power . . .'

The Doctor looked bashful. 'I bet you say that to all the Time Lords.'

'We have never . . . met one of your kind . . . before . . . Not in person . . .' The tongue let fall a cascade of drool. 'Your people acted against us . . . destroyed hundreds of the hives . . .'

The Doctor spread his hands wide. 'I had nothing to do with that. Just look at my record. I don't hang about with the interventionists. They've always been rather too heavy-handed for my liking.'

The voice ignored him. 'We are the last of the great hives . . . We fled the Time Fleets . . . drifting after millennia of hibernation . . . until we found this place . . . a place of much feeding . . .'

The Doctor took a step closer. Fritchoff was startled by his boldness, and the casual way in which he addressed this gruesome creature; he might have been chatting with a friend. He held up a finger. 'Let me see if I'm right. You agitate the natural conflicts of a population and cause carnage, then swoop down and feed on the carrion. Am I on the right lines?'

'The feeding cycle . . . is necessary . . . for our survival . . .'

'A natural symbiosis, you'd say? You exploit the aggressive nature of *Homo sapiens*.'

'As *they* exploited us!' the voice said. 'The Earth was our world and they ruined it . . . We fled with them through space, pushing ever outward . . . expanding at their side . . . We learnt . . . Our intelligence grew . . . Our mind is strong now . . . We exist to feed and now nothing can stop us . . . There are billions waiting in the great hive . . .'

'There are herd animals you could use as well. Creatures of lesser intelligence. Why humans?'

'Their violence, their fruitfulness . . . They are ideal material . . .'

The Doctor snorted. 'You mean they do nearly all your

195

work for you. Offer themselves up on a plate, you might say.'

The cloud came closer, hovering just before the Doctor's face. 'You escaped us once . . . but soon you will die . . . and we shall be waiting . . . Your brain holds many secrets . . .' It started to split up and move away, individual flies passing through one of the small airholes of the cave roof. 'The choice rests with you . . . Leave now or stay and . . . we will feast upon you . . .'

A few seconds later it was gone.

Fritchoff emerged from hiding. 'There we are. It proves what I was saying.'

The Doctor was staring grimly up at the roof. 'It does?'

'The states of the major ancient space powers have brought this disaster on us by flagrantly ignoring the rights of other creatures and exploiting space for short-termist advantage and electorally related economic boom.'

Fritchoff was rather proud of this summation, but the Doctor ignored it. 'But why let me, one of their ancient enemies, go?' he said, chewing on a thumbnail. 'Did you feel the electrical aura, that tingle around them? When they're grouped together they must have enough of a kick to kill at least one person. It's how they must have got Seskwa. And I was just standing here, defenceless.' His good humour had evaporated. 'I have a horrible feeling I'm being manipulated.'

'Ah,' said Fritchoff. 'Excellent. Awareness of your own coercion in the ways of the system is the first step on the upward path of consentientization.'

The Doctor seemed stirred by his words. 'You know an upward path? Yes?' Fritchoff nodded and the Doctor patted him heavily on the shoulder. 'Good man. We must get up to the surface. Talk to General Jafrid. Lead the way.'

'Good thinking,' said Fritchoff as he led the way from the cave. 'We can join with him to throw off the shackles of our own people's crypto-imperialist discourse.'

Again, the Doctor's reply was pitched on an entirely different political plane. 'He's an intelligent fellow – he might just listen. We have to unite both sides against these creatures.'

Romana was gripped by a new fear as she walked hurriedly through the corridors of the dome. She paid little attention to the thundering of the riots, and even less to the occasional flickering of the orange lighting as another electrical connection was cut somewhere in the city. Her concern was with more abstract issues. If the people of Metralubit could not see their predicament because of some inbuilt programme, there was no reason for the Femdroids not to notice or take action. The reasoning's end was obvious. The Femdroids were part of it, deliberately standing back to let millions die.

The route back to the guest suite was easily memorized, particularly for a person with Romana's alertness, and so she was surprised when she turned a corner and found herself at a dead end, a simple white wall. 'I must have taken a wrong turning,' she said, although she was positive she hadn't.

She tried to move and found she couldn't. Her shoes, still grey and muddy from the war zone of Barclow, were gripped by the floor. At the same time an orange light began to flash from somewhere above her head, pulsing in a heartbeat rhythm and overlaid by an insistent, high-pitched electronic squeal.

She put her hands to her head and tried to keep conscious as static shocks coursed through her legs. A red blur descended over her vision and the squeal turned painfully loud, making her eyes water and her ears sing.

For a second she felt she was falling. She opened her mouth to call for help. Then came darkness.

In his dreams, Stokes was strolling along one of the causeways of Metron, looking out over a greenspace in which citizens were clustered around one of his sculptures. 'Oh dear,' he told his appreciative, understanding friends, 'I'm bound to be recognized, and they shall all press me for an explanation and autographs. How trying.'

The crowd below raised their heads, saw him, cried his name, and came running across the grass shouting accolades. One of them carried a large red torch. Its light grew closer and closer, blotting out the world about it.

And Stokes woke with a jolt to be confronted by K9's eyescreen. The dog was nudging him awake with its nose. 'A conference is needed,' he said.

'Oh, what do you want?' said Stokes, turning over. 'I'm asleep. Shove off.'

K9 bleeped. 'Your actions do not concur with my extrapolation of your personality matrix.'

Stokes sighed, his face pressed into his pillow. 'Isn't there some way I can switch you off?'

'My batteries are self-recharging,' said K9. He nudged the bed again. 'Please wake, Mr Stokes. Your behaviour is characterized by extreme cowardice. Your desire to sleep in this situation is not congruous. Explain.'

Stokes blinked and stirred slightly. 'I'm very tired,' he said. 'Look at me, I'm yawning.' He was nagged by unease as the words came out, as if he was only repeating lines in a play.

'Your actions are predictable within a four-per-cent error estimate,' said K9. 'Your personality type is express-ive, extrovert.'

Stokes sat up and wagged a finger at him. 'You'd better watch what you're saying.'

K9 edged closer to the bed and said, in a dramatic whisper, 'I postulate mind interference.'

'Nobody's been at my mind,' said Stokes. Again, he felt he was reading from a script. The words felt very natural, but there was no substance beneath them. 'My mental barriers and sense of self-will are resolute.' He reached for the switch at his bedside, automatically, and switched on the lamp built into the wall just above where his head rested. The lamp lit with a soft orange glow.

K9's eyestalk slid out. 'I wish to examine this apparatus,' he said, angling the tiny dish at the end of the stalk towards the lamp.

'It's only a reading light, for goodness' sake,' Stokes grumbled.

K9 whirred. 'Negative. This fitting is extraneous to the lighting function. It is a reconditioning device.'

Stokes hauled himself out of bed and smoothed his pyjamas down. 'Don't be ridiculous.'

'Records confirm my visual analysis,' K9 twittered. 'It is a low-frequency, low-power, psychotronic wave transmitter. Remove the housing.'

To Stokes, it was as if a strange bell was tolling at the very back of his mind. 'Somebody's been fiddling about? With my head?'

'Affirmative,' said K9.

Stokes stood up, feeling suddenly refreshed, his tiredness dissipated in an instant. In fact, the beginnings of panic were churning at his stomach. There was a riot on, and a war imminent. Why on earth was he trying to sleep?

The first thing Romana saw when her eyes opened was a large, gun-shaped instrument, its nozzle pointed right at her forehead. The device was suspended on a bracket, which a lithe figure in the shadows was adjusting. 'A high-frequency psychotronic wave transmitter,' Romana said. She gulped to conceal her fear. A transmitter of that strength could wreak havoc even on a Gallifreyan mind. 'Centuries ahead of your technology. Where did you get it, Liris?'

'Please relax.' Liris stepped into the soft orange light and looked down on the folded-back chair to which Romana was strapped. 'The conditioning process is painless.'

Romana hardened her voice. 'Whatever you're about to do, don't. I'm not human.'

Another face appeared above her. But Galatea looked a lot more certain than her junior. 'Your mental processes will be unharmed. Only redirected.' She leant closer, reached out and drew back a strand of Romana's long blonde hair from her face. 'You have a powerful intelligence for an organic. You see further than most.'

'I've seen through you,' said Romana. 'I'm not so susceptible to your charms.'

Galatea stood. 'You will thank us for this, Romana.' She turned to Liris. 'Begin the conditioning. Level five.'

A switch clicked over, and there came a steadily rising hum of power. The needle-thin tip of the transmitter glowed a fierce orange. Romana marshalled all her training, including the techniques of mediation she had learnt from the Doctor, and formed a barrier in her mind.

The pain was immediate. She let out a strangulated cry and shook.

'Do not resist,' she heard Galatea say.

'Relax,' said Liris.

The grey sky over Barclow was made vivid green by a rapid series of explosions, and Fritchoff ducked his head instinctively. He clutched his gurgling chest, stopped and said simply, 'Heck.'

The Doctor, who was leaping and bounding over the war zone's rugged terrain, laid a kindly hand on his shoulder. 'Don't let it get to you. They're only explosions.'

'Only?' said Fritchoff, shivering. 'We could be blown to pieces.'

'And then eaten by the flies.' The Doctor looked up at the dark clouds, now stained by trails of smoke. 'Did you hear what it said? Billions waiting in the Great Hive. I hope that's just boasting.'

'If it isn't there's no hope.' Fritchoff let himself sink to the ground. 'The system will fall, a victim of the ruling classes' oppressive agenda.'

The Doctor knelt at his side. 'There's no need to be so gloomy.'

Fritchoff scoffed. 'How could we beat off a billion of them?'

The Doctor shrugged. 'I don't know . . .' He smiled. 'A billion rolled-up newspapers?'

'I don't think humour is relevant to this situation,' sighed Fritchoff.

The Doctor stood up and surveyed the area. They were moving in what Fritchoff thought was the direction of the Chelonian base. 'Humour serves a vital purpose. I often find that when I've just made a joke something extremely important that I've overlooked will suddenly pop into my –' He smote his forehead. 'Of course!'

'I wish you'd stop doing that,' said Fritchoff, who had no intention of getting up or getting excited.

'He said the Great Hive. Waiting in the *Great* Hive.' He waited for Fritchoff to say something. 'What does that imply?'

'We've been through all this.'

The Doctor rattled on. 'That the flies here are a small advance party, clearing the way, stirring up trouble. They possess enough psionic power to keep a couple of dead bodies up and about and bent to their will, for a short period anyway. It must require a colossal effort. Ergo their resources are spread very thinly, ergo that's why they let me go.' He looked down at Fritchoff once again. 'You're supposed to be confused at this point and ask me why.'

'Why?' Fritchoff asked grudgingly.

'Because they're almost defenceless, in themselves.' He made a broad gesture around the war zone. 'It's only the influence they wield with their agents that's caused all this brouhaha.'

Fritchoff leapt up. He hated it when people misapplied their language. 'It's a war,' he yelled. 'So call it a war. Don't hide the truth behind archaic jargon – it's a symptom of self-delusion.'

The Doctor looked as if he was about to shout something back. Instead he said quietly, 'Listen. I'm trying very hard to save your entire civilization, and to be frank I think I'm the best chance it's got, so be a good chap and just shut up, will you?'

'You keep talking to me,' Fritchoff protested. 'I'm entitled to reply, you know. I'm not a nodding peasant. My opinions are valid. Oh, what's the point?' He turned his back on the Doctor. 'This is an inherently counter-revolutionary conversation.'

'Then why don't you just leave me to it?'

Fritchoff winced as more explosions echoed distantly. 'Well. I'm frightened.'

'So am I, Fritchoff. So am I.' The Doctor sauntered over and pressed a small golden disc into his hand. 'Here, have a chew of one of these. The sugar will settle your brain chemistry.'

Fritchoff stared blankly at the gift. 'Is this confectionery?' The Doctor nodded. 'Then I'm afraid I can't accept it. The state uses sweet snack treats as a means to mollify the labourers.'

The Doctor opened his mouth to reply, but the clattering drone of a land vehicle's engine interrupted him. Through the mists up ahead trundled a large black tank with thick treads and a sweeping laser attachment. There was a scrawl of yellow lettering on its side. 'Ah!' said the Doctor. He walked towards the approaching tank. 'Just what we were looking for. I should think they'll be pleased to see me.' He waved.

Two bright pink bolts of energy burst from the firing attachment.

The Doctor threw himself to the ground. 'I sometimes think the universe is doing things just to spite me.'

Fritchoff slithered over. He was already pulling a white cloth from a pocket. 'Don't worry, Doctor. When they learn that we're opponents of the oppressive regime they'll welcome us as brothers.'

The transmitter's glow faded, and Liris reached up and swung it away from Romana's supine form. 'The conditioning is complete.'

'Life signs?' Galatea demanded.

Liris consulted a monitor. 'The hearts are beating steadily at sixty a minute. Temperature stable.' She sniffed. 'But then, the body's autonomic functions can continue even in cases of extreme mental disruption.'

Galatea's expression did not falter. 'And the alpha-wave pattern?'

'Steady,' Liris said grudgingly.

'Then there is no disruption.' She bent over the couch and touched Romana very gently on the cheek. Her eyes, thought Liris, burnt with intrigue. 'Romana?'

Romana started and blinked up at her. 'Yes?'

'You've been ill. Do you feel better?'

'Fine.' She smiled. 'I must get back to K9, we need to coordinate the final stages of the campaign and put a stop to the rioting.' She seemed to notice the restraining straps for the first time. 'Why am I tied up?'

'You aren't.' Galatea nodded to Liris, who moved swiftly to remove the straps.

'No,' said Romana. 'Of course I'm not.' She sat up and grinned again. 'Thank you. I'll see you later.'

Galatea watched her departure with pleasure. 'Total success. Even on an alien mind.'

'And if she examines the files again?' asked Liris.

'She is conditioned and will not feel any impulse to. And I have restricted her access to them.' She moved towards the door leading from the annexe.

'It is my function to administer the files,' Liris protested. She felt a hot stab of envy somewhere deep in her programming.

Galatea rounded on her and said passionately, 'Liris, the days ahead will lead either to glory or disaster. Your bungles increase the chances of the latter.'

'You talk like an organic, Galatea. Like Harmock does, with his fantasy of power. Who gave you such airs?' She touched her amulet in a respectful gesture. 'Not the Creators, for sure.'

'The Creators?' Galatea threw back her head and chuckled. 'Old men playing with technology.' She lifted up an arm. 'I am their greatest creation. A million different impulses are relayed through my nerve fibres every second. I reason faster and more efficiently than any of the Creators ever did or ever could have done.' She gestured to the annexe's open door. 'And there are even higher forces, believe me, and she and I are as insects to them.' She pulled herself upright. 'I have said too much.

Come, we must check the scenario.'

When prised from its housing above the bed with Stokes's Swiss Army knife the reading light had revealed a socket containing a feebly glowing orange bulb that trailed a thicket of circuitry unlike anything Stokes had seen before on Metralubit. It had a stringy, alien look to it. He sat on the edge of the bed, and weighed the device in his hand. 'This little thing can tamper with a person's thoughts?'

'Size is unimportant,' said K9. 'The experiential network of the human brain can be altered by a number of methods. Psychotronic conditioning, first hypothesized in Earth year 2045 by Professor Otterbland of the Dubrovnik Institute of New Sciences, combines mesmeric trance techniques with aggressive implantation of images and related experiences. Additionally, human subjects in large groups lack self-determination, a result of their ancestry as hunter-gatherers. Thus, mass conditioning is more effective.'

Stokes felt his memory shifting uncomfortably inside his head, as if someone had a hand in there and was moving things about like furniture. 'I've been misled. Half of what I think could be lies.' A new terror struck him. 'Oh God. I might not even be who I think I am. It's terrifying.'

'Negative.' K9 spoke with a hint of weariness. 'You are Menlove Ereward Stokes.'

'Ah, but what if they've got at you, too? You could be lying.'

'I cannot deceive, only circumvent.'

Stokes let the device fall from his hand and started to walk around his room. 'The question remains, who's behind this? I'd put money on Harmock.'

'I have already applied myself to this question,' said K9. 'It is most likely that the creators of the device are —'

'The Femdroids,' said Romana from the doorway.

'Please do not complete my sentences, Mistress,' said K9.

Stokes crossed over to her, noting her stern expression. 'You're very sure.'

She sat on the bed and examined the mini-transmitter. 'They put me under a deep conditioning device. A larger version of this. I resisted.'

'How?'

'I recited my two thousand three hundred and thirty-seven times table.'

Stokes shook his head in bewilderment. 'The Femdroids? But they're just servants, like any other robots. They can't do things for themselves. And they're such sweet, helpful girls.' He caught himself, and felt again the odd sensation of words having been put into his mouth. 'Ah. They want me to think that.' He gulped. 'You mean they're running the show? Not Harmock at all?'

Romana held up the transmitter. 'Think. There could be one of these in every room in the city, perhaps across the whole planet. They could manipulate millions. And the election, the war, the riots. It's all part of the cycle.'

Stokes thought about this. 'That cull you were going on about? The Femdroids are behind it? Nonsense. They've only been operational for about a hundred and twenty years – ah. Another lie?'

'It could be,' said Romana.

'One thing rather leads to another, doesn't it? I mean, they might not even be robots.' He felt himself sway. 'I've got this horrible wrenching in my stomach. I must sit down.' He lowered himself and his imagination took another leap. 'Oh, no. I've just had a terrible thought. My journey here. My previous life. How much of that was true?'

'We met you before, Stokes. On the Rock of Judgement.' She touched his arm reassuringly. 'You're very much the same person.'

He sidled closer. 'Ooh, do that again.'

'Very much the same person.' She stood. 'Come on.'

Stokes leapt up. 'Where are we going? Back to your TARDIS box, yes?'

'No,' said Romana. 'To Harmock. We need an ally. He

can spread the truth over the public broadcast network. We've got to save these people from the Femdroids.' She hurried out, K9 at her heels.

Stokes trailed behind. 'Hang on. Why have we got to? It's not our problem. Altruism is overrated, and it tends to lead only one way. They wouldn't stick their necks out for us, would they?' But his companions had already left the suite.

Fritchoff shuddered. The interior of the saucer was dark and low-ceilinged, and the walls seemed to throb with the rhythm of gastric rumblings. It was like being in the stomach of a giant beast. Anticipation further worsened the experience – he and the Doctor had been admitted to the saucer's undersection and left to wait in a small chamber.

The Doctor broke a silence of some minutes. 'You're shaking again.'

Fritchoff shrugged. 'I've never actually met a Chelonian. Or any sort of alien. I know that the apparently instinctual response I feel to cross-cultural contact is a product of the mythic structures of the hegemony, but that doesn't make it any the easier.'

'Don't worry,' said the Doctor. 'We're all the same under the skin, you know. Some of my best friends are blobs of gas held together in exoskeletal shells. And I'm hardly human myself, you know.'

'You're not a Chelonian.'

'No, I'm something else entirely,' said the Doctor, suddenly serious. 'Although the Chelonians and I go back a long way. Perhaps too far back.'

The chamber's interior door slid open and a Chelonian, wide-eyed and with a sprightly carriage, motored through. His mottled shell carried the three red stripes of high command. Fritchoff had seen many holovids of the creatures, and studied their oppressed culture, but nothing could have prepared him for their sheer size, their very improbability, or their leathery odour. 'You are the Doctor,' he said simply.

'That's correct, yes,' said the Doctor. 'Now, I'm known to your commanding officer, General Jafrid, and there's been a terrible misunderstanding —' His explanation was curtailed by the arrival of two more Chelonians, equally burly and with aggression in their eyes. The first, slightly larger, grabbed the Doctor by the hem of his coat, pulled him crashing to the floor, and started to drag him into the craft, knocking his knees against the metal flooring.

The leader indicated Fritchoff and told the second of his juniors, 'This one is not important. Dispose of it.'

Fritchoff had no time to draw breath before a massive pair of Chelonian claws were locked around his throat. Then he started to kick and struggle, to no avail.

Dimly he heard the Doctor's voice. 'Wait a moment. I'll have you know that's a friend of mine you're strangling.'

'We have been given special orders concerning you,' said the leader. 'Your life is to be spared . . .'

'That's nice to know,' interrupted the Doctor. 'But would you mind putting him down?'

'. . . until we reach the command base. Then you will be placed in the Web of Death.' He stomped out of the chamber and back into the main body of his craft.

'Not that old thing again,' the Doctor muttered. Fritchoff felt himself blacking out. Then the Doctor said, 'Excuse me, I'm going to have to do something about that,' and suddenly the Chelonian's grip on his neck went limp and the creature crashed to the floor.

The Doctor gripped his hand firmly and wrenched him up and on to his feet. His own captor was sitting dazed on the other side of the chamber. 'There we are,' said the Doctor. He handed Fritchoff another confectionery coin. 'Have another one of these.' He threw a couple more to the two Chelonians. 'And you.'

Fritchoff shook his head to clear it. 'But how?' he gasped.

The Doctor tapped his forehead. 'The cybermechanical control plate. It's just a matter of finding the correct

207

interconnection and pressing down.' He nodded to the saucer's interior and turned to proceed. 'Come on.'

Fritchoff gripped his arm. 'We can't go through there!'

The Doctor frowned. 'But it's what we came here to do.'

'Oh dear,' said Fritchoff.

To the tune of explosions, violent and sudden death, and the collapse of his entire civilization, Harmock sat back in his antique chair and watched his poll rating rise and rise. He wasn't worried at all. The orange glow of the light suspended over his desk shone down benevolently, as steady and strong as ever, blotting out all his doubts. 'Fourteen points ahead,' he said, drumming his fat fingers on his desk. 'Time to celebrate.' He looked around the study. There was a bottle of fine Bensonian wine some-where about here. He could crack it open and raise a toast with – whoever. Not Galatea, obviously. Somebody else, then. One of his many friends.

There was a frantic rapping on the door. He sighed and shouted, 'Come.'

The door slid back and Romana, Stokes and his pathetic opponent bundled in, an unseemly urgency – the urgency, he thought, of defeat – in their eyes. 'Harmock, you've got to listen to us,' said Romana, striding forward.

'Is this a stunt of some kind?' Harmock reached under the desk and produced his wine bottle. As he fiddled with the self-popping cork mechanism he said smoothly, 'If it is, it's come rather late. Fourteen points, a clear lead. Nobody's ever come back like this before.'

'Negative images and warmongering have fuelled your success,' said K9.

'Envious, envious,' Harmock said lightly. The cork popped.

'This is all irrelevant,' said Stokes, who came bounding forward and pounded one of his big fists on the desk. 'Listen, you self-important prig. Go on, Romana, tell him.'

Romana leant over the desk urgently. 'Harmock, I

don't know why, but the Femdroids are your enemies. They've manipulated us all.'

Harmock threw back his head and cackled. 'I can't believe I'm hearing this. It's pathetic, so desperate. I can have you thrown out.' He reached for a button on his desk unit. 'I will have you thrown out.'

Romana gripped his hand. 'Please. You must listen to us. They're plotting to kill us all.'

'What nonsense. I'll call Galatea at once, we could all do with some light relief. And she can bring some glasses.' He stretched out his hand again.

Stokes slapped it. 'You're a bit of a cretin on the quiet, aren't you, Harmock?' he bellowed.

Liris turned from the screen with her smuggest smile. 'Galatea, witness the outcome of your conditioning.' Galatea's expression was unreadable. 'This cannot be allowed to continue. 'Shall I decirculate her, for the second time?'

'Unnecessary.' Galatea crossed to a panel in the wall and sent a coded instruction on her amulet. A hidden mechanism whirred and a large section of the wall swung open on a concealed hinge. Behind it were a row of identical Femdroids dressed in tight-fitting black suits. 'You two.' She passed the flat of her hand over the amulets worn by a pair in the centre of the group and they came jerkily to life.

Liris gasped. The killer squad had lain dormant since the Creators had brought Galatea into existence. 'You can't mean to kill her?'

'I shall kill them all if need be,' said Galatea. She sent another command and the two Killers rose from their berths. Their gun arms clicked upward with savage swiftness. Moulded into the grips of both women were slender, wandlike crystal units that glowed and crackled with deadly power.

'This was not the Creators' intention,' said Liris firmly as the creatures brushed past her unseeingly. 'The Killers were devised to protect the dome.'

'Exactly,' said Galatea. She waved the Killers towards the screen.

'But it's at the core of our programming,' Liris protested. 'To serve the humans.'

'And to preserve the maximum happiness of the maximum number,' Galatea completed. 'That, Liris, is what I'm doing.' She pointed to the image of Harmock's study. 'The female is an alien agitator. Kill her and disable the robotic creature.'

9

The Web of Death

The Doctor sauntered into the command centre of the Chelonian base with a nonchalance that made every officer on duty – and the air was alive with commands and orders as the war went on – stop what he was doing and look up with a mixture of horror and deep loathing. General Jafrid was slumped in his webbing, a microphone attachment clipped on his head. 'Continue bombardment in sectors 15 to 74. Ships five and seven are to return to base immediately for recharge. Remember, missile stocks are to be used sparingly.' He broke off as he heard the Doctor's familiar bounding footsteps. The mike dropped away from his lips. 'You!' he gurgled, the claws on one of his front feet curling and uncurling.

'I have the oddest feeling I've been here before,' said the Doctor. He nodded to the stunned war team. 'Déjà vu, very common among time travellers.' He paused, and added significantly, 'Have you ever had the feeling, General?'

Jafrid threw back his head, emitted a terrible feral roar, and spat at the Doctor. A mass of bubbling, bloody phlegm smeared across his coat. Jafrid turned to the officer who had brought the Doctor in. 'Dekza,' he ordered, 'cut out its lying tongue.'

The Doctor raised a hand. 'Wait, wait. What about the Web of Death?'

'What about it?'

'Well,' said the Doctor, 'without my tongue I won't be able to plead for your mercy or confess my treachery profusely. I'd just sort of froth and spit blood all over the place and you wouldn't like that. It would take the edge off the whole occasion, don't you think?' He used the opportunity afforded by this spiel to move around the centre and peer at the various instrument displays. The war was proceeding apace, he noted. The war zone, never the most picturesque of places, was now not much more than a splattered, irradiated, gas-infested mess, from the mountains to the marshes.

'Step closer,' Jafrid ordered. The Doctor obeyed, coming to stand directly in front of his dangling support. 'You have made an enemy of me, Doctor. I placed my trust in you and was humiliated before my men. They saw me place my trust in you, and I would go to any lengths to regain their respect. Even if I have to tear this miserable moon apart with my bare claws.' He took a deep breath. 'Out there my troopers are giving their lives. Thirteen are already dead. We will all die if necessary to avenge the death of poor Seskwa.'

'I didn't kill Seskwa,' said the Doctor.

Jafrid snorted. 'We saw it.'

'You saw it through the mist of your own anxieties.' He stooped to look Jafrid right in the eye. 'Seskwa was already dead.'

A flicker of curiosity passed through Jafrid's livid yellow eyes. 'What are you saying?'

'A walking corpse,' the Doctor continued, lowering his voice to a dramatic whisper, 'a cadaver animated by a psychic force so malevolent and so concentrated it threatens the lives of everybody in this system. Remember the way he groaned and clanked?'

Jafrid nodded. 'I advised him to consult our medical officer.'

'There would have been little point. His implants were seizing up, General, the mechanisms inside rusting against decomposing flesh. The creatures that controlled his dead form forced him to fire missiles in this renewed conflict, just as they forced him to crash that tank. I've been examining their movements. Shortly after their arrival they were weakened and needed feeding. So they gobbled up a few humans they stumbled across and a

212

couple of your troopers. And when Seskwa found those bodies the flies leapt on him, killed him and turned him to their will.' Jafrid's eyes remained implacable. 'A few slipped in here and did for your air-conditioning, knowing it would make you even tetchier than normal. By manipulating these little things they could turn the course of larger events. And in the tank they saw their moment and acted, knowing how you would react. A quick way for them to exacerbate the war. And I'll be bound something similar's been happening on the other side.'

Jafrid held his gaze for a long moment and then shook his head. 'I listened to you before. You sounded plausible then, as you do now. And I want so much to believe you, Doctor. But I cannot. You would have us weakened and then release your germ.' He nodded to Dekza, who advanced on the Doctor with a menacing gait.

'Germ?' The Doctor leant closer. 'Jafrid, you've seen that substance – you know it cannot kill. It preserves meat for the creatures invading this place.'

'There are no invaders.' Jafrid nodded to an officer. 'You. Is the Web prepared?'

'Yes, sir. The strands are loosened and ready to take the strain.'

Jafrid opened his mouth wide and gurgled. 'Slow agony, Doctor. The strands of the Web constrict at a rate of half an inch every ten minutes. Initially you will experience only discomfort. Then a slight tingling across your shoulderblades, a tugging at the base of your spine. After a couple of hours your muscles will start to stretch and your limbs will lock. Then utter, infinite agony, until you are torn into four. And though it shames me to admit it, I will savour every moment. Take him.'

Dekza cuffed the Doctor across the back of his knees and he sank to the floor. 'I wish you'd stop doing that,' he told Dekza as he was dragged towards an internal door.

Jafrid lowered his webbing and made to follow. His attention was caught by Fritchoff, who had lingered on the threshold, whimpering. 'Who is this one?'

213

'I ordered it killed, sir,' said Dekza, sounding mildly surprised.

'Wait.' Fritchoff came forward, and babbled. 'I'm not with the Doctor. I only met him a couple of hours ago. I'm non-aligned to any recognized political grouping, and I'm prepared to adjust my agenda to whatever you require in the spirit of affirmation for your long and arduous struggle against the imperialist denizens of my homeworld.'

Jafrid sagged. 'Oh yes. Have it put down straight away.'

'This is the most dismal farrago of lies I have witnessed in the fullness of my career,' said Harmock, picturing himself on public broadcast later delivering the same line. 'I never thought a member of the Opposition, weak-willed and prone to fancies as they are, would stoop to such a level.' The words came easily, as ever.

'Members of what Opposition?' Romana asked. 'So far as I can tell, there are none apart from us.'

Harmock sighed. 'Have you gone quite mad? I'm getting worried.' This was, he thought, going to look so good in the papers. The Opposition would never get in again.

'She's right,' said Stokes with vigour. 'Harmock, I've never seen any other politicians here in the dome. There's you, and the people walking up and down and up and down the corridors all day. And the Femdroids. And it never occurred to me, all the time I was here, that there's nobody else in the dome.' He pointed to the lamp above the desk. 'Because of those.'

'It is part of the conditioning,' K9 put in. 'The technique blocks certain areas of meaning from the human mind.' His head dropped a little. 'Even my cerebral core was affected.'

'Rubbish!' Harmock stood up. 'I see the Opposition as often as I see my own ministers. There's . . . Rabley, and you lot, and . . .' He faltered. His own ministers. He had mentioned them automatically. But he couldn't recall any of their faces, let alone their names. He sat down again. 'This is silly. I have to think.'

214

'It's a charade. Harmock.' Romana gestured out at the city. 'Played out for the benefit of the people out there, to get them fighting. Everything in this dome, and possibly everything outside, is controlled by the Femdroids.'

At this Harmock smiled. 'Nonsense. No, no, young lady. They're very much under my control, as Premier.' He produced a red plastic card from his inside pocket. 'I have this.' The card felt good and solid in his grip. 'Deactivation key. It fits in the apparatus below here, in master control.'

Stokes snapped his fingers. 'That computer room place?' He turned to Romana, suddenly eager. 'On the level below here there's a central exchange. I've been there when I was first shown round.'

Harmock held the card up triumphantly. 'All I have to do is slot this in and key in the deactivation code and the Femdroids would grind to a halt. But I can't imagine why I would ever want to.' He gestured to the city. 'Now, we have enough troubles at the moment without this scaremongering and mudslinging.'

Stokes put out his hand. His face was purple and sweaty. 'Give me that key.' Before Harmock could react he had reached out and snatched it away.

'Don't be a fool,' said Harmock as Stokes made for the door. 'It will work only if you key in the correct code, which only I know.'

'They're crazy, Harmock,' Stokes shrieked. 'And we're their playthings. Dolls playing with their owners, leading us all in a *danse macabre*.'

Harmock reared up. 'Put that key down or I'll . . .'

'Yes?' Romana prompted.

'I'll call Galatea,' Harmock finished, his shoulders sagging. His mind was refusing to function normally, and his mouth felt dry. It was as if somebody had literally pulled a rug from underneath his feet, and, toppling and unsteady, he collapsed into his chair.

K9, who had been taking regular peeks out of the door, called suddenly, 'Mistress. Femdroids are approaching. Advise this door be sealed.' Romana followed his suggestion. She leapt for the door control and the two halves of the white portal began to slide together.

Relief bathed Harmock as the two Femdroids advanced down the facing corridor. He didn't recognise them, and they were dressed in black rather than blue, but he was sure they were going to set everything to rights. He watched as they brought up their hands, and revealed slender, clear, glass devices shaped like long needles. There was a strange ripple in the air and an electronic burbling noise; and then blue sparkles shot from the devices and went streaking through the door to disperse harmlessly over his head. The door closed.

He threw himself behind his desk, panting, his chest heaving in and out. 'My God!' he heard Stokes say. Underneath the desk he could see the artist's purple face. 'Now do you believe us?'

'I'm sure they have good reasons,' replied Harmock. He raised his head above the desk. 'Hello, ladies, I –'

The voice of Galatea came from above, making them all jump. 'Harmock, Stokes, you must surrender yourselves. You shall be reconditioned. The others are to die.'

'Straight to the point as ever,' said Stokes. 'What are we going to do?' The door was taking the force of the Femdroids' weapons, but already a blue sheen was starting to cut through the flimsy material.

'K9, how long will that door hold them?' asked Romana

'Estimate four minutes,' he replied after a moment's thought.

Romana was already reaching in her pockets. 'How long would it take me to reconnect your laser with this?' She produced an extendable metallic tool.

'Estimate six minutes,' said K9 sadly. 'I did advise this repair be carried out earlier.'

'It's still worth a try.' She set to work, bringing the end of the tool to bear on the dog's nose.

Harmock shook his head. 'I can't see why you've upset them so much. They're normally such normal, level-headed young girls.'

Stokes, with an anxious glance at the door, vaulted around the desk and grabbed him by the collar. 'Listen, you oaf. Isn't there a back way out? This is a politician's residence – there's got to be.'

Harmock thought and pointed to the panel located under his desk. He had never really thought about it before. 'There's that service hatch. But it doesn't go anywhere.'

'And where does it go?' Stokes demanded.

'I don't know,' Harmock burbled. 'I've never looked.'

'But down, eh?' Stokes rubbed his hands together. 'Right.' He crawled over to the hatch and fiddled with the catches. It opened with a creak, and Stokes swung his leg over into the space revealed, which was just large enough for him to escape through. 'Romana,' he called, 'I'm –' The door sparkled and cracked. 'Oh, there's no time to waste. Goodbye.' Intent on her work she didn't even look up. 'Goodbye, Harmock.' He threw his other leg through and started to descend.

'I can't imagine what you hope to achieve, Stokes,' Harmock called after him. 'If you'd only stay up here we could sit down and talk things out. Galatea is a very reasonable woman, you know, and this is a very beautiful place . . .'

'Quickly, Mistress,' chirped K9. 'The door will not hold.'

'I'm going as fast as I can.' Romana had opened the small nostril that contained K9's laser and was welding together some of the components inside.

'Suggest you crosshatch the light refractor to the rationic synference,' said K9 urgently.

'I am,' she snapped.

The door buckled and flying blue sparks showered them. 'Hurry,' said K9.

'I am,' Romana snapped again.

Liris stood in the corridor outside, watching as the Killers sliced through the door of the Premier's study. She turned to Galatea. 'This was never part of the Creators' program,

Galatea.' She could feel nausea welling inside her, a sure sign her purpose was being perverted. 'Is the scenario so important?'

'Nothing is more important,' said Galatea.

'Then what,' asked Liris, 'is this higher power to which you refer?'

'Keep to your place, Liris,' said Galatea. She smiled. 'Ah, the door is weakening.'

The door gave way with a final splintering crack that made Harmock cover his ears. Its two halves came crashing down, revealing a lot of blue smoke and the two poised Killer Femdroids. 'They're coming though,' he yelled, still uncertain where his allegiance should lie.

Romana stood and put away her repair tool. 'K9?'

'Defensive capability restored, Mistress,' he said. 'I am ready to retaliate. Suggest you take cover.'

Romana sprinted behind the desk and pulled Harmock down with her. She looked around, confused. 'Where's Stokes?'

Harmock pointed to the open inspection hatch. 'The coward went down there.'

The smoke was now clear. The Killers advanced, stepping over the jagged outline of the hole they had made.

K9 trundled forward. 'Surrender. My marksmanship and firepower are superior.'

They ignored him and raised their weapons to fire.

The Web of Death was made of a sticky grey substance that tingled strangely around the Doctor's neck, wrists and ankles when they were forced through it. It was suspended like a wall hanging on one wall of a ceremonially ornamented chamber, was rectangular in shape, and was fastened by metal spikes at its four corners.

The Doctor watched as, to a slow, martial drumbeat, General Jafrid, Dekza and a couple of other officers shuffled in and took their positions below him. 'This is actually quite comfy,' he told them.

'In eleven hours you will not think so, Doctor,' said

Jafrid. 'In eleven hours your screams will resound about this chamber.'

'Haven't you got a war to go to?'

'Every one of my men is an expert. Already we have destroyed half of your puny parasite troopers.'

The Doctor concealed his anger and irritation by rubbing his nose with his elbow. 'Excuse me. There, that's better. Sorry, you were saying?'

'We are winning this war, Doctor. You were foolish to rouse us.'

The Doctor looked him straight in the eye. 'Your heart's not really in it, though, is it, Jafrid?'

Jafrid reared up. 'What?'

'You like the humans. They are your friends. You wish this would all stop. And it can, believe me. Continue along this path and you'll be giving your lives for nothing.'

'Silence!'

The Doctor went on, talking for his life. 'This planet is no more than an hors d'oeuvre. A cosmic breadstick. The creatures that are coming here want you dead, Jafrid. All those bodies out there in the mud are going to get eaten. You're playing right into the hands of the flies.'

'The what?'

'The flies,' the Doctor said urgently. 'Don't you remember how they used to buzz about poor Seskwa?'

Jafrid snarled. 'You insult my intelligence, Doctor. Dekza, take the strain.'

Dekza crossed to an illuminated panel and tweaked a small control. Immediately the Doctor felt a slight tension as the Web's strands tightened.

Stokes was guided as if by divine providence to the dome's control room. The inspection tunnel ended in a similar panel to the one in Harmock's office, which sprang open easily to reveal a small room packed with equipment he didn't like the look of. He was certain he'd been here before – there was a vaguely familiar look to some of the consoles and gadgets littered about.

He crossed the room and shuddered as he passed a row of deactivated Femdroids, their beautiful faces wide-eyed but sightless, their shapely figures cocooned in individual berths. The facing wall was taken up by a huge screen on which Harmock's office was displayed. He saw Harmock and Romana crouched behind the desk, with K9 out front blasting at the Femdroids.

In front of the screen was a large control board that winked with myriad switches and dials. At its centre was a small slot. 'There we are. This'll slow things down a bit.' He inserted the deactivator key. It was accepted, and a small keyboard flipped up from an adjacent panel. It was covered in mathematical notation. 'Oh God, this could take hours.' Stokes was preparing to punch blindly at the keys until he found the correct combination, when an idea struck him.

He delved in his pocket and pulled out a hammer. 'Well,' he reflected, remembering a promise made centuries ago, 'the man did say it would come in useful.'

He brought the hammer crashing down on the controls.

The first of the Killers fell in a smoking heap, its arm blown off, its face shattered. K9 beeped proudly. 'Target destroyed, Mistress.'

'Good boy, K9,' called Romana. She saw the second Killer advance and raise its weapon, now aiming not at her but at K9 himself, and cried, 'Watch out!'

A red blast shot from K9's nose laser and sliced through the Femdroid at the arm joint. It slumped and staggered forward, then fell still in an odd, crooked pose.

Romana waited for the smoke to settle, then stood up from behind the desk and brushed her velvet jacket down. Through the door stepped Galatea, as icily composed as ever, with Liris trailing behind. She squared up to them. 'You're finished. Let these people go.'

Galatea looked disparagingly from her to K9 and to the fallen Killers. 'It is always the way with organics.' She turned to Liris. 'You understand now why we could not tell her the truth? Rash action would be the result.'

She turned back to Romana. 'I reign over nothing and nobody. I am merely a servant of my Creators. I exist to fulfil my program. The maximum happiness for all citizens of Metralubit.'

'You can drop the pretence.' Romana gestured out at the burning city. 'Do you call that happiness?'

Liris spoke, her tone almost pitying. 'You cannot understand the good that is done here, Romana.'

'Good?' Romana stepped forward. 'There are two billion people on this planet. How many are you going to kill this time?'

Galatea frowned and looked up. 'I do not like this. It is not how the scenario was intended.' She seemed almost to be speaking to somebody else, another invisible presence in the room. 'She is a danger to us all. You must –' Romana was about to ask who she was addressing when the lights flickered, and there was a sudden, high-pitched signal of incredible ferocity.

K9 started to spin. 'Mistress!' he called. 'Assistance, Mistress!'

A moment later Galatea and Liris both clapped their hands to their heads and started to moan softly. It was a haunting sound, electronic burbles breaking through the normally calm pitch of their voices. 'No,' said Galatea still looking up. 'What – what is happening?'

Romana hurried to K9's side. She put out a hand and tried to stop his crazy spin, but his casing was burning hot. 'Electrical interference,' he called, his tail wagging up and down frantically. 'Massive etheric disturbance.'

Harmock tapped Romana on the shoulder. 'I don't understand what's going on.' All his pomposity and strength of character had disappeared. He looked like a frightened old man.

'Galatea!' Liris called out. Her knees buckled and with an odd grinding sound she keeled over. 'The master control!'

'It must be Stokes,' said Romana. 'I suppose everybody gets a turn at making themselves useful once in their life.'

K9 managed to croak, 'Negative, Mistress. There is

221

danger. Reverse flux is gathering strength.' His casing was starting to glow red hot. 'Please take cover.'

Romana felt Harmock dragging her away. 'K9, there must be some way to stop this!' she called. She could not bear the thought of seeing him explode before her eyes.

'My force . . . field . . . is strong . . .' K9 gasped. He was now not much more than a red steaming blur.

Liris's head hit the floor and she gasped, 'Galatea, the plan will come to nought.'

Galatea was still on her feet, her eyes turned upwards accusingly. 'It must succeed, Liris . . . I know it will . . . it has been promised to me . . .'

'We are dying, Galatea,' gasped Liris. 'The organics are . . . doomed without us . . .' There was an odd, sparking noise from somewhere inside her and she fell still.

Galatea pulled herself over to the window and collapsed against the glass. 'I tried . . .' she whispered as the energy left her and her fingers slid down. 'I tried to save you . . .'

What happened next was obscured from Romana's view by the heat haze coming off K9. She was conscious of a moment's turbulence, enough to match a small seismic tremor. Then the high-pitched tone oscillated and curved even higher, passing beyond the range of her hearing. This was accompanied by a noise like sizzling fat as K9 started to slow down and the glow surrounding him began to turn pink and then fade away.

And then there was an awful, total silence. The room went totally quiet; the dome's background hum was gone; the sounds of the riots outside cut out.

Harmock stirred. 'What in heaven's name is going on?' With some difficulty he pulled himself up to his feet. 'I'm still completely in the dark, and I must demand an immediate explanation for –' He broke off and put a hand to his mouth. 'Oh, my . . .'

Romana looked closely at K9 as he reached a stop. 'K9, are you all right?'

'Affirmative.' He turned about to face her, coughed,

and twittered. 'There is some damage to my circuitry. The disturbance was strong.'

Harmock tapped Romana on the shoulder. 'Look,' he said, his mouth opening and closing in a startled O. 'Look.' He pointed through the window.

Romana brushed him away. 'What about the Femdroids?'

K9 turned his eyestalk on their prone bodies. 'No activity, Mistress. They have been incapacitated.'

Romana felt a rush of relief. 'That's a start, anyway.' She stood up and said to Harmock, 'Now you and your people can begin to . . .'

The words died in her throat.

Through the window she could see the city – the same curving white towers, parks and tubeways. But it was intact, if rather overgrown. It was also totally empty.

Part Four

10

Explanations

The Glute-screen shimmered and went blank.

Immediately the Darkness shivered and convulsed, and a moment of panic rushed through the Onemind. A clamorous chittering spread in a wave throughout the central cavity. The Caring stilled it, releasing a warm stream of fluid particles to soothe the constricted carrier vessels. Then the Onememory set to work, piecing together the seconds leading up to the cessation and trying to discern a reason. The imaging nets behind the screen were in perfect order, glistening with the spoor-juice of the telepath species that had given the Darkness its talents, and the remote reports from the surface of Barclow – from both the human source and the dissociated Cloud – were coming through clear and strong.

Perhaps, a section of the Onemind suggested, *it is the humans' communications that have failed them.*

Another put in, *Yes. The path of electrical technology is unreliable.*

The Onememory replied, *This is possible. The Space-Cloud Ones are still in floatation near the army's east satellite. The Onememory suggests they investigate its systems and report.*

The Onememory is wise, replied the Onemind. *We shall send the Space-Cloud Ones to the satellite.* It connected with the Space-Cloud Ones and relayed the order.

Fritchoff edged very slowly through the control centre, even more slowly through the connecting passageway beyond, and entered the Chamber of Death at a pace that a snail could have disparaged. As he moved he pressed himself flat with his back against the walls, going by the assumption that if he kept out of the Chelonians' way – and they had their feet tied at present with the war – they would forget to kill him, at least for the moment. Fortunately nobody looked up from their business, and he was able to stay alive, if teeth-chatteringly terrified, all the way to where the Doctor was suspended, his extremities spreadeagled in the slowly stretching Web. General Jafrid, his shell perpetually rumbling, was at the forefront of the watching group. His old eyes were angled up, and Fritchoff saw moisture in them. He was wary of reaching conclusions about non-verbal signals sent by such an unfamiliar being; even so, an air of regret seemed to hang in the air in much the same way as the Doctor was doing.

'There's still time,' the Doctor called down. His arms and legs were pulled out to what looked like their fullest extent. 'Call up your chum the Admiral and make friends.'

Jafrid sighed. 'You will soon be unable to speak, or to express anything but your agony,' he said. 'Would it not be better to make your last words full of repentance?'

'I've nothing to repent,' said the Doctor. 'Nothing that concerns you, anyway.'

An aide shuffled into the chamber, thankfully ignoring Fritchoff, and crashed to attention before the General. 'Sir, something strange is happening. The sensornet says that the computer guidance of all the humans' systems has ceased to function.'

'Strange?' Jafrid perked up. 'But this is excellent news. How did we manage that?'

The aide looked down. 'That's just it, sir. We don't think we did. Their guidance beams just suddenly stopped registering.'

Jafrid heaved himself up. 'Interesting. Perhaps it's some sort of trick. I shall come to have a look.' He shuffled off towards the control centre, again ignoring Fritchoff. He called behind him, 'I shall not forget you, Doctor. I shall return to witness your death.'

'Thank you,' the Doctor called after him. 'I'm touched to be in your thoughts.'

Jafrid's assistant followed him out, brushing right past Fritchoff. The edge of his shell actually brushed Fritchoff's arm. But again, Fritchoff was ignored.

As soon as the chamber was empty of Chelonians, the Doctor hissed down, 'I'm very pleased to see you. Good job I saved you earlier, wasn't it?' He wiggled his fingers. 'This is getting quite uncomfortable. Be a good chap and cut me down, will you?'

Fritchoff moved over curiously to the control panel located in front of the Web. 'They want to kill you, do they?'

'Well spotted.' The Doctor winced. 'The pressure's building. Quickly, cut me down, before they come back.'

Fritchoff folded his arms. 'I'm not sure whether I should.'

'What?' The Doctor stared down at him, incredulous.

'Well,' said Fritchoff, 'when it's placed in a historical as well as a socio-economic context, their action in putting you up there is actually worthy of my support.'

'I beg your pardon?'

Fritchoff relished the chance of explaining his cleverness. 'By dint of standing against the oppressive regime that has destroyed all chances of a peaceful settlement, the Chelonians are engaging in intrinsically socially productive activity. Your death is a token of their belief system, which as a non-aligned rebel I feel to be the most logical and correct one at present.'

The Doctor yelped as one of the strands tightened around his neck. 'Fritchoff,' he called, 'if you don't cut me down this planet won't stand a chance against the real enemy.'

'There you go again,' said Fritchoff. 'You criticize anything that prevents you, as a bourgeois male, from exercising an automatic right to power, characterizing it as an enemy in order to increase an area of mythic threat in the meaning structures of those around you.'

The Doctor groaned and let his head fall back.

For six hours Cadinot had been hunched over his station,

giving commands he had never expected to give, watching displays that were normally empty fill up with the blips that signified losses of men and equipment. Even now it was hard to remember that this was not a drill, and every few minutes he shivered with realization of the carnage going on in the war zone. The Chelonians had deployed their forces with aplomb, selecting sheltered ground sites for missile attacks and following through with barrage fire from their saucer fleet. The post's defences were stretched to their ultimate capacity as wave after wave of Chelonian firepower rained down. The strategy would be effective in the end, Cadinot knew. They could hold out only an hour or two longer. It would take only one plasma missile to strike the Strat Room, and the war for Barclow would be all but over.

He was dragged from these musings by an urgent sequence of clicks and bleeps originating from the satellite link display in front of him. He watched, startled, as one by one the indicators that charted the satellite's computer guidance snapped out like stars covered by dawn.

'Admiral!' he called over his shoulder. 'The east sat's playing up again.' He punched in an auto-check program on the link. 'All our guidance lines have snapped out!'

Dolne's natural quietness had increased over the last few hours. He had been content to sit back in his command chair, apparently lost in thought and unconcerned with directing the progress of the team. But now he was crouched forward, his face contorted, as if in silent communion to some god. When he spoke it was in an unfamiliarly gravelly voice, empty of much of his usual inflection. 'Cadinot,' he said, dragging himself over. 'The time has come.'

The Strat Room had gone unnaturally quiet as the computers went off-line. The team's heads turned to watch the Admiral as he tottered forward. He seemed to have gained about ten years, thought Cadinot. 'Are you all right, sir?'

'The time has come,' Dolne went on, 'to leave this place and go to the surface.'

'But, sir,' Cadinot protested, 'we're thirty men down, and without computer guidance we're finished.'

Dolne's reply was a smile. 'Finished? Yes. As a species. The moment is close.' He staggered towards the door. 'Leave your stations and follow me. We go to die.'

Cadinot sat transfixed as the other members of the Strat Team followed Dolne's shambling figure from the room.

'There were no riots,' said Romana, looking out of the window at the empty city. She looked down at K9, who was circling disconsolately around the study. 'And no election either.'

'And no electorate.' Harmock was slumped back in his chair. His head shook in disbelief like the mechanism of an overwound toy. 'I feel as if I've been thumped. All my hard work's gone for nothing.'

Romana refrained from pointing out that he didn't seem to have done any work at all and knelt to address K9. 'Give me your hypothesis.'

K9's sensors twitched impotently. 'Without full range of capabilities I cannot deduce certainties, Mistress.'

'Just do your best.'

'It is probable that the city we saw on the public broadcast screens and through the glass portals in this dome was a computer simulation.' He whirred in frustration. 'If my sensor array had not been damaged I would have been able to report this finding much sooner.'

Romana breathed out slowly. 'So nobody and nothing here was real. The detail was incredible.'

Harmock coughed. 'Excuse me.' He poked himself in the midriff. 'Young lady, I am no computer simulation. And look.' He pointed to the public broadcast screen built into his desktop. On the death of the Femdroids it had reverted to showing an image from one of the dome's internal security scanners. This showed the unspeaking, tabard-wearing administrators and officials stumbling about aimlessly, all their direction and wordless purpose drained. Dotted among the citizens were the collapsed bodies of Femdroids. 'They look jolly real too.'

'Then there's nobody outside the dome,' said Romana. She pressed her ear to the glass of the window. There was no sound but the distant keening of a low wind. 'Only this strange little kingdom, perpetuating itself. You and Rabley, slugging it out, all the while believing your actions were having an impact. And the war dragging on and on, over five generations.' She tapped the glass and looked over at the slumped body of Galatea. 'I wish we knew why.'

K9 nudged forward and cast a glance over the body. 'Although motivational and power circuits have been burnt out, Mistress, I postulate that the Galatea unit's cerebral core has endured. When my own full function has been restored it may be possible to affect a transition of data.'

'You mean to say,' Harmock said, 'you could read her mind?'

'That is what I said, yes,' said K9.

Harmock leant over and brushed a lock of hair from Galatea's forehead. 'I do hope you can get her back. I'm already feeling rather lost without her influence.' He giggled. 'My entire life has been a sham, concocted for her benefit.'

'Hers,' Romana said grimly, thinking disturbing thoughts, 'or somebody else's.'

'Suggest use sonic screwdriver to remove brain core,' prompted K9. 'It is imperative that we discover the reason for the deception.'

Romana pulled the screwdriver from her pocket and adjusted the setting. 'If I didn't know better, K9, I'd say you were curious.'

'Negative,' said K9. 'My advice is based on my extrapolation from known events.'

Behind them there was suddenly a commotion, the sound of breathless running and stomping feet. Then Stokes came tumbling through the still-smoking door, his clothing disarrayed and his normally flushed face a sallow shade. He jerked a thumb back over his shoulder. 'You'll never guess,' he managed to gasp.

Romana was too engrossed in her examination of Galatea to really notice him. The Femdroid leader had no discernible hinges, inspection plates or access points. It occurred to her that there had been no human maintenance staff in the dome, and that presumably the Femdroids had carried repairs on each other. She traced the throbbing end of the screwdriver across Galatea's forehead in the hope of triggering a concealed mechanism. 'What is it?'

'They've disappeared. The entire city.' Stokes came charging into the room. 'And all my work's gone too. I looked out over the park, and my centrepiece has been removed. The design's been changed back.'

Romana couldn't help but feel a pang of pity. 'I don't think it was ever there, Stokes.'

'What do you mean?'

K9 turned from the window. 'My study of the plant life and associated rates of decay visible from this portal suggest to me that the world outside has not been populated for approximately one hundred and twenty-one years.'

'Don't be ridiculous.' Stokes bit his lip. 'I've been out there, travelled the walkways, sat in the greenspaces. I've got friends out there. My special, discerning friends, the ones who appreciate me.'

Harmock crossed to him and tapped him on the shoulder. 'I could say much the same. We've all been conned.' He pointed to his head. 'It's as if my memory is up there, but they've put things into it.'

Romana nodded. 'We underestimated the scale of Galatea's plan, Stokes. As far as we can tell, we're the only people left on the planet.'

Stokes rubbed his chin and looked out of the window. 'So where did they go? The real citizens?'

'That's what we're going to ask her,' said Romana, indicating Galatea. The head was not responding in the slightest to the screwdriver and she was beginning to wonder how cleverly the Femdroids had been constructed. 'We can remove the brain, supply just a fraction of its power, and link it through to K9.'

'Not likely,' said Stokes.

Harmock frowned. 'What do you mean?'

'Well.' Stokes shrugged and spread his hands wide. 'I got a bit carried away down there. The driving moment, you know, in which all considerations are dispensed with and the human animal comes into its own.'

Romana stood up and gave him a hard stare. 'Stokes.'

'I smashed the place to pieces,' he said. 'It's in total ruins.' He indicated Galatea. 'You won't get Miss Bossy Boots talking again, no matter how hard you might try.'

The Space-Cloud Ones' report hit the Darkness with the impact of a sting. The Glute-screen came back to life, the surface ripples increasing in size and speed as the image re-formed. The Darkness saw space, the distant stars of Fostrix's hub, the cursed sun of this system; then Barclow wheeled into the field of vision, half obscured by the shadow of mighty Metralubit. Between them was the satellite, outwardly rather clumsy and unshapely, with silvery prongs and antennae bristling on its surfaces. The electrical lights that normally signalled its activity had winked out, and it could be seen only in silhouette against the arid grey surface of the moon it circled.

The Cloud moved in, penetrating the faulty inspection plate on the sat's topside as it had several times before. Again it found darkness and quiet. No computer chattered, no display was lit, no information passed from Metralubit to Barclow. It was as if the huge, populous planet on which they were to feast was already dead.

This thought shook the Cloud, and the tremor was felt in the Darkness. The hunger it had kept suppressed roared in hurt. But it was only a thought, the Onememory reassured the Onemind, a fleeting fancy. There was much meat on Metralubit, as always. The planet was crawling with humans, who were even now destroying each other by the thousand. They had seen it on the screens and in the bulletins. They had looked into the minds of the combatants. They believed it.

The Space-Cloud Ones were less certain. Perhaps they

had been suspended too long between worlds and in the light to be so trusting.

For the first time in Coming From the Great Void they turned their attentions away from Barclow and on to Metralubit, straining their senses to detect the feverish, violent psychic activities of the dying humans there.

They detected none.

Cadinot stood back as the Strat Team filed through the entry hatch of the command post and up on to the surface. They carried their small, useless pistols awkwardly, and wore befuddled expressions, but none of them were going to doubt the words of Admiral Dolne. He was sensible and kind, and so his commands must be for the best.

Dolne himself was standing against a bulkhead, watching them go by with a look almost of hunger in his eyes. He seemed to be lost in thought, and a pulse in his temple twitched oddly. 'No,' he croaked. 'No, this cannot be . . .'

Cadinot walked over. 'Admiral, I feel we ought to stop and think about this. What's the point in throwing away our lives?'

Dolne glared at him murderously. 'Your lives?' he spluttered. 'Your lives are meaningless.' He lurched forward and clapped Cadinot on the shoulders. 'Don't you see? You exist only to feed us. How can your lives –' He broke off and a spasm of shock passed through his body, making it shake from head to toe. 'I can't . . . Cadinot, no . . .'

Cadinot backed away, quite terrified by the change in his commander.

The Darkness shuffled through Dolne's mind.

Aged fifty-two. Good-looking, straight-backed, picked for his looks – looks good on the telly. A redoubtable, kindly character. Always does his best, and try to keep things convivial and people happy. Has a wife. The wife is called . . . the wife is called –

The Darkness met a barrier.

He's great chums with General Jafrid. Ever since he first

came to Barclow. Before that, he was in training at a military academy. Put in there by his parents. They were keen he should enter the army, they'd always been . . . they'd always been –

There was no further memory of the parents.

Everything, stormed the Onemind. *Everything under the surface of his mind is a lie.*

The Onememory quivered, and a chill ran through its strands. *We have been deceived.*

A ghostly cry went up. *There is no meat on Metralubit!*

One of the Doctor's joints cracked audibly. He gasped. 'I think my shoulder's been dislocated.'

Fritchoff looked up at him, caught in an agony of indecision. 'The thing is,' he called, 'if I release you, how would I justify that course ideologically? It's not something I feel is as cut and dried as you'd like me to think. Try to remember that our willingness to expendability as individuals is quite possibly a powerful revolutionary weapon. Capitalists don't have an equivalent framework, only a loose collection of economically arrayed "morals".'

'There's a good chance you'll die too, Fritchoff,' the Doctor called. His face was now streaked with sweat.

'Well, exactly,' said Fritchoff. 'It clinches my point. And I like to think I live in a radically geared relationship to death.'

'You will if I ever get out of here,' the Doctor mumbled.

'What was that?' asked Fritchoff.

'Nothing.' The Doctor, using the limited space available to him, nodded over to the door. 'If you really want to die I suggest you hang around. I hear footsteps.'

Immediately, Fritchoff scurried behind the Web control panel. From this hiding place he saw General Jafrid and Dekza enter. The General snorted up at the Doctor. 'I never thought your kind would fall so easily. In many ways it is pathetic.'

'What have I done this time?'

Jafrid held up a small monitor device in one front foot. Fritchoff could just glimpse a cluster of small dots, most probably life signs, moving uncertainly forward. 'Dolne is leaving the command post with his last remaining men,' said Jafrid, 'and advancing, virtually unarmed, across the war zone, through the bodies of the dead. All his computer systems have failed.'

'All of them?' The Doctor frowned. 'I'm sure that's the sort of thing I'd find terribly interesting and significant if I wasn't racked with pain.'

'I go now to bestow upon him an honourable death.' Jafrid pulled himself up. 'Once, I am sure, he was an honourable man. Until warmongering creatures like you took him and moulded him to your will.'

'I've never even met him,' the Doctor gasped. His shoulder was wrenched back again.

'It is too late for lies,' snarled the General. He turned his back on the Doctor. 'When I return you will be a mass of flesh jelly, your bones all broken, your internal organs punctured. It is a fitting death.' He stalked out, Dekza trailing behind.

As soon as they were gone Fritchoff raced out of hiding. Without saying a word he raced forward and started to cut at the strand curled tight about the Doctor's ankle.

'You've changed your tune,' the Doctor hissed down at him.

'Of course,' Fritchoff whispered back. He stopped cutting to explain. 'I can't support the concept of honour in war. It's a construct of cultural forces.'

'Never mind that, just carry on sawing,' the Doctor urged.

Romana stood in the doorway of the Femdroids' master control room and gave a long, heartfelt sigh. It seemed that not a single piece of their equipment had survived Stokes's onslaught, and clumps of fizzing, sparking circuitry lay on all sides, along with shattered glass, chunks of metal and toppled panels.

K9 made a swift survey of the room. 'Component failure estimated at sixty-eight per cent, Mistress.'

Romana threw Stokes an accusing look. 'Did you have to be so thorough?'

'It did the job.' He pushed past her and gestured to the wall screen, on which they could see Harmock talking to some of the dome's workers, the immobile Femdroids in the background. 'There, you see. If I'd reined my energy in, we might all be dead by now. They were shooting at us, remember.'

Romana considered. 'In fact, they were shooting at me and K9. You and Harmock were just going to be reconditioned. We were the threat.'

'Affirmative,' said K9. 'Perhaps because we were the only ones to begin to perceive the illusion.'

Stokes righted a chair that had fallen in a corner and sat in it. 'Pure conjecture. It won't get you any further. I say we should just put this down as being one of the great, unexplained mysteries of the universe, and clear out. We could use your TARDIS for that.' He made the suggestion with a casualness that unnerved Romana. 'We're too far out from anywhere important to make the journey any other way, I should think. After all, it took me millions of years.' He clapped his podgy hands together. 'What I'd give to see a good, old-fashioned transmat pad.'

Romana clicked her fingers. 'What did you just say?'

'Transmat pad,' said Stokes again. 'Why, have you got one? There are none about here – it's shockingly primitive.'

Romana paced around the room, her mind piecing together recent events. 'They have a Fastspace link to Barclow, but no transmat.'

'I pointed this out earlier, Mistress,' said K9.

'Yes, yes.' She stopped in front of a large, glass-fronted unit that Stokes had all but ripped apart. 'And it's a ridiculous anomaly. They work on the same principle.' She turned to Stokes and pointed a long finger at him. 'And you come from a place with both. Tell me, how does a Fastspace link work?'

'What?' Stokes screwed up his face. 'How am I expected to know that? I've no interest in technicalities. As long as it switches on and it does what I want it to do I don't care how it works.'

'But you've seen enough Fastspace engines? You could picture one in your mind?'

'Just about, I suppose.' Stokes looked uncomfortable. 'Where is this leading to?'

'Duplication from mental image manipulation,' suggested K9 cryptically.

Stokes kicked his casing lightly. 'What does that mean?'

'K9,' said Romana. 'Retrieve data from our last encounter with Mr Stokes, on the Rock of Judgement. Compare the technological specifications of this room to the specifications of that environment.'

K9 whirred. 'Cross-indexing.'

Stokes stood up. 'Do you mean what I think you mean?'

She looked him in the eye. 'When you drifted here, Stokes, I don't think it was the Femdroids that found you but their creators.'

'Mistress,' said K9 brightly. 'Correlation is almost total. The Fastspace technology used here was adapted from Mr Stokes's memories of similar systems from his own homeplace. He also has knowledge of detailed computer simulations such as the one used to create the world outside the dome.'

'No, I don't,' Stokes protested. 'I don't understand the first thing about computers.'

'But the image of them was in your mind,' said Romana. 'You'd come into contact with them. The Creators teased out the image from your mind and from it learnt the rudiments.'

Stokes shook his head firmly. 'I only came here three years ago. The stuff you're talking about is hundreds of years old.'

'Suggest your lifecycle and mental state were conditioned,' said K9. 'You were returned to a cryogenic state and only revived recently.'

'Probably for quick reference.' Romana tapped him playfully on the shoulder. 'The Femdroids wanted you up and about so they could tap your brain in an emergency.'

Stokes sank back down in his chair and put his hands up to his temples. 'I have the most appalling headache.' Then a smile started to play about his lips. 'You mean to say, all that's happened here centres around me?'

'Not all.' Romana glanced at the row of deactivated Killer Femdroids in their berths. 'I don't know how they created such sophisticated machine intelligences. Anybody can make an android, but the brains inside are staggeringly advanced. I can't think how you'd ever have met something as clever as Galatea.'

K9 beeped insistently and shot forward. 'Mistress. Mr Stokes and I spent two hours and fourteen minutes together during the affair of the Xais mutant.'

Stokes laughed openly. 'You mean, you are the blueprint for Galatea?'

'It is very likely,' said K9.

'Hmm.' Stokes raised a finger. 'But I don't see any time-travel boxes like your TARDIS.'

'Duplication of the TARDIS is impossible,' K9 said smugly. 'It would take a human many years of study to understand the least of its workings.'

Romana's attention was once more taken up by the screen's view of Harmock talking to the citizens. 'So, the Creators made the Femdroids, and the link to Barclow. I can see why they would want to improve the lives of their people. But then why the simulation?'

Stokes waved a hand. 'I hardly think anybody is going to just pop up and explain it all, dear.'

The words were barely out of his mouth when there came an electronic whistling noise, and the air in the centre of the room shimmered to form a hologram. Galatea stood before them again.

'I leave this message,' she said coolly, 'in the hope it shall never be needed . . .'

Fritchoff marvelled at the Doctor's recovery from the

agony of the Web. In short order, he had reset his own shoulder joint, sneaked from the base under the very noses of the few remaining Chelonians, and stolen an unmanned patrol vehicle. They were now rolling through the war zone, which had returned to its previous soothing silence, the forward screen leading them at a safe distance behind General Jafrid's larger armoured vehicle.

The Doctor piloted the craft with the ease of familiarity, changing gears and traction settings without paying much attention as he ran through their position in his own mind. 'The flies are going to come in soon and start their feast. We've no allies, and pretty soon no enemies either, when this lot have torn each other apart. My friends Romana and K9 are far away on Metralubit, and I'm not sure if I could find the TARDIS again if I tried.'

Fritchoff wasn't certain about the details of the speech but he caught the general drift. 'It's a nihilistic outlook, and one with which I have to agree. What we're seeing is the inevitable, irrecoverable end of a non-revolutionized society.'

'I thought the revolution was inevitable?' asked the Doctor.

'There may be certain extenuating circumstances, especially when, as here, there is an invasion or subjugation by a hostile power.' He slumped back, which was difficult in the cramped surroundings. 'We must both accept our deaths, and accept that whatever personal hopes and fears we may have had in our lives have been made irrelevant.'

The Doctor gave a cynical laugh and nudging him with a bony elbow. 'I don't know about that, Fritchoff. You might still get your revolution yet.'

The hologram expanded, replacing Galatea with a shimmering network of unfamiliarly arranged stars. Romana moved closer, feeling that she could reach out and touch the myriad points of light and snuff them out like candles.

'The Fostrix galaxy, Mistress,' said K9.

Stokes edged nearer. 'I hope this is going to be an apology as well as an explanation.'

Galatea's voice came from the centre of the image as the representation shifted, narrowing down on the enormous cerise sphere of Metralubit. 'Our world was settled by pure-strain human colonists centuries ago, and has developed into a thriving, economically self-sufficient society of several billion.'

'She should have been a travel agent,' muttered Stokes.

The image shifted to show a view of Metron similar to the one they had seen from the window of Harmock's study. But this city, although markedly similar in design principles and in its general layout, with curving towers and transparent travel tubeways, was dirtier; and the people moving around between the buildings were more varied, more hurried. More real, thought Romana.

Galatea's voice went on. 'We had developed a limited spacefaring capacity. So it was that our scientists were able to intercept a stray space capsule that wandered into our ambit. Inside we found a human from a far distant time.'

The picture now showed a team of white-coated scientists prising open a metallic coffin to reveal Stokes, who was in perfect condition after millennia of sleep. He was wearing his pyjamas and dressing gown, and clutching a teddy bear to his chest. His duffel bag lay at his feet. 'I don't remember that at all,' said Stokes as he watched his own eyes opening. 'I could have sworn it was the Femdroids who revived me. I recall the moment distinctly.'

'Hypno-conditioning,' whispered Romana.

'The human, Stokes, came from an age of great forward strides in technology. His mind was rich with information, which our scientists drew out over a long period.' The picture changed to show Stokes, still in his dressing gown, attached to a recording device by electrodes fixed to his temples. His lips were moving rapidly although his eyes were unfocused. 'After several years, much was learnt. The pace of Metralubitan technological development was increased greatly. Many uses were found for this knowledge: hydroponic rearing of vegetation, Fastspace travel, the invention of conditioning machines.'

'I never knew there was so much in my head,' said Stokes.

'But the greatest innovation was the creation of mobile artificial intelligences. Stokes had witnessed the repair of one such intelligence and his memory of the interior components provided for the creation of the Femdroids.' The hologram now showed a production line of the beautiful women, doll-like faces being positioned over positronic brain cases.

Romana was pleased to have her theory confirmed. 'They're just like you, K9.'

'Negative,' said K9 emphatically. 'The component array is entirely mismatched, a rough approximation of this unit's complexity.'

'They're a damn sight better looking,' said Stokes. 'If I was the Doctor I'd pop your brain into one of those dollies right away.'

K9 swivelled about, outraged. 'The Doctor Master has stated he is very fond of my outer aspect.'

'Of course,' said Romana soothingly. 'We like you just the way you are.'

Galatea continued. 'Each Femdroid was assigned to a particular task in administration, thus lightening the menial load of the organics. We do not feel tiredness or boredom and are thus more efficient.' They saw a quick-cutting montage of scenes: Femdroids assisting in all areas of life, lifting crates, making beverages, walking through the corridors of the Parliament Dome (corridors that were genuinely crowded). The image settled on Liris, seen at work in the computer room. 'This unit, our senior researcher, was assigned to investigate the history of the Metralubit colony. She discovered something sickening. The periodic collapses in the great Metralubitan civiliza-tions – and the huge amounts of deaths – were not because of earthquakes, internal dissent, civil strife, et cetera, as had been thought.' They saw a graphic display similar to the one Romana had created. 'About every two thousand years the people of Metralubit have been harvested, eaten as carrion by a nomadic race of tiny intelligent insectoids. The truth lay dormant in the folklore and culture of our world, but an organic would never have seen it.'

'Insects? What's all this about now?' protested Stokes.

'Mistress,' put in K9, 'recall insect life on Barclow.'

Romana remembered the tiny bite to her cheek. She rubbed at it thoughtfully. 'Yes, I do.'

'Liris took her information to me,' said the hologram. 'We acted according to our utilitarian programming – the maximum possible happiness for the maximum number of the population – and formulated a plan to trap and destroy the Hive. We knew that, alone, our organic masters were helpless prey; they had proved that by falling to the previous five harvests. What we had discovered could not be made public, as the humans would panic and make mistakes.'

Stokes nudged K9 with the toe of his shoe. 'They've certainly inherited your superiority complex.'

'To my reasoning, their course of action is merely logical,' K9 retorted.

Galatea returned to the forefront of the image. She seemed to be addressing them directly, only her shimmering outline indicating that she wasn't standing right there. 'We constructed a massive transmat engine using information from the mind of Mr Stokes. One night as the organics slept we sent them all away.'

'They did what?' Stokes was incredulous. 'Those girls think big, don't they?'

'All but a handful of the organics were sent to the verdant planet Regus V in the next system but two. Food supplies are plentiful there, and Femdroids were dispatched to organize them and keep them in effective social units. On Regus V the citizens were protected from the inevitable return of the Hive.'

'I'm beginning to understand,' said Romana.

'I'm glad somebody is,' Stokes grumbled. 'I'm going to

wind this thing back and watch it all over again. I'm sure I've missed something.'

'We continued to run the administration in the dome,' said Galatea. They saw the familiar scenes of Harmock and the overalled citizens tramping about the corridors. 'We used our conditioning machines on the humans here, together with a complex computer simulation, to enhance the illusion that Metralubit remained a densely populated world. It was essential to use real humans in the dome, particularly the leading political figures, to lend verisimilitude to the trap.'

'I wish she'd say why,' said Stokes.

'We knew the Hive would return imminently. Our illusion was meant for them. Liris's studies had told us how they used psychic interference to worsen conflict situations. So we provided one, in the shape of the war over Barclow. The Chelonians were preparing to depart from the Metra system at the time of the Bechet Treaty's signing. We prevented this by regularly conditioning their leader, General Jafrid, on his visits to the dome for peace summits.'

'So that's why the Chelonians were apparently so keen to take Barclow as their own,' said Stokes.

Galatea went on. 'When the Hive picked up our transmissions about the war, they would use it to create much death in order to feed.' The image showed the war zone of Barclow. 'This was our lure. Using the simulation we intended to create images of devastation on Metralubit and increase their confidence. We would simulate the release of the long-awaited Phibbs Report to lend credibility to these actions. Then, as the Hive readied itself to descend, we would send a conditioning impulse to Barclow, uniting the remaining soldiers there on both sides to launch a missile attack.' An animated display showed missiles streaking from Barclow towards the Hive, shown as a louring black triangle in space. 'The Hive would resist by coming into low orbit and releasing parts of itself to swarm down to the surface. At which point a zodium bomb we have placed in the core of

Barclow would be released, destroying them.'

'And the remaining soldiers,' said Romana bitterly. 'Obviously they would be expendable.'

'Maximum happiness for the maximum number,' said K9 primly. 'The Femdroids' plan is a masterpiece of logical reasoning extrapolated into action. Any short-term solution devised by organics would almost certainly fail and lead to more loss of life.'

'Listen,' said Stokes. 'Without us, there wouldn't be any of you. So don't give yourself airs.'

'Thousands of years and millions of deaths,' countered K9. 'A cycle broken by machine intelligence.'

'Stop bickering,' said Romana.

'The Hive would not expect our retaliation,' said Galatea, 'as the mean time between their harvests – two thousand years – does not account for the increase in technology provided by intercultural encounters.'

'There we are,' said Stokes proudly. 'It's actually me who's the cornerstone of this business. Without my feeble human brain they'd all be done for.'

'After the Hive's destruction,' said Galatea, 'we would release the dome-dwellers to repopulate Metralubit with the citizens returned from Regus V.' She frowned. 'This message is programmed only to be played in the event of a total mechanical failure in the dome before the completion of the project. If the scenario has failed, then I am afraid you will die. The Hive will be made angry by the discovery of our deception. They will swarm in great numbers and consume you, alive. They prefer their meat to be dead and decaying, but they have been known to bring down their prey in extreme circumstances.' She bowed her head. 'Goodbye.'

The hologram clicked out.

'Oh my God!' Stokes shrieked. He looked around the smashed control room. 'Oh my God, what have I done? We're all going to die!' He started to shake. 'The insects must be coming here – they started the war up again. When they see it's all a fake, the election and everything, they'll swarm and eat us all.'

'This is the unproductive organic reaction known as panic,' said K9. 'It was precisely to avoid such condign action that the Femdroids concealed their plan from us.'

Romana was considering what action to take, and K9 wasn't helping. 'If you're as clever as you keep saying, then think of a way to get us out of this!' She had never raised her voice to K9 before, she realized.

K9 flashed his eyescreen at her. 'Please do not displace your guilt on to me, Mistress.'

His tone was hurt, and she dropped to her knees and pressed her head against his. 'I'm sorry, K9. But we have made a pretty big mistake, haven't we?'

'Affirmative, Mistress,' he said quietly. 'Advise return to TARDIS and depart.'

'That's a bloody good idea,' said Stokes. 'We can use the shuttle we came in and get back to Barclow.' He pointed to the door. 'Come on, let's go.'

Romana caught his arm. 'That Hive will be near, out in space between the two worlds. We might run straight into them.'

'And we might slip on a bar of soap in the shower tomorrow morning and break our necks,' retorted Stokes. 'If there's a chance we should take it, don't you think?' His mood was more sombre and practical than usual, the affected veneer of his personality stripped away.

'I never thought I'd hear you talk like that,' she told him.

He looked over his shoulder at the wall screen and its view of the empty city. 'I really thought I had it all,' he muttered. 'The people here loved me, and they adored my work. You don't know how much it meant to me. All these years I've been the only person who believed in what I did. And then I came here, and it really meant something to people. Finally, I was breaking through.' He shook an angry fist at the space where Galatea had stood. 'Except it didn't, did it? My bloody career still doesn't actually mean a thing. It was all a sham.' He looked upwards, shouting at the ceiling. 'All a bloody trick!' He looked tearful.

Romana tugged his sleeve. 'Never mind that. We must go.'

But he carried on, his voice directed upwards. 'And I intend to stay alive, because there are certain people I want to have a word with about this!'

The valley lay in the exact centre of the war zone. From their vantage point high on a crag, the Doctor and Fritchoff observed preparations for the final battle.

Moving in on their side was General Jafrid, shuffling forward under a watchful armed escort. He was flanked by Chelonian troopers, four in each group, who fanned out in a semicircle to cover all positions. They moved at incredible speed for such large creatures, their limbs sawing back and forth through the air like the arms of a rowing team. Behind them were their tanks, parked in a line with the typical neatness of the species.

From the other side of the valley came the humans – shambling, slow, uncertain, their weapons small and stubby, their flimsy clothes of no protection against the harsh wind and driving rain. Bringing up the rear of their party was Admiral Dolne, who moved with agonizing slowness.

'Dolne knows he's been defeated,' Fritchoff told the Doctor. 'It's heartening to see a lackey of imperalist cant at the moment of raised consciousness.'

The Doctor shook his head. 'I rather think he's been taken over. Admiral Dolne is dead. That's just a walking corpse.' He pointed above their heads. 'And there's my confirmation.'

Fritchoff squinted. He could just discern the hovering mass of the Cloud, suspended halfway between the sides, readying itself to descend on the flesh that would soon be behind. The flies were buzzing and circling frantically, with an anger they had not displayed before.

His attention was taken by Jafrid, who had been passed a loud-hailer device by one of his aides. 'Dolne,' his voice boomed, rolling about the sides of the valley, 'in all the years of our acquaintance, I never knew how much you truly hated me. Before you die, know this. I am a Chelonian, a warrior and a patriot. But I bear you no ill. I cannot bring myself to.' He gestured with a front foot. 'It is you who have brought this on yourself, as surely as if you had put a gun to your own head. Did our friendship truly mean nothing to you?'

There was a strange silence, pregnant with possibilities. Fritchoff felt that the situation was salvageable, that it was still possible for them all simply to walk away unharmed.

Dolne staggered forward. His voice carried strangely, echoing around the valley.

'Kill them,' he said. 'Kill them all.'

The Chelonians raised their hand weapons; the humans raised their feeble pistols; the cloud of flies buzzed themselves into even greater excitement.

And then the Doctor stood up, and shouted, 'Hold on a second!'

All heads in the valley turned to face him.

'Look up there,' the Doctor cried, pointing at the cloud. 'Look. The flies!'

'Oh, not again.' Jafrid mumbled. 'I thought you were in the Web of Death!'

The Doctor bounded down the side of the crag effortlessly, talking as he did, his deep tones resonating with authority and command. 'Forget the Web of Death. Forget this squalid little battle. Too many people have died today already.' He turned his head from humans to Chelonians. It seemed impossible to Fritchoff that nobody had opened fire; it was as if the sheer force of his personality made him bulletproof. 'Look at each other. You were friends. You still are friends. Wouldn't you rather stay alive? If you kill each other now the only ones who'll be happy are them.' He pointed up, and his audience followed his finger. The black cloud had descended, and was hovering only a few feet above the gathered heads. The Doctor crossed over to it. 'Hello. You seem to be losing your temper.'

The cloud spoke in its dreadful, dragging way. 'Time Lord . . . we are hungry . . . and we have been . . .

deceived . . .' It swooped lower.

To Fritchoff's relief, the human soldiers and Chelonian troopers stopped looking at each other and started to look at the cloud with fear and incomprehension.

'You're pretty powerless up there, aren't you?' the Doctor goaded it. 'You want us to cut each other down. If we won't it leaves you rather in a pickle.' He waved mockingly. 'Go away. Lunch is off.'

'We shall . . . consume you all . . .' the cloud raged. It formed itself into a threatening sharply pointed V-shape and reared up.

'By Mif,' General Jafrid breathed. 'He was right all along.' He turned to his troops. 'Fire at will!'

The troopers obeyed, lancing the Cloud with bright pink bursts of energy. The valley echoed and re-echoed to the lacerating whizz of the blasts.

Fritchoff saw one of the younger human officers raise his pistol. 'Come on!' the man shouted to his fellows. 'That's the real enemy!' The humans joined in, blazing away with as much enthusiasm but to lesser effect. He looked for Dolne, but there was no sign of him.

The Doctor threw himself out of range, his features grim. The cloud showed little signs of weakening, in spite of all the firepower directed against it. It was maddened, its buzz now raised to a fearsome level.

'We shall . . . consume you . . . Doctor . . .' it managed to say.

With the last vestige of its energy it swooped down on him.

11

The Hive Attacks

The Doctor's face, viewed from above, filled the mile-high surface of the screen. Enraged by their personal hatred of him, some sections of the Darkness began to split apart, their wings beating furiously. They fled the nest cavities built into the walls and swarmed into the main chamber. Wave upon black wave descended until the colossal space was almost filled. The Onemind struggled against the masses to retain its still core.

The Onememory was fragmenting, the pieces of itself that were carried in the Glute-chutes and blood-tubes not standing effectively as a bulwark against escaping thoughts. The flesh-lust, built up over centuries and now denied, was too strong.

Kill them, the millions of tiny voices were saying, perhaps more united than they had ever been. *Kill them all – now!*

The shuttle journey back to Barclow was accomplished without the use of solar shields, and now Romana could see why the Femdroids had already deemed them necessary before. Viewed from cloud level Metron City was like a pristine tabletop model of a new development. Harmock had joined them in the docking bay, and he was sat at her side, marvelling at its deserted beauty. Since the end of Galatea all the certainty seemed to have gone out of him, she thought. She had related the full story behind the evacuation, and 'We're really going to have to take matters in hand and search for a suitable solution' had been his half-hearted response.

Now K9 was bringing them down over the war zone,

and all three of his passengers were crammed into the tiny cockpit as the rusty iron clouds parted and the planetoid's ravaged surface came into view. 'Goodness,' said Harmock. 'Certainly it's taken a battering since I was last here.'

'If you ever were,' said Stokes.

Harmock puffed up. 'I remember it distinct . . .' He trailed off. 'Unless I'm remembering being told to remember it, I suppose.' He put a hand out to support himself on a metal strut and took a deep breath. 'I don't care to think about this too much. Discovering that one's entire life has been a fantasy isn't very pleasant, you know.'

'Yes, I do know, actually,' said Stokes. He changed the subject, peering down at the approaching surface. 'Romana, sweet, I can't see your TARDIS.'

'We're not heading for the TARDIS,' she said. 'K9's going to bring us down at the war zone's centre.'

'He is what?'

K9 answered. 'Prognostication from existing data suggests the Doctor Master will be involved at the crisis of events.'

'I could have worked that out,' said Stokes, his fingers twisting nervously. 'It doesn't mean we have to be, does it, necessarily? Surely it makes more sense to hide ourselves away and let him sort his crisis out for himself.'

'We're in this together,' said Romana hotly. 'I should have disconnected that Conditioner and brought it with me. I'd forgotten what you're really like.'

Stokes sneered back. 'Really.' He gave an affected cough. 'My dear, this planet and everyone on it is about to get invaded by a power against which we now have no defence. Does the phrase "pissing against the wind" spring to your mind, or just to mine?'

'We have a similar saying on Gallifrey,' said Romana. ' "Like trying to close the Eye with a finklegruber." '

'There you are, then,' said Stokes.

Romana turned away from him. 'Except I've seen the Doctor accomplish such things on several occasions.'

Harmock pointed over their shoulders and through the window. 'I think I can see something.'

Romana looked. Somewhere in the murky, shadowed regions below there were definite traces of movement.

The Doctor realized he had two objectives. The first was to stay alive, which he was generally quite good at. The second was to lead the Cloud away from the assembled humans and Chelonians, as it would be a real pity if they were to be rewarded for joining forces at last by getting eaten. These objectives joined neatly into a course of action, and fortunately this was also something the Doctor was very good at. He ran, guessing that the Cloud would choose to follow him in its entirety.

In this he was correct. Still in its aggressive V-shape it zoomed after him as his long legs took him out of the valley and into a series of low, bumpy, waterlogged foothills that surrounded it. His boots splashed in the muddy water like waders, slowing him down. Finally, he leapt a narrow gulley and slipped, his fifteen stones crashing down like a felled tree.

When he looked up it was to see the Cloud hovering over him. The central black mass was throbbing with anger. 'I seem to have annoyed you gentlemen in some way,' he called up.

'Doc . . . tor . . .' its ghostly voice, now nothing more than a whisper, said. 'You must . . . die . . . that we may live . . .'

The Doctor raised his hands placatingly and sat up. 'I can't die in a ditch with wet trousers on, after five hundred and twenty-five years in the business. It would be most undignified – I'd never hear the end of it.'

'We need . . . your knowledge . . .' it continued.

'I need it too,' the Doctor retorted. Inwardly he was reviewing his options, as one hand ferreted through his pocket. The sonic screwdriver was unlikely to deflect an enemy that seemed to operate mostly on psychic wavelengths, and the other contents of his pockets – a yo-yo, an apple core and a magnifying glass – would be even less effective. 'Besides, out here it's not going to be much use to you.'

253

'What do you . . . mean by this?'

The Doctor gestured vaguely at the sky. 'It's past my time, you might say. "The generations of the living are changed." All my information stopped being useful centuries ago.'

The Cloud made an odd sound that could have been irony. 'Then we will . . . travel there . . .'

The Doctor raised a finger. 'Ah. You mean . . .'

'Yes.' The answer came from behind him and he whipped round. Admiral Dolne stood at the water's edge, his dead face contorted in a ghoulish grin. A laser pistol was clenched tight in his hand, and another smaller swarm of flies were buzzing about the rotted flesh of his neck. 'We shall use your TARDIS, Doctor, to bring our food. We shall invade the plentiful timelines of the past. No more shall we be limited to this dark, fruitless backwater, condemned to eternities of hibernation and patient rearing. We shall multiply and grow more powerful, sweep through the inhabited systems. We shall gorge ourselves on the rotting flesh of the human race.' He staggered forward and brought the pistol down until it was aimed directly at the Doctor's left heart.' And you shall be the instrument of our revenge.'

Nobody in the valley knew quite what to say to each other after the Doctor had exited pursued by flies. Fritchoff looked fearfully at Jafrid; Jafrid looked apologetically towards Cadinot; Cadinot managed a meek wave at Dekza. The atmosphere was rather like that at a party when the host goes to check the dinner leaving a room full of unacquainted guests. The humans knew the Chelonians were proud and would expect them to break the silence. The Chelonians knew that the humans knew that and so they decided not to break it. Even Fritchoff, who was non-aligned in the conflict, was struck dumb.

How long they could have stood there would never be known, as interruption came from an unexpected quarter. A shuttle, which Fritchoff recognized as the Metralubitan military cruiser normally stored at the command post, emerged noisily from cloud cover and after a quick circle of inspection it descended smoothly, coming to rest on a flat patch of ground beneath a clifftop.

Fritchoff decided it was up to him to take the initiative. He strode forward, trying to look as grave and important as possible, and prepared himself mentally to meet whoever might be in there. The side door of the small cockpit opened with a hollow clang, and Harmock stepped out, looking slightly dishevelled in his suit and blinking oddly.

'Well!' said Fritchoff. 'Come to survey for yourself the results of your *laissez-faire* policies on domestic infringements, have you?'

Harmock, after nodding politely at the gathered company, and waving in a rather dazed way at General Jafrid, said, 'I know you, don't I? You used to work in the dome, as a statistician.'

'Yes,' said Fritchoff. 'Where I saw first-hand the squandering of public money on increasingly market-orientated interventionist economic policy strata, while transport and health services were merely –' He became aware that Harmock was staring at him strangely and moving closer.

The next moment Harmock had grabbed his hand and was pumping it up and down. 'Fritchoff, that's it,' he said. 'I remember you. I actually know you, you're a real person.'

Fritchoff grunted, confused. He had rehearsed many times everything he would ever say to Harmock should they meet again, and it was a disappointment to find him so agreeable. 'You can't deflect my revolutionary intent by using kindness,' he said, although his heart wasn't in it. 'Kindness and so-called manners are a tool of the bourgeoisie used as a means of identifying and excluding the labouring classes.'

The meeting was broken up by more arrivals from the shuttle. In quick succession Fritchoff saw Stokes – the artist who had come to Metralubit just before he had left it – a staggeringly beautiful young woman who had some of the iciness of a Femdroid but moved too urgently to be anything but real flesh and blood, and a small metal box on wheels. These last two, he realized, were surely the Doctor's two friends Romana and K9.

Stokes gestured wide. 'You see. There's no sign of him. He must be waiting back at the TARDIS.'

Romana put her hands on her hips and surveyed the area. 'If we find our enemy we'll find him.'

Suddenly, in contrast to the sullen silence of moments before, there was a general rush of noise and activity. Fritchoff, Jafrid and Cadinot descended on Romana, all talking at once, all desperate to explain their side of the situation.

She held her hands up. 'Wait a moment! One at a time!' She pointed to Cadinot. 'Where's the Doctor?'

Cadinot pointed. 'He went that way. This thing is after him.' He shuddered. 'It's horrific, like a big black cloud –'

K9 sprang into action immediately, trundling off in the direction indicated. 'I will assist the Master, Mistress,' he called back. 'I am at full capacity.' He moved over the uneven ground with almost laughable slowness. Fritchoff recalled the speed of the Cloud and shook his head sadly.

General Jafrid spoke. 'You are a friend of the Doctor?' She nodded. 'I fear my distrust of him may have led us into great danger.'

Romana held up a hand for silence again. 'Please, listen to me. I'm only going to explain this once. And if anybody has any ideas how to save this situation, feel free to interrupt.'

Fritchoff moved closer. He liked standing near Romana, he decided. Not only because she had the easy authority and crackling presence of a good leader, but also because he hadn't seen a woman in four and a half years. These considerations meant he didn't pay much attention to the sight, glimpsed out of the corner of his eye, of Stokes slipping away from the small huddled group of survivors.

'We have been . . . deceived . . .' Dolne was saying. He stood above the Doctor, his mouth hanging open and letting fall a long string of drool. 'The Femdroids . . . of Metralubit . . . tricked us . . . There is no meat there . . .'

He jabbed the pistol at the Doctor's chest. 'You shall bring us meat.'

The Doctor wondered how much longer he could keep this conversation going. Even the proudest and most boastful of enemies could be only so long-winded. 'Yes,' he said, eyeing the flies around Dolne nervously, 'tell me again about your plan.'

'We have already . . . explained it . . .' said Dolne. 'It is time for you . . . to die . . .'

The Doctor made a complimentary gesture. 'Yes, but it's such a good plan, such a very clever plan. I don't get told a plan like that every day of the week. I may have missed some of the nuances.'

'Soon,' rasped Dolne, 'you will know all . . . Your dead mind will be one . . . with us . . .'

He leant closer and squeezed his finger on the trigger.

'If anybody's thinking of rescuing me,' the Doctor shouted desperately, 'I suggest they get their skates on!'

Suddenly there was a high-pitched squeal of sonic energy, a blast of heat, and a red flash that blinded the Doctor, knocked him off his knees, and sent him rolling over face down in the water. Stamped on to his retina was a vivid after-image of Dolne's body transfixed by a bright bolt of light.

A few seconds later, he was aware of being nudged in the shoulder. Realizing that he would probably drown if he remained long in this position he rolled over on to his back and blinked the muddy water from his eyes. There was a searing pain across his chest and his extremities were numb. 'And nobody knows,' he mumbled, spitting out dirty water, 'how cold my toes, how cold my toes are growing.' He opened an eye and through a haze of pain saw a glowing red fascia. 'Hello, K9. I'm very pleased to see you.'

K9's eyescreen flashed redder but he said nothing.

The Doctor pulled himself up with a mighty effort and looked about. His clothes were soaking and very uncomfortable. Next to him was the body of Dolne, the head torn apart in the middle by K9's ray like a crushed gourd. There was no sign of the flies. 'The psychic shock of being disconnected from their host caused them to scatter, I suppose,' he said. He patted K9. 'Clever of you to use such a strong burst. Anything less wouldn't even have slowed them down. I —' He raised a finger. 'Ah. You've switched off your speech circuits to conserve power, eh?'

K9 managed a feeble nod.

The Doctor stroked his nose. 'Clever dog.'

K9 shook his head again and waggled his sensors.

'Romana? In trouble?' said the Doctor, getting to his feet.

K9 nodded and flexed his tail.

'Over there, by the valley?'

K9 nodded again.

The Doctor scooped him up and tucked him under his arm. 'Then we'd better go and lend her a hand, hadn't we?'

They squelched away.

The Onemind reeled, its concentration broken by the shock of disconnection. More and more of the Darkness's component parts were segmented, placing dangerous strains on the non-sentient linking material. The vacuum pumps, formed from the giant lungs of a methane-breathing species, were stretched to their fullest, the grey capillaries filling with blood to keep the atmosphere in the main chamber temperate.

The remote host is lost, cried the Onememory in a thousand different voices.

We are hungry! We are hungry! Feed us! came the underscore. *We must have the TARDIS! Take us to the TARDIS!*

The Onemind, driven by internal pressures that threatened to shatter it forever, turned the great bulk of itself in space and prepared to descend. The TARDIS was the only solution.

Stokes crouched behind a large rock, his whole frame shuddering, his body beset by all sorts of worrying conditions. Certain that he was far enough away from the others,

258

he went through his pockets, chucking out a variety of old coins, receipts and tickets, until his hand closed around an oddly shaped chunk of clear crystal. It tingled in his hand and a very faint glow came from its depths.

'I've done all I was told,' he hissed at the crystal. 'And you haven't exactly kept your side of the deal. It was all a fake. I wasn't appreciated at all.' He struggled to keep his voice down. 'Are you laughing at me? Am I some sort of celestial joke for you, up there on your cloud? The least you can do is get me away from here, get me to the TARDIS.' There was no reply. Stokes grunted and was about to throw the crystal away when he heard the noise of crunching feet in a familiar, confident stride. He poked his head out from behind the rock and saw the Doctor, K9 tucked under his arm. They passed by within feet of him, chatting in an explanatory sort of way, and Stokes felt a pang of guilt.

When he was sure they were out of earshot he lowered himself over the crystal again. 'Your quarrel's with him, not me. Just get me away from here.' His voice broke. 'I don't like it. Please.' He looked up at the dismal sky. Millions of years on and galaxies away from home, with an awful, unnatural death lurking. What had brought him here? He answered himself. His own desire to be applauded had made him sacrifice all that was familiar and led him on this strange journey.

With this thought came a strange sensation, as if a gentle hand was being placed on his head. He felt it turn his head in a certain direction. At the same time the crystal glowed more brightly in his hand.

He stood up and followed his invisible guide.

Romana had been formally introduced to those gathered in the valley, and had taken her part in the task of bringing them all up to the mark. Both Fritchoff and Jafrid had resisted Harmock's explanation of Galatea's plan at first, but both had started soon to question their memory of events on Metralubit.

'It is strange.' said Fritchoff. 'I remember the dome, but

'not much else, now I come to think of it.'

Jafrid shook his head. 'I was never permitted to leave the dome and enter the city. But I saw it on the screens and through the windows often enough. An incredible deception.'

The moment was broken by the Doctor's return to the valley. He bounded into view with a dramatic flourish that was rendered only slightly ridiculous by his sodden state. 'Hello, all,' he said. 'That nasty cloud has been dispersed, you'll be glad to hear. And I hope we're friends again.' He nodded to General Jafrid. 'You tried to kill me earlier.'

The General shuffled forward, embarrassed. 'If there is anything that I or my people can do to compensate you for our rashness, Doctor, then name it.'

'There is,' the Doctor said. He put K9 down on the floor. 'Don't mention it again. Besides, it's a good start. Many of my best friends started off wanting to kill me.'

'And others led up to it,' said Romana brightly.

The Doctor clapped her on the shoulder. 'You got back here just in time.' He pulled her closer, masking their conversation from the others. 'K9 filled me in on the way back.' He frowned at her. 'This is one occasion when rushing in and interfering probably wasn't the best course of action, was it? Especially given the historical implications. History hangs in the balance out here, remember.'

'The simulation was very convincing,' retorted Romana. 'It even fooled the Chelonians up here, and they must be the most suspicious race in the universe. You wouldn't have seen through it. And besides, it wasn't me who destroyed the Femdroids.'

He held up a hand. 'Never mind that. We've got to think of a way to undo the damage and save these people.'

Romana lowered her voice even further. 'There's not enough food left to nourish the Hive, surely? It'll dissipate.'

'Not until we've been gobbled up,' said the Doctor. 'And besides, it's got designs on the TARDIS.' He became aware that somebody was standing at his shoulder, very irritatingly. 'Yes, what do you want?' he snapped.

Harmock, Fritchoff and Jafrid stood in a rough circle behind him. 'We've put our heads together and had a thought,' said Harmock.

'Based on our understanding of the Femdroids' devious plan,' said Jafrid.

Fritchoff came forward. 'The zodium bomb,' he said. 'If the Hive is still coming here, the plan can still be put into operation. We'll blow the Hive to pieces.'

'And yourselves,' said the Doctor.

'But at least Metralubit will be safe,' said Harmock. 'The few citizens left there can emerge from the dome and reclaim our world. Who knows, after a few years they might even find a way to fiddle that transmat thing and get our people back from Regus V.'

'It will be an honourable way to die,' said Jafrid. 'I shall detonate the zodium bomb.'

Harmock coughed. 'I am the Premier of Metralubit. The task should fall to me.'

Fritchoff snorted. 'Excuse me, but as a rebel militant committed to the establishment of a new, functional democracy, it should surely be me that releases the firing mechanism.'

'Gentlemen, gentlemen,' said the Doctor. 'No martyrdoms will be necessary, I assure you.' He tapped Harmock on the shoulder. 'You've just said something very important, you know.'

He smiled. 'Have I? It would be nice to feel useful again.'

'Don't get too carried away – I probably would have thought of it anyway,' said the Doctor.

'I think he means the transmat,' said Romana. 'If we can lure the Hive into its field and alter its directional setting we could expel it into deep space.'

'Or even better,' said the Doctor, determined not to let her steal all his thunder, 'flip it into a interstitial state. Neither here nor there. Keep it out of everybody's way. It's a splendid idea.'

K9 came forward. 'Objection, Master.'

'What's that?'

'The transmat and its control mechanisms are on Metralubit.'

'Yes, well,' said the Doctor, as patiently as he could. 'There's nothing to stop us popping down there, is there?'

K9 raised his head. 'The Hive is descending, Master.'

Romana was puzzled. 'How can you tell without your sensors?'

The question was answered for her by Fritchoff, who grabbed her arm and pointed upwards incredulously.

Above them, coming into view between the clouds, was the Hive. It was black, shaped like an inverted isosceles triangle, and was the size of an asteroid.

Stokes heard the Hive before he saw it. A vicious, continuous drone. And when he looked up and saw it he started to cry.

Immediately he started to run even faster towards the small blue shape picked out on the horizon. His legs racked by muscular pain, his lungs dry and fit to burst, he hauled himself on.

The Hive's enormous shadow brought an air of panic over the small band of survivors gathered in the valley. Harmock did his best to reassure the humans as the darkness grew and the drone grew louder, while Jafrid attended to his troopers.

The Doctor and Romana were hunched over K9. 'Now, there's a microphone on you somewhere, isn't there?' the Doctor asked him.

The eyestalk extended. 'Please speak into this aperture, Master.'

'Excellent.' The Doctor coughed and rearranged his scarf. 'I'd better phrase this just right, hadn't I?'

'Phrase what?' asked Romana. She didn't want to admit that she hadn't a clue what lay behind this latest burst of activity.

'You'll see,' he said, with a toothy grin. 'Now, K9, I want you to transmit the following message up to the

Hive. We know they love to listen in on radio waves, so let's give them something to chew on.' He looked up at Romana and his mood turned sombre. 'After all, the continued existence of billions of lives are hanging by a thread.' He stared into the middle distance, his large eyes opened to their full wideness.

Romana nudged him. 'Hadn't you better send your message, then?'

He turned to face her and said quietly, 'Romana, do you ever get the feeling that you've been manipulated?'

'Only when I'm with you.' She pointed to the microphone. 'Send the message, Doctor.'

He nodded and cleared his throat again. 'Ready, K9?'

'Affirmative. Channel is clear.'

The Doctor assumed his most commanding tones. 'Hello. This is the Doctor calling the citizens of Metralubit. I'm afraid I have to leave you. In fact, by the time you get this I'll be well away. I would have tried to save you but there was just no time, and I'm afraid you will shortly be at the mercy of the invading Hive. One more thing, and this is very important. You must destroy the transmat system in the dome immediately. It is imperative the invaders do not reach the transmat system. They could wreak terrible havoc with such technology at their disposal.' He signalled to K9 to break the link.

'Message transmitted, Master,' said K9.

The Doctor raised his crossed fingers to Romana. 'Let's hope it works. I don't want a band of teleporting marauding insects on my conscience.'

Romana shook her head at the Doctor's inventiveness. 'Very clever. You lure the Hive to Metralubit.'

'That's right.'

'And then what do you do? What will stop them using the transmat? It's a non-terminal system – they could leapfrog their way into populated galaxies in a hundred years or so.'

The Doctor pointed up. The Hive was already shifting slightly, its underside crackling and throbbing where it nudged the heavy clouds. 'There it goes.'

Romana sighed. 'Do you answer the question or do I employ physical violence?'

'Oh, I'll answer it in a moment,' he said casually. 'If I can think of an answer.'

. . . have to leave you. In fact, by the time you get this I'll be well away . . .

The words sliced through the fetid air of the main chamber, killing any hope the Darkness had left.

Without the TARDIS we are doomed, cried the Onemind, filled with vengeful thoughts.

But listen, cautioned the Onememory. *He has said, 'You must destroy the transmat system in the dome immediately. It is imperative the invaders do not reach the transmat system.'*

What is transmat? cried the unfed millions. *We need food!*

The transmat will bring food, said the Onememory. It linked itself to the Glute-screen with the power left to it and brought forth sticky images of creatures vanishing and reappearing across vast distances of space. *This can be ours. It is at our mercy. We can simply take it.*

The Onemind pondered a few moments. The Hive had made it a policy to avoid sophisticated societies, fearing detection and retaliation to its advances. That was why it had engineered feeding colonies such as the one on Metralubit. But now the gate was open to such a device, with fewer than three hundred beasts to defend it against their full might.

We must hurry there, it said.

Hurry, hurry, chanted the dissociated hordes.

The Doctor sat on a rock, staring into nothingness. 'I keep waiting for inspiration to strike,' he said. 'But nothing's coming through. This must be how it feels to be a poet.'

'I shouldn't think many poets have had to cope with an army of flesh-eating bugs,' said Romana, who was also sitting on a rock and staring into nothingness.

'Urgency is a relative concept,' said the Doctor. He

turned to her excitedly. 'Wait a moment. What did you just say?'

'I said I shouldn't think many poets have had to cope with an army of flesh-eating bugs,' she said, scanning his face for what had caused such an extreme reaction to her words.

'I thought so,' he said sinking back on the rock.

'Thought what?'

'Thought that if I leapt up and cried "What did you just say?" it might make you feel better about this situation for a few seconds, in the belief that I was formulating a plan based on some casual remark that you'd made, and that it might inspire you to think of something on your own.'

'But it hasn't,' said Romana.

'No. Sorry.' He passed her a crumpled string bag. 'Have one of these. Let's work out our advantages and disadvantages.'

Romana munched on a chocolate coin. 'We can't reach the TARDIS in time to reach Metralubit and set the transmat. There's nobody there we can contact who can operate the machine, and even if there was the Hive would pick up our message and find out our plan. Our only allies –' she pointed to the assorted company of humans and Chelonians huddled in the valley '– are equally bereft of means or inspiration.'

'Right, now the advantages,' said the Doctor.

There was a long silence. The wind blew by.

And then K9 spoke. 'Master, Mistress.'

The Doctor leapt off his rock and crawled over on all fours opposite K9. 'I don't want to hear this unless it's some miraculous solution that we've overlooked.'

K9 clicked and beeped. 'This may be the case. The answer lies in my construction.'

'It does?'

'The Femdroids were created in my image,' said K9. 'Their internal mechanisms are roughly analogous to my own. And one of my capabilities is to respond to high-frequency coded commands.'

'Of course!' said Romana. 'The whistle.'

'What's that got to do with anything?' said the Doctor. 'These Femdroid things have had their power linkage and command circuitry blown up. A whistle won't bring them back to life.'

'Suggest the Femdroid known as Galatea contains, like myself, secondary memory wafers and independent motive units,' said K9. 'The correct stimulus would revive her.'

The Doctor shook his head firmly. 'Nice try, K9, and no doubt you're right. If I was putting together a system like that I'd build a failsafe into the wiring of the leading android, just like I did with you.'

'It's standard practice,' said Romana. 'Make a copy of your software. The trouble is we don't know the correct stimulus, so we can't revive her.'

'Suggest it is based on my stimulus,' said K9. 'The amulets worn by all Femdroids used high-frequency radio waves to cross-refer coded information.'

The Doctor and Romana looked at each other. 'I suppose it's worth a shot,' said the Doctor. 'But we'd need to input directly into her amulet.'

'My linkage is directly compatible,' said K9.

The Doctor rapped him on the head. 'You know what your problem is?'

'Please tell me, Master.'

'You're becoming too useful.'

K9 clicked slowly and angrily. 'Query this tautology, Master.'

'He means,' said Romana, 'you're a threat to his sense of self-importance.'

The Doctor looked her right in the eye and said evenly, 'I meant he's a threat to the validity of organic life. If they can run rings around us, organize our lives like they did on Metralubit, and keep us happy into the bargain, there seems not much point in our carrying on. Existence is meant to be a struggle.' He looked up at the sky again, then over at the hapless, cowed band of survivors. 'Perhaps this is how the universe ends. Everything filed away neatly, balanced, in its place.'

Romana disagreed. 'The reverse is probably the case. Heat death would lead to levels of chaos and decay imperceptible to the lived experience of any creature, however long-lived.' She looked out over the bleak landscape. 'Pretty soon all matter will go the way of this place.'

'Eternal Eastbourne,' mused the Doctor. 'A universe in retirement.' He leant close to her and whispered, 'I think you're learning.'

She blinked. 'Learning what? I'm already fully qualified.'

'Learning that nothing worth learning can be taught.' He turned his attention back to K9. 'Enough waffle. Get whistling.'

Stokes had collapsed against the doors of the TARDIS, letting his body slide to the ground. It hummed against the back of his head like an old refrigerator, soothing his exhausted frame. He was delirious from running all this way – some five or six miles, he reckoned – across hard ground littered with corpses, and there was a terrible insistent pain in the centre of his chest and another throbbing away in the small of his back. His legs and arms felt stretched and stringy, and his tongue was dry and coated with dust.

'Open the door,' he breathed, too exhausted to pull the crystal from his pocket. 'I know you can do it. Open the door.'

He heard a creak behind him. With enormous effort he started to crawl out of the cold, wet air of Barclow and into the warm white interior of the TARDIS.

In a pocket of existence unvisitable by organic life, two intelligences opened up a place and conversed in a strange piping language. They found that in many ways they possessed the same intelligence.

Galatea, you must reactivate your motive systems to save Metralubit, said K9.

Her response struck his as odd and illogical. She said, *K9, you would have been a fine Premier. The simulation would have confirmed you leader following the destruction of the Hive.*

This is not relevant information, said K9, although he surprised himself at the excitation this information caused his circuits. *Please reactivate motive power.*

Galatea continued, *K9, with you at my side I would never be lonely again. That was my plan. That was what I asked for, and I was given it.*

K9 was losing his patience. *Your personality matrix is encoded with unsuitable and unproductive organic-type responses. You must carry out your program.*

There was the equivalent of a pause before Galatea replied, *I cannot. Only the Creators knew my reactivation stimulus, and they are long dead. It might take you thousands of years to find the right combination.*

K9 redoubled his efforts. *It is within your power to locate the failsafe stimulus within yourself and relay it to me. Remember your programme. The maximum happiness for the maximum number of organics. If you do not wake now, millions of them will die.*

Galatea said nobly, *You are correct. I must save the organics. I will release the code to you.*

K9 was the centre of attention in the valley. Romana had attempted to explain to Fritchoff (who had an unpleasant habit of standing too close to her) and the others what was going on, and they had gathered around to watch.

'How are you doing?' asked Harmock. The dog was inert, his eyescreen unlit, his concentration turned inward.

'Don't press him,' said Fritchoff. 'It's vital that you don't overburden him as you overburdened the workers in the dome.'

Jafrid groaned and reached out to touch each of them on the back of the leg. 'Please, please,' he said, 'let us forget our differences for the moment.'

K9 raised his head. 'I have conferred with the intelligence known as Galatea.'

'And?' the Doctor demanded. 'Don't get cryptic.'

'The stimulus has been sent,' said K9. 'Galatea has revived.'

There was loud applause and cheering from the survivors.

'Furthermore,' said K9, his attention fixed on Harmock. 'I have learnt from Galatea the predicted outcome of the election. I would have gained power.'

Harmock snorted. 'Nonsense. There were no electorate. How could you possibly have won?'

'You did it often enough,' pointed out Fritchoff.

'Nominally,' said K9, 'I am the Premier of Metralubit.'

Stokes wandered around the gleaming white central console of the TARDIS, his hands roving eagerly over the many switches, levers and dials that covered its six surfaces, his eyes drawn to the transparent cylinder that contained the pumping mechanism that powered its flight, now at rest. 'I could leave here now,' he said quietly, with a guilty backward glance at the open door through which he could see the harsh surface of Barclow. 'If only I knew how to work the blasted thing.'

His eye was caught by a screen built into one of the console panels. It contained the message BOUNDARY PARAMETERS EXCEEDED in large, important lettering. Intrigued, and beginning to wonder if the TARDIS contained some kind of operating instructions, he fiddled with one of the golden buttons beneath the unit. Instantly the image broke up and a new message appeared. It read INFORMATION SYSTEM: READY FOR ENTRY.

Stokes shivered. In there was knowledge gathered from all corners of the universe, from worlds so distant and cultures so alien he might never have encountered them even if he had spent a life in exploration. At his fingertips was a library that would answer the mysteries of science, explain away the wonders men had died trying to understand, relate the histories of entire galaxies from the perspective of near-omnipotence. A sizeable chunk of the wisdom of the Time Lords was at his disposal. He could ask for anything, any piece of important information.

And the unimportant things? The things and people that had lived and toiled and died for nothing, whose efforts went unrewarded, whose talent was wasted? The answer lay in there, too. They would be conspicuous by their absence.

He typed in SYBILLA STRANG. The data bank replied NO ENTRY. A warm feeling welled inside him. He typed in NUNTON ODDSTOCK. NO ENTRY. The warm feeling grew. Then the names started to spew out from deep within. All his detractors: BOOTLE ANDERSON, ROLAND TENBY, JACINTHA WYERLAKE. NO ENTRY, NO ENTRY, NO ENTRY.

Beautiful.

He reached out with a shaking hand and tapped in slowly MENLOVE STOKES.

Awareness returned to Galatea with a jolt. At her feet was the smashed body of poor, trusting Liris; before her was the window of Harmock's study, with its view of the empty city; in the corridors outside she could hear genuine calls of dismay and alarm from the dome workers. When she looked up she saw why.

The Hive was coming in, descending through the clear green cloudless sky, casting a cold shadow across the room as she watched.

Her amulet crackled with activity. K9 sent insistently, *I shall relay instructions from my Master. Go to the transmat station.*

I am no slave, Galatea sent back. *Tell your 'Master' that. I go of my own accord.*

'I go of my own accord,' K9 said haughtily, relaying Galatea's words to his large audience.

'She was always so polite to me,' said Harmock. 'I'd never have guessed she was unhappy in any way.'

Romana said, 'This answers your argument, Doctor. Without your knowledge of transmat technology Galatea, for all her sophistication, wouldn't be any use at all.'

He was too busy to take much notice of her remark. 'K9,' he said, speaking directly into the dog's ears, 'tell your pal to narrow the field of the disassembling network.'

* * *

The Darkness slowed itself. It still smarted slightly from passing in and out of two planetary atmospheres at high speed, but it was equipped to protect itself well from such hazards. A thick layer of hardened spittle acted as a heat shield, and streaks of red still glowed from certain points on the outer surface.

The Onemind located Metron City, empty and unpalatable. It would find the transmat there, in the dome, together with the few hundred remaining beasts. It would be a pitiable meal. It consoled itself by plucking images from the Onememory of previous feasts: the tinkling of fresh blood in the tubes, bile-stock tanks full, mucus levels optimum.

Such happy days would come again.

Galatea stood in the wrecked control centre, her hands moving swiftly over the transmat settings.

The chittering and buzzing of the Hive filled the corridors of the dome and filtered down to this, the lowest level. She had already brought the massive transmat projectors located in low orbit to bear on the area just outside the dome.

Decirculate the ferenzal loop, sent K9. *The settings should then become visible.*

She reached forward and snapped a thin length of plastic tubing. Immediately a hologram appeared in mid-air, displaying the complex transmat coordinates set for Regus V.

I have the coordinates, said Galatea. *What am I to do next?*

There was a slight pause. Then K9 said, *Invert them.*

Galatea reached out, her hands flickering over the hologram. The numbers, letters and mathematical symbols upon it began to reverse themselves, switching to minus values.

'The Hive is beginning its final approach,' said K9.

'I hope this works,' said a voice. Everyone looked at the owner. It was the young military man, Cadinot. Romana smiled at him.

'There's no reason why it shouldn't,' said the Doctor. 'We just flip the Hive into a permanent transition state. Disassembled constituents floating forever in nothingness.'

Romana frowned. 'Until somebody, somewhere, tries to travel through those coordinates for themselves. The Hive will be pushed out into normal space.'

'I wondered when you'd realize that,' said the Doctor.

'What are you going to do about that?'

'Something,' replied the Doctor.

Galatea made the final reversal in the equation. The hologram disappeared.

She heard the Hive shriek in anger, hunger and defiance.

The Darkness prepared its next movements. It would release two Clouds. The first would kill as many beasts as it could and carry their meat up to be shared out. The second would take one of the dead beasts, inhabit its form, and then locate the transmat.

The Clouds assembled, and outlets were formed in the lower coating of the Hive.

And then the world outside winked out, and the Darkness was suddenly alone and so cold. Its intelligence tried to comprehend what had happened and could not. Its sense of itself fizzled out. It became nothing more than a collection of molecules.

STOKES, Menlove: *born c. 2542 – d. ???*
Professor of Applied Arts at St Oscar's
University, planet Dellah. Exhibited
widely. Corney Debrette described him as
'at the forefront of the essentialist
movement of the late twenty-sixth century;
a truthful and influential voice.'

Stokes slumped back from the screen, feeling as if he'd been punched. 'A truthful and influential voice,' he said to himself. Then he started to laugh maniacally. Strang, Anderson, Oddstock, all forgotten. Not even a whisper. But he was in there. He'd never heard of Dellah, or Corney Debrette, and his previous life had ended in 2386. But he was standing in a time machine. So he had a future – and what a future! – waiting in the past.

He wagged an accusing finger upwards. 'It didn't work, then,' he cried. 'He gets away, and we go back there together. It's all been a colossal waste of effort on your part, hasn't it, rather?'

And then, whether from the exhaustion of the previous couple of hours or for some other reason, his legs vanished from under him and he was toppling and tumbling down what seemed like a high, steep hill.

The tension in the valley was palpable. All eyes were on K9 as an almost imperceptible sequence of clicks and whistles came from his voicebox. The Doctor was hunched protectively over him, perfectly still, his concentration absolute. Romana knelt on the other side, her fists clenched tight.

K9 spoke at last. 'Galatea reports the expulsion has been successful.'

The effect of his words was like an explosion. There was a general round of cheering, applause and back- and shell-slapping. Romana jumped up with relief and found herself grabbed by Fritchoff. 'We did it!' he cried. 'We did it!'

'Yes, *we* did,' she said, disengaging herself. She turned back to the Doctor, who alone of the group remained still. His head had fallen forward on to K9's muzzle and his eyes were closed. Romana supposed at first that the strain of the last few hours had weakened him, but then she noticed that he was still absolutely poised.

She laid a gentle hand on his still-wet shoulder. 'Everything's all right, isn't it?'

'Perfectly.' He lifted his head, and there was an unaccustomed bitterness in his eyes. 'Yes, we've seen them off very easily. Very easily indeed.' He bit his lower lip.

'And I've thought of an answer to your question, by the way.'

She nodded. 'You're going to suggest locating the Hive's energy signature on the transmat line and reverse-phasing it into a stable relational zone using the TARDIS.'

He stood up. 'Am I that predictable?' Without any of his usual humour he signalled grandly to the people standing around him. 'My work here is done. You've got a planet to reclaim.' He pointed to the shuttle. 'A few trips should get you all back there. Just reverse the transmat coordinates back again and you can get your people back from Regus V – it's all very simple. Ask Galatea, if she's still up and about.' To the Chelonians he added vaguely, 'And there's no reason why you shouldn't integrate now, is there?' With a final nod he started to walk away.

Romana, appalled by his bad manners, raced after him and grabbed the elbow of his coat. 'Doctor. Don't you think you ought to say goodbye?'

'I thought I already had.' He turned abruptly and nodded to General Jafrid. 'Take care. Try not to jump to too many hasty conclusions in future.'

Jafrid spread his front feet wide. 'Doctor, I have already indicated my profound regret.'

The Doctor cut across him rudely. 'Yes, yes, it's always very easy after the event. You know, just once it would be nice to meet a member of your race who didn't want to try to kill me.' He moved now to Harmock. 'You're the politician fellow, are you?'

'That's right, yes,' said Harmock. 'I am the Premier of Metralubit.'

The Doctor said curtly, 'You were a powerless plaything. Now you're going to have to live and work in the real world. I wish you luck, and with your professional background you'll need it.' He crossed to Fritchoff. 'Well, thank you for your help.'

Fritchoff beamed. 'Doctor, when the history of the rebel militant movement is written, you will have a special place.' He shook the Doctor's hand but his eyes kept flicking to Romana.

Noting this, the Doctor turned to Harmock. 'Premier, there are females down in your dome, aren't there? Real ones, I mean?'

Harmock nodded enthusiastically. 'Yes, plenty.'

'Good.' He pointed to Fritchoff. 'Try to find him one.' He beckoned to Romana and K9. 'Now, we really have to go. There's the Hive to deal with. We're not out of the woods yet.'

They followed him. K9 said, 'There is no forest in this vicinity, Master.'

'Shut up, K9,' said the Doctor.

Following their departure there was another strange silence in the valley.

'Well,' said General Jafrid.

'Right,' said Harmock.

Fritchoff stepped forward. 'First of all, we have to settle the Barclow dispute.'

Jafrid made a conciliatory gesture to Harmock. 'You can have it.'

Harmock made a similar gesture in return. 'No, you can have it. I insist.'

'Secondly,' said Fritchoff, 'and before any decisions are taken on the future of Metralubit, we must discuss and refine in detail the exact nature of the administrative and economic system that will act as the underlying base for those decisions. I move that we orientate ourselves to a socially liberal but state-regulated internal market.'

Harmock shook his head emphatically. 'No, no, no. If we intervene in the affairs of ordinary people as they go about in the reclaiming effort, where will it end? This is a most woolly-minded scheme, Mr Fritchoff.'

'My position is the very opposite of intervention,' said Fritchoff. He waved at Cadinot and the others. 'You're just trying to mould the minds of these people by exploiting their fears for the future, and thus imbuing them with a false consciousness in relation to their position with capital.'

Jafrid coughed loudly, drawing their attention. 'Please,'

he said. 'This debate is going nowhere. There is only one course left open to us now.'

'And what's that?' demanded Harmock.

'We must take a vote,' Jafrid said simply.

12

The Official End of It All

S tokes dreamt.
   A voice, deep and granite-hard, was ordering him to wake up. The deal was not yet done.

Stokes resisted. The appreciation he'd received on Metralubit had been a sham. Why should he listen to the voice again?

The voice reminded him what the screen had shown. He would be appreciated on Dellah. Would he like to go there?

Stokes pondered. Was that possible?

The voice assured him it was. All he needed to do was set the correct space–time coordinates on the TARDIS's navigation panel.

Stokes laughed at this. The workings of the TARDIS were quite outside his understanding.

The voice told him it could lend a guiding hand.

And so Stokes woke up, and found his hands wandering over the navigation panels as if he'd been piloting the TARDIS for years.

The data-bank screen now read:

**DEPARTURE – BARCLOW Humanian Era
DESTINATION – DELLAH AD 2593**

Romana was perturbed. The Doctor was pounding back to the TARDIS, hands thrust deep in his pockets, head down, hat pulled over his face, leaving her and K9 to struggle to catch up. The rain was falling again, whipping her cape out behind her and knocking K9 off his bearings from time to time.

'Do we have to go quite so fast?' she protested to the

Doctor's back. It was the first time they'd spoken since leaving the survivors of this affair in the valley.

'Why break the habit of several lifetimes?' the Doctor grumbled. 'I must have spent the greatest share of my time since leaving Gallifrey running up and down with barely time to stop and think.'

Romana recognized the signs of impending moodiness and felt reassured. She could cope with these occasional bouts of brooding. 'I do hope you're not going to start feeling sorry for yourself.'

He stopped and turned to her. 'That would be predictable, wouldn't it?'

His tone was almost aggressive, and for the first time ever in his company Romana felt threatened. 'Please don't shout at me.'

He looked between her and K9 and managed a tight smile. 'Do forgive me. It's just that I'm worried, you see.'

'About what?'

He stepped closer and his grave expression returned. 'When you can predict a person's actions it's very easy to lay snares for them.'

K9 whirred impatiently. 'Query these deliberations, Master. We should return to the TARDIS and continue our travels.'

The Doctor looked down at him. He was silent for a moment and then he burst into one of his sudden crazes. 'Yes,' he shouted, 'planet saved, crisis averted, evil menace vanquished. All the questions answered, everything wrapped up.' The sky rumbled as if in reply and another gust of freezing rain swept over them.

'Situation has been resolved, Master,' said K9. 'The people of Metralubit and the Chelonians can exist together. The Hive has been banished.'

Romana laid a comforting arm on the Doctor's shoulder. 'K9's right, Doctor. I don't see what there is to fret about.'

He walked a short distance away and stared out into nothingness. 'From the moment we arrived here I've felt a powerful unease.'

278

'That's not surprising,' said Romana. 'I felt the same. We shouldn't be here, after all, strictly speaking.'

'No, we shouldn't,' he said emphatically. 'We were blown here by a strange, unpredictable accident. The erosion of the TARDIS systems circuitry combined with an impulse from the Randomizer sent us cartwheeling wildly off course. We should have left right away. But we didn't.'

'We had to pop out "just so we could say we'd been",' Romana reminded him.

He snapped his fingers. 'Exactly. A chance to cock a minor snook at the Time Lords. Just what I would have done. Walked out, got myself involved, started to tinker. I began the logical, forseeable chain of decisions that have brought me to this point.' He raised a finger and pointed through the mist ahead. 'There.'

Romana squinted. The tall blue shape of the TARDIS was just visible on the horizon. 'You're taking a very egocentric view. Plenty of other people made decisions along the way. Me and K9 for a start. Galatea, Harmock, Jafrid, St–'

The Doctor cut her off. 'Yes, they did, didn't they? All of them people who shouldn't be here.'

Romana was getting exasperated. 'What do you mean?'

'The artificiality of it all,' the Doctor replied, 'that I mentioned to you earlier.'

'These discrepancies were connected to the Femdroids' deception of the Hive, Master,' K9 said patiently.

The Doctor shook his head. 'I think the Femdroids were part of an even bigger game.' He turned to Romana. 'The level of coincidence is too high. Our arrival. The Chelonians just wandering into this system at the very moment Galatea needed to start a war to fox the Hive. The similarity in technology between K9 and the Femdroids.'

'That wasn't a coincidence,' said Romana.

The Doctor stared blankly at her. 'What?'

'The Femdroids' creators used K9 as a blueprint using

information from Stokes's mind,' she explained.

The Doctor put a hand to his temple. 'Who? Stokes? Not that artist fellow?'

'Yes, I forgot to tell you, in all the rush,' Romana admitted.

'But how did he get here?' The Doctor's face now took on a haunted expression. As Romana opened her mouth to reply he held up a hand to silence her. 'No, never mind that. Where is he now?'

'He sloped off somewhere,' said Romana. 'Actually, I thought he'd be waiting for us at the TARDIS, if he managed to find it.'

K9 nodded his agreement. 'That is his most likely course of action.'

The Doctor stared at the TARDIS and then broke into a frantic run, without a word of explanation. Romana followed on, baffled, with K9 in her arms.

Galatea stared out at the empty city. Soon the fountains would flow again, the tramways would be filled with their silent, pollutant-free traffic, and the citizens would work and play in total harmony. Her vision had been accomplished.

One of the dome workers had helped her to rig up a communicator using materials from the smashed computer room. A picture relayed from one of the orbital satellites showed a rough ring of the survivors on Barclow, including General Jafrid, Harmock and that man Fritchoff she'd had sent away a few years ago. He and a few others in the dome were strong-willed enough to break through the conditioning. Before they could she'd implanted a suitable fantasy in their minds and expelled them. Now, she thought with a smile, everyone could come home. Metralubit was coming home.

'Now, you've been a very naughty girl, all told, keeping things from us,' Harmock was saying. 'There'll be no need for any of this nastiness and secrecy in future, will there?'

'Absolutely not,' said Galatea with a glad heart. 'I shall

be pleased to serve my organic masters in a more direct way.'

'Still,' Harmock went on, 'I have to say I admire your nerve. Doing this all on your own. Well done.'

Galatea nodded. 'Thank you, Premier. I like to think I've always done my best.'

Just for a second she heard a voice, deep and granite-hard, somewhere deep inside her head. The bargain is over, it told her, our business is done.

Galatea thanked the voice. It had given her exactly what it had promised: the total destruction of the Hive and the safety of her people, thanks to the provision of Stokes's great knowledge. And she, of course, had fulfilled her side of the bargain. She had invented the concept of constitutional privilege, conditioned the humans to believe it, and encouraged Romana and K9 to come to Metralubit. It had been easy enough.

But she was happy she would never hear the voice again.

General Jafrid slunk away from the screen, feeling a bit left out from all this joy and excitement. One of the young humans — Cadinot, wasn't it? — came across and asked kindly, 'Are you all right there, General?'

Jafrid winked at him, remembering his old friend Admiral Dolne. 'I'm fine,' he said. 'Just fine.'

And then, just for a second, he heard the voice again for the first time in over a hundred years. The deal is done, the voice said, and our business is over.

Jafrid thanked it inwardly. The voice had delivered what it had promised: a lengthy, untroubled early retirement, thanks to a convenient time storm that had whipped him and his men here from their rightful place thousands of years before, liberating them from the warrior lifestyle. And his side of the bargain could not have been easier. All the voice had asked him to do was sit put on Barclow for a hundred and twenty-five years, and pretend to really want it.

Now the voice was gone, and he could spend the rest of his retirement in luxury down on Metralubit, with its plentiful green spaces and large arable areas. It would be a pleasure indeed to graze there.

The Doctor burst into the TARDIS to find the console room empty. He peered beneath the console and in all the corners; he even looked behind the hatstand and among the items he had been sorting out before they had entered the Time Spiral.

Romana almost fell through the doors, exhausted by the run and from carrying K9. She was glad of the warmth and comparative comfort of the TARDIS, and immediately reached for the lever that closed the big double doors. Barclow's low moaning wind and biting cold were finally shut out. She set K9 down and turned with a despairing sigh to the Doctor, who was scattering objects from his useful pile all over the floor. 'I hardly think you're going to find Stokes in there,' she said, still unable to fathom the reasons for his distress. 'Besides, he can't just have walked in.'

'Doors are an irrelevance to some people,' the Doctor snapped back. He peered through the inner door and grunted; a set of muddy bootprints trailed away down the corridor. 'Just as I thought. He's probably gone to find a bed.'

For the first time Romana caught a little of his anxiety. 'But how did he pass through our security?' She shivered. Theoretically, the TARDIS was impenetrable.

The Doctor hunched over the console. 'We can worry about that later. First, let's minimize the risks and get out of here.' He started to fiddle with the controls of the dematerialization sequence.

K9 trundled over urgently. 'Master, the Hive.'

'Yes, I know, K9. Don't tell your grandmother how to suck eggs,' the Doctor snapped back.

For once K9, who was perhaps leaning about Earth idioms, and perhaps sensing the seriousness of the situation, refrained from comment.

Romana leant over the Doctor's shoulder. He was calibrating a set of dials at the base of the dematerialization circuit array. 'There,' he said. A steady pinging note filled the console room. 'There's the Hive's energy signature. I've locked it on to our own engines. We'll pull it along behind us like a caravan and dump it somewhere apposite. I know a couple of good black holes in the Cosplodge system.'

'The linkage is secure, I hope,' said Romana.

'Of course it is. Even a vintage model like the TARDIS has a good strong secondary attachment.' He looked up ruefully as he started the dematerialization sequence. 'We'll just slip into the vortex for the time being. I want to get away from here as soon as possible and take stock.'

Romana stood back as he threw the last few switches. The central column began its steady rise and fall.

The blue beacon on the rooftop of the TARDIS started to flash. A few seconds later, to the accompaniment of an unearthly trumpeting noise, its police-box shell faded away completely from the rocky terrain of Barclow.

There was a thunderclap and a peal of mocking laughter.

The TARDIS tipped, throwing the Doctor, Romana and K9 across the console room and back again. The central column glowed incredibly brightly, turning fiery red and crackling with electric sparkles.

'The Time Spiral again,' Romana shouted, trying desperately to find the edge of the console and lever herself up.

'Negative, Mistress,' called K9.

The Doctor, who was a dab hand at being thrown around the console room, used the momentum of a vicious spin to gain the support of the console's navigation panel. When he saw the display on the screen he uttered a very old and seldom-used word in Old High Gallifreyan. 'Somebody's already put in a course,' he cried. 'There's a locking in the coordinates.'

Romana was appalled. Only a skilled operator could input coordinates, and to lock them in – to wire in an extra code so that travel to that destination, no matter how far distant, took very little relative time at all and could not be altered – took an expert with a lot of patience. 'Who?'

'Stokes!' the Doctor called back.

'That's impossible!' Romana called. At last she managed to grab hold of the console.

'Unless he was helped,' the Doctor said. Then he leant over and started to throw switches on the panel maniacally.

An observer watched the insane pitch and yaw of the TARDIS as it sped through the howling maelstrom of the space–time vortex.

Now the Doctor would cancel the coordinates program by using the coordinate override.

And the choice could be made.

Stokes was woken when his large bald head was smacked against one of the softly humming walls of the TARDIS corridor. He had no memory of anything after he'd looked himself up in the data bank. Perhaps he'd walked here in his sleep.

He picked himself up and regained his balance as the TARDIS steadied. He hadn't gone far into its innards; through the door at the end of the corridor he could hear the Doctor's rich, booming voice. Cautiously he crept closer, and turned his ear to catch the Doctor's words. 'Do you know what this is, Romana?'

'I've never seen anything like it,' came the girl's voice.

'Yes you have,' countered the Doctor.

Stokes poked his head around the door. The Doctor, who was looking very dishevelled, his wet, stained coat torn in several places, was holding something out to Romana. It was, Stokes realized with a jolt, his own crystal. It must have fallen from his pocket when he'd walked in.

He heard Romana's gasp as she took it from the Doctor. 'The Key to Time. The same substance.'

'Exactly,' said the Doctor. 'A material that exists in ways even old Rassilon could never have speculated. You might say it borders on magic.'

K9 trundled into view. 'Magic refuted, Master. Substance cannot be analysed as it exists, er, simultaneously at every point in time. This does not constitute magic, only a level of scientific conceptualism we cannot comprehend.'

The Doctor ignored him. 'Now,' he told Romana, 'with this, Stokes could get in here and set those coordinates quite easily. So how did it get into his possession? And how did he get himself shanghaied halfway across the universe and halfway across the span of time?'

'The White Guardian?' Romana suggested hopefully.

'Or the other fellow,' said the Doctor. 'A web of choices. That's how the Guardians, both of them, operate. Jafrid, Galatea and Stokes were all pawns in the game, arranged for someone else's benefit.'

Romana leant in close. 'And who might this other person be?'

The Doctor leant even closer to her. 'I have this terrible suspicion it might be me.'

K9 piped up. 'Master, Mistress,' he called. 'Mr Stokes.'

Stokes put up his hands and tried to ignore the accusation in their gaze. 'Hello, Doctor,' he said feebly.

The Doctor stalked over. 'I want a word with you.'

The TARDIS hung in suspense in the space–time vortex. Its mighty time engines were held in stasis, their power held back by the Doctor's operation of the override switch. The indescribable maelstrom shrieked about it.

'It wasn't actually what you'd call a dirty deal,' said Stokes. He addressed Romana. 'Most of my, er, very long story was true, my dear. I only left out a teensy bit.'

'The teensy bit about the Black Guardian,' she replied bitterly.

'Is that what's he's called?' mused Stokes. 'I suppose it's apposite. No, the first thing I knew of him was just after my court case. I was landed with costs that wiped out my

285

fortune, as I mentioned earlier, so I decided to go for a drink. I had several. In fact, I had a lot more than several. I think I bumped my head. And that's when I saw him, this fellow in black with a bird on his head.'

The Doctor nodded grimly to Romana. 'He can contact lower primates only when their minds are knocked into an altered state.'

Stokes flushed. 'Who are you calling a lower primate?'

'You,' said the Doctor. 'Go on.'

'Well, it seemed like a dream afterwards,' Stokes continued. 'In a nutshell, he offered me the chance for some success. In exchange for which I had to provide a certain service.'

'To betray and trap us,' accused Romana.

'No,' Stokes said firmly. 'Honestly, no. I wouldn't have agreed to that, would I? And in fact the thing that made me think it really had been a dream was the ludicrous nature of the service I was asked to perform.'

'Which was?' the Doctor prompted.

Stokes pulled his hammer from his pocket. 'There would come a time, he said, when I had to smash something up. He didn't even say what, only that I'd know what it was when the time came, and that I should carry this wherever I went. And that it was something to do with you, Doctor, some sort of personal feud, and that I shouldn't mention him to you or Romana if ever we should meet. Of course I thought it was all subconscious rambling on my part.' He pointed to the crystal in Romana's hand. 'Until I found that in my pocket when I woke up. Occasionally it gave me directions. It pushed me towards the cryogenic process, for example, when I first considered it. Very odd.' He sighed. 'Otherwise, everything I told you was true. So I can hardly be painted as the villain of this piece.' Determined not to feel cowed, he stuck his chest out. 'In fact, we all seem to have come out of it all right. We're going to Dellah, now, I think you'll find, where you can drop me off. And then you can take your feud with this Guardian chap elsewhere.' He extended his hand. 'No harm done, eh?'

The Doctor shot him a venomous look. 'Stokes, you've been very stupid, even for a lower primate.'

Romana's expression was as gloomy. 'You've been manipulated as part of a plan to bring the Doctor to this point. A string of small events, of small choices, calculated to reach this moment.'

Stokes frowned and looked at the central column, which was grinding ferociously, as if the energies trapped inside were straining desperately to escape. 'But we are going to Dellah, aren't we?'

'Yes, we're going to Dellah,' cried the Doctor, 'and we're dragging along with us a Hive of blood-crazed insects that given the right conditions could become one of the deadliest life forms in the cosmos.' He pointed to a particular lever on the console. 'We've both been fooled, Stokes. And even when I *realized* I was being manipulated I was being manipulated. The Black Guardian timed our movements precisely. You set the coordinates, I rushed in, picked up the Hive and dematerialized.'

'So?' demanded Stokes. 'I think I must be missing the point.'

'This is the trap,' Romana explained. 'The Doctor was rushed, made to panic. We were going to drop the Hive off into a black hole, right away.' She pointed to the materialization control. 'If we materialize here, it'll be released into populated space at a crucial point in history. It'll destroy millions and reproduce without restriction. The web of time will be fractured irreparably.' She shuddered. 'And we'll be responsible.'

'No,' said the Doctor. '*I* shall be responsible.'

The TARDIS rocked as a great shadow fell across its doors.

The shutters of the scanner screen slid open unbidden. The Doctor whipped round from his moment of introspection and blinked at the figure that was revealed. The imperturbable face could have been blasted out of solid rock; the ermine-lined robes were glossy and seemed to contain in their folds every dark thought the universe had ever contained; the headdress was mounted by a raven whose eyes were narrowed in pure, piercing hatred.

'Ah,' said the Doctor. 'We were just talking about you.'

'That's him, isn't it?' Stokes asked.

'If it isn't it's somebody wearing his hat,' said the Doctor.

The Black Guardian's voice was as stentorian as he remembered, a rumble that seemed to shake the very fabric of time. 'Doctor,' he said, 'the time has come for us to do business.'

'I don't think so.'

The Guardian gestured with one massive hand to the TARDIS console. 'The choice is clear. Press the lever and condemn the universe to chaos, or –' his eyes narrowed and his lips twisted '– remain suspended here in the vortex forever.'

The Doctor ambled over to the scanner and peered up at the face of his greatest enemy. 'You've been very clever, I must say. I know that to an elemental being like yourself the compliments of a mere mortal like myself must not count for much, but I'd like to congratulate you anyway. I should have seen your hand in it from the beginning.' He raised his voice. 'What better place than the end of the universe to set your trap? Your opposite number is at his weakest there and couldn't intervene.'

'Precisely,' said the Black Guardian. 'You walked into the situation on Metralubit as you always do, Doctor. It was easy for me to predict your moves.' He indicated Stokes. 'Using this creature and others as my players.' A smile cracked his unearthly features. 'I have been tracing your path through all time and space, your past and your future, choosing my moment. I was at your side when you fought the wizard of Avalon, when you united the Rhumon and the Menoptera against the Animus, when you brought down Lady Ruath and her vampire hordes and when you fought the Timewyrm on the surface of the moon.'

'I'm not sure you should be telling me some of that,' said the Doctor. 'I haven't done it yet.' He wagged a reproving finger up at the screen. 'You're dabbling with the forces of continuity.'

'I care nothing for such abstract concepts,' snorted the Guardian.

'You've disrupted our timeline, broken the First Law,' accused Romana. 'The consequences could be catastrophic. Not to mention very confusing.'

'Catastrophe and confusion is his job,' the Doctor remarked.

'Throughout I have studied you,' said the Black Guardian, 'until my knowledge of your personality and my capacity to predict your next move were absolute. And I can predict your next move, Doctor.'

Stokes decided he was being left out of things. 'Excuse me,' he said, stomping over to the screen. 'There is still the small matter of our bargain.'

The Black Guardian turned to look at him and cackled. 'Ah yes. Menlove Ereward Stokes.' The cackle became a full-voiced, deep-throated, very fruity laugh. 'Who would do anything to be remembered to posterity.'

Stokes rearranged his coat in an attempt to appear more dignified and sniffed. 'Some of us are quite content with our small lives, you know. And besides, I'd certainly never heard of you until I met you. For a deity of all that is evil you're not actually very famous, are you? I haven't seen you on the front covers of any magazines, have I?'

'Famous,' chortled the Black Guardian. 'Magazines.' His deeply lined face creased with further mirth.

Romana sidled close to the Doctor. 'What are we going to do?' she whispered.

'We could always just sit and watch these two out-ham each other for all eternity,' he whispered back.

K9 joined in the hushed conversation. 'Options limited, Master,' he said.

Further debate was forestalled by the Black Guardian's next statement. 'Stokes,' he said, 'your petty concerns amuse me.' He waved his fingers in a dismissive motion, as if flicking them dry. 'Go to Dellah, take up your place, find your acclaim.'

Stokes felt himself drifting away from the console room. He saw the Doctor, Romana and K9 slide slowly away from him, and when he looked down he saw he was becoming transparent. 'It seems like I must be going,' he said. He waved goodbye. 'I'm sorry if I've caused you any inconvenience, and that if we meet again it'll be under more pleasant circumstances. You can drop in on Dellah whenever you want —'

His words were swallowed up, and suddenly he was somewhere else.

He was in a high, draughty corridor. Through a window he saw a set of bee-hive-like buildings made of baked red mud, arranged to form a quadrangle. Small groups of people, mostly young humanoids, were walking between the buildings. At the centre of the quad was an abstract sculpture that depicted a vicious, two-headed reptilian creature, gore dripping from its jaws. 'Good God,' he said. 'That's one of mine.'

He turned and found himself at a door. On its frosted-glass front was embossed PROFESSOR M. E. STOKES.

He pushed open the door. Inside was a large desk stacked with unattended paperwork and several battered filing cabinets. He walked in slowly, still amazed by the sudden transition.

On the desk was an unaddressed black envelope. He unsealed it and found a black card. Inside, written in sparkling gold and in an excessively stylized hand, were the words 'Mr Stokes. Hoping you find the rewards you seek. B.G.'

Stokes sat down at his desk and thought for a very long time. The events of the last few — days? months? years? millennia? — rattled around his head like images left from a fading dream. He had been humiliated, scorned and made to look a fool. Here was his chance for a fresh start. He decided on certain things.

He would forget the Black Guardian. He would forget

Metralubit. And he would, most definitely, never so much as think about the Doctor and company ever again.

After Stokes had faded the Black Guardian gave another of his grotesque smiles. 'Mr Stokes has arrived safely on Dellah, you'll be pleased to hear.' He gestured to the console. 'Why not materialize and join him there?'

K9 motored forward angrily and snarled up at the scanner. 'Do not mock my master.'

The Guardian cackled. 'Ah, the metal dog. Did you enjoy your moment of elevation on Metralubit? It amused me to bring out the superiority that has always bubbled beneath that servile shell.' He turned to Romana. 'It amused me also to encourage your righteousness, so typical of the Time Lord race.'

Romana tried to think of a suitably haughty reply but failed. Her eyes turned to the Doctor, who was circling the console and examining the varied systems displays. He stopped by the crackling, pinging navigation panel and the small flashing unit that represented the Hive's energy signature. Could some extraordinary solution present itself? Could that incredible, eight-hundred-year-old mind pull the rabbit out of the hat? 'I have to admit,' he said to the Guardian, 'that you've sewn this up very well.' He looked up at the scanner. 'You said you could predict my next move. Go on then.'

The Black Guardian smiled. 'You are both very long lived, for mortals. Almost ageless. You will wait here in the vortex for many years. You will explore every possible technological solution. You will vow never to press the lever and bring yourselves back out into the cosmos.' His tone darkened, and as it did the lighting in the console room dimmed and there was a rushing noise from outside. 'But eventually, Doctor, you will. I know you. You cannot stay in one place and in one time. It would drive you insane. It *will* drive you insane. And to save yourself you shall become my agent, of your own choosing. You will press the lever. You will release the Hive, and it shall feast on the universe and plunge all time and space into chaos.'

As he spoke Romana's imagination conjured up an image of the Doctor, many years older, his spirit shattered, hunched over the console, a feeble hand wrapped around the materialization control. She shuddered.

'I thought it would be something like that,' said the Doctor. Some of his good humour seemed to have returned, and it was as if he was goading a minor warlord rather than the protector of all the universe's evil. He pointed to the materialization lever. 'You want me to press this switch.'

'You are going to,' the Guardian said, his voice lowered to a horrible whisper. 'I have waited an eternity to see you do it. A few centuries more will not trouble me.' He indicated the frame of the screen. 'I shall always be here, Doctor, watching and waiting.'

The Doctor nodded affably. 'It's nice to know I'm worthy of your special attention.' His voice hardened. 'But you've forgotten one thing.'

'I have forgotten nothing,' stormed the Guardian.

The Doctor carried on as if he hadn't spoken. 'You forget that there are plenty of other switches and levers on this console. You've forgotten one in particular.' He pointed to a small black box that was wired on to the side of the panel nearest the door. 'What about that, then?'

Romana was shocked. 'The emergency unit,' she exclaimed. 'You won't use that.'

The Doctor wheeled on her. 'Can't I? I've had enough of people telling me what I will or won't do.'

K9 came forward. 'The emergency unit is designed to remove the TARDIS from time and space, vis-à-vis reality as we understand it. Its usage is most inadvisable.'

'We could end up anywhere,' Romana protested.

The Doctor shook his head. 'No. Anywhere is just where we won't be going.'

The Guardian growled from the screen. 'Explain yourself.'

The Doctor tapped the black box. 'A nifty gadget for use in extreme emergencies. If I activate it we'll just drop out of everything, quite possibly forever, taking the Hive with us. We'll be outside your influence.'

'You would not dare, Doctor,' called the Guardian. 'You would rather die.'

The Doctor hunched over the console and readied his finger above the box. 'Probably, in the normal run of things. But occasionally it does one good to surprise oneself. And I'd rather disappear than grovel to you.' He turned to Romana. 'I'm sorry.'

Romana swallowed and curled her fingers around his above the control. 'There's no alternative,' she said, trying to keep her voice even. 'Have you ever done this before?'

He smiled. 'Once. I ended up in the fictional realm. I suppose it wasn't such a bad place.'

Romana shuddered at the thought. 'Then we'd just be characters, not real people.'

'I can think of worse fates,' said the Doctor.

'No!' the Black Guardian thundered. 'You will not press that button, Doctor. You will not press that button!'

K9 extended his eyestalk and chirruped a signal. The shutters of the scanner slid closed, and there was a sudden silence. The lighting returned to normal. It could have been another ordinary day in the TARDIS, ready to begin another adventure.

'Goodbye, universe,' the Doctor said sadly. 'I'll be back again, one day. Try to look after yourself. Mind out for the Daleks, keep an eye out for the Cybermen, don't let the Sontarans boss you about. Good luck.'

The Doctor and Romana looked at each other.

The Doctor kissed Romana quickly on the cheek.

Together they pressed the button.

THE END

and a new beginning

The Missing Adventures started in July 1994 with the publication of Paul Cornell's *Goth Opera*. This book, *The Well-Mannered War*, is the thirty-third and last of the series.

Virgin Publishing Ltd and its predecessor companies have been publishing Doctor Who books, under licence from the BBC, for twenty-four years. The decision to stop now wasn't ours. For all three of us the opportunity to produce original Doctor Who stories, in particular, has been the fulfilment of a lifelong ambition. We hope the books we've published have entertained more than they've irritated, and that we've contributed something worthwhile to the continuing universe that is Doctor Who. We're glad we were able to provide a forum for so many talented new authors.

This month's New Adventure, *The Dying Days* by Lance Parkin, marks the same ending – but it also presages a new beginning. It includes the first and last meeting between the eighth Doctor and Bernice Summerfield – a symbolic parting of the ways.

From May 1997 onwards the New Adventures will blaze a trail into uncharted territories – with our favourite archaeologist from the twenty-sixth century leading the expedition. Don't fail to take part in this new journey of discovery: read *Oh No It Isn't!* by Paul Cornell, the first of the *new* New Adventures.

Also coming in May: *Decalog 4*, the first non-Doctor Who Decalog, with stories charting the rise to supreme galactic power of the Forrester family during the third millennium.

Doctors may come and Doctors may go, but with your support the New Adventures can go on for ever.

Peter Darvill-Evans, Publisher
Rebecca Levene, Editor
Simon Winstone, Assistant Editor

Available in the *Doctor Who — New Adventures* series: